Henry Morton Stanley

**The Life, Labours and Adventures of David Livingstone**

Henry Morton Stanley

**The Life, Labours and Adventures of David Livingstone**

ISBN/EAN: 9783744759014

Printed in Europe, USA, Canada, Australia, Japan

Cover: Foto ©Raphael Reischuk / pixelio.de

More available books at **www.hansebooks.com**

# THE

## LIFE, LABOURS, AND ADVENTURES

### OF

# DAVID LIVINGSTONE,

### LL.D., D.C.L.,

ABOUT THIRTY YEARS A MISSIONARY IN THE WILDS OF
AFRICA; HIS DISCOVERY AND RELIEF

BY

## H. M. STANLEY.

*WITH AN ACCOUNT OF HIS DEATH, AND THE DEPOSITING
OF HIS REMAINS IN WESTMINSTER ABBEY,*
1874.

TORONTO:
MACLEAR & CO., PUBLISHERS.

# PREFACE.

THIS volume is intended as a sequel to one issued last year by the same publishers, entitled " The Life and Labours of Dr. Livingstone." In the latter work the story of the great missionary and explorer was brought down to the time when he was discovered by Mr. H. M. Stanley, the energetic agent of the *N. Y. Herald.* At that juncture every one hoped that the next accounts we should receive of the result of Livingstone's researches in Central Africa would come from his own lips, and fall upon English ears. It seemed meet, however, to that Divine Providence, which had so long guided his steps in safety through difficulty and danger, to ordain that his brave heart should cease to beat while he was in his cherished field of labour, with the harness on his back. Soon after our work was published, he succumbed to disease after a few days' illness; and the patient, hopeful, dauntless, and untiring spirit entered into its everlasting rest.

The labours of an earnest and self-denying life were thus

brought to a close, and their history—so far as the materials are accessible—may now be told in its entirety. We propose, therefore, in this volume, to complete our work by giving as full an account as possible of the great explorer, from the day (March 14th, 1872) when Mr. Stanley took leave of him at Unyanyembe until April 18th, 1874, when his honoured remains were laid

> "In the great Minster's transept,
>     Where light-like glories fall;
> And the sweet choir sings,
> And the organ rings
>     Along the emblazoned wall."

We shall endeavour to trace the course of his last wanderings; to indicate the geographical discoveries he made up to his last illness; and show the unfaltering hopefulness which sustained him in his work until he laid him down to die. The pathetic story of that death, with the many touching incidents which attended it, the fidelity of his native servants—"faithful among the faithless found "—and, finally, England's recognition of the value of a life spent in labouring for Christian civilization, for human freedom, and for scientific discovery will complete the narrative we have undertaken.

Although, as we have said, the primary object of this

work is to render our history of the Life and Labours of Dr. Livingstone, a finished biography of its distinguished subject,—and it will therefore, properly speaking, begin with the year 1872—it seems proper to prefix, in a somewhat condensed form, the record of the preceding years from 1813, the year of his birth. This we think due to those who have not had the opportunity of reading the former volume. The preliminary sketch, together with the main body of the work, will thus render this book a complete and compendious biography of the great missionary. Every effort has been made to render the narrative full and correct in every part. No source of information at our command has been neglected; we, therefore, commend it to the public as the fullest, the cheapest, and the most accurate biography of Dr. Livingstone hitherto published.

# DR. LIVINGSTONE.

IF any one about fifty years ago had ventured to predict that a poor lad, the son of humble parents, who was then toiling daily at the loom in a Lanarkshire town, would one day achieve fame and admiration without seeking it, and would be laid to rest amongst the nation's honoured dead, the prophecy would have been received with a smile of incredulity. Nor would the prophet have strengthened his case, if he had descended to particulars :— if he had told the world that the poor weaver-boy, without wealthy friends, with no resources but a stout heart, a persistent will, and a firm trust in God, would one day carry the blessings of Christian civilization into the heart of Africa, and explore that continent from ocean to ocean; and, further, that, while living, his safety would become the source of the deepest solicitude to nations; that in death he would be mourned by millions, from the banks of the Ganges far westward to the shores of the Pacific. Yet such a prophecy was fulfilled by the brave man who now rests beside Stephenson and Outram in Westminster Abbey.

David Livingstone was born at Blantyre, a manufacturing town on the Clyde, about eight miles from Glasgow.

His parents, as we have said, were poor but they were also pious, and there can be no doubt that home influences early determined the future of their illustrious son. Such instruction as David enjoyed in his early years he must have obtained at the parish school. To the old parochial school system of Scotland was due the superiority of the Scottish people in elementary education over their brethren of the sister kingdoms ; and many men, whose names are illustrious in the annals of the Empire, took their first step on the road to eminence under the direction of the parish " dominie.''

At the early age of ten it became necessary that David Livingstone should begin to earn a livelihood for himself. He was accordingly placed in the Blantyre Cotton Works as a " piecer "—that is, on the lowest round of the factory ladder. Neither his employers, nor probably himself, could then have conceived the notion that there was a loftier ladder which David was destined to mount, ending in a more ethereal air and an ampler sunshine. It is quite evident, however, that the young weaver did not mean to bury his talent in the earth. He at once took advantage of an evening-school—the master of which was in part paid by the mill-owners—and, equipping himself with that venerable manual—" Ruddiman's Rudiments of Latin," commenced the study of the classics. In the course of five years he had read Virgil and Horace, reserving miscellaneous reading in science and travels for his evening, and often his midnight hours. His delight in works of the latter class had doubtless the effect it has frequently

exerted on others destined to be themselves explorers.
Whether Livingstone had already sketched in outline his
future career as a missionary, or whether, unknown to
him, it was being shaped by Divine Providence alone may
be a matter of dispute.  Still, we can hardly believe that
one of so practical a mind would have entered upon the
study of Latin without some definite end in view.

At the age of nineteen, having previously passed through
the various grades of his apprenticeship, Livingstone became a cotton-spinner in the full sense of the term.  At
this time without doubt the great and lofty aim of his
life was clearly defined.  He had determined to go forth
into the heathen world as a minister of the Gospel of
Christ—a herald of salvation in those dark places of the
earth which are the habitations of cruelty and superstition.
He wisely determined to acquire, at the same time, a medical, as well as a theological, training.  To the inestimable
benefits which have flowed from this double equipment,
Livingstone's history is not the only evidence which might
be adduced.  Finding that he could save sufficient from
his wages at the factory, by working during the summer months, to maintain himself at college during the
winter, he entered his name at the Glasgow University as
a student of Greek, medicine, and divinity.  In due time
he graduated in medicine.  Livingstone's first intention
evidently was to enter the missionary field as an independent labourer, untrammelled by outside control, and free
to work out his own plans in his own way.  Yielding,
however, to the advice of friends, he finally resolved to go

forth under the auspices of the London Missionary Society
as a medical missionary. With that view he presented
himself for examination in September, 1838, and, having
satisfied the directors as to his qualifications, he was placed
in the Society's Training College at Ongar, in Essex, under
the immediate care of the Rev. Mr. Cecil. As every reader
is aware, the London Missionary Society is non-sectarian
in character, its object being to send the Gospel to the
heathen without regard to differences of creed, which,
however important they may be in Christian countries,
are not found dividing the missionaries from one another
in their work amongst the heathen. There it is absolutely
necessary that the champions of the truth should draw
closely together if they would successfully encounter the
powers of darkness. The nearest approach to a Union of
the Evangelical Churches which will perhaps ever be
attained on earth may be witnessed in the brotherly co-
operation of missionaries of all denominations in heathen
countries, whither they have gone to proclaim the truths
and the blessings of a common Christianity. At this time
Livingstone was moderately tall in stature, but slim in
build. His, however, was one of those wiry, closely-knit
frames which are often indicative of great powers of bodily
endurance ; and this form of physical organization is
usually accompanied with strong determination and un-
yielding tenacity of purpose.. All these Livingstone possessed in an eminent degree, as the steady and unfaltering
perseverance of his early years has sufficiently shown.
That such a man should fail in the high and holy work he

had set himself to do was, even humanly speaking, improbable; but when we consider that he was upheld by an
arm that was mightier than his, we know that it was impossible.   His first intention had been to go out as a missionary to China; but the opium war had for a time
closed the Celestial Empire against the missionaries, and
thus his attention was providentially directed to Africa, in which he was destined to achieve so much for
God, and to reap undying renown amongst men.   Accordingly, in 1840, he sailed for the Cape, where he
arrived in safety after a voyage of three months.   Filled
with a burning zeal to commence the work of his life
without delay, Livingstone immediately departed by way
of Algoa Bay for the scene of his labours at Kuruman, or
Latakoo as it is sometimes called, in the country of the
Bechuanas.   This mission-station, which had been established thirty years before, by Messrs. Hamilton and
Moffat, was seven hundred miles from Cape Town. It was,
in fact, the most advanced station yet occupied by the
soldiers of the cross—the out-post of the Christian army
which Dr. Livingstone was destined to push far forward
into the kingdom of heathen darkness, barbarism, and
cruelty.   At Kuruman he found a comfortable mission-
house, a stone church, and well-cultivated lands abounding in vegetables and fruit.   Robert Moffat received the
young missionary with gladness, and the latter, after
tarrying here for a season, resolved to proceed to the northward.   The Bakuenas or Backwains was the name of the
tribe he visited; it is in fact a branch of the larger nation

of Bechuanas. The tribe itself is divided into clans called by the names of animals—a trace, it has been suggested, of an animal worship like that of the ancient Egyptians. Livingstone next went to Lepelôle or Lituruba, where he made preparations for a settlement, meanwhile proceeding southward as far as the Cakaa mountains. Most of this journey was performed on foot, because of the sickness which had fallen upon the draught oxen. The Doctor appeared to be so slim and weak that the natives ridiculed the idea of his attempting to accomplish the journey. They were not aware that he was acquainted with their language and he overheard them saying:—" See, he is not strong he is quite thin, and only appears stout because he puts himself into those bags (meaning his trousers); he will soon knock up." They soon found out their mistake, however; for, thin as he was, he was also tough and active, and found no difficulty in out-stripping them all. On his return to Kuruman, he learned that his Backwains had been driven out of Lituruba by a hostile tribe; for the present, therefore, he abandoned his hope of settling there, and did not again visit the place for some years. A conspicuous comet visible about this time had a curious effect upon the warlike African tribes. Amongst civilized nations the effect of these strange visitants of our planetary system in the times of astronomical ignorance, was to check military ardour; in Africa, on the contrary, their appearauce is always the signal for a sanguinary onslaught on the neighbouring tribes. After having travelled northward again, in order to reconcile to their chief Sekomi, some of the disaffected Banangwatos, he returned in the direction of Kuruman, and selected Mabtoso, a beautiful valley, as the site of a mission-station. It was here, in 1843, that his career was well nigh brought to an abrupt termination by a conflict with a lion. The king of beasts, as he is not unfitly called, is the terror not only of all other animals even to the rhinoceros, who would appear to be impregnable, but he inspires even the heart of man with dread. The cattle, of course, are his prey; and not at night only, but even in broad day he often assails the cattle-pens of the settlers. The Bakatla, in Livingstone's vicinity, were in terror on account of a sudden invasion of these ferocious animals. Believing that they were given over to the power of the lions by witchcraft, they had not the courage to attack them. It is known that if one of a troop of lions be killed, the rest will immediately leave the country, Livingstone, therefore, resolved to lay one of them low. Going out with the natives, the party soon discovered the objects of their search on the summit of a low hill. Forming a circle, they found that they had enclosed three lions, but a shot, fired by one of the natives, having missed, one of the beasts bounded through the circle. The natives should have speared him, but in their trepidation they failed to do so. They still had two lions there, but they were in such a position that to fire upon them would be to run the risk of wounding their comrades on the other side of the circle. Thus one after the other of the animals they were hunting escaped. They had not yet done with them, however; for, on their way back to the village, they saw one of them quietly sitting on a rock, apparently enjoying their defeat. Livingstone immediately raised his gun and discharged both barrels at the lion, each bullet taking effect. The natives raised a shout of joy, but their triumph was but momentary, for just as Livingstone was re-loading his gun, the infuriated animal raised his tail aloft in anger, and sprang upon him. His description of what followed is terribly vivid. He is conscious only of a blow which makes him reel and fall to the ground; of two glaring eyes, and hot breath upon his face; a momentary anguish, as he is seized by the shoulder and shaken as a rat by a terrier; then comes a stupor which was afterwards a sort of drowsiness, in which there was no sense of pain, no feeling of terror, although there was a perfect consciousness of all that was happening. This condition is compared to that of patients under the influence of chloroform; they see the operation but do not feel the knife, and Livingstone thinks that this is probably the state of all animals when being killed by carnivora, and he regards it as a merciful provision of the Creator for lessening the pain of death. He knew that the lion had one paw upon his head, and, turning round to relieve himself of the pressure, saw the creature's eyes directed to Mebalwe, at a distance of ten or fifteen yards, who was aiming a gun at him. It missed fire, and immediately the native teacher was attacked and bitten in the thigh; another man, who attempted to spear the lion, was seized by the shoulder. But then the bullets he had received took effect, and, with a quiver through his

Livingstone under the Lion's Paw

... they saw ... them quietly sitting on a
... greatly ... their defeat. Livingstone im-
... raised his gun and discharged both barrels at
... m, each but ...king effect. The natives raised a
... shout of joy but ... rush ... was but momentary, for
... as Livingstone ... re... his gun, the infuriated
... mal rise ... ... and sprang upon him.
... ip... ... singularly vivid. He is
... conscious ... saw ... him ... and fall to
... ground ... y... eyes, and hot breath upon
... face ... tar. ...guish, as he is seized by the
shoulder and ...ken as a rat by a terrier, then comes a
stupor which was afterwards a sort of drowsiness, in
which there was ...signs of pain, no feeling of terror,
although ... a perfect consciousness of all that
was happen... ... ... compared to that of
patients under ... chloroform ... they see the
operation ... ... Livingstone thinks
that this is ... ... all animals who, being
killed by carnivora ... is it a merciful provision
of the Creator ... ...ing ... pain of death. He knew
that the lion ... ... upon his head, and, turning
round to relieve himself of the pressure, saw the creature's
eyes directed to Mebalwe, at a distance of ten or fifteen
yards, who was aiming a gun at him. It missed fire, and
immediately the ... teacher was attacked and bitten
in the thigh; another man, who attempted to spear the
lion, was seized by the shoulder. But then the bullets he
had received took effect, and, with a quiver through his

Livingstone under the Lion's Paw.

huge frame, he rolled over on his side dead. No less than eleven of the lion's teeth had penetrated the flesh of Livingstone's arm and crushed the bone, which not having been properly set, was felt all through the intrepid missionary's life, and served to identify his remains in England nearly a year after his death. In 1844, he was united in marriage to Mary Moffat, the eldest daughter of the founder of the Kuruman Mission. She was in every respect the model of a missionary's wife. To her husband she was, in the highest sense, a helpmeet—as he expressed it, "the best spoke in his wheel." In household matters no one could be more expert; she could make candles, soap, clothes, or whatever else was needed. She taught the native children, nursed the sick, and never seemed weary in well-doing. Except during the years 1852–6, when she and her family were in England for their health, she was the constant companion of her husband in his travels, whenever her health and strength permitted it. It must have been with a heavy heart that Livingstone buried her beneath the baobab tree on the banks of the Zambesi. We may mention here that they had four children, three sons and one daughter.

After his marriage, he removed to Chonuane amongst the Bakwains, a tribe to which he was much attached. The Chief Sechele was a man of great intelligence and his conversion had a powerful effect upon the tribe. He learned to read that he might study the Scripture, and aid in prosecuting the work of the mission. The Bakwains are a shrewd people in all matters of worldly in-

terest, good judges of cattle, and expert hunters. They
are of course rude and uneducated, and also slow in ap-
prehending the truths of Christianity, notwithstanding
their statements to the missionary. On questioning intelligent men among them as to their former knowledge of
good and evil—of God and the future state—Livingstone
says that they scouted the idea of any of them ever
having been without a tolerably clear conception on all
these subjects. Respecting their sense of right and wrong,
they profess that nothing we indicate as sin ever appeared
to them to be otherwise, except polygamy; and they
declare that they spoke in the same way of the direct influence exercised by God in giving rain in answer to the
prayers of the rain-makers, and in granting deliverance in
times of danger, as they do now, before they ever heard
of white men. They have no public worship, idols or sacri-
fices, which makes both them and the Caffres appear among
the most godless races of men. The belief in "rain-mak-
ing" was firmly held by the tribe. Sechele confessed
that the requirement to surrender this favourite superstition had been the greatest obstacle to his acceptance of
Christianity. The rain-makers reproached Livingstone
with not being able to open the clouds and send down
rain. "What is the use," they said, "of your everlasting
preaching and praying if it brings not rain?" They also
claimed to possess an infinity of charms to procure desired
blessings.

The frequent droughts which afflicted the village induced
Livingstone to prevail on Sechele to remove the entire

tribe to the Kolobeng, a stream forty miles distant.   Here
he remained with them until 1849, teaching and endeavouring to civilize his dusky friends.   He never affected
the exercise of authority, or employed any other means
than argument or quiet persuasion.   In addition to preaching and teaching, he was the physician of the sick and
the almoner of the poor.   To use his own words:—" The
smallest acts of friendship, even an obliging word and civil
look, are, as St. Xavier thought, no despicable part of the
missionary armour.   Nor ought the good opinion of the
most abject to be neglected, when politeness may secure it.
Their good word, in the aggregate, forms a reputation
which procures favour for the Gospel.   Show kindness to
the reckless opponents of Christianity on the bed of sickness, and they can never become your personal enemies.
Here, if anywhere, ' Love begets love.' "  Besides his other
labours, his hands were not idle.   He was bricklayer, carpenter, stone-mason, and general director of the social economy of the settlement.  Whatever his head or hand found
to do, he did it with all his might.

And now, in 1849, occurred his first great geographical
discovery, that of Lake Ngami.  Previous, however, to
his departure, an untoward event occurred.   The Dutch
Boers had long been the enemies of the missionaries, whom
they suspected of a design to elevate the Bechuanas to
their own level, to the injury of Boerish trade.   They
assailed the stations one by one, and at last attacked and
scattered the settlers of Kolobeng.   They were successful,
but with a loss for the first time, however, of six men.

Laying this at Livingstone's door, most unjustly as they probably knew, these so-called Christians plundered his house, destroyed his books and medicines, and carried off the furniture and clothing, together with large quantities of stores left in the keeping of the natives by some English gentlemen who had passed through Kolobeng on their way to hunt in the country beyond. Livingstone, nothing daunted, commenced his journey across the Kalahari desert in search of Lake Ngami, which, though mentioned by the natives, was not marked on any of the maps. Two African travellers, Colonel Steele and Mr. Oswell, the latter of whom paid the guides, accompanied him. They started on the 1st of June, 1849, with eighty oxen, twenty horses, and twenty men. This journey was a long and harassing one. To attempt to cross the desert at that point was out of the question ; the travellers were, therefore, obliged to skirt it for a considerable distance, and then cross at its narrowest part. Moreover, as the main object of the Dutch Boers in assailing the Bechuanas had been to prevent their migrating to the lake by depriving them of their arms, so now Sekomi, Chief of the Bamanangwâto, refused Livingstone his assistance likewise under a false pretext. The fact was, that it was from Lake Ngami that the Boers obtained their principal supplies of ivory, and much of this passed through Sekomi's hands. Both, therefore, were interested in keeping the Bechuanas and their instructor out of the field. In some parts of the Kalahari desert, watermelons were found in such abundance that a traveller they met stated that his cattle had sub-

sisted on the fluid contained in them no less than twenty-
one days. The hot air of the desert is at times so strongly
charged with electricity, that a bunch of ostrich feathers
held a few seconds against it becomes as strongly charged
as if attached to a powerful electrical machine, and clasps
the advancing hand with a sharp cracking sound. Livingstone thinks that the borders of this wilderness would be
found to afford relief to persons suffering from pulmonary
complaints. Those who now recommend Florida, Madeira,
or Mentone, may perhaps be induced, at some future
time, to direct their attention to the desert of Kalahari.
We need not describe in detail the difficulties of this
long and tedious journey. Suffice it to say, that both men
and animals suffered fearfully from the scorching rays of
the sun, the burning sand, and the terrible thirst which,
too often, there was no water to assuage. At length, to
their joy and relief, they reached a beautiful river the
Zouga, and finally on the 1st of August, exactly two
months after they set out, they looked with thankful
hearts upon the broad expanse of Lake Ngami. Livingstone estimated it to be from seventy to one hundred
miles in circumference. He and his two friends were
probably the first Europeans who had ever beheld it; but
its discovery was as nothing compared with the intelligence they gathered from the natives who had come from
the northward. They soon found upon inquiry, that
stretching for hundreds of miles, was an immense country
abounding in woods, lakes, and rivers. This at once dispelled the delusion prevalent in Europthat the interior

of South Central Africa was an arid desert of sand. Here
then was the bright vision of a new field for the exercise
of Livingstone's noble abilities. If the country were well-
wooded and well-watered, it must also be well-populated,
and ripe for the harvest of Christian civilization. The
missionary's heart throbbed more quickly, and he longed
to press forward to explore it for himself. But it was
now October and, as Oswell had volunteered to go to the
Cape for a boat, they resolved to return. Livingstone remained at Kolobeng till April, 1850. The next object he
had in view was to reach the country of the Makololo,
whose Chief, Sebituane, lived two hundred miles beyond
Lake Ngami. He therefore set out with his wife and
three children ; the Chief, Sechele, also accompanied him.
This time they kept more to the eastward, and crossed the
Zouga at its lowest extremity, going up the northern bank.
This last step proved to be a mistake, and they were compelled to retrace their steps. Hearing that a party in
search of ivory were stricken down with fever, sixty
miles off, Livingstone, with his usual alacrity, hurried off
to their assistance, and succeeded in saving the lives of all
but one. He then returned to the settlement and thence
to Kuruman, to recruit his own health and that of his
family. While he was there, messengers arrived at Kolobeng, from Sebituane, Chief of the Makololo, who had
heard of the attempt of the white men to reach him, and
promising to render every assistance in his power. He
also sent presents of cattle, &c., to Sechele, Sekomi, and
the other chiefs in the neighbourhood. Unfortunately

hey had departed before Livingstone returned, and he
thus lost much valuable information touching the best
routes to their country. He soon managed to learn what
he desired to know by other means. The Bosjesmen or
Bushmen were well acquainted with the difficult ap-
proaches to the Makololo territory, and it so happened
that a man who had had dealings with the former people,
broke the mainspring of his gun. Livingstone promised
to mend it on condition that its owner would put him in
communication with the desert people. He thus contrived
to gather all the intelligence he required. This was at the
Zouga, and he immediately crossed that river, made his
way as directed to the Chobe, and entered the country of
the Makololo. Learning that Sebituane the Chief, who had
come a hundred miles to meet them, was at a place twenty
miles down the stream, Livingstone and Oswell went
down in a canoe to visit him. They were most hospitably
received by the chief, who had long desired to open up
independent relations with the white men. Unhappily
he died, just as his desire was being fulfilled, of inflam-
mation of the lungs, the result mainly of an old wound
received in battle. " Never," says Livingstone, " was I so
much grieved by the loss of a black man before ; and it
was impossible not to follow him in thought into the
other world, and to realize somewhat of the feelings of
those who pray for the dead. The dark question of ' What
is to become of such as he ?' must be left, however, where
we find it. ' The Judge of all the earth will do right.' "
Sebituane's daughter, who, contrary to custom, suc-

ceeded him, gave Livingstone full liberty to visit the country. At the end of 1851, he discovered the Zambesi in the centre of the continent, a river destined in the future to be the great highway of traffic in South Central Africa. At this time it was from three hundred to six hundred yards in width of deep water. Every year it rises about thirty feet, overflowing and fertilizing lands for fifteen or twenty miles on each side and resembling a vast lake. Not finding a suitable place of settlement near at hand, Livingstone resolved to take his family to the Cape, whence they could embark for England to recover their health and strength. He could then return alone and seek for a healthy district, free from marsh, in which to found a station. His family sailed in April, 1852, Livingstone promising to follow them in two years; yet four years and a half rolled by before they received any tidings of him. Meanwhile every inquiry possible was set on foot, and yet no intelligence could be obtained, and there was too much reason to fear that he had fallen a victim to the climate, the wild beast or the savage. It was not so, however; he was battling on in the new field he had discovered, like a faithful soldier of the cross. It was during this period that he accomplished " that wonderful journey," which, as Sir Bartle Frere says, " first made his name known throughout Christendom, by crossing and re-crossing the continent of Africa, from the mouths of the Zambesi to St. Paul de Loando, through regions which it was not supposed that a white man had ever crossed before. His

erty to visit the
 discovered the
ent, a river des-
ighway of traffic
it was from three
th of deep water.
 overflowing and
niles on each side
g a suitable place
 resolved to take
ould embark for
ngth. He could
thy district, free
on. His family
g to follow them
rolled by before
eanwhile every
 no intelligence
h reason to fear
 the wild beast
he was battling
like a faithful
period that he
which, as Sir
own through-
ng the conti-
ambesi to St.
was not sup-
before. His



first step was to penetrate to Linyante, on the Zambesi, the capital of the Makololo nation. It is situated at the confluence of the Chobe with the great river, and in its neighbourhood are to be found all the land animals, and all the amphibia, together with the varied forms of luxuriant vegetation peculiar to tropical Africa. Here in the royal hut Livingstone began to preach the Gospel to the Makololo, and continued to do so for some time. His first movement in the way of exploration was a voyage up the Zambesi, escorted by Sekeletu, the chief, and a body-guard of well-armed men. Sekeletu, we may remark, had assumed the chieftainship at the request of Sebituane's daughter. The party passed though the territory of the Banyeti and other nations tributary to the Makololo. The country, as Livingstone describes it, is surpassingly rich, so that the accounts previously received from the natives were fully corroborated. It is covered with beautiful trees with open glades between them, stretching away in every direction. The grass is particularly luxuriant, and amongst the animals which browse on the plains beyond are, the elephant, the rhinoceros, the antelope, and the zebra; on the banks of the river, the hippopotamus. Returning, they shot down the river, now at its height, in canoes, accomplishing sixty miles in a day. Livingstone now commenced his wonderful journey to the sea. We take advantage of a condensed account, based upon the explorer's own narrative. Accompanied by a band of Makololo provided by Sekeletu, he left Linyante for Loando in September in 1853, and on the 30th of November reached

Gonye Falls. On the 17th of December he was at Libonta, where he was detained for days collecting contributions of fat and butter as presents to the Bolonda chiefs. Libonta is the last town of the Makololo.

On the 27th of December, Dr. Livingstone was at the confluence of the Leeba and Leeambye, the former of which he ascended to the small stream Makondo, having in the meantime declined an invitation from a female chief to visit her. On the 6th of January, 1854, he reached the village of another female chief, Nyamoana, and interviewed her. He left on the 11th, after receiving presents from Nyamoana. We learn from the doctor that the Balonda are real negroes, having much more wool on their heads and bodies than any of the Bechuana or Caffre tribes, which may be a matter of some interest to the physiologists. A grand reception by the chief, Shinte, shows how far the African of that region has progressed in the art of court etiquette.

On the 1st of February, in the country called Mokwankwa, the doctor was surprised to find English cotton cloth more eagerly inquired after than beads and ornaments, not because the tribes were more modest, but because the climate was colder. During the entire month of February, 1854, the doctor kept on travelling towards his objective point, occasionally tarrying in villages, and receiving the hospitalities of the chiefs. His description of the geography of the country through which he passed is of the greatest interest to civilized people.

The month of March was characterized (on the 6th) by

change of route on account of the visits of slave traders,
n traversing a succession of open lawns and deep forests,
n being taken sick, partially recovering, encountering
hostile parties, paying tribute to be allowed to pass
through some countries—a system established by slave
traders to curry favour with the chiefs—in obtaining
guides to get into the Portuguese territory, and on the 30th
coming to a sudden descent from the high land. Below
him lay the great Quango valley. This valley equals that
of the Mississippi in fertility. The doctor's reflections on
its geographical formations, its people, and its productions
are fresh contributions to science and civilization.

Reaching Ambaca, he was kindly received by the Portuguese Commandant, who recommended wine for his de-
bility, and here he took the first glass of that beverage
he had taken in Africa. He felt much refreshed, and
could then realize and meditate upon the weakening
effects of the fever.

They were, he says, curious to even himself, for, " though
he had tried several times since he had left Ngio to take
lunar observations, he could not avoid confusion of time
and distance, neither could he hold the instrument steady
nor perform a simple calculation." Hence many of the
positions of this part of the route were left till his return
from Loando. Often, on getting up in the morning, he
found his clothing as wet from perspiration as if he had
been dipped in water. In vain had he tried to learn or
collect words of the Bunda, or dialect spoken in Angola.
He forgot the days of the week and the names of his com-

panions, and had he been asked, he says, he probably could not have told his own. The complaint itself occupied many of his thoughts. One day he supposed he had got the true theory of it, and would certainly cure the next attack, whether in himself or his companions ; but some new symptoms would appear and scatter all the fine speculations which had sprung up, with extraordinary fertility, in one department of his brain.

These attacks of fever delayed him many times upon his journeyings. Both in going to Loando and in returning, he was frequently stricken down. He arrived at the Portuguese settlement of St. Paul de Loando on the 31st of May, 1854. Here he was hospitably received both by the authorities and by Mr. Gabriel, the British Commissioner for the suppression of the slave trade. Fever and dysentery detained him for four months, during which time he was carefully nursed and tended by those around him. He had the services of the government physician, and every means was used to restore him to health. So terribly was he reduced, however, that had he not possessed a constitution of iron, he must have succumbed beneath the repeated attacks of disease.

On looking about Loando, he found it to be nothing more or less than a great convict establishment, that is, as far as the European inhabitants are concerned ; most of them had been sent into exile for some political or other offence against the laws ; they are, however, greatly outnumbered by the blacks and half-castes ; there are 9,000 of the former, of whom 5,000 are slaves.

But little religious instruction among the natives seems
to be attempted ; the convents of the Jesuits, who were
formerly zealous teachers here, are now waste and tenant-
less.   Sugar and rice and cotton, and most other tropical
products might be cultivated with great success; but the
curse of slavery seems to rest like a blight upon every
useful branch of commercial enterprise.   The wild excitement and horrible greed, fostered by this lawless traffic in
human beings, seems to possess every mind so that there
are few who will engage in the calmer pursuits of agriculture or manufacturing industry.   Livingstone noted that
the cotton-plant was growing wild all about, and wasting
its silky filaments ; that indigo and coffee, and other valuable products might be had almost for the gathering ;
and that several sugar and other manufactories which he
visited were not so successful as they might be, if more
spirit and capital were thrown into their management ;
and he sighed over the folly and inhumanity of man, in
neglecting the bounteous gifts of God and exercising
cruelty and oppression on his fellows.

At length, on the 20th of September, 1854, he mustered
all his remaining strength for a fresh effort. Passing round
by sea to the mouth of the Bengo, he sailed up that river
through a country admirably adapted for the culture of
the sugar-cane.   He visited some of the tribes in this
region, and took advantage of a delay caused by the illness
of some of his men to examine the resources of the country
and the best means of opening it up for commerce and
cultivation.   It is stated that the district of Angola com-

prises some 40,000 people, many of whom can read and write; that of Golungo Alto about 104,000, many of whom have trades. The doctor here makes some useful suggestions in regard to the carrying trade to the coast and traffic with Europeans generally. He visited the deserted convent of St. Hilarion at Bango, and heard the Jesuits and other missionaries well spoken of for their instruction of the children.

On January 1st, 1855, the doctor left Pungo Andongo, and found the whole country drained by the Lucalla and its feeders extremely fertile, with wild coffee in abundance. The Portuguese authority extends inland about 300 miles to the River Quango, the sixteen districts including about 600,000 souls. The doctor has no hesitation in asserting that if the country had been in possession of England, it would now have been yielding as much or more of the raw material for her manufactures as an equal extent of territory in the cotton-growing States of America. A railroad from Loando to this valley is wanted. As he proceeds, the doctor describes the characteristics of this wonderfully humid region, and says they may account in some measure for the periodical floods of the Zambesi and perhaps the Nile.

At Cassange, he found the people groaning under the most degrading superstition. It is true that they appeared to recognize the Barimo, or Great Spirit—a dim notion of a Supreme Being; but they did not approach him in worship. Such a deity as they acknowledge is only used as an object to strike awe into their dupes by

those who deal in divination and witchcraft. The most
horrid cruelties, including the sacrifice of human victims,
are perpetrated by these people. Livingstone's spirit
groaned within him when he found the gross darkness in
which the poor creatures were involved, and he thus
contrasts it with the prodigal fertility of loveliness of the
land in which they lived:—

"How fearful," he says, "is the contrast between this
inward gloom and the brightness of the outer world, between the undefined terrors of the spirit and the peace
and beauty that pervade the scenes around me! I have
often thought, in travelling through this land, that it presents pictures of beauty which angels might enjoy. How
often have I beheld, in still mornings, scenes the very
essence of beauty, and all bathed in an atmosphere of
delicious warmth, to which the soft breeze imparts a
pleasing sensation of coolness as if from a fan! Green,
grassy meadows, the cattle feeding, the goats browsing,
the kids skipping, the groups of herdsboys, with miniature bows, arrows, and spears; the women winding their
way to the river, with watering-pots poised jauntily on
their heads; men sewing under the shady bananas; and
the old, gray-headed fathers sitting on the ground, with
staff in hand, listening to the morning gossip, while others
carry branches to repair their hedges. Such scenes,
flooded with the bright African sun, and enlivened by the
songs of the birds before the heat of the day becomes intense, form pictures which can never be forgotten."

Leaving Cassange, the party proceeded to the Quango,

and came in contact with the Ambakistas, "the Jews of Angola," as they are called, although they have nothing of the Jew about them, except his subtlety and intelligence. Being shrewd business men, they are employed as clerks and writers, their penmanship being characterized by a female delicacy which is much esteemed among the Portuguese. They have considerable knowledge of the history and laws of Portugal, that being, however, the only European country of which they know anything. Livingstone was soon after again prostrated by fever, and remained for eight days tossing on a sleepless bed, made up like a grave in a country churchyard with grass on the top. The kind attention of the Portuguese, who had accompanied the missionary, contrasted very favourably with the conscienceless extortion of the villagers when they were solicited to render any assistance. Having mounted his ox, the doctor again proceeded on his journey. Their progress for a while was very slow, seven miles being about the extent travelled on each day when they moved on, which was not above one-third of the time—two-thirds being consumed in stoppages occasioned by sickness or the necessity for seeking food. After crossing the Loango, they made a *détour* to the southward to get cheaper provisions; they were now more out of the path of the slave-traders, and found the inhabitants more timid and civil. Onward they travel by zig-zag paths through the forest, their way beset by climbing paths. They soon reach another river, abounding in crocodiles and hippopotami, the glens on whose

, " the Jews of
r have nothing
y and intelli-
are employed
being charac-
uch esteemed
lerable know-
l, that being,
ch they know
ain prostrated
ng on a sleep-
y churchyard
of the Portu-
ry, contrasted
ortion of the
er any assist-
or again pro-
a while was
t travelled on
ot above one-
ned in stop-
r for seeking
a *détour* to
y were now
d found the
they travel
ay beset by
ver, abound-
s on whose



banks are green and shady, and the woods enlivened by
the song of birds. Thence through bogs, surrounded by
clumps of straight evergreens. More streams, and yet
more; the Kanesi and the Fombeji are crossed, and they
reach Cabango, on the banks of the Chihombo. They are
coming into a more densely populated part of the country,
where provisions are cheap and plentiful; four persons
can be well fed upon vegetable and animal food at the
rate of about a penny a day, paid in cloth or beads. Cabango is a considerable village of some two hundred huts,
and several real square houses, constructed of poles, with
grass woven between. In these dwell the half-caste
Portuguese agents for the Cassange traders. No business could be transacted for four days, because a person
had died there and the funeral obsequies lasted during
all that time. Livingstone now passed through Matia-
moo's well-peopled country. It has but little trade;
what there is consists of an exchange of calico, salt,
gunpowder, coarse earthenware, and beads for ivory
and slaves. There are no cattle, except a herd kept
by the chief to supply him with meat. He is mild
in his government, and more just than African chiefs
generally are. We are now among the Balonda, who are
better looking than the people nearer the coast. They
are a sprightly, vivacious race, spending their time chiefly
in gossip, and marriage, and funeral ceremonies, at the
latter of which they are most merry and uproarious, probably to conceal their grief, which they manage to do
most effectually. The party now strike to the south-east

to visit Katema, an old friend. Passing through the territory of a chief named Bango, and crossing the Loembwe, on the second of June, they reach the village of Kawawa, where a very noisy wake is going on over a dead man— rather more picturesque than an Irish wake, and not quite so quarrelsome. So the party journeyed on till they arrived again at Linyante at the end of the winter season—that is, in August—where they were received with every demonstration of joy. After a short sojourn of two months and some earnest consultations with the natives as to the means to be taken for opening up a trade with the west coast on the one hand, or Zanzibar and the Mozambique Channel on the other, Livingstone resolved to follow, as closely as possible, the course of the Zambesi, and see what facilities that great river affords for opening up the heart of South Africa to Christianity and commerce. Accordingly, on the 27th of October, 1855, when the first continuous rain of the season begins to fall, he and his party made ready for their departure ; and on the 3rd of November they set out, accompanied by Sekeletu and two hundred Makololo. The mother of the chief had prepared for Livingstone a bag of ground nuts fried in cream with a little salt, which is considered a great delicacy ; and Mamire, her second husband, made a farewell speech, expressive of hope for his safety and quick return with his wife, whose coming to dwell among them they all seemed greatly to desire. So the cavalcade set out as it had done before, with Livingstone for a leader, and the friendly chief bearing him company on the way with a numerous escort. The doctor's clothes had been sent on ahead, and he was drenched to the skin in a thunderstorm, so Sekeletu gave him his own blanket to sleep on, going without himself—an act of kindness of which few savages would be capable. Afterwards he presented him with twelve oxen, with hoes, beads, &c., sufficient to purchase a canoe when they reach the Zambesi, beyond the celebrated Mosi-oa-tunya or " Smoke-resounding " Falls, which, after travelling for about a fortnight, they were now approaching. These falls, since called the Victoria Falls and described as as large and more magnificent than Niagara, are caused by a deep fissure in the hard, black basaltic rock, which forms the bed of the river, into which the mighty volume of water leaps down a sheer descent of unknown depth, with tremendous sound and a shaking of the earth which can be heard and felt many miles away. The river is here about 1,860 yards broad, flowing from north to south, and the crack in its bed, caused by some great convulsion of nature, lies right across it, being about as long as the stream is wide. The width of the crack at its narrowest part is about eighty yards. So into this tremendous chasm, which has been plumbed to twice the depth of Niagara, plunges that mile-wide sheet of water— a spectacle the most sublime, perhaps, that all the earth affords. On the verge of this awful precipice, and in the midst of the water, dividing it into two nearly equal streams, stands Garden Island, a little spot of ground, which by skilful paddling may be approached in a canoe; and, looking from thence down the sheer descent of that crystal wall, one may see nearly half a mile of water, collected in a channel, from twenty to thirty yards wide, flowing to the left, at exactly right angles to its previous course, while the other portion of the fall flows to the right. These two streams meet midway in a boiling whirlpool, and dash off, foaming and seething, through another rocky fissure at right angles to the crack down which they were first precipitated, and from the eastern end of which this outlet is about 1,170 yards, but not more than 600 from its western end. Through this narrow escape-channel, which does not appear to be more than twenty or thirty yards wide, the Zambesi rushes southward for about the distance of 130 yards, when it enters a second chasm, somewhat deeper than the first, and nearly parallel to it. The eastern half of this chasm is left dry, and has large trees growing in it, while the volume of water goes steadily off to the west, forming a promontory which has at its point the second escape-channel, about 1,170 yards long and 416 broad at the base; after reaching which the river turns abruptly round the head of another promontory, flowing away to the east through a third chasm; it then glides round a third promontory and away back to the west by a fourth chasm, and in the distance it seems to round yet another promontory and bend once more back to the east in a fifth chasm. There has been no wearing away of the rocks by the long-continued action of the water, as at the Great American Falls. They are right through the course of this gigantic zigzag so sharply cut and angular, that it can at once be seen that the hard

e of water, col-
ty yards wide,
to its previous
1 flows to the
boiling whirl-
rough another
wn which they
end of which
nore than 600
scape-channel,
nty or thirty
for about the
econd chasm,
parallel to it.
and has large
r goes steadily
ch has at its
'0 yards long
hich the river
promontory,
asm; it then
back to the
it seems to
e more back
no wearing
ction of the
ey are right
sharply cut
at the hard



basalt has been broken by a force acting from beneath, into their present form—how many ages since no one can tell, but Livingstone conjectures it was probably done when the ancient inland seas were let off by similar fissures nearer the ocean. From the different promontories views of the falls may be obtained under varying aspects, all agreeing in the one element of sublime grandeur; but perhaps there is none finer than that from Garden Island, where the whole body of water runs clear over the mountain, quite unbroken, but, after a descent of ten or more feet, the whole mass suddenly assumes the appearance of a mighty snow-drift; portions of it, like comets with streaming tails, leaping off in every direction, twisting and twirling i.. a mad dance that dazzles the eye and makes the brain giddy to look upon. Clouds of these aqueous comets, invested in finer spray, rush up in columns as it were of steam to the height of 200 or 300 feet; they may be seen at the Batoka village, Moachemba, about twenty miles off, and it is f . these and the sounds like thunder, which may be heard as far as they can be seen, that the name "smoke-resounding" has been applied to the falls. This vapour becoming condensed falls in constant, showers upon the evergreen trees on the island and banks from whose leaves the heavy drops roll like globules of quicksilver, and form rivulets which, running down the face of the rocks, are licked off their perpendicular beds by the uprising columns, and sent again into the air, to be again returned in showers upon the trees, and again thwarted in their efforts to find the level of the main stream, that goes rushing and roaring in the narrow escape-channels, or gliding with a smoothness that indicates the vast depths of the hollows which receive it round the tree-covered promontories, on which one can stand and view the amazing spectacle. When the morning sun gilds these smoke-like columns, double and treble rainbows flash and coruscate about them. In the evening there is a yellow sulphurous haze, as if from the mouth of the bottomless pit. Livingstone declared that of all the wonders of the lands he had visited he had seen no such stupendous spectacle as this, and there is no doubt that he was the first European who had ever gazed upon it. As he could not detain Sekeletu and his two hundred followers unnecessarily, he did not make a lengthened examination of the falls at this time, but in 1860 he had more time at his disposal, and paid greater attention to the wonders of the place. On the latter occasion he was accompanied by his brother Charles, who had seen Niagara, and he unhesitatingly gave the palm to the African cataract. The latter was seen, it must be remembered, during the season of drought; at flood the volume of waters here must greatly exceed that at Niagara; and the tortuous course of the channel, the many deep chasms into which the current leaps, the numerous points of views from which it may be seen, and the effects produced are so strange and startling that it must ever be an object of wonder and reverential awe.

Now, bidding adieu to Sekeletu, who left with him one hundred and fourteen men, he turned his face to the north-

e narrow escape-
1at indicates the
t round the tree-
stand and view
g sun gilds these
nbows flash and
here is a yellow
' the bottomless
wonders of the
:upendous spec-
he was the first
As he could not
lowers unneces-
nination of the
time at his dis-
wonders of the
npanied by his
1 he unhesitat-
t. The latter
the season of
a must greatly
course of the
h the current
which it may
' strange and
f wonder and

with him one
a to the north-

ward and resumed his toilsome journey to the sea. ' Crossing successively the Lekone and the Kalome (Nov. 30th),
both tributaries of the Zambesi, they reached the Mozuma,
with the Taba Cheu, or White Mountains, to the south-
east. Between the banks of the river, in which no water
was then flowing, Livingstone observes with much satisfaction pieces of lignite, probably indicating the existence
of coal—everywhere a great adjunct to civilization. Here,
also, were ruins of large towns which had been depopulated by wars, most probably caused by the atrocious slave-
trade. Sunday, the tenth of December, was passed in the
village of Monze, the principal chief of the Batoka. Various chiefs of this tribe and the Batonga were also visited.
Crossing the Nakachinta, a small branch of the Zambesi,
with a low range of forest-clad hills before them, they
descend into a fertile plain. As they pass along, the people
supply them with food in abundance. They had somehow
found out that Livingstone had medicine, and they brought
their children and sick folk to be cured by him, much to
the disgust of his followers, who wished to monopolize his
skill and remedies. Here, for the first time, was heard
the curious cry "*Pula, pula,*" signifying, " rain, rain,'
uttered by a bird, probably a kind of cuckoo. The natives
call it *Mokwa reza*—" Son-in-law of God," and say that
its cry predicts heavy falls of rain. This is a bird of good
repute ; not so the crow, whose nests are destroyed in
times of drought to break the charm which it is said seals
up the windows of heaven. The country grows more and
more beautiful as they proceeded, being furrowed by deep

valleys abounding in large game, such as buffaloes and
elephants; three of the latter were shot, and an abundance
of meat obtained, in which the natives gladly shared.
Having visited the residence of the chief Semalembue, on
the Kafue, here about two hundred yards wide, they follow its course to its confluence with the Zambesi. Passing through the territories of various tribes, they found
them uniformly friendly, with one exception. The Selole
had been deceived by an Italian named Simoens, who had
married a chief's daughter, and they suspected Livingstone
to be another Italian, or Simoens, who had been killed in
an expedition, come to life again. It required all the
tact and address which Livingstone possessed to pacify
these people and secure his personal safety. They then
took in their heads that he possessed some supernatural
power to propitiate their deity, and came to him for potions
to give them success in hunting and such other vocations
as they followed. The missionary pointed them to a
higher power for aid in all their good undertakings. A
strong, muscular race of people were those about this part
of the course of the Zambesi, which was their great highway. Both men and women cultivate the ground. They
have the lower lip deformed by artificial means, which so
disfigures most of the tribes. Their villages are pictur-
esquely situated among the hills, and their valleys are
occupied by gardens, where maize and native corn grow
luxuriantly. They cannot keep oxen for the tsetse, and
look upon white men as marauders, having been much
robbed by the half-caste Portuguese, whom they call

Bazunga. " They have words of peace all very fine," they say, " but lies only, as the Bazunga are great liars." They knew not then that they might trust the *Makoa*, the " English." The next stage reached was the confluence of the Loangwa with the Zambesi. In this neighbourhood the Portuguese had at one time a flourishing establishment, and it was clear that the reminiscences of the natives touching European dealings were by no means agreeable. From the crowds of armed men who appeared at his approach, Livingstone was apprehensive of an attack, but he managed to re-assure the people. At Inpende they surrounded the encampment with strange, wild cries, and seemed to be meditating an attack. Livingstone sent word to the chief that he was an Englishman; his reply was, " We don't know that tribe; we suppose you are a Mazunga (Portuguese), the tribe with which we have been fighting." Assured that this was not the case, something like the truth dawned upon the native mind, and the exclamation broke forth, " You must be one of that tribe that loves the black man." What an honourable distinction was this! This established friendly relations, and the chief did all he could to aid their progress. Some men were detailed to ferry them across the river, here 1,200 yards wide and 700 or 800 feet deep. This is the country of the Babisa. To the north lies Senga, which abounds in iron ore. English cotton goods begin to be abundant, and the name of an Englishman is a passport to the favour of the natives. " He is a man," said they, " his countrymen are enemies to the slave trade." And when the slaves

4

themselves reported Livingstone's approach to Tette, then about ten days' journey off, they said, " Oh, this is our brother who is coming ! "

Tette was reached on the third of March. It is situated on a slope up from the river, close by the bank of which stands the fort which, though it mounts but few guns and has only thatched dwellings for the troops, was strong enough to keep the natives in awe, and prove the salvation of the Portuguese. Major Sicard, the Commandant of Tette when Livingstone reached the place, had considerable influence with the natives, which he had exerted to restore peace ; that, however, had not lasted long. He had been told by some natives that "The Son of God, who was able to take the sun down from the heavens, and place it under his arm (this was in allusion to the sextant and artificial horizon), had come ;" and, having previously heard that Livingstone was on his way thither, felt sure that this was he, and prepared to receive him. In the vicinity of Tette there is abundance of coal and iron, and also a gold-field partially worked by the natives. Large crops might be raised of maize, indigo, and cotton, with other tropical products but for the accursed slave-trade which depopulates the country and deprives it of labourers who would gladly work for low wages. As it is, a fine country is made comparatively unproductive, and what might be a thriving and industrious population is thinned and converted into blood-thirsty ruffians by the odious traffic. Livingstone, therefore, always insisted that the first step to Christianize and civilize the African, was the utter ex-

ette, then
is is our

s situated
of which
guns and
as strong
salvation
andant of
consider-
xerted to
long. ¦ He
i of God,
heavens,
in to the
d, having
y thither,
e him. In
and iron,
e natives.
nd cotton,
lave-trade
of labour-
it is, a fine
and what
is thinned
he odious
at the first
e utter ex-

tinction of the trade in human flesh and blood. On the 22nd of April, after curing the commandant and others of the fever, Livingstone started for the coast. Passing through Senna and Manica, he left the main stream at Mazaro, which had already been explored up to this point from the sea, by Captain Parker, and followed the Mutu on the direct route to Quillimane or Killimane on the Mozambique Channel. This place he reached on the 26th of May, 1856, about four years after he set out from the Cape. During the whole of this time no news of him had reached Europe, and the worst apprehensions were entertained by his friends. Here he was compelled to remain six weeks in a most unhealthy locality. At length H. M. brig *Frolic* arrived off the bar. An offer of a passage to the Mauritius was gladly accepted, and Livingstone left Africa on the 12th of July, and, after a short sojourn at the Mauritius to recover his health, sailed for England, where he arrived on the 12th of December. He had been absent sixteen years, and during that time had travelled, in the wearisome African fashion, 9,000 miles. He records his thankfulness in these words :—" No one has cause for more abundant gratitude to his fellow-man and to his Maker than I have ; and may God grant that the effect on my mind be such that I may be more humbly devoted to the services of the Author of all our mercies ! "

Livingstone had come among his friends like a man from the dead, and related such particulars of his wonderful travels and discoveries as he could within the compass of public addresses, with the modest reticence which characterized the man, and the hesitancy of speech of one long unaccustomed to the use of his mother tongue. Everywhere he was hailed and honoured as a great discoverer and philanthropist. The gold medal of the Royal Geographical Societies of London and Paris were awarded to him, and our national universities conferred on him the honorary degrees of LL.D. and D.C.L. respectively. Other distinctions were also conferred upon him. Wherever he went crowds assembled to listen to his descriptions of regions hitherto unexplored, and savage tribes, of whose existence the civilized world had, till then, been unaware. Strange and startling as were the revelations which he made, yet no one doubted their truth. Every word that he uttered bore the stamp of veracity.

The newspapers of the day give some accounts of the great discoverer which are deserving of notice. In announcing his arrival at Marseilles, the London *Times* stated "that when taken on board H. M. S. *Frolic*, on the Mozambique coast, he had great difficulty in speaking a sentence of English, having disused it so long while travelling in Africa." This must surely have been a fancy; it was only four years and a half since he parted with his wife and family at the Cape; he frequently came in contact with Englishmen, hunting and exploring, and besides regularly kept a journal in his native language. The notion probably arose from a pleasantry of the Doctor's, like that mentioned below, afterwards repeated as a sober fact. The *Nonconformist* gives the following description of the explorer at this time :—" A foreign-looking person, plainly

and rather carelessly dressed, of middle height, bony frame
and Gaelic countenance, with short cropped hair and mus-
tachios, and generally plain exterior, rises to address the
meeting. He appears to be about forty years of age. His
face is deeply furrowed and pretty well tanned. It indicates a man of quick and keen discernment, strong im-
pulses, inflexible resolution, and habitual self-command.
Unanimated, its most characteristic expression is that of
severity; when excited, a varied expression of earnest and
benevolent feeling, and remarkable enjoyment of the ludicrous in circumstances and character, passes over it.
The meeting rises to welcome him with deafening cheers.
When he speaks you think him at first to be a Frenchman,
but, as he tells you a Scotch anecdote in true Glas-
gowegian dialect, you make up your mind that he must
be, as his face indicates, a countryman from the north. His
command of his mother tongue being imperfect, he apolo-
gizes for his broken, hesitating speech by informing you
that he has not spoken your language for nearly sixteen
years; and then he tells you as best a modest man can
concerning his travels. In doing this he leaves out all
about his personal sufferings, just remarking that he in-
tends to save those anecdotes for his ' garrulous dotage.'
Much of what he says, he has already, of course, written
in his journals, and of some circumstances he has before
told at other places; but he is one from whom you could
hear the same thing more than three times. His narrative is not very connected, and his manner is awkward,
excepting once when he justifies his enthusiasm, and

once when he graphically describes the Mosiatunya—the great cataract of Central Africa. He ends a speech of natural eloquence and witty simplicity by saying that he has begun his work and will carry it on. His broken thanks are drowned by the applause of the audience." The London *Leader* concluded a review of Livingstone's work as follows:—"For seventeen years, smitten by more than thirty attacks of fever, endangered by seven attempts on his life, continually exposed to fatigue, hunger, and the chance of perishing miserably in the wilderness, shut out from the knowledge of civilized men, the missionary pursued his way, an apostle and a pioneer, without fear, without egotism, without desire of reward. Such a work, accomplished by such a man, deserves all the eulogy that can be bestowed upon it, for nothing is more rare than brilliant and unsullied success." It was during his residence in England that Livingstone wrote his "Missionary Travels in South Africa," containing a complete narrative of his labours and discoveries between 1840 and 1856. The unpretending style of the work, and the native modesty of its author, sometimes conceal from the reader the full extent of his labours ; yet sufficient is disclosed, in a casual manner, to give some idea of his careful observation of the minutest details regarding the natural history of the country, and its capabilities for agriculture, trade, and metallurgy. He had carefully arranged a sort of African materia medica, after an accurate examination of the properties of the wild plants. The cases of fever which he cured at Tette were treated by him, after his stock of quinine had been exhausted, with a native plant, whose febrifuge qualities he had discovered. Even the diseases of wild animals did not escape Livingstone's attention, and he "furnishes a very interesting chapter on the domestic habits and diseases of wild beasts in Africa, as well as those of the native population, throwing much new and original light on these topics. The serpents of the country are also scientifically treated."

On the 10th of March, 1858, Livingstone again left England, in H. M. Colonial steamer, the *Pearl*, with the object of exploring the Zambesi and its mouths and tributaries, and ascertaining their availability as highways for commerce and Christianity to pass into the heart of Africa. His first destination was the Cape, as before; on this occasion he was accompanied by his brother Charles, Dr. Kirk, the naturalist of the party, and Mr. R. Thornton, who was acquainted with geology. At Cape Town, Mr. F. Skead, R.N., joined them as surveyor, and they proceeded round to the east coast, which was reached in May. It was found on examination that the Zambesi pours its waters into the ocean by four mouths, the Milambe, which is most westerly; the Kongone, the Luabo, and the Timbwe or Muselo. There is also a natural canal when the river is in flood, which winds very much among the swamps, and is used as a secret way for conveying slaves from Quillimane to the bays, from whence they can be shipped. The best entrance was found to be the Kongone, and into it the *Pearl* was taken, and also a small steam launch, named *Ma-Robert*, the name given by the natives to Mrs. Livingstone.

Very broad generally is the river Zambesi, but the deep channel, or *Quete*, as the canoemen call it, is narrow, and winding between sand-banks, which make the navigation difficult. When the wind freshens and blows up the river, which it usually does from May to November, the waves upon this channel are larger than elsewhere, and a line of small breakers marks the edge of the shoal-banks. The draft of the *Pearl* was found to be too great for the river, so the goods belonging to the expedition were taken out, and placed on an island, about forty miles from the bar, and the vessel returned to the sea, with Mr. Skead, the surveyor, so that the party were left very much to their own resources. Boats were employed to carry luggage up to Shupanga and Senna, and this was a source of some danger, as the country was still in a state of war.

Every year the warlike Landeen, the lords of the right bank of the Zambesi, come in force to Senna and Shupanga, for the tribute which the Portuguese pay, and the more land they find under cultivation the more tribute they demand; so that it is like a tax on improvement and operates to retard it.

The Governor of the Province of Mozambique made Shupanga his head-quarters during the Mariano war. His residence stands on a gentle slope which leads down to the Zambesi, with a fine mango-orchard to the south, while to the north stretch away cultivated fields and forests of palms and other tropical trees, beyond which towers the lofty mountain, Morambala, amidst the white clouds, while yet more distant hills are seen faint and far in the blue horizon. Beautiful are the green islands in front, reposing on the sunny bosom of the tranquil waters; and pleasant the shade beneath the great baobab-tree, where now, far from their native land, rest in peace those who were very dear to the leader of this expedition—one especially, whose grave is marked with a white cross, of whom we shall by and by have more to say.

The month of August was spent chiefly at Senna, where Livingstone endeavoured to enlist the chief and people in the cause of Christianity. Henceforth, however, whilst he never allowed an opportunity to escape without unfolding in the simplest language the truths of religion, he seems to have been convinced that Christianity could not secure an extensive and permanent foothold in Africa until the country was fully opened up to commerce and civilization. The great obstacle to this material development is the accursed traffic in human flesh—the slave-trade. Livingstone urged persistently, up to the hour of his death, the necessity, nay the duty incumbent on Britain, of exterminating the trade with a strong hand, as the first and most essential step to the civilization of this part of Africa. He had shown that instead of being the sandy desert the geographers imagined, South Central Africa was found to be a well-watered country, with large tracts of fertile soil, covered with forest and beautiful grassy valleys and occupied by a considerable population. He had found also that this population was shrewd, intelligent, and tractable; and all that was needed, after the extinction of the slave-trade and the cessation of the wars caused by it, was European enterprize and skill, to be employed in developing the vast resources of a fertile country. On the 8th of September, 1858, the ship anchored off Tette, and Livingstone was once more among his faithful Makololo, who rushed into the water to embrace him, but were restrained by the fear of spoiling his new clothes. Thirty of the band had died of small-pox, and six, who had got tired of cutting firewood for a living and had taken to dancing instead, had been killed by the half-caste Portuguese chief, Bonga, on the pretence that they had brought witchcraft medicine to kill him. According to the belief of the Makololo, the victims of the small-pox had been bewitched by the people of Tette. "We do not mourn for them," said the survivors; "but our hearts are sore for the six youths who were murdered by Bonga." Regret, however, was useless, and justice on the murderer out of the question. He still held his stockade, and the home government winked at his offences against its authority, hoping thus to coax him into a recognition of it.

It had been promised that the Portuguese government should support the Makololo during Livingstone's absence, and this had greatly relieved his mind while away from them; but no orders to that effect had been issued, and therefore the poor fellows had to live as best they could by hunting and cutting wood.

The Makololo regretted that they had no oxen, only

pigs, to give their friend. " We shall sleep now he is come back," they said; and the minstrel of their party extemporized a song, which he sung to the jingling of his native bells, in praise of the good missionary to whom Major Sicard had kindly granted the use of the government house for a temporary residence.

The people of Tette are superstitious above all others. Droughts and every other trouble which overtake them are ascribed to evil spirits and witchcraft. They worship the serpent, hang hideous little images about the dead and dying, and propitiate the invisible spirits of the earth and air by offerings of meat and drink. Livingstone put up a rain-gauge in his garden, and this was looked upon with great dread and suspicion, as a kind of machine for the performance of incantations; " it frightened away the clouds," said some of the knowing ones among them. There is much slavery in Tette; but the Portuguese do not make bad masters—it is the half-castes who commit the greatest enormities. Men cunning in the preparation of charms abound there—the elephant doctor, the crocodile doctor, the gun-doctor, and a host of others, all "medicine men," who, for a consideration, will furnish charms, each one of which gives immunity from some particular kind of danger, or ensures success in some particular pursuit. The dice-doctor is a diviner; by casting his cubes, and reading the numbers, he can tell where stolen property is hidden, and all that it is the business of the detective to find out. The party next reached that part of the Zambesi where its course is crossed

by a range of hills called the Kebrabasa or Kaorabasa,
meaning finish or break of the service, in reference to the
change which here takes place from water to land transit,
as the canoes cannot pass up the rapids, and baggage has
to be conveyed overland to Chicova.  The rapids were
explored with a view of ascertaining if they were navigable—so also was the cataract of Morumbwa.  Higher up
the travellers scrambled over rocks so hot that they
blistered the soles of their feet.  It is now Christmas, but
Christmas in a summer dress.  The birds are singing, the
corn is springing, the flowers are in bloom and the hum of
busy insect life is heard everywhere over the fertile plains.
Not only is there this difference in the climate but almost
everything one meets with in Africa is at variance with
our pre-conceived notions.  This was remarked long ago
by one who said that " wool grows on the heads of men
and hair on the backs of sheep."  " And," says Livingstone, " in feeble imitation of this dogma, let us add that
the men often wear their hair long, the women scarcely
ever.  Where there are cattle, the women till the land,
plant the corn, and build the huts; the men stay at home
to sow, spin, weave, and talk, and milk the cows.  The
men seem to pay a dowry with their wives instead of
getting one with them.  The mountaineers of Europe are
reckoned hospitable, generous, and brave; those of this
part of Africa are feeble, spiritless, and cowardly, even
when contrasted with their own countrymen on the
plains.  Some Europeans aver that Africans and themselves are descended from monkeys; some Africans be-

lieve that souls at death pass into the bodies of apes;
most writers believe the blacks to be savages; nearly all
blacks believe the whites to be cannibals. The nursery
hobgoblin of the one is black, of the other white. Without going further on with these unwise comparisons, we
must smile at the heaps of nonsense which have been
written about the negro intellect." After going on to remark on the absurdities which are often addressed to abori-
gines by travellers, as if they were children, and the ludicrous mistakes which are made through ignorance of their
language, he continues, "Quite as sensible, if not more
pertinent, answers will usually be given by Africans to
those who know their language, as are obtained from our
uneducated poor; and could we but forget that a couple of
centuries back the ancestors of the common people in
England, probably our own great-great-grandfathers, were
as unenlightened as the Africans are now, we might
maunder away about intellect, and fancy that the tacit influence would be drawn that our own is arch-angelic. The
low motives which often actuate the barbarians do,
unfortunately, bear abundant crops of mean actions among
servants, and even in higher ranks of more civilized people; but we hope that these may decrease in the general
improvement of our race by the diffusion of pure religion."

As it was impossible to ascend the Zambesi beyond the
rapids of Kebrabasa with a steamer like the *Ma-Robert* of
only ten-horse power, Livingstone sent an application to
the Government for a more suitable vessel. Meanwhile,
the party proceeded up the Shire. The first attempt was

made in January, 1859, and was opposed by Tingane and
five hundred men.　They were observed taking aim at
the vessel from behind the trees, but Livingstone, nothing
daunted, went on shore and explained to the excited
savages that he was English, and had come neither to take
slaves nor to fight, but to open a way to his countrymen
to come and purchase cotton or whatever else they had to
sell, except slaves.　His boldness and candour had their
effect, and Tingane became quite friendly.

Proceeding up the river, their progress was at length
interrupted by a series of cataracts, to the lowest of which
was given the name of the distinguished president of the
Geographical Society, Sir Roderick Murchison.　Not deem-
ing it prudent to risk a land journey beyond the falls
among a strange and savage people, who evidently looked
with suspicion on their movements, they resolved to return
to Tette.　They were now about a hundred miles up the
Shire, as the crow flies, but had probably gone double that
distance in following the windings of the river.　Down
stream their progress was, of course, much faster than it
had been up, being aided by the current.　In the middle
of March, 1859, Livingstone again started up the Shire.
About ten miles below the cataracts he found the chief,
Chibisba, a remarkably shrewd and intelligent man, with
whom he entered into amicable relations.　He had sent
an invitation to the white man to come and drink beer
when he first visited the spot; but his messengers were
so terrified at the sight of the steamer, that they jumped
out of their canoe, which they left to drift down stream,

and swam away to the shore as for dear life, first shouting
out the invitation, which nobody understood. From
Chibisba's village, the party set out in search of Lake
Shirwa, of which they had heard, and which, after many
difficulties and dangers, they reached on the 18th of April.
It is a considerable body of bitter, brackish water, with
islands like hills rising out of it. It abounds in leeches,
fish, crocodiles and hippopotami; the shores are covered
with weeds and papyrus; the length of the lake is from
sixty to eighty miles by about twenty broad. But this,
they were told, was nothing in extent when compared
with another lake to the north, separated only by a narrow neck of land. Finding the natives in this neighbourhood still suspicious and occasionally even hostile, they
resolved to return to their vessel; and on the 23rd of June,
the *Ma-Robert* again anchored before Tette. In August,
they commenced a third expedition up the Shire. On the
25th they again reach Chibisba's village; on the 28th leave
the ship, bent on the discovery of Lake Nyassa. The
party consisted of forty-two, four being whites, thirty-six
Makololo, and two native guides. Their first task was to
surmount the Manganja hills by a toilsome road. There
are three terraces during the ascent, and they finally
reached the uppermost, three thousand feet above the sea-
level.

The fertile plains, the wooded hills, the majestic mountains, and other features of this splendid scenery, now
gazed on with delight for the first time by European eyes,
were seen to great advantage from this elevated plateau.

The air was fresh and bracing as that of the Scottish
mountains, and here in some of the passes they found
bramble-berries, reminding them of home and its thous-
and endearing associations. They spent a week crossing
the highlands in a northerly direction ; then descended
into the upper Shire Valley, which has an elevation above
the sea of 1,200 feet. It is wonderfully fertile, and supports a large population. A pleasant and well-watered
land is this Manganja country; rivers and streams abound
in it ; its highlands are well wooded, and along its water-
courses grow trees of great size and height ; it is a country
good for cattle, yet the people have only goats and sheep.

After many obstacles and dangers the party at length
stood by Lake Nyassa, a little before noon on the 16th of
September, 1859, undoubtedly the first Europeans who
had looked upon it, although the Portuguese and one or
two other travellers have set up claims to its discovery.
Dr. Roscher, a German, visited it about two months after
Livingstone, but he was unhappily murdered by the natives, and all the account left of his exploration was what
could be gathered from his servant. It is satisfactory to
know that the murderers of poor Roscher were captured,
taken to Zanzibar, and executed. It was here that Livingstone came into direct contact with the great plague-spot of
Central Africa. Close to the confluence of the lake with
the River Shire is one of the great slave-paths from the
interior, and Livingstone was told by an old chief who
entertained him hospitably, that a large slave-party led by
Arabs was encamped close by. They were returning

from the interior with slaves, ivory and malachite. Some of them actually visited Livingstone's party, and offered young children, whom they wished to get rid of, for sale. On learning that these were English, however, they hastily broke up their camp, and disappeared in the night. The consequences of this odious traffic at Lake Nyassa are most deplorable. A country of surpassing richness which might be settled by a large and thriving population is little better than an uncultivated wilderness.

Constantly, in his explorations up the Shire and around Lake Nyassa, did Livingstone come upon ruined villages, and fugitives hiding among the reeds and tall grasses, perishing of hunger and exposure, while skeletons and human forms in every stage of decomposition attested the frightful character of the deeds which are committed in carrying on this horrible traffic, which has converted a peaceful and industrious people into idle and dissolute robbers and assassins, or miserable crouching creatures who scarcely dare to call their souls their own—who look upon every stranger as an enemy, and have no confidence even in their own friends and relatives. Urged by the greed of gain, one portion of a tribe will not unfrequently set upon and overcome the other, that they may sell the conquered ones—some members of a family will seize and sell the rest; hence all social ties are broken, and a state of demoralization ensues, compared with which a simple state of primitive savagery is innocence itself.

Under these circumstances, it was not to be wondered
5

at that the Manganja tribes were more suspicious and less hospitable than those on the Zambesi. They had often been deceived before by treacherous visitors who settled down in villages under the pretence of trading, and then suddenly in the night, throwing off the mask, attacked the village, killing those who resisted, and carrying off the rest into slavery. Livingstone compares the outline of Lake Nyassa to that of Italy, it being somewhat like a boot in shape. The narrowest part, about the ankle, is eighteen or twenty miles broad. From this it widens to the north, until it becomes fifty or sixty miles over. The entire length is about two hundred miles, in a direction nearly due north and south. On the western shore is a succession of bays, the depth varying, at a mile out, from nine to fifteen fathoms. In rocky bays where soundings were taken it was one hundred fathoms. It seems likely that no anchorage can be found far from the shore. The lake appears to be surrounded by mountains; those on the west being the edges of the table-land. Like other bodies of water so enclosed, Nyassa is subject to sudden and violent storms. The annual rise of the water is about three feet. This does not take place till January, although the rain begins in November. The men on the lake fish chiefly by night. They have fine canoes which they manage with great dexterity, standing erect while they paddle. All the natives are tattoed from head to foot; and the women make themselves hideous with lip-rings and other ornaments, as they consider them. Livingstone says, "Some ladies, not content with the upper

pelele, go to extremes, as ladies will, and insert another in
the under lip through a hole opposite the lower gums.
A few peleles are made of a blood-red kind of pipe-clay,
much in fashion, sweet things in the way of lip-rings, so
hideous to behold that no time or usage could make our
eyes rest on them without aversion." On being informed
that these ornaments were not used in the traveller's
country, a chief and his wife immediately presented him
with a set, with a view, we may presume, to their introduction in England. The slave trade was going on at a
terrible rate on the lake; an Arab "dhow," crowded with
wretched captives, was running regularly across it. Nineteen thousand slaves from this Nyassa country alone pass
annually through the custom-house at Zanzibar, and it
has been estimated that not above one in ten of those in
the interior reaches the coast. A great many of the facts
collected by Livingstone regarding this region were obtained during his second visit, extending from September
the 2nd to October the 27th, 1861. Meanwhile he re-
visited Tette and Senna, and then proceeded to redeem
his promise to take the Makololo back to their own
country. Some of these men had married slave-women
and preferred to remain. With the rest, the missionary
set out on the 15th of May, and reached Sesheke, the new
town of Sekeletu, on August 18th. After going on a visit
to Sinamane, a tributary chief of the Makololo and the Batoka, a great tobacco-growing people below the great falls,
he proceeds again to Tette. The new ship, the *Pioneer*,
arrived at the mouth of the Rovuma on the 25th Febru-

ary, 1861. She was an excellent vessel in every respect, except her draught of water, which was too great for the upper portion of the river, where she frequently grounded. The next step was to ascend the Shire, where Charles Livingstone had succeeded in inducing some of the natives to cultivate cotton. They were accompanied by Bishop Mackenzie and the Oxford and Cambridge Missions to the tribes of the Shire and Lake Nyassa. It had been settled to establish, if possible, a mission station on the high ground in Chibisba's territory, and now having reached that point, they learned that there was war in the Manganja country, and that marauding parties of the Ajawa were desolating the country to supply the slave-market. It was therefore resolved to take the goods up the hills and establish the mission there.

Accordingly, on the 25th of July they started for the highlands, to show the bishop his new scene of operation. Halting at a village the second day, they were told that a slave-party on its way to Tette would presently pass that road, and, in a few minutes, a long train of manacled men, women and children came along the road; the black drivers armed with muskets, and decked with finery, marched before, behind, and at the middle of the line in a jaunty manner, and ever and anon blew exultant notes out of long tin horns. Seeing the white men, they darted off into the forest as fast as their legs would carry them. The chief of the party alone remained, and could not well escape, because he had his hand tightly clasped in that of the leading slave. He was at once recognized by Living-

stone as a well-known slave of the late Commandant of
Tette. He said he had bought the captives; but they
asserted that they had been taken in war, and while the
inquiry was going on, he, too, darted off, and escaped with
the rest. Then all hands were busy, cutting free the women and children, and releasing the necks of the men from
the forked sticks into which they were firmly penned.
The poor people could hardly believe their ears when told
that they were free, and might go where they liked, or
remain under the protection of their liberators. This they
at once decided on doing, and set to work with alacrity,
making a fire with the slave sticks and bonds, wherewith
to cook the meal which they carried with them for break-
fast. Eighty-four slaves, chiefly women and children, were
thus liberated. Sixty-four more were freed in the course
of the journey to the highlands. The party now resolved
to visit the Ajawa chief and remonstrate with him. On
their way they met crowds of the Manganja fleeing in
terror, and passed through field after field of maize or beans
ripe for the harvest, but with none there to cut it down.
Then came the smoke of burning villages, and finally they
were face to face with a long line of Ajawa warriors. The
appearance of the missionaries made the savages more
furious. The party were surrounded and attacked, and
found themselves compelled to fire their rifles and drive
them off. This was a bad commencement of a missionary
enterprise, and it led to other troubles, which eventually
broke up the mission, and caused the death of Bishop Mackenzie, who appears to have been a very earnest, ener-

getic, and estimable man. He was placed in a very difficult position, and no doubt made some very grave mistakes, for some of which it has been said Livingstone was
to a certain extent answerable. But had his advice been
followed, many of those disasters which occurred would
have, no doubt, been avoided. The connection of the
members of the Zambesi Expedition with the Bishop's
Mission ceased immediately after the above events took
place, for the ship then returned to prepare for the second
journey to Lake Nyassa, to which reference has already
been made.

With the after collisions which took place between the
bishop and the slavers, Livingstone not only had no part,
but the steps which led to them were taken contrary to
his advice. In the end, the fever—the result of wet, hunger,
and exposure—seized the bishop, and he died in a native's
hut, the wretched shelter of which was grudged by the
owner. Livingstone's party also suffered from fever on
the Shire, and one young man died from its effects. They
got down to the Zambesi on the 10th of January, and
then made for the coast. On the 30th, H. M. S. *Gorgon*
arrived with Mrs. Livingstone, and the ladies who were to
join the Universities' Mission. The sections of an iron
steamer for the navigation of Lake Nyassa also arrived;
but they were detained six months in the Delta, the
*Pioneer* not being equal to the task of bringing them up.
The ladies were conveyed in the captain's gig to the mouth
of the Ruo, where they expected to meet the bishop.
Not finding him there they proceeded to the station, to

hear the melancholy intelligence of his death. Bereaved and sorrow-stricken they were brought back to the *Pioneer*. Soon a greater grief than any he had yet known fell upon Livingstone.

Captain Wilson and Dr. Kirk, who had accompanied him, became dangerously ill of fever; and, for a time, only one of his men was fit for duty, all the rest being sick with malaria, or the vile spirits sold to them by the Portuguese officials; and, saddest of all, that dear wife from whom he had been so long parted, also took the infection. About the middle of April she sickened, and speedily sank. Obstinate vomiting came on, which nothing could allay; all medical aid was useless, and her eyes were closed in the sleep of death as the sun set on the eve of the Christian Sabbath, April 27th, 1862. What a sad Sabbath was that for the bereaved missionary, so far away from the comforting and sustaining influences of home! It required fortitude and faith to enable him to bear up against this blow, and to say to his heavenly Father, " Thy will be done!" No Ma-Robert now for the expectant Makololo; no helpmate now for the lonely man who had suffered and done so much in the cause of Christ. Calmly she sleeps under the shade of the baobab-tree at Shupanga. The white cross planted on her grave shines out of the gloom on that green slope that margins the Zambesi river. Many who pass that way will see it, and ask about her and her brave husband who shared together the toils and the perils of missionary life in the centre of Africa, and laid down their lives in the field of their labours. Charles

Livingstone, in a letter, thus writes the epitaph of his sister-in-law :—" Those who are not aware how this brave, good English wife made a delightful home at Kolobeng, a thousand miles inland from the Cape, and, as the daughter of Moffat, and a Christian lady, exercised a most beneficial influence over the rude tribes of the interior, may wonder that she should have braved the dangers and toils of this down-trodden land.  She knew them all; and, in the disinterested and dutiful attempt to renew her labours, was called to her rest instead.  *'Fiat Domine voluntas tua!'* "

The following year Mr. Thornton fell a victim to his generosity in endeavouring to carry provisions to the survivors of Bishop Mackenzie's mission.  Soon after, nearly the whole expedition were attacked by dysentery.  Dr. Kirk and Charles Livingstone suffered so severely that it was deemed advisable to send them home.  Previous to these events, the *Lady Nyassa*, as the new steamer was called, was put together and launched.  She entered the Shire, towed by the *Pioneer*, on the 10th of January, 1863; was taken to pieces at the foot of the first cataract, and carried over forty miles of portage.  Livingstone thoroughly explored the lake, and was proceeding to settle down to his work, when the Government instructed him to return with the expedition.

To Christianize South Africa,—this was now the cherished object of his life, and when, in obedience to orders, he turned his back upon this great mission-field, now so familiar and so dear to him,—doubly dear as the last resting-place of her whom he first loved and married there, and steamed out of Zanzibar in the little *Lady Nyassa*, bound on a voyage of 2,500 miles to Bombay, he resolved to return as soon as opportunity served, and renew his efforts for the conversion and civilization of the black people, who were indeed to him "men and brethren."

The *Lady Nyassa* proved to be a capital seaboat. She left Zanzibar on the 30th of April, 1864, and reached Bombay in the beginning of June, having encountered much stormy weather. Her crew consisted of thirteen souls, seven native Zambesians, two boys, and four Europeans, viz., one stoker, one carpenter, one sailor, and Livingstone himself, captain and navigator. The Africans proved excellent sailors, although not one of them had ever seen the sea before they volunteered for the service. The intrepid explorer reached London on the 20th of July, 1864, and was received with even greater enthusiasm than in 1856. During a portion of his brief sojourn in England, he was the guest of Mr. Webb, the present proprietor of Byron's ancestral home, Newstead Abbey. Here he wrote a large portion of his second work, where Byron had years before composed many of his poems. It would be curious to contrast the characters and careers of the two men whose names were thus accidentally associated together. The wayward, unsteady genius of the one had little or nothing in common with the earnest, persevering, unwavering strength of purpose which characterized the life and labours of the other. Yet, each of them succumbed to disease, self-exiled, and far from his native land; the

one at Missolonghi, fighting for the freedom of Greece ;
the other at Ulala, battling with darkness, slavery, and
idolatry in the wilds of Africa.   What Livingstone in his
former journeys effected may be appropriately summed
up here.

He was the first of all Europeans to cross the inhospitable Kalahari desert; first to stand by Lake Ngami ; first to
view the broad expanse of Lake Nyassa; first to make
his way through obstacles and difficulties which scarcely
any other man would have braved and overcome, from the
central country to the western coast, then back again
eastward to the sea, a fever-stricken, famished man whom
nothing could daunt or turn from his course.  He explored
rivers of great length, whose names even were unknown
to geographers ; made observations of the greatest utility
to future missionaries and travellers ; opened to commerce
and religion realms of exhaustless fertility, rich in animal,
mineral, and vegetable productions and tribes of men,
gentle and teachable, who only need the influence of
Christian civilization to raise them from a state of
degradation ; and, finally, he first exposed the cancer
which is eating into the heart of Africa and retarding its
progress,—the foul traffic in human flesh.  In referring to
Livingstone's achievements, the N. Y. *Herald* thus connects him with the other explorers of Africa : "These
discoveries were sufficient to establish the fame of any
man for a generation, but they did not satisfy the crav-
ings of the intrepid Livingstone.  New light had been
thrown on other portions of the continent by the travels

of Dr. Barth, by the researches of Krapf, Erkhardt, and
Rebman, by the efforts of Dr. Blaikie (a martyr, unfortunately; alas, not the last to the climate!), by the journey
of Francis Galton, and by the discoveries of Lakes Tanganyika and Victoria Nyanza by Captain Burton and
Captain Speke, 'whose untimely death,' remarked the
warm-hearted Livingstone, 'we all deplore.'  Then followed the researches of Van der Decken, Thornton and
others; and, last of all, the grand discovery of the main
source of the Nile by Speke and Grant.  The fabulous
torrid zone of parched and burning sand was now proved
to be a well-watered region, resembling North America
in its fresh-water lakes, and India in its hot, humid lowlands, jungles, and cool highlands."  Livingstone's object
in the expedition we have been describing may be given
in his own words, from a speech delivered before his departure from England:—

"I will explain to you how I mean to endeavour to
follow up the discoveries which have been made.  The
central part of the African continent was supposed for a
long time to be a great sandy plain.  Certain rivers were
known to be flowing in towards the centre, but they were
not known farther, and they were supposed in consequence
to become lost.  But, instead of that, the grand view
burst gradually on my mind of a very fine, well-watered
country; and not only that, but of certain well-watered
healthy localities on both sides of the country, which were
suitable for a European residence.  Efforts have been
made for centuries to get into the interior of Africa, but,

unfortunately, it has always been attempted through the unhealthy parts near the coast. On the southern part of the country we had the Kalihari desert, and the expedition which was sent out from Cape Town under Dr. Smith was prevented from penetrating the interior by this same Kalihari desert. The unhealthy coasts presented a barrier on both sides, and this desert presented an obstacle on the south; but when Messrs. Oswell, Murray, and myself succeeded in passing round that desert, then we came into a new and well-watered country beyond. When I passed into that country, I had not the smallest idea that there was such a want of cotton as I found to be the case when I went home to England. But there I saw the cotton growing wild and almost everywhere, and that sugar was collected all over the country (although the people did not know that it could be produced from the sugarcane); and I found, further, that this was a great market for labour. When I lived at Kolenbeng, men left that tribe, and I found some of them within 200 miles of Cape Town seeking to obtain work. Now, here we have the produce and here we have the labour, and I hope we may secure a healthy standing point, from which Europeans may push their commercial and their missionary enterprise to the unhealthy regions beyond."

Dr. Livingstone then proceeds to describe the coal-fields of Central Africa, and urges that his expedition is a practical one. "It is not," he says, "like those that have been sent to the North Pole. We hope to have something to show when we come back." And again :—

" What I hope to effect is this : I don't hope to send down cargoes of cotton and sugar; perhaps that result will not be in my lifetime. But I hope we shall make a beginning, and get in the thin edge of the wedge, and that we shall open up a pathway into the interior of the country, and, by getting right into the centre, have a speedy passage by an open pathway, working from the centre out towards the sides.

" When going into the country, we don't mean to leave our Christianity behind us. I think we made somewhat of a mistake, indeed, a very great mistake, in India; but where we are going, we snall have no need to be ashamed of our Christianity. We go as Christians ; we go to speak to the people about our Christianity, and to try and recommend our religion to those with whom we come in contact.

" I have received the greatest kindness from all classes of people in the interior. I have found that in proportion as we approach the confines of civilization, do the people become worse. Such is the fact; the nearer we come to civilization, we find the people very much worse than those who never had any contact with the white man."

We now come to Livingstone's last expedition, extending between the years 1865 and 1873. He left England for the last time, on the 14th of August in the former year, his immediate destination being Bombay. Here he organized his mission, which consisted of eleven Christianized Africans, from a Church Mission there, two of them being young Ajawa, whom Livingstone had brought

to India with him; eleven Sepoys of the Bombay Native
Infantry; and some Johanna men, the chief of whom
Ali Moosa, had been with him during the two years of his
last exploration. From Bombay he proceeded to Zanzibar,
and on the 28th of March, 1866, the great explorer crossed
from Zanzibar for the mainland, and at once started for the
interior by way of the River Rovuma. The first information we have directly from him after his departure is
contained in a despatch sent by him to Earl Clarendon,
dated Bemba, latitude 10 degrees 10 minutes south, longitude 31 degrees 50 minutes east, February 1, 1867; and in
a letter to Sir Robert Murchison, dated at the same place
on the 2nd of the same month (and received in England
about the 27th of April, 1868). In these communications,
Livingstone stated that he was then at the confluence of
the Niende, and the Rovuma, in the same route as the
unfortunate Roscher. He crossed the Rovuma at a place
called Ngomano. This was the furthest point which had
been reached by a white man, as all the country round
was devastated by the Mafite, a marauding tribe of Zulus.
There was in addition a drought prevailing. In spite of
difficulties, however, Livingstone pushed on to the westward, leaving the Rovuma, and passing through the territory of the Waino and Makua who proved friendly. The
party had been weakened by desertions; all the Sepoys
except the leader had deserted; some of the educated
Africans had also disappeared; so that the whole number
was reduced to twenty. Crossing Nyassa at its northern
end, they passed through the country of the dreaded

Mafite, on their way to the yet undiscovered Lake Tanganyika, which they knew lay somewhere in this direction, and was perhaps the greatest of the chain of lakes which furnish the head-waters of the mysterious Nile. It was here that the Johanna men pretended that Livingstone had fallen in a skirmish with the Mafite. The account was so circumstantial, and there was such an air of verisimilitude about it, that only a few were bold enough to dispute it. They urged that the Johanna men were known to be great liars, and Moosa their leader, from whom the particulars were gleaned, had given two or more irreconcilable versions of it. Still Moosa's story was almost universally believed. The *Times of India*, for example, said, "The hopes raised by the news of the rumoured safety of Dr. Livingstone have speedily been dispelled, and there can no longer be any doubt that he was killed by a savage of the Mafite tribe. The narrative of the Sepoy belonging to the marine battalion who formed one of the doctor's escort, and who arrived from Zanzibar on the 14th of May, turns out to be altogether inaccurate ; and substantially, the tale told by Moosa is proved correct." Dr. Kirk believed the story, and Dr. Seward, Consul at Zanzibar, in his despatch expressed his entire reliance upon the narrative of the Johanna men. On the other hand, Sir Roderick Murchison dissected the story, and had very little difficulty in pulling it to pieces; and Mr. J. S. Moffat, Livingstone's brother-in-law, was equally emphatic in the expression of his doubts. The entire narrative was, as we now know, a mere fabrication intended by the Johanna men as an excuse for their desertion, and had not the slightest foundation in fact. Steps were immediately taken to send an expedition under the command of Mr. Edward Young, an officer in the Royal Navy. On reaching Lake Nyassa, they found traces of Livingstone, and as they proceeded, they discovered that he had passed through places far beyond the alleged scene of his death. There appeared not the slightest reason to doubt the substantial correctness of the information obtained, that Livingstone had passed through the most dangerous part of his journey, and had made good his advance into the interior with the apparent intention of descending the Nile into Egypt.

On the 8th of April, 1868, letters were received from Livingstone, dated from a district far beyond the place where he was said to have been murdered, and announcing that he was in good health. In July, 1868, he was near Lake Bangweolo in South Central Africa, whence he wrote to say that he believed he might safely assert that the chief sources of the Nile arise between 10° and 12° south latitude, or nearly in the position assigned to them by Ptolemy, whose river Rhapta was probably the Rovuma. Another communication was received from the traveller, dated Ujiji, May 13th, 1869; and on January 24th, 1871, news arrived in this country that he had made an extensive journey to the west of Lake Tanganyika. In his letter from Ujiji, he thus gives a sketch of the work which he intended to accomplish:—" As to the work to be done by me, it is only to connect the sources which I have discovered, from five hundred to seven hundred miles south of Speke and Baker's, with their Nile. The volume of water which flows north from lat. 12° S. is so large, I suspect that I have been working at the sources of the Congo as well as those of the Nile. I have to go down the eastern line of drainage to Baker's turning-point. Tanganyika, Nzige Chowambe are one water, and the head of it is three hundred miles south of this. The western and central lines of drainage converge into an unvisited lake, west or south-west of this. The outflow of this, whether to the Congo or the Nile, I have to ascertain. The people west of this, called the Manyema, are cannibals, if Arabs speak truly. I may have to go there first, and down Tanganyika, if I come out uneaten, and find my new squad from Zanzibar. I earnestly hope that you will do what you can to help me with the goods and men. £400, to be sent by Mr. Young, must surely have come to you through Fleming and Company." We may now glance back over the period covered by the letters, for a summary of which we are indebted to the New York *Herald*. These letters contain almost all the information yet obtainable of Livingstone's work, between 1867 and 1871.

In his despatch to Earl Clarendon (1867) he states that he could not go round the northern end of Lake Nyassa as he intended, partly because the country had been swept of provisions by Zulu marauders, and partly because he believed some of his own men would flee at the sight of danger. By striking southward he passed through a depopulated tract of about 100 miles, but became acquainted with Mataka, the most influential chief on the watershed

between the coast and the lake. Some of his people had
gone to Lake Nyassa to plunder without his knowledge,
and he had ordered the captives and cattle to be sent back.
His town consists of 1,000 houses, [altitude 3,000 feet,
the climate [cold in July. Meeting after starting with
three Wajssau chiefs, they were found to be the greatest
slave traders in the country, and seemed astonished at
hearing the protests made against the traffic, it being the
first time they had heard their conduct condemned.

The doctor had remained with Mataka from July to
the end of September (1867), and in the beginning of
October tried to go westward; but the people of Katosa,
or Klemasura, were afraid to take him up to Kirk's range,
because some Arab slaveholders had been driven thence
by the exasperated inhabitants. The range is only the
edge of a high plateau, where the people, all Manganja,
had not been led into buying and selling each other. As
he went westward to avoid the Magitu, he turned northward as soon as he was past the longitude of their country, and came near being captured. Crossing the Loangwa
and the great valley in which it flows—the bed of an ancient lake—he entered the Lobisa, a country of the Babisa, and obtained information as to the route the Portuguese followed in going to Cazembe. It is placed by the
map makers too far east, so Dr. Livingstone trod on new
ground. It will enable one to form an idea of the way
he went if he conceives him going westward from Kalosas,
and then northward until he takes up the point at which
he left off in 1863. The watershed between the Loangwa

and Zambesi rises up 6,000 feet. The Zambesi was crossed in latitude 10 deg. 34 min. south. It had flooded all its banks, but the lines of trees showing its actual size were not more than forty yards apart. He says he thinks he is now in the watershed, although not the highest part of it, between Zambesi and Soapuila. He and his party here suffered a great deal from gnawing hunger. The Babisa, who were among the first natives to engage in slavery, have suffered its usual effects. Their country is almost depopulated, and the few inhabitants have nothing to sell. He found no difficulty in the Loangwa and Zambesi valleys in securing supplies of meat with the rifle; but Lobisa had no animals, and he had hard times in marching through its dripping forests, but no serious difficulty with the natives.

Bemba, from which his first letter was addressed, has a treble line of stockades and a deep ditch around the inner one. Dr. Livingstone w ites:—"The chief seems a frank, jolly person, and having cattle, we mean to rest a little while with him. We are very much emaciated, but, like certain races of pigs, take on fat kindly. Our sorest loss has been all our medicines. We are 4,500 feet above the level of the sea, but, having rains every day, feel that we need, like the cattle of the people, the protection of huts." He regrets that his geographical notes are so scanty, but hopes to send fuller information from Tanganyika.

In his letter to Sir Roderick Murchison, he states that he had had no news whatever from the coast since he left, but hopes for letters and a second stock of goods at Ujiji.

He had also been unable to send anything. Some letters he had written in hopes of meeting an Arab slave trader, but he says they all "skedaddled" as soon as they heard the English were coming.

In another letter to the British Secretary for Foreign Affairs, dated "Near Lake Bangweolo, South Central Africa, July, 1868," (and read before the Royal Geographical Society, November 8, 1869,) Dr. Livingstone refers to his letter of February, 1867, in which he stated that he had the impression that he was then on the watershed between Zambesi and either the Congo or the Nile. He now states that more extended observation has since convinced him of the essential correctness of that impression, and from what he has seen, together with what he learned from intelligent natives, he thinks he may safely assert that the chief sources of the Nile arise between 10 deg. and 12 deg. south latitude, or nearly in the position assigned to them by Ptolemy, whose river, Rhapta, is probably the Rovuma. Aware that others have been mistaken, and laying no claim to infallibility, particularly as to the parts west and north-west of Tanganyika, because these had not yet come under his observation; but according to his previous discoveries the springs of the Nile have hitherto been searched for very much too far to the north. They rise some 400 miles south of the most southerly portion of the Victoria Nyanza, and, indeed, south of all the lakes except Bangweolo.

The doctor here entered into a lengthy, but very interesting and important recital of his geographical discoveries up to the period of his present writing. In giving an idea of an inundation, which, in a small way, enacts the part of the Nile lower down, he said he had to cross two rivulets which flow into the north end of the Moero; one was thirty, the other forty yards broad, crossed by bridges. One had a quarter, the other half a mile of flood on each side. The Luo had covered a plain abreast of Moero, so that the water on a great part reached from the knees to the upper part of the chest. The plain was of black mud, with grass higher than his head. In places, while walking in paths, he was plunged ankle deep in soft mud, while hundreds of soft bubbles rushed up, and, bursting, emitted a frightful odour. The state of the rivers and country made him go in the very lightest marching order. He took nothing but the most necessary instruments, and no paper except a copy of note books and the Bible. Only one of his attendants would come where he then was; the others, on various pretences, absconded. " The fact is," he exclaims, "they are all tired of this everlasting tramping, and so verily am I." Were it not for an inveterate dislike to give in to difficulties without doing his utmost to overcome them, he says he would abscond too.

The doctor expresses dissatisfaction at the manipulation which some of his sketches had undergone after he had sent them home. He thus expresses himself:—

" After all my care, and risk of health and even of life, it is not very inspiring to find 200 miles of lake tacked on to the north-west end of Nyassa, and these 200 miles perched up on an upland region, and passed over some 3,000 feet higher than the rest of the lakes. We shall probably hear that the author of this feat in fancography claims therefrom to be considered a theoretical discoverer of the source of the Nile."

He shows the folly of thus intermeddling, and says that to his " gentle remonstrances he received only a giggle." The doctor was evidently in low spirits when he penned this portion of his letter. It is in this letter the doctor refers to the tribe that lives in underground houses in Rua—a matter that has already excited the attention of the curious and scientific. Some excavations are said to be thirty miles long, have running rills in them, and a whole district can stand a siege in them. The "writings" therein, the doctor was told by some of the people, are on the wings of animals, and not letters. The people were described as very dark, well made, and eyes slantingwards.

On the 7th September, 1869, Dr. John Kirk, at Zanzibar, received a letter from Dr. Livingstone from the same place (giving the date as July 8th, 1868), as those mentioned above, and probably forwarded by the same courier. In this letter the great explorer speaks a little more plainly about some home matters. He says :—

" I shall not follow the Lualaba by canoes, as we did the Zambesi, from near the Victoria Falls to the Kebrabasa. That was insanity, and I am not going to do any more mad things merely to please geographers, who are mostly insane. My positions have been altered for the most idi-

otic reason at places where no one else observed or will
observe in our day." [He then refers to the Nyassa inter-
pretation, of which he complains in his letters to the British Secretary for Foreign Affairs.]

The receipt of these letters did not re-assure the public
mind; and, as time wore on, bringing no further intelligence from the great traveller, the conviction began to
force itself daily on the public mind that after all he had
either been murdered by hostile tribes engaged in the slave
trade or had fallen a victim to the climate. In his address to the Geographical Society (November 8th, 1869,)
Sir Roderick Murchison expressed the general feeling
when he said that if Livingstone had gone upon the
Congo, they were as uncertain of his safety as before, and
the work would have to be done over again. He urged
strongly upon the Government the duty of making some
permanent provision for Livingstone. " In his wonderful
labours," said he, " Livingstone has not merely been the
Christian Missionary and Geographical Explorer; he is
also accredited as Her Majesty's Consul to all the native
states in the interior. Such being the public mission with
which the great traveller is entrusted, let us now confidently believe that Her Majesty's Government will autho-
rize, on his return, the grant of a suitable pension to the
man whose labours have shed so much renown on Bri'  ';
and that our gracious Sovereign who has, I know, taken   e
deepest interest in his career, will reward him wi.  some
appropriate token of her goodwill." The result was the grant
of a pension of £200 per annum. We may mention here

that Livingstone had spent all the money he had made by his works and otherwise, in equipping the *Lady Nyassa*, which cost £6000 and only sold for £2000 in Bombay. To his other anxieties was added the fear that his children were in want. Notwithstanding the gereral desire to learn something of the fate of Livingstone, neither the Geographical Society nor the Government took any steps in the matter. So, as the New York *Herald* says, with pardonable pride, it was left to private enterprise to search him out. Towards the close of 1869, Mr. James Gordon Bennett, jr., son of the founder and proprietor of the New York *Herald*, conceived the idea of sending one of the correspondents of that paper as a special commissioner. The boldness and novelty of the idea, as well as the liberality with which it was carried out, reflected great credit upon Mr. Bennett's enterprise; and in spite of all that was said as to the pure speculative prospect kept in view, there is no reason why the projector of the search expedition should not have full credit for those generous and disinterestod motives which must unquestionably have been stronger than any mercenary hopes could possibly be under the circumstances. Mr. Henry M. Stanley, the correspondent instructed with the arduous duty of conducting the search, entered upon his task with praiseworthy intrepidity. The success of the expedition was more than problematical, while its dangers and difficulties were great, perhaps insurmountable. Mr. Stanley, however, without a moment's hesitation undertook the duty; and with a pertinacity and perseverance worthy of Livingstone himself conducted the enterprise to a successful issue. His account of the commission he received at Paris has been often published, but it ought not to be omitted here. About the middle of October, 1869, the correspondent who had been engaged in describing the Civil war in Spain, was in Madrid when he was hastily summoned to Paris by Mr. Bennett, the younger. Within four hours he was on the way to the French capital; a delay at Bayonne prevented his arrival there till the following night. He at once made his way to Mr. Bennett's hotel and found that gentleman in bed. The following dialogue then ensued :—

"Who are you?" he asked.

"My name is Stanley," I answered.

"Ah, yes! sit down; I have important business for you."

Mr. Bennett then rose, and, throwing on his dressing-gown, entered into the heart of the subject at once.

"Where do you think Livingstone is?"

"I really don't know, sir."

"Do you think he is alive?"

"He may be and he may not be," I answered.

"Well, I think he is alive, and that he can be found, and I am going to send you to find him."

"What," said I, "do you think I can really find Livingstone? Do you mean me to go to Central Africa?"

"Yes; I mean that you shall go and find him, wherever you may hear that he is, and to get what news you may of him, and perhaps," he added, slowly and thoughtfully,

" the old man may be in want; take enough with you to
help him should he require it.  You will act according to
your own plans, and do what you think best—*but find
Livingstone.*"   Stanley was a little staggered at the coolness with which Bennett ordered him off to Central
Africa in search of a man whom everybody believed to be
dead; so he ventured to suggest a difficulty.

" Have you considered seriously," said he, " the great
expense you are likely to incur on account of this little
journey ? "

" What will it cost ? " asked Bennett.

" Burton and Speke's journey cost between £3,000 and
£5,000, and I fear it cannot be done under £2,500."

Mr. Bennett's reply was characteristic both of the man
and of the great nation to which he belongs:

" Well, I will tell you what you will do.  Draw a
thousand pounds now;  and when you have gone
through that draw another thousand; and when that is
spent draw another thousand, and when you have finished
that draw another thousand, and so on: but *find Livingstone.*"   Stanley says that he was well aware that when
Mr. Bennett had fixed his mind upon anything he was
not easily diverted from his purpose; at the same time
the correspondent thought that, considering the important
nature of the scheme, it had not been coolly considered
in all its bearings.   He therefore hinted at a rumour that,
on the death of Bennett's father, the son intended to dispose
of the *Herald.*  This he denied, and added, " that he meant

the paper to publish whatever news would be interesting
to the world, at no matter what cost."

"After that," rejoined Stanley, "I have nothing more
to say. Do you mean me to go straight to Africa to search
for Dr. Livingstone?" With a keen eye to the interests
of his journal, Mr. Bennett had half a dozen preliminary
errands for his indefatigable agent, and in going about
these a full year was spent. He was to go to the inaugu-
ration of the Suez Canal, then up the Nile, to encounter
the Baker expedition, and then to write a practical guide
to Lower Egypt. In the next place, he "might as well
go to Jerusalem," to examine what the exploring party
were doing there; next to Constantinople, to ascertain the
merits of the dispute between the Sultan and the Khedive.
As he was not so very far away, he "might as well visit
the Crimea, and the old battle grounds;" thence by the
Caucasus to the Caspian, to pick up information about the
Russian expedition to Khiva. From the Caspian the way
was easy through Persia to India, and, on the way, a
telling letter might be sent from Persepolis. Nor was this
all—"Bagdad will be close on your way to India, and
something might be written about the Euphrates Valley
Railroad." Mr. Bennett concluded in these words: "Then,
when you have come to India, you can go after Livingstone. Perhaps you will hear by that time that he is on
his way to Zanzibar; but, if not, go into the interior and
find him. If alive, get what news of his discoveries you
can; and if you find he is dead, bring all possible proofs
of his being dead. That is all; good night, and God be

with you."   "Good night, sir," said Stanley ; " what it is
in the power of human nature to do I will do ; and on
such an errand as I go upon, God will be with me."  And
bravely Stanley fulfilled his mission.  Yet we cannot help
thinking that it was a mistake to waste an entire year in
by-wanderings, considering that Livingstone was possibly
at the moment in want and danger ; and, further, that
Stanley's energies might have been exhausted, and perhaps his life sacrificed before he had entered upon the
great task he had undertaken.  Our American friends,
however, have their own way of doing things; they are
rapid travellers, and are fond of attending to a dozen things
at once.  In the present case everything turned out well,
and Mr. Bennett's plan was justified by the event.  He
evidently knew his man, and had the utmost confidence
in the indomitable push and perseverance of Mr. Stanley.
Two months after the Paris instructions were given, the
indefatigable correspondent was at Philæ, on the Nile,
"interviewing" a member of Sir Samuel Baker's expedition.  In the meantime he had witnessed the inaugural
ceremonies at the opening of the Suez Canal.  About the
middle of January he arrived at Jerusalem, next month
at Constantinople, and the month after (March, 1870) at the
Crimea.  Thence he passed, by the route Mr. Bennett had
marked out, by Teheran and Ispahan to Muscat in Arabia,
and thence to Bombay, where he arrived on the 12th of
July.  It was October before he left for the Mauritius,
and he at last arrived at Zanzibar on the 6th of January,
1871.  A month after, the party arrived at Bagamoyo.

Much time was necessarily taken in equipping and dispatching the five caravans which preceded the correspondent, and it was not till the 23rd of June, 1871, that Mr. Stanley arrived at Unyanyembe. His first letter, dated September 21st, 1871, gives an exceedingly graphic account of his arrival, and of the vicissitudes of his journey to the point at which he had arrived at the time of writing. The only blemish in the narrative contained in this and the succeeding letters is a tendency to sneer at Livingstone's countrymen, and even to attempt to discredit the authenticity of the letters of 1867–8. With regard to his hostility to Dr. Kirk, we may have something to say in the sequel: here it is only necessary to quote a few words from this first letter. It shows two things :—First, that Stanley had no belief in the accounts received in England, or that he knew nothing about them ; and, secondly, that he was not above sending from Africa an ironical eulogy of the venerable President of the Geographical Society, whom, when better informed, he called the " staunch and enduring friend of Dr. Livingstone." We quote the passage to show that, after all, Sir Roderick's faith based on knowledge was superior to Mr. Stanley's incredulity founded on ignorance :—

" Amid these many scraps of clippings, all about Livingstone, there are many more which contain as ludicrous mistakes, mostly all of them having emanated from the same scientific pen as the above. I find one wherein Sir R. Murchison, President of the Royal Geographical Society, stoutly maintains that Livingstone's tenacity of purpose,

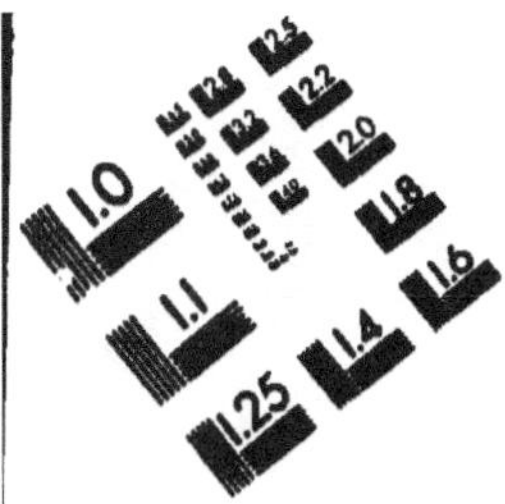

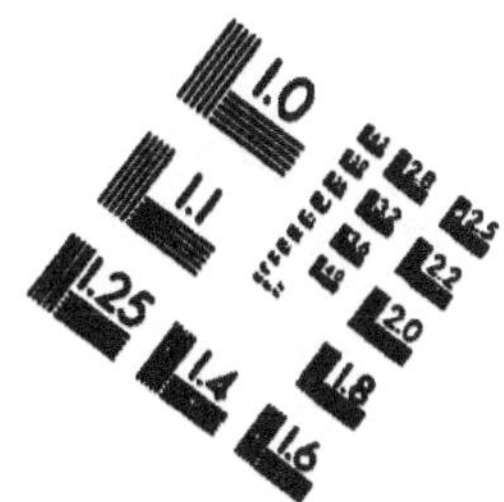

## IMAGE EVALUATION
## TEST TARGET (MT-3)

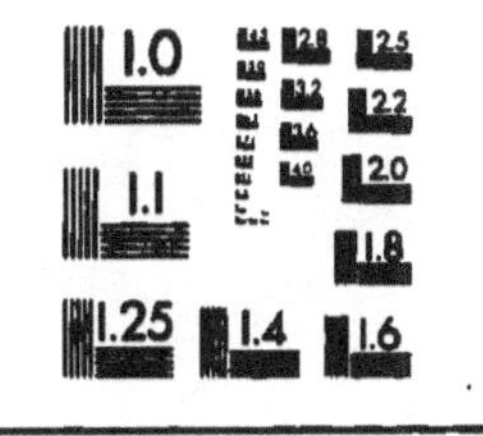

6"

Photographic
Sciences
Corporation

23 WEST MAIN STREET
WEBSTER, N.Y. 14580
(716) 872-4503

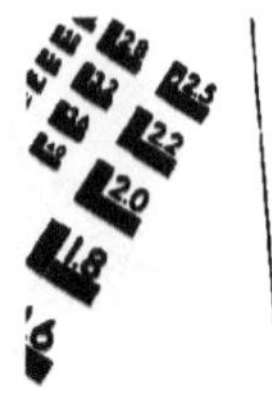

undying resolution and herculean frame will overcome every obstacle. Through several scraps runs a vein of doubt and unbelief in the existence of the explorer. The writers seem to incline that he has at last succumbed. But to the very latest date Sir Roderick rides triumphant over all doubts and fears. At the very nick of time he has always a letter from Livingstone himself, or a despatch from Livingstone to Lord Clarendon, or a private note from Dr. Livingstone to his friend Kirk at Zanzibar. Happy Sir Roderick! Good Sir Roderick! a healthy, soul-inspiring faith is thine. Well, I am glad to tell you the outspoken truth, tormented by the same doubts and fears that people in America and England are—to-day uncommonly so. I blame the fever. *Yet, though I have heard nothing that would lead me to believe Livingstone is alive,* I derive much comfort in reading Sir Roderick's speech to the society of which he is president. But though he has tenacity of purpose and is the most resolute of travellers, he is but a man, who, if alive, is old in years."

The cynical tone of Mr. Stanley's early letters to the *Herald* is much to be regretted. It detracts from the otherwise unqualified admiration we feel for his energy and perseverance, and makes his expedition look rather too much like an African mission in the interest of spread-eagleism. Perhaps, however, as our entertaining correspondent remarks, much of this uncomplimentary criticism may have been due to the fever of which he received the first touch about this time. Unyanyembe is the chief district of Unyamwezi of which Stanley relates his experiences as follows :—

" Unyamwezi is a romantic name. It is the 'Land of the Moon,' rendered into English—as romantic and sweet in Kinyamwezi as any that Stamboul or Ispahan can boast is to a Turk or a Persian. The attraction, however, to a European, lies only in the name. There is nothing of the mystic, nothing of the poetical, nothing of the romantic, in the country of Unyamwezi. I shudder at the sound of the name. It is pregnant in its every syllable to me. Whenever I think of the word immediately come thoughts of colocynth, rhubarb, calomel, tartar emetic, ipecacuanha and quinine into my head, and I feel qualmish about the gastric regions, and I wish I were a thousand miles away from it. If I look abroad over the country I see the most inane and the most prosaic country one could ever imagine. It is the most unlikely country to a European for settlement; it is so repulsive, owing to the notoriety it has gained for its fevers. A white missionary would shrink back with horror at the thought of settling in it. An agriculturist might be tempted; but then there are so many better countries where he could do so much better, he would be a madman if he ignored those to settle in this."

These of course were first impressions which Mr. Stanley saw occasion after to correct. There cannot be a greater contrast in description than there is between the tone of these early letters and that of his writing after he had encountered Livingstone, acquired some of his knowledge, and caught the magic of his enthusiasm. It had been Stanley's intention to press on immediately from Unyanyembe to Ujiji; but it turned out that they were not to leave the district as soon as they anticipated. They had arrived at the former place on the 23rd of June, and on the 6th of July they heard that Mirambo, a chief of "The Land of the Moon," had taken heavy tribute from a caravan on the road to Ujiji and turned it back, declaring that no Arab caravan should pass through his country while he was alive. This declaration, it appears, was the result of a long standing feud between Mirambo and Mkasiwa, king of Unyanyembe, who was on terms of friendship with the Arabs. Stanley's attitude under the circumstances may be given in his own words :—

"On the 15th July war was declared between Mirambo and the Arabs. Such being the case, my position was as follows :—Mirambo occupies the country which lies between the object of my search and Unyanyembe. I cannot possibly reach Livingstone unless this man is out of the way—or peace is declared—nor can Livingstone reach Unyanyembe unless Mirambo is killed. The Arabs have plenty of guns if they will only fight, and as their success will help me forward on my journey, I will go and help them.

"On the 20th July a force of 2,000 men, the slaves and soldiers of the Arabs, marched from Unyanyembe to fight Mirambo. The soldiers of the *Herald* expedition, to the number of forty, under my leadership, accompanied them. Of the Arab's mode of fighting I was totally ignorant, but

I intended to be governed by circumstances. We made a most imposing show, as you may imagine. Every slave and soldier was decorated with a crown of feathers, and had a lengthy crimson cloak flowing from his shoulders and trailing on the ground. Each was armed with either a flint-lock or percussion gun—the Balocches with matchlocks, profusely decorated with silver bands. Our progress was noisy in the extreme—as if noise would avail much in the expected battle. While traversing the Unyanyembe plains, the column was very irregular, owing to the extravagant show of wild fight which they indulged in as we advanced. On the second day we arrived at Mfuto, where we all feasted on meat freely slaughtered for the braves. Here I was attacked with a severe fever, but as the army was for advancing I had myself carried in my hammock, almost delirious. On the fourth day we arrived at the village of Zimbizo, which was taken without much trouble. We had arrived in the enemy's country. I was still suffering from fever, and, while conscious, had given strict orders that unless all the Arabs went together, that none of my men should go to fight with any small detachment."

On the fifth day, the Arabs, growing unusually bold after the capture and execution of a spy, went forth to capture a village in which Mirambo then was. As they were entering one gate of the village the hostile chief quietly retreated by another, and placed his available force in ambush. Meanwhile the Arabs encumbered themselves with the plunder of the village, consisting of ivory and slaves, and proceeded to return again by the road. When they reached the spot where Mirambo had planted his ambush, the signal was given, and the enemy rose as one man. Each of them taking possession of his man, speared him and cut off his head. Not an Arab escaped, and it was only from some of the slaves who made their way to the camp that the story of the disaster was made known. The result was a general panic and a general stampede. Mr. Stanley, with his usual coolness and intrepidity, attempted to rally the Arabs and others who were still at the camp. They retreated in as orderly a manner as they could be induced to do. Mr. Stanley goes on to say :—

" The next day was but a continuation of the retreat to Unyanyembe with the Arabs ; but I ordered a halt, and on the third day went on leisurely. The Arabs had become demoralized ; in their hurry they had left their tents and ammunition for Mirambo.

" Ten days after this, and what I had forewarned the Arabs of came to pass, Mirambo, with 1,000 guns and 1,500 Watudas, his allies, invaded Unyanyembe, and pitched their camp insolently within view of the Arab capital of Tabora. Tabora is a large collection of Arab settlements, or tembes, as they are called here. Each Arab house is isolated by the fence which surrounds it. Not one is more than two hundred yards off from the other, and each has its own name known, however, but to few outsiders."

It was this place which Mirambo proceeded to invest, and Stanley immediately prepared to defend it. One can hardly help smiling at the national spirit of the energetic correspondent as he describes the construction of the earth-fortifications. "First of all," he says, as if that were by far the most essential part of the defences, "a lofty bamboo pole was procured and planted on the top of our fortlet, and the American flag was run up, where it waved joyously and grandly, an omen to all fugitives and their hunters." The subordinate matters of ditch-making and the construction of rifle pits followed, and all night the besieged stood on guard; but the morning came, and "Mirambo departed with the ivory and cattle he had captured, and the people of Kwihara and Tabora breathed freer." This little taste of active service with such worthless allies does not seem to have been to Mr. Stanley's liking, and no wonder at it. He concludes his first letter in these words:—

"And now I am going to say farewell to Unyanyembe for a while. I shall never help an Arab again. He is no fighting man, or, I should say, does not know how to fight, but knows, personally, how to die. They will not conquer Mirambo within a year, and I cannot stop to see that play out. There is a good old man waiting for me somewhere, and that impels me on. There is a journal afar off which expects me to do my duty, and I must do it. Good bye; I am off the day after to morrow for Ujiji; then, perhaps, the Congo River."

When next the *Herald* correspondent wrote, a great transformation had taken place in his views of Africa, for he had accomplished his mission. This letter is dated

November 23rd, 1871, from Bunder, Ujiji, on Lake Tanganyika. We quote the opening sentences :—

"Only two months gone, and what a change in my feelings! But two months ago, what a peevish, fretful soul was mine! What a hopeless prospect presented itself before your correspondent! Arabs vowing that I would never behold the Tanganyika; Sheikh, the son of Nasib, declaring me a madman to his fellows because I would not heed his words. My men deserting, my servants whining day by day, and my white men endeavouring to impress me with the belief that we were all doomed men! And the only answer to it all is—Livingstone, the hero traveller, is alongside of me, writing as hard as he can to his friends in England, India and America, and I am quite safe and sound in health and limb. Wonderful, is it not, that such a thing should be, when the seers had foretold that it would be otherwise—that all my schemes, that all my determination would avail me nothing? But probably you are in as much of a hurry to know how it all took place as I am to relate. So, to the recital."

The journey from Unyanyembe, which Stanley left on the 23rd of September, was not altogether a smooth one. In the first place, there was a general stampede amongst his native followers during an attack of fever which seized the correspondent. The fellows, however, either came back voluntarily or were captured. Stanley took care to mete out a proper measure of punishment to the worst cases. Passing through the extensive forest between Unyanyembe and Ugunda, he arrived at the capital of the latter place, wherein " one may laugh at Mirambo and his forest thieves." From this town, Ma-manyara, where the party were hospitably treated, Marefu in Ukonongo was reached in five days' march. We cannot follow in detail the progress of Mr. Stanley to Lake Tanganyika and Ujiji. The journey was continued through many dangers and with great difficulty, but the perseverance of the American carried him through all, and finally he stood on the last hill, and " the port of Ujiji, embowered in palms, with the tiny waves of the silver waters of Tanganyika rolling at its feet, was directly below." The following extract will best describe the peculiar feelings of the *Herald* correspondent at this juncture :—

" We are now about descending—in a few minutes we shall have reached the spot where we imagine the object of our search is—our fate will soon be decided. No one in that town knows we are coming ; least of all do they know we are so close to them. If any of them ever heard of the white man at Unyanyembe they must believe we are there yet. We shall take them all by surprise, for no other but a white man would dare leave Unyanyembe for Ujiji with the country in such a distracted state—no other but a crazy white man, whom Sheikh, the son of Nasib, is going to report to Syed or Prince Burghash for not taking his advice.

" Well, we are but a mile from Ujiji now, and it is high time we should let them know that a caravan is coming ; so ' Commence firing ' is the word passed along the length of the column, and gladly do they begin. They have loaded their muskets half full, and they roar like the broadside of a line-of-battle ship. Down go the ramrods, sending huge charges home to the breech, and volley after volley is fired. The flags are fluttered; the banner of America is in front, waving joyfully; the guide is in the zenith of his glory. The former residents of Zanzita will know it directly, and will wonder—as well they may —as to what it means. Never were the Stars and Stripes so beautiful to my mind—the breeze of the Tanganyika has such an effect on them. The guide blows his horn, and the shrill, wild clamour of it is far and near, and still the cannon muskets tell the noisy seconds. By this time the Arabs are fully alarmed; the natives of Ujiji, Wag-uhha, Warundi, Wanguana, and I know not whom, hurry up by the hundreds to ask what it all means—this fusi-lading, shouting and blowing of horns and flag-flying."

The most graphic account of the meeting of Stanley and Livingstone is contained in a speech delivered by the former before the Geographical Society on his return to England. It connects well with the extract we have just given from his letter :—

"So we were firing away, shouting, blowing horns beating drums. All the people came out, and the great Arabs from Muscat came out.

"Hearing we were from Zanzibar and were friendly, and brought news of their relatives, they welcomed us. And while we were travelling down that steep hill, down to this little town, I heard a voice saying, 'Good morning, sir.' I turned, and said sharply, 'Who the mischief are

you?'  'I am the servant of Dr. Livingstone, sir.'  'What!
is Dr. Livingstone here?'  'Yes, he is here.  I saw him
just now.'  I said, 'Do you mean to say Dr. Livingstone
is here?'  'Sure.'  'Go and tell him I am coming.'  Do
you think it possible for me to describe my emotions as I
walked down those few hundred yards?

"This man, David Livingstone, that I believed to be a
myth, was in front of me a few yards.  I confess to you
that were it not for certain feelings of pride, I should have
turned over a somersault.  But I was ineffably happy.  I
had found Livingstone; my work is ended.  It is only a
march home quick; carry the news to the first telegraph
station, and so give the word to the world.  A great many
people gathered around us.  My attention was directed to
where a group of Arabs were standing, and in the centre
of this group a pale, careworn, gray-bearded old man,
dressed in a red shirt, with a crimson joho, with a gold
band round his cap, an old tweed pair of pants, his shoes
looking the worse for wear.  Who is this old man? I ask
myself.  Is it Livingstone?  Yes, it is.  No, it is not.
Yes, it is.  'Dr. Livingstone, I presume?'  'Yes?'  Now
it would never have done in the presence of the grave
Arabs, who stood there stroking their beards, for two white
men to kick up their heels.  No; the Arabs must be
attended to.  They would carry the story that we were
children—fools.  So we walked, side by side, into the
verandah.  There we sat—the man, the myth, and I.  This
was the man; and what a woeful tale of calamities that
wrinkled face, those gray hairs in his beard, those silver

lines in his head—what a woeful tale they told! Now we begin to talk. I don't know about what. I know we talk, and by and by come plenty of presents from the Arabs. We eat and talk, and whether Livingstone eats most or I eat most I cannot tell. I tell him many things. He asks, 'Do you know such a one?' 'Yes,' 'How is he?' 'Dead.' 'Oh, oh!' 'And such a one?' 'Alive and well.' 'Thanks be to God.' 'And what are they all doing in Europe now?' 'Well, the French are kicking up a fuss; and the Prussians are around Paris, and the world is turned topsy-turvy.' It is all a matter of wonder for Livingstone. He soon turned in to read his letters. And who shall stand between this man and the outer world?"

Stanley appears to have had some curious notions about Livingstone, whom he expected to find brusque in manner and morose in temper. We quote from his letter of Dec. 26th, 1871:—

"Besides, I had heard all sorts of things from a quondam companion of his about him. He was eccentric, I was told; nay, almost a misanthrope, who hated the sight of Europeans; who if Burton, Speke, Grant, or anybody of that kind were coming to see him, would make haste to put as many miles as possible between himself and such a person. He was a man, also, whom no one could get along with—it was almost impossible to please him; he was a man who kept no journal, whose discoveries would certainly perish with him unless he himself came back. This was the man I was shaking hands

with, whom I had done my utmost to surprise, lest
he should run away. Consequently you may know
why I did not dare manifest any extraordinary joy
upon my success. But, really, had there been no one
present—none of those cynical-minded Arabs I mean
—I think I should have betrayed the emotion which
possessed me, instead of which I only said, 'Doctor, I
thank God I have been permitted to shake hands with
you.' Which he returned with a grateful and welcome
smile."

Mr. Stanley's description of Livingstone's personal appearance is exceedingly interesting. He tells us that, on
his first introduction, the great traveller was as a closed
volume to him, roughly bound. Whatever of value the
book might contain, its exterior gave no sign of it. As
to the general form and figure of the man the correspondent says :—

"He is a man of unpretending appearance enough, has
quiet, composed features, from which the freshness of
youth has quite departed, but which retains the nobility
of prime age just enough to show that there yet lives
much endurance and vigour within his frame. The eyes,
which are hazel, are remarkably bright, not dimmed in the
least, though the whiskers and mustache are very gray.
The hair, originally brown, is streaked here and there with
gray over the temples, otherwise it might have belonged
to a man of thirty. The teeth above show indications of
being worn out. The hard fare of Londa and Manyema
have made havoc in their ranks. His form is stoutish, a

little over the ordinary in height, with slightly bowed
shoulders. When walking he has the heavy step of an
overworked and fatigued man.　On his head he wears the
naval cap with a round vizor, with which he has been
identified throughout Africa. His dress shows that at
times he has had to resort to the needle to repair and re-
place what travel has worn.　Such is Livingstone externally."

Stanley had brought letters for the explorer from his
family and friends in Europe, but the perusal of them
was postponed till evening in order that he might hear
what had been going on in the outside world during his
prolonged absence.　He was thus informed of the opening
of the Suez Canal and the Pacific Railway; the Spanish
Revolution and King Amadeus, with the assassination of
General Prim; General Grant's election; the Franco-
German war and its issue; besides a long obituary list,
containing more than one personal friend of Livingstone's.

Under the genial influence of Stanley's companionship
the doctor gradually disclosed his real nature which at
the first meeting seemed an enigma.　The haggard and
stern features which had shocked the correspondent, the
heavy step, the gray beard and bowed shoulders had
not truly indicated the spring and youthfulness of Livingstone's character.　" Underneath that aged and well-spent
exterior lay an endless fund of high spirits, which now
and then broke into peals of hearty laughter—the rugged
frame enclosed a very young and exuberant soul."　His

memory also struck Stanley as being wonderfully reten-
tive—which the latter curiously enough attributes to the
fact that Livingstone did not smoke. He could repeat
entire poems and knew more of Whittier and Lowell than
Stanley himself did. The same faculty was also noticeable
in the recollection of ",an endless number of facts and
names of persons connected with America." The correspondent then refers to the strong and abiding piety which
was the guiding influence of his life. Mr. Stanley is no
doubt right when he attributes the mellowing and sub-
duing of a naturally stern character to the influence of
religion. Without it, instead of being beloved by his
servants and the natives with whom he came in contact,
he would probably have been a. hard task-master, with
cold and distant human sympathies. The two white men
had not been together long when Stanley offered to spend
a few months with Livingstone in order to complete the
exploration of Lake Tanganyika. The correspondent's
motive was a generous one; he had reliable attendants, and a good supply of cloth and other necessaries and the journey could thus be made in comparative comfort. Livingstone gratefully accepted the
offer, and the combined parties immediately set out across
the Lake from Ujiji. This was on the 20th of November,
1871, ten days after Stanley's arrival. The expedition
occupied from that date to the 18th of February, 1872,
during which time nearly 800 miles had been travelled.
It was about a month after (14th of March) that Livingstone
and Stanley parted, the latter arriving at Zanzibar on the

17th of May. The despatches to the Foreign Office were
delivered to the Foreign Secretary immediately on
Stanley's arrival in London, that is, on August the 1st.
The narrative of the correspondent's travels with the
explorer will naturally come in its proper place as a part
of the general sketch of Livingstone's last expedition.
This we propose to give in a connected form in the next
part. The mass of letters from which the story is ex-
tracted are so disconnected as to be confusing to the reader
We shall endeavour, therefore, to make a consecutive account of the whole from 1866 to 1873, the date of Livingstone's death. No sooner was the news transmitted from
Bombay that Stanley had succeeded in discovering Livingstone than the story was received with loud expressions
of incredulity. The *Telegraph*, which may be called the
New York *Herald* of London, alone took Stanley's part
and defended his veracity from the first. Even his arrival
in England did not dissipate the doubts which still ling-
ered in some minds, as to the truth of his narrative. So
late as the end of 1872, when it was reported that Dr.
Livingstone was on his way to Zanzibar, *en route* for
England, it was hinted that Stanley "had better make
himself scarce" before the doctor's arrival to confront
him and disprove the statements he had made. We fear it
must be confessed that national jealousy was at the bottom
of this distrust; and this feeling was rather aggravated
by the contemptuous tone of Stanley, when speaking of
Burton, Speke, Baker, and Beke, and also of the British
relief expeditions which had not met with his success,

The fact—which, however, ought not to lessen our admiration of Stanley's energy—appears to be, that the American "was in luck." He arrived at Ujiji only ten days after Livingstone's return there; and, as he says himself, had he gone directly to Zanzibar, when he received his instructions, or at any time except that which was accidentally chosen, he might have followed the explorer far westward to Manyema, and then missed him after all—with the chance of perishing in fight, or of fever by the way. It was scarcely in good taste, therefore, to assail with ridicule those who had laboured in the same cause, under less favourable circumstances. The proofs of the truth of Stanley's story were so overwhelming, however, that we wonder how any one could express a doubt on the subject. He was the bearer of despatches to the Foreign Office; letters to his family, including one to Mr. John Livingstone, a brother, of Listowel, Ontario; to Sir Roderick Murchison, Sir Bartle Frere, Mr. James Gordon Bennett, jr., and others, Besides this, there was his diary sealed up and committed to Stanley's care for transmission to Livingstone's daughter, Agnes. Shortly after his arrival in England, Mr. Stanley appeared in public before the Royal Geographical Society, presided over by Mr. Francis Galton. Amongst those present were Sir Thomas Fowell Buxton, Professor Fawcett, M.P., Mr. Edwin Chadwick, Dr. Carpenter, Baroness Coutts, Sir John Bowring, Dr. Price, and Admiral Richards, the Hydrographer of the Navy; Sir Henry Rawlinson, Dr. Beke, and Consul Petherick occupied seats on the platform. The ex-Emperor and Empress of the

French, and the Prince Imperial, were also present, and took great interest in the proceedings. One venerable form, however, was wanting, that of Sir Roderick Murchison, the constant and unflinching friend of the explorer. The president had sunk under a stroke of paralysis just before Stanley discovered Livingstone, and had been laid in his grave sometime before the latter penned these lines to Sir Bartle Frere:—"I am distressed to hear no tidings of Sir Roderick, except that he has been ill. It awakens fears for the dearest friend in life." When he appeared before the meeting, Mr. Stanley, after his introduction by the president, gave a brief but succinct account of his discovery of Livingstone. The theory held by the explorer as to the true fountain-head of the Nile waters, of which we shall speak more fully hereafter, was warmly discussed and objected to in a paper sent by Col. Grant, and in a speech by Consul Petherick. Sir Henry Rawlinson's remarks were non-committal, although he expressed himself in doubt. He concluded by expressing a hope that the traveller "would soon ascertain where the river-system debouched, which would be the crowning result of his African travels." Mr. Oswell, Livingstone's old friend, contented himself with returning his warmest thanks to the correspondent, for what he had accomplished by his expedition. Mr. Stanley again took the floor and defended Livingstone's views in a characteristic, perhaps it may be called a "slashing," speech. He replied to Colonel Grant's objections and Sir Henry Rawlinson's doubts, and was particularly severe on Dr. Beke. Mr. Stanley subsequently read

before the British Association for the Advancement of
Science, at its annual meeting at Brighton, a carefully
prepared paper on the exploration of Tanganyika, by
Livingstone and himself. Before closing this section of
the work, we may as well get rid of a disagreeable subject,
the alleged misconduct of Dr. Kirk, the acting British
consul at Zanzibar. In his very first letter from Unyanyembe, Mr. Stanley opened his batteries upon the doctor. The
charge then made was briefly this:—That Dr. Kirk, on
November 1st, 1870, dispatched a sealed bag of letters for
Dr. Livingstone, on a caravan laden with provisions. On
the 4th of February, after much culpable delay on the part
of the escort, they had only got as far as Bagomoyo, and on
the 18th, Dr. Kirk and a party arrived there in the gun-
boat *Columbine.* Three days before, hearing that the
consul was approaching, and probably fearing his anger
at the delay, those in charge of the caravan had hastily
departed for the interior. Stanley says, that in the meantime Kirk and his friends were shooting wild beasts of
the Knigani. The accusations against the consul were :—
First, that he had not a word to say or a word to write
to his old friend, from the 1st of November, 1870, to about
the 15th of February, 1871, though how he was to send it
after the departure of the caravan does not appear; and
secondly, the question is put, whether "this man, Dr.
John Kirk," the professed friend of Livingstone, had shown
his friendship for Livingstone, in leaving his caravan
three and a half months at Bagomoyo; or whether, when
he went over to Bagomoyo in the character of "showman

of wild beasts," to gratify the sporting instincts of the officers of Her Britannic Majesty's ship *Columbine*, he showed any very kinc *y* feeling to the hero traveller, in leaving the duty of looking up that caravan of the doctor's till the last thing on the programme.

To this Dr. Kirk's answer would obviously be, that he had every right to suppose that the caravan was far beyond his reach before he could arrive at Bagomoyo. It did, in fact, take care to get out of the way before he appeared there. The fate of this expedition certainly could not be laid at Dr. Kirk's door, for Dr. Livingstone himself expressly states in his despatch to Earl Granville, under date November 14th, 1871, "that the Banians, who advanced their goods for retail by Shereef, had, in fact, taken advantage of the notorious East African Moslem duplicity to interpose their own trade speculations between two government officers, and almost within the shadow of the Consulate, *supplant Dr. Kirk's attempt to aid me* by a fraudulent conversion of the help expedition to the gratification of their own greed. Shereef was their ready tool, and having at Ujiji finished the Banian trade, he acted as if he had forgotten having ever been employed by any one else. Here the drunken half-caste Moslem tailor lay intoxicated at times for a whole month ; the drink—palm toddy and tombe—all bought with my beads, of course."

We regret to say anything that would seem to detract from the credit due to Mr. Stanley, but it is abundantly evident that, from some dislike he had taken to Kirk, he persistently poisoned Livingstone's mind against the doctor. On hearsay evidence, of the truth of which nothing could be known, Kirk was unjustly condemned; and, as will be seen from the letter below, published by Mr. John Livingstone for the first time in the *Portland Press*, in July, 1874, the traveller had come to believe that Dr. Kirk had not only been careless in forwarding supplies, but that he had actually attempted to thwart him in a malicious manner. Dr. Livingstone's brother, in publishing this letter, states that his indignation had been moved by reading that Dr. Kirk had been a pall-bearer at his brother's funeral, and that had he been there, he would have protested against it. We give the letter *in extenso*, that our readers may see how; under skilful manipulation, the story had grown :—

LAKE BANGWEOLO,

Central Africa, Dec. 1872.

MY DEAR BROTHER,—You may have heard how I was baffled and nearly taken by a coterie or ring of slave-trading-Arabs and Banians, the latter our Indian fellow-subjects, by whose money, arms, and ammunition, the Arab agents carry on all the cruelties and murders necessary in their enterprises. I lost two years in time, about a thousand pounds in money, had two thousand miles of useless tramping, and was subject to the imminent risk of a violent death four several times,—all through my agent, in killing simplicity, handing over the affair of supplying me with men and goods to his friend, Ludha Damji, the head and chief money-lender of the ring. He sent his own

8

and other Banian slaves instead of men, and at three times
the highest freeman's pay. Then the goods were placed
in charge of a thief by the name of Shereef Bosher, and
he sold all off for slaves and ivory to himself. The Banians would not kill a flea for the world, but by their
money means, they are the worst cannibals in all Africa.
Their slaves came loudly declaring that they were ordered
by the English vice-consul to force me back. This was
of course false. He could not be such a fool as to place
himself in their power. But slaves are in some respects
like children, and quite overacted their part. This is the
way in which I view their asseverations. A little American girl is said to have asked a visitor who was received
with great cordiality by mamma :—" Is your next door
neighbour a fool ?" " No, my dear, he is a very sensible
man. Why do you ask that ?" " Because mamma said
you was next door to a fool." Public advice was sent by
the English vice-consul to the Foreign Office, and published by the Royal Geographical Society, that I ought to
retire and leave the rest of the work to others. That
means himself. Astute Banians may have learned the
proclivities of my public advisers, and delivered them un-
diluted to their slaves. When consulted by Sir Roderick
Murchison, I recommended this same vice-consul as a
leader of this expedition, and he afterwards told me it
was declined unless he had as good salary and position to
fall back upon as Speke and Grant had in their pay and
commissions. The salary and position he now holds were
procured by my own intercession. Then followed the

following self-invitation : "You cannot imagine how much I long to have a run again with you in the wilds ; I feel as if I must have it sometime." No response followed this appeal.

No sooner was Lake Bangweolo discovered and announced at the coast, than an official description of it was sent to the Bombay Government, in which it was gravely stated that it is like Nyassa, Tanganyika, and the Albert Nyanza, overhung by high mountain slopes, which open out in bays and valleys or leave great plains which, during the rainy season, become flooded, so that caravans march for days through water knee-deep, seeking for higher ground on which to pass the night. Now I found the Lake to be 4,000 feet above the sea—the height at which I now write—but the country around is remarkable only for extreme flatness. When I first reached it the only mountain slopes were ant hills, some of them about twenty feet high. Their slopes could scarcely be called high except on the top of the 4,000 feet. There was no more slope from the land generally, than there is from the Isle of Dogs down to the level of the Thames.

The news I got at Ujiji—to which I was forced back by the Banian slaves—was that the vice-consul was in Ludha Damji's hands. I had been plundered of my goods, wholly or partially, four times, but the consular agent paid expressly to give information, seems to have been kept silent by the Banians, who have the custom house and all the public revenue entirely in their hands. There was nothing immoral in the vice-consul's friendship for

Ludha, but it was highly impolitic, for it gave all the members of the ring the persuasion that Ludha would make all safe. I was in misery. I was still determined not to give in to their villanies; but was resolved to make my way down to Baker for aid.

I have the prospect of going home to poverty, for my salary was stopped by a Mr. Murray, clerk in the Foreign Office, who was put in as a third under-secretary when the slave trade was rife on the west coast, and now it has ceased tries to save his own pay by cutting down others. The superiors know little about these matters. I shall not go a begging, but as soon as I get a set of new teeth, launch out into foreign parts to seek my fortune—a nice reward for the discovery of the sources of the Nile, is it not? If the paid consular agents concealed the robberies from the vice-consul they are culpable. When my formal complaint of all I have suffered from the people employed by Dr. Kirk came down by Stanley, it was like a clap of thunder to him, and before he had collected all his thoughts he raved against me. The English relief and search expedition were strongly advised by him to wait till the rains should cease, and they seemed to have dawdled on a most unhealthy island until all their good intentions oozed out at their finger ends. Kirk wrote that he felt the greatest grief and indignation at my losses—the direct result of the misbehaviour and dishonesty of those engaged—but nine days after he declared before five gentlemen that he would not send over the consular agent to Bagamoyo to see the men secured by

Stanley off (the steamer was starting) nor do anything for Dr. Livingstone, because he believed niggers would only insult him. It was his own belief in Ludha and his slaves that caused all my losses, and it is his own inference entirely that I believed the slaves when they swore that he instructed them to force me back. But it is my belief that possibly the difficulties may have had a remote connection with his eagerness to share the honour of discovery after I had helped him to his perquisites, position, and salary. His wrath and babbling out that he was charged with the instruction of the slaves is ominous. The fascination of mixing up his name with discoveries seems pretty strong, and there may be a little lurking hope of enhancing his standing in the community. I never said aught to him.

The Government also had another plan than sending out the search and relief expedition, which was, that if they had no offer for one already out, to take a few Arabs, run in and settle the Nile question by looking at the north end of Tanganyika, and call me out of Manyema, where his truthful Arabs reported me as living like an Arab. And I went up quite sure that, if anywhere, the Nile was west at the Lualaba where I was working. The idea seems to have come from Kirk, but it has not prevailed over me, and if the good Lord above gives me strength and influence to complete the task in spite of everything, I shall not grudge my hunger and toil.

Affectionately yours,

DAVID LIVINGSTONE.

It will be observed that the traveller was in no position to know the truth or falsehood of the accusations made against his old friend and fellow-explorer. We can easily understand the bitterness of feeling which must have taken possession of Livingstone's mind when he was persistently informed that Dr. Kirk was acting, not only an unfriendly, but an absolutely hostile part. He was alone, half-starved, and in the midst of dangers of various kinds, and when he was positively assured that the Consul had played false, and that by the first white man who had come to him with succour, we can hardly blame him for forming a precipitate judgment. But there is another side to the question. There was no possible reason for such extraordinary conduct. Up to the moment when Stanley arrived at Ujiji, they had been intimate friends. Kirk, as we have already stated, was a valued member of the Zambesi expedition, and only left it with Charles Livingstone, when they had both been brought to the gates of death by repeated attacks of fever and dysentery. That a man who had taken the deepest interest in Livingstone's explorations and manifested the liveliest sympathy with him should thus, from no assigned reason, change his whole course of conduct, is of itself antecedently improbable in the highest degree. Livingstone knew well by experience the difficulties which encompassed any expedition to relieve him, and ought, therefore, to have paused before he credited the accusations against his fellow-countryman. Dr. Livingstone's own son, who was at Zanzibar, and therefore in the very best position to learn

the truth, entirely acquitted Dr. Kirk; what he thinks of
Mr. Stanley's share in his father's misapprehensions plainly
appears.

In answer to the various statements that have recently
been made concerning Dr. Kirk and Dr. Livingstone, the
son of the latter, Mr. Oswell Livingstone, has felt it his
duty to publish the following letter. It will be remembered that this gentleman accompanied the Search Expedition organized by the Royal Geographical Society :—

TO THE EDITOR OF "THE DAILY TELEGRAPH."

Sir,—May I ask for a few remarks of my own concerning Dr. Kirk and my father, the same prominent publicity
which is afforded to your correspondent's details, as your
readers have them in your publication of to-day ?

I will preface what I have to say by stating that the
extreme happiness which was borne to me whilst at Zanzibar, upon the news of my father's safety, was sadly
marred by the impression which had evidently entered
his mind concerning his old and true friend, Dr. Kirk, *at
some time previous to his parting with Mr. Stanley.*

Before leaving the coast I used all my own exertions,
in letters to Dr. Livingstone, to remove this misconcep-
tion, and I ardently hope that I have done so with success
before now. But in the mean time Dr. Kirk had received
some astonishing and strongly-expressed surmises in
letters from my father, concerning the results he had experienced from the sending off of various expeditions for
his relief, both by Dr. Kirk and such other officials as had

preceded him in office.   Dr. Kirk had also been made
aware of that which *Mr. Stanley had forcibly and pub-
licly retailed as coming from my father*, so that he felt
the claims of friendship (which had been ignored on Dr.
Livingstone's part) must be laid aside in all further intercourse, for the stiff routine of consular action, to which
my father had alone appealed in his letters.

It would seem from what I read to-day that Dr. Kirk
did not conceal this when speaking to the American
Consul and a gentleman with him at the time.   Mr.
Stanley has so far omitted to furnish your correspondent
with this very necessary context—namely, that the speech
was made after the whole order of things had been so
disastrously interfered with, and your readers are left
to infer that Dr. Kirk's apathy is exposed, and that the
conduct attributed to him is really founded on fact.   Let
me state at once that Dr. Kirk is totally unworthy of the
accusations which are daily reaching the public, *and
which can have but one source.*   I may add that nothing
could exceed the kindness that we, the members of the
Search Expedition, experienced from him and Mrs. Kirk
during the whole time we were at Zanzibar and guests in
their house.

Both to Mr. Keene and myself Dr. Kirk plainly stated
that henceforth it only was left for him to deal with Dr.
Livingstone in a purely official capacity, and that the old
friendship between them had been laid aside.   I repeat
that I trust it is only for a time that this determination
must *perforce* be adhered to, and that I live in hope that

the earnest representations of myself and others who know my father, and also know Dr. Kirk, and the exertions he has really made, may speedily restore a balance which nothing should have overset.

I am, sir, yours faithfully,

W. OSWELL LIVINGSTONE,
*Of the Livingstone Search Expedition.*

The Royal Geographical Society,
1, Saville Row, July 27.

To which it is only necessary to add that, when he arrived in England, Mr. Stanley made no accusation against Dr. Kirk, but consented to be a fellow pall-bearer with him at the funeral—a step he could not have taken with honour if he still believed in the Doctor's treachery. The latter is still an intimate friend of Livingstone's children, and it will take a great deal more evidence than has yet been adduced to convince any candid mind that he did act or could have acted in the manner attributed to him. And here we very gladly take leave of a very unsavoury subject, and pass on to our sketch of the last expedition and last days of him whom Mr. Oswell called "their dear old Livingstone."

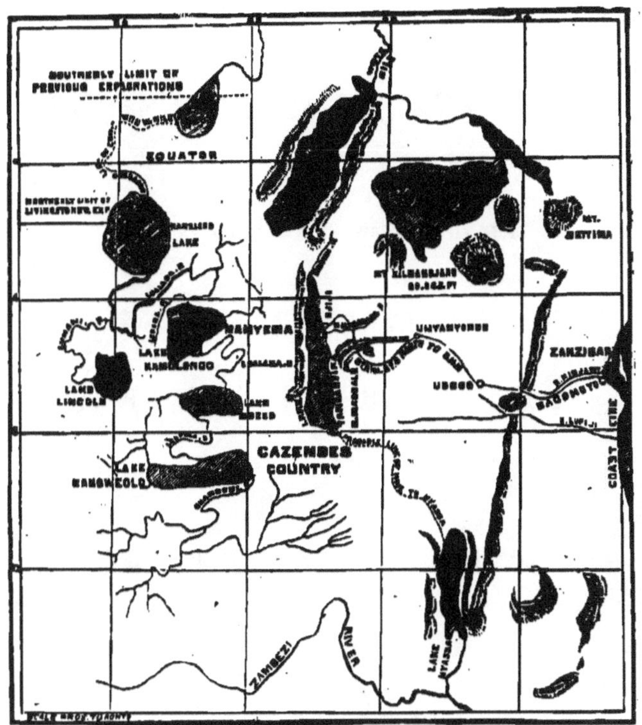


Map of Livingstone's Later Discoveries.

# THE
# LAST YEARS OF LIVINGSTONE;

BEING A NARRATIVE OF THE GREAT MISSIONARY'S
LAST JOURNEY OF EXPLORATION IN AFRICA

WITH THE

## PARTICULARS OF HIS DEATH

AND AN ACCOUNT OF

## HIS BURIAL IN WESTMINSTER ABBEY.

Toronto:
PUBLISHED BY MACLEAR & CO.
1874.

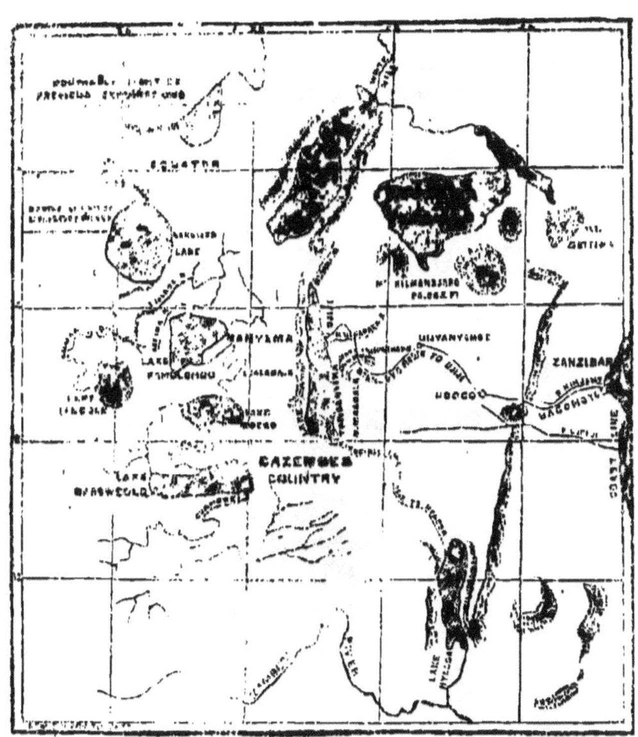

Map of Livingstone's Later Discoveries.

# THE

# LAST YEARS OF LIVINGSTONE;

### BEING A NARRATIVE OF THE GREAT MISSIONARY'S LAST JOURNEY OF EXPLORATION IN AFRICA

#### WITH THE

# PARTICULARS OF HIS DEATH

#### AND AN ACCOUNT OF

## HIS BURIAL IN WESTMINSTER ABBEY.

Toronto:
PUBLISHED BY MACLEAR & CO.
1874.

a
of
th
lit
be
'
ine
pro

# PREFACE.

IN the pages that follow, we have endeavoured to present to the public in a consecutive narrative, a full account of the last journey of Dr. Livingstone, the full particulars of his premature death, and the last honours paid to him by the Queen and people of Great Britain.

We have had some difficulty in presenting the facts in a connected form, owing mainly to the miscellaneous and often contradicting sources of information from which they are drawn. Without flattering ourselves that our little work is entirely free from error, we believe it will be found as accurate as circumstances will permit.

The repetition of much of the correspondence has been inevitable; and the variations in the spelling of African proper names, whose autography is necessarily unsettled and arbitrary, have also been unavoidable.

Our aim has been to give to our readers all the information we could gather regarding the wonderful man whose death has been deplored, we may almost venture to say, by the entire race of man.

As supplementary to the work we have inserted in Appendices a concise account of previous journeys of exploration in Africa by earlier travellers, and also a full exposition of a new expedition undertaken jointly by the *N. Y. Herald* and the London *Daily Telegraph* under the command of Mr. Stanley, to confirm and complete the discoveries of the lamented Livingstone.

August, 1874.

# THE LAST YEARS OF LIVINGSTONE.

THE last expedition of Dr. Livingstone had for its object
the thorough and complete exploration of the headwaters of the great rivers which flow from the heights of
Central Africa, viz., the Nile flowing to the north; the Congo, to the west, and the Zambesi to the east. Upon the satisfactory solution of the disputed geographical questions
involved, depended, of course, the direction in which commerce and missionary effort ought to be made. The first
thing to be done was evidently to settle the course of the
great highways to the sea, and afterwards to take measures
for the suppression of the slave-trade, and the opening up
of the country to civilization and Christianity. Dr.
Livingstone left the island of Zanzibar in March, 1866,
and on the 7th of April, he departed from Mikindini Bay
for the interior. His expedition consisted of twelve Sepoys from Bombay, who were afterwards sent back to
the coast; nine men from Johanna, of the Comoro Islands
off Hindostan, and these afterwards deserted him, and
spread a false report of his death ; seven liberated slaves
and two Zambesi men, six camels, three buffaloes, two
mules, and three donkeys. Reaching Lake Tanganyika at
its southern end, he crossed Marangu, and came to Lake
Moero. He followed this lake to its southern end, and

found that a river called Luapula entered it from the
south. He was thus on the direct course of the great
water-system, and he therefore followed this river till he
found it issuing from another lake, the Bangweolo, which
is of about the same size as Tanganyika, but of a rectan-
gular form, and lying east and west instead of north and
south. A number of rivers flow into this lake, but far the
largest is the Chambezi. There was a similarity in name
between this river and the Zambesi, but he was quite satisfied that the two rivers had no connexion, as he had
traced the Chambezi running north through three
degrees of latitude. And now, we may go back to some
of the troubles which befell the intrepid explorer. During
the early part of the journey, the expedition travelled up
the Rovuma on its left bank—a route full of difficulties.
In order to make a path for their beasts of burden, especially the camels, Livingstone and his men were compelled
to ply their axes through dense, and almost impassable
jungles. This hard work was distasteful to the Sepoys and
the Johanna men, and they very soon began to murmur.
At every step they invented pretexts for impeding the
advance of the expedition. Not content with this, they
soon began to ill-treat the animals until not one was left
alive. Finding that Livingstone was not induced to retrace his steps by this means, they incited the natives
against him by charging him with strange practices. As
this conspiracy against the doctor was likely to prove a serious danger, he determined to send the Sepoys back to the
coast, which he did, after furnishing them with the means

of subsistence.   These fellows were intended as a body-guard to the explorer, and were armed with Enfield rifles for that purpose by the Bombay government.   A more worthless escort could hardly be imagined.   They were too lazy to carry their own guns, impressing any boy or woman they met to carry them either by threats or promises, neither of which they had any right to make or power to fulfil.   An hour's march would knock them up, and then they would throw themselves upon the ground, and mourn over their cruel fate, or plot some new mischief against the white man.   When they were got rid of, the Johanna men took their innings, and were guilty of a worse crime soon afterwards.   The party arrived on the 18th of July, 1866, at a village belonging to a chief of the Mahiyau.   It is situated "about eight days' march south of the Rovuma overlooking the water-shed of Lake Nyassa."   Two of the liberated slaves next deserted him, but pressing onward he arrived at the country of Mponda, a chief living near Lake Nyassa.   Here another defection took place which must have touched Livingstone more keenly.   Wakotani, whom the doctor had taken to Bombay, and educated, asked for his discharge, forging several plausible lies to excuse his request.   Livingstone was not deceived but, with his usual generosity, gave him ample means of subsistence, and even writing paper to use if he should ever be disposed to communicate with him.   The faithless Wakotani almost succeeded in enticing Chuma, another protégé of the doctor's to leave the service, but ultimately without success. Leaving this country, Living-

9

stone next proceeded to the southern extremity of Lake Nyassa. The village at which they stopped, belonged to a Babisa chief, whom the traveller cured of a skin disease. While here, a half-caste Arab came in with a story that the Ma-Zitu had plundered him at a place at least one hundred and fifty miles away. No one knew better than Mousa, the leader of the Johanna men, that this story was false, but it furnished him and his band with a new reason for going back to the coast. He accordingly went to Livingstone, and told the story with such embellishments as his fancy and power of invention suggested. Livingstone asked him if he believed the tale; to which he replied that he did, saying—" he tells me true, true. I ask him good, and he tell me true, true." The doctor knew better, for the Ma-Zitu never do things by halves, and to say nothing of the topographical difficulty in the way, it was certain that if they had robbed the Arab, they would also have murdered him. The Babisa chief at once pronounced the story a pure invention, because, as he said, if the Ma-Zitu had been in the vicinity, he should have heard it soon enough. From this time, however, Livingstone had no peace from the Johanna men. Mousa, although he knew perfectly well that the Arab's tale was false, chose to simulate great terror of the Ma-Zitu. He cried out to the doctor: " I no want to go to Ma-Zitu. I no want Ma-Zitu to kill me. I want to see my father, my mother, my child in Johanna," &c. The explorer protested that he did not want the Ma-Zitu to kill him either, and that as Mousa was afraid of them, he would not go near them, but go straight west till he cleared the track in which they moved.

Mousa did not seem satisfied; indeed, he did not intend to be, and as soon as Livingstone started westward, he and the rest of the Johanna men deserted in a body. Mousa's conduct was less excusable than that of his comrades; he had been of Livingstone's party on the Zambesi for two years, and had been treated with that fatherly tenderness and consideration which endeared the traveller to all his dependents. In his just resentment at the ingratitude of these men, Livingstone states that he was at first inclined to shoot Mousa and another of the ringleaders, but he rejoiced afterwards that he had not stained his hands with their blood. There is no doubt that they well deserved death for their treachery, not merely at the desertion, but long previously. We need not repeat the "lie with circumstance" which they told when they reached the coast. As liars they were certainly no mean proficients, and, for a time, they actually deluded some of the acutest of Englishmen into the belief that Livingstone had really been murdered by natives before the eyes of Mousa and his false comrades. A few days after the Johanna gang left, another of the party came to express his fears of the Ma-Zitu, but, as Mr. Stanley says, Livingstone soon "shut him up" by forbidding him to mention the tribe again. It was only by native help that he was enabled to get through his difficulties; without it he must have sunk under the obstacles in his path. "Fortunately," as the doctor says with unction, "I was in a country now, after leaving the shores of the Nyassa, where the feet of the slave-trader had not trodden. It was a new and virgin land, and of course, as I have always found it in such cases, the natives were really good and hospitable, and for very small portions of cloth my baggage was conveyed from village to village by them." In many other ways the traveller in his extremity was kindly treated by the undefiled and unspoiled natives. In December, 1866, Livingstone entered a country which had been desolated by the dreaded Ma-Zitu, and his party had the greatest difficulty in obtaining food enough to keep them alive. Desertions which, under these circumstances, were more excusable than those of the Johanna men, took place from time to time, and sometimes the delinquents took with them the doctor's clothes and linen. Misfortunes of various kinds attended him during the time he traversed the countries from Babisa to Londa, which lies west of Tanganyika and north of Bangweolo. In the Londa country he encountered the celebrated Cazembe, made known to Europeans first by a Portuguese traveller, Dr. Lacerda. He appears to have been a fine, stalwart man of singular intelligence. In a strange sort of state attire, the king received Livingstone at the head of his chiefs and body guards. Mr. Stanley thus describes this extraordinary court ceremonial as he heard it from the lips of the doctor himself:—"A chief who had been deputed by the king and elders to find out all about the white man, then stood up before the assembly and in a loud voice gave the result of the inquiry he had instituted.

He had heard the white man had come to look for waters, for rivers and seas.  Though he did not understand what the white man could want with such things he had no doubt that the object was good.  Then Cazembe asked what the doctor proposed doing, and where he thought of going.  The doctor replied that he had thought of going south, as he had heard of lakes and rivers being in that direction.  Cazembe asked:

'What can you want to go there for?  The water is close here.  There is plenty of large water in this neigh. bourhood.'

Before breaking up the assembly, Cazembe gave orders to let the white man go where he would through his country, undisturbed and unmolested.  He was the first Englishman he had seen, he said, and he liked him."

Cazembe evidently could not understand how any one could be chimerical enough to search for more water when he had plenty and to spare where he then was.  The interview with the queen must have been very amusing.  Like her husband, she was tall in person and handsome also; but she had evidently, like her more civilized sisters, a desire to make a sensation.  Her efforts at the toilette, however, proved too much for Livingstone's keen sense of the ludicrous, and he could not help laughing in the royal presence.  His laugh proved contagious, and her majesty and her maids of honour laughed also.  It was previous to his reception by Cazembe that the explorer first saw the Chambezi in the Londa country.  The similarity of the name of this river and the Zambesi at first led Livingstone astray, and therefore he did not pay much attention to it, as he regarded the former simply as the headwaters of the latter. From the beginning of 1867 until he arrived atUjiji in March, 1869, he was engaged for the most part in correcting the errors of previous travellers, especially the Portuguese, who had caused considerable confusion by speaking of the two rivers as if they were identical. In exposing these errors, Livingstone traversed and re-traversed the valley of the Chambezi until he found it emptying itself into Lake Bangweolo—its direction being north and west. It was, therefore, clearly shown that Chambezi was a distinct river from the Zambesi, and, as the traveller contended, none other than the most southerly feeder of the Nile The real name of the Zambesi, moreover, he found to be Dombazi. North-west of Cazembe's country, the traveller came to a lake called Liemba by the natives, but which was ascertained to be the lower end of Tanganyika, in latitude nine degrees south. Its entire length, therefore, would be 560 geographical miles. We are now in a position to consider the conclusions to which Livingstone came regarding the water-system. These were in brief, that the lake and river-system beginning with Tanganyika and passing through the Victoria and Albert Nyanza, were not the ultimate sources of the Nile; and that the parallel system from the Chambezi was the true river. The remaining years of Dr. Livingstone's life were spent in verifying his view of the hydrography of Central Africa. We may here insert the lucid explanation Stanley obtained from Livingstone, premising that the name Webb's River was substituted for the Lualaba—the name being given in honour of Livingstone's old friend of Newstead Abbey. "It is hoped that the most superficial reader, as well as the student of geography will comprehend this grand system of lakes connected together by Webb's River. To assist him, let him procure a map of Africa, by Keith Johnston, embracing the latest discoveries. Two degrees south of the Tanganyika, and two degrees west, let him draw the outlines of a lake, its greatest length from east to west, and let him call it Bangweolo. One degree or thereabout to the northwest, let him sketch the outlines of another but smaller lake, and call it Moero; a degree again north of Moero, another lake of similar size, and call it Kamolondo, and still a degree north of Kamolondo, another lake, large and as yet of undefined limits, which, in the absence of any specific term, we will call the Nameless Lake. Then let him connect these several lakes by a river called after different names. Thus, the main feeder of Bangweolo, the Chambezi; the river which issues out of Bangweolo, and runs into Moero, the Luapula; the river connecting Moero with Kamolondo, Webb's River; that which runs from Kamolondo into the Nameless Lake northward, Lualaba; and let him write in bold letters over the rivers Chambezi, Luapula, Webb's River, and the Lualaba the ' Nile,' for these are all one and the same river. Again, west of Moero Lake, about one degree or thereabouts, another large lake may be placed on his map, with a river running diagonally across to meet the Lualaba north of Lake

Kamolondo. This new lake is Lake Lincoln, and the river is the Lomami River, the confluence of which with the Lualaba is between Kamolondo and the Nameless Lake. Taken altogether, the reader may be said to have a very fair idea of what Dr. Livingstone has been doing these long years, and what additions he has made to the study of African geography. That this river, distinguised under several titles, flowing from one lake into another in a northerly direction, with all its crooked bends and sinuosities, is the Nile, the true Nile, the doctor has not the least doubt. For a long time he did doubt, because of its deep bends and curves—west, and south-west even—but having traced it through its headwaters, the Chambezi, through seven degrees of latitude—that is, from latitude eleven degrees south to a little north of four degrees south—he has been compelled to come to the conclusion that it can be no other river than the Nile. He at first thought it was the Congo, but he afterwards found that the source of this great river was the Kasai and the Quango, two rivers which rise, as might be expected, on the western side of the Nile water-shed in about the latitude of Bangweolo. That the Lualaba cannot be the Congo would seem evident from its great volume, it being broader and much deeper than the Mississippi; and, in addition, it has a steady northward course. It is probable, Livingstone thinks, that this river may turn out to be what is known as Petherick's branch of the White Nile. The entire question will eventually turn on the comparative altitudes of the two rivers. Meanwhile, the other English geographers look upon Livingstone's theory as untenable. At the meeting of the Geographical Society addressed by Stanley, the principal objectors were Col. Grant and Consul Petherick. The former urged that, at that time, there were still 1000 miles unexplored by Livingstone, and that he had adopted his conclusions too hastily; that in this distance there are Speke's Mountains of the Moon, and the great bend to the west of the Nile at seven degrees, eight minutes, north latitude. There are also 300 miles of longitude between the two positions; besides which Schweinfurth, the botanist, visited the source of the Gazal, and found it north of the equator and not, as Livingstone supposes it, eleven degrees south of it, Consul Petherick, the first Englishman who had navigated the Bahr-il-Gazal, also thought the explorer mistaken. He believed that there must be a water-shed, running east and west separate from that of the Gazal; and that the waters that Livingstone was pursuing northward must find some other outlet—where he did not profess to say. To these objections Mr. Stanley replied at length, dwelling particularly on the fact that though the objectors denied that this mighty water-system was a feeder of the Nile, they could not tell what became of it. " If the Nile has not been discovered," said he, " what, let me ask, has been discovered ? What is that great and mighty river, the Lualaba ? Where does it go to ? Does it go into a lake, as Sir Henry Rawlinson supposes ? What the Lualaba flow into a lake !—into a marsh !—into a

swamp!    Why, you might just as well say that the
Mississippi flows into a swamp!"    He further urged that
the rivers flowing from Tanganyika were insignificant
compared with the Lualaba, which, at some places, is from
three to five miles broad.    "If the Lualaba enters a
swamp, where does the water go to?"    The first letter
received during this period from Livingstone was written
from Bemba in the Lobemba Country S. S. W. of Tanganyika.    It was dated February the 2nd, 1867, and
effectually disposed of the lying story of the Johanna
men.    It was in the Lobisa country immediately to the
south of Lobemba that Livingstone breathed his last.
The general features of both districts are described in this
letter.    The former it appears to consist mainly of a
plateau six thousand six hundred feet above the level of
the sea, and is the water-shed of the Chambezi of which
we have already spoken and the various streams called
Loangwa which flow in a south-easterly direction into
Lake Nyassa.    In the same communication he explains
that he could not send any letters, after he left Nyassa
till he reached Bemba, where he had found a party of
black Arab slave-traders from Bagamoyo near Zanzibar
This next letter was dated the 8th of July, 1868, from
Lake Bangweolo.    The interval had been spent, as we
have already shewn, in examining the course of the
Chambezi and its tributaries.    When he fully explored
this district, including Lake Moero, he returned by
Cazembe's country.    It was here that he found an old
white-bearded half-caste named Mohammed ben Salib,

who was kept as a kind of prisoner at large by the king because of certain suspicious circumstances attending his advent and stay in his country.  Through Livingstone's influence Mohammed ben Salib obtained his release.   On the road to Ujiji he had bitter cause to regret having exerted himself in the half-caste's behalf.  He turned out to be a most ungrateful wretch, who poisoned the minds of the doctor's few followers and ingratiated himself in their favour by selling the favours of his concubines to them, thus reducing them to a kind of bondage under him. From the day he had the vile old man in his company manifold and bitter misfortunes followed the doctor up to his arrival in Ujiji, in March, 1869.

He remained at this place till the end of June, 1869 It was during this time that he wrote the last letters received from him, prior to the return of the *Herald* expedition.   In a letter dated the 30th of May, addressed to Dr. Kirk, he complains of the bad conduct of the buffalo-driver sent him, and asks for a supply of cloth, beads and sheeting, and a few pairs of shoes.   What he proposed to accomplish in the Tanganyika district and west of it, he thus states: " As to the work to be done by me, it is only to connect the sources which I have discovered from five hundred to seven hundred miles south of Speke and Baker's, with their Nile.  The volume of water which flows north from lat. 12° S. is so large, I suspect I have been working at the sources of the Congo, as well as the Nile."  (In this, as we have seen, he afterwards found that he was mistaken.)  " I have to go down the eastern line of drainage to Baker's turning-point. Tanganyika, Nzige Chowambe (Baker's ?) are one water, and the head of it is three hundred miles south of this. The western and central lines of drainage converge into an unvisited lake west or south-west of this. The out-flow of this, whether to the Congo or the Nile, I have to ascertain. The people west of this, called Manyema, are canibals, if the Arabs speak truly. I may have to go there first, and down Tanganyika, if I come out uneaten, and find my new squad from Zanzibar. I earnestly hope that you will do what you can to help me with the goods and men. £400 to be sent by Mr. Young, must surely have come to you through Fleming & Co."* When this letter was read before the Royal Geographical Society, Sir Roderick Murchison remarked, that "if Livingstone should be supplied with carriers and provisions; he will, I doubt not, follow these waters, and thus being led on, perhaps, to the Congo, we may be once more subjected to a long and anxious period of suspense." This, unfortunately, proved to be the case, and Sir Roderick's devotion to his friend was unrewarded by the tidings of his safety, for he died before news came that the enterprise of Mr. Gordon Bennett, and the energy and pluck of Stanley, had been crowned with success.

As soon as Livingstone had recovered strength, at the end of June, 1869, he again started westward. Taking a *dhow* at Ujiji, he crossed over to Uguhha, on the western shore. It had been his intention to sail round Tanganyika,

---

* This extract appears in another part of this volume ; but it was necessary to repeat it here in order to make the narrative consecutive and complete.

but he found that the Arabs were so bent on plundering him that he was compelled to abandon the idea. The result of this last and most important of his expeditions was the discovery of a series of lakes of great size, connected by a large river, called by different names as it flowed from one lake into another. From Uguhha he journeyed in company with a party of traders about sixty miles up Tanganyika, and then struck into the interior in a north-westerly direction, for the country of the Manyema or Manyuema. Livingstone's design was to trace the river which flowed into Lake Bangweolo as the Chambezi, and out of it as the Luapula, in its northward course. He was persuaded that, in doing so, he was on the central line of drainage of the Great Nile Valley. It was known to him that, in issuing from Lake Moero, the river was called the Lualaba (Webb's River), and on forming a third lake, Kamolondo, became again a great river-lake itself, studded with many islands. On this occasion he struck the great stream at the large bend made by its flowing west about one hundred and twenty miles, and then sweeping round to the north. Owing to recent illness the indefatigable traveller was only able to accomplish two hours a day. They were now (in July) approaching Bambarre, where Moenekuss, the most intelligent of the Manyema chiefs resided. Two days before their arrival there, however, they met a company of Ujiji traders, with 18,000 pounds weight of ivory, which they had bought for a mere trifle in coarse copper bracelets and beads. The slaves of this party gave a very unfavourable account of the Manyema, and they agreed with the Arabs that they were bad and cannibals into the bargain.   This, however, as Livingstone said, was only one side of the story.   Proceeding west of Bambarro, so as to embark on the Lualaba, he went down the Luamo, a stream about 150 yards wide, rising in the mountains opposite Ujiji, and across the great bend already spoken of.  The people had been badly treated by the armed slaves just spoken of, and unfortunately regarded Livingstone as of the same tribe.  In one of his despatches he says: —" Africans are not generally unreasonable, though smarting under wrongs, if you can fairly make them understand your claim to innocence, and do not appear as having your ' back up.' "   On this occasion, however, it was very difficult to convince them, and the women especially were particularly positive.  When one lady was asked to look at Livingstone's colour as a proof that he could not be the head-trader she supposed him to be, she failed to be convinced, and exclaimed, " Then you must be his father." As for the men, the only harm they did was to turn out armed, and show the party out of the district.  The latter returned to Bambarre, and then with their friend Muhamad Bogharit, and his trading party already mentioned, started due north, Muhamad to buy ivory, and Livingstone to reach another part of the Lualaba and obtain a canoe. When he reached that broad, lacustrine river, he found its crooks and bends very confusing.  At one time it flowed northward, then westward, and occasionally southward. The country here is described as very beautiful, but exceedingly difficult to travel.  As this portion of Livingstone's journey led to very serious results shortly after, we may quote from his despatch to Lord Granville, dated November 15th, 1870, but only delivered at the Foreign Office by Mr. Stanley on the 1st of August, 1872, a passage which gives a graphic description of the kind of country through which he had to pass :—

" The mountains of light gray granite stand like islands in new red sandstone, and mountain and valley are all clad in a mantle of different shades of green.  The vegetation is indescribably rank.  Through the grass—if grass it can be called, which is over half an inch in diameter in the stalk and from ten to twelve feet high—nothing but elephants can walk.  The leaves of this megatherium grass are armed with minute spikes, which, as we worm our way along elephant walks, rub disagreeably on the side of the face where the gun is held, and the hand is made sore by fending it off on the other side for hours.  The rains were fairly set in by November; and in the mornings, or after a shower, these leaves were loaded with moisture which wet us to the bone.  The valleys are deeply undulating, and in each innumerable dells have to be crossed. There may be only a thread of water at the bottom, but the mud, mire or (*Scottice*) " glaur " is grievous; thirty or forty yards of the path on each side of the stream are worked by the feet of passengers into an adhesive compound.  By placing a foot on each side of the narrow way one may waddle a little distance along, but the rank crop of grasses, gingers and bushes cannot spare the few inches of soil required for the side of the foot, and down he comes into the slough. The path often runs along the bed of the rivulet for sixty or more yards, as if he who first cut it out went that distance seeking for a part of the forest less dense for his axe. In other cases the muale palm, from which here, as in Madagascar, grass-cloth is woven and called by the same name, " lamba," has taken possession of the valley. The leaf stalks, as thick as a strong man's arm, fall off and block up all passage save by a path made and mixed up by the feet of elephants and buffaloes; the slough therein is groan-compelling and deep.

"Every now and then the traders, with rueful faces, stand panting; the sweat trickles down my face, and I suppose that I look as grim as they, though I try to cheer them with the hope that good prices will reward them at the coast for ivory obtained with so much toil. In some cases the subsoil has given way beneath the elephant's enormous weight, the deep hole is filled with mud, and one, taking it all to be about calf deep, steps in to the top of the thigh and flops on to a seat soft enough, but not luxurious; a merry laugh relaxes the facial muscles— though I have no other reason for it than than it is better to laugh than to cry."

Some of the many rivers flowing into the Lualaba are crossed by the singular means of a vegetable bridge. This is entirely natural in its construction, and consists of a tangled mass of thick grass, whose blades form a kind of mat over the surface of the stream. In the shallower places, the water-lily and lotus forms part of it. Crossing on one of these bridges is like wading in deep snow. The foot has to be lifted above the mass and planted on the next verdant spot, the leg sinks up to the knee, and the hole is immediately filled with water. Occasionally there are deep holes the bottom of which could not be reached by a stick six feet long. The name given to this species of bridge by the Manyema is very significant of its nature, " as if he who first coined it was gasping for breath after plunging over a mile of it." Here and there over the Manyema district are large belts of the " forest primeval," through which the sun scarcely penetrates. In addition to the huge trees, there are climbing plants of all sizes. Travelling in these shady woods is very agreeable. On the summit of the trees are vast numbers of parrots and guinea fowls inaccessible to the shot of the rifleman. Livingstone states that he has heard gorillas, called " sokos" by the natives, growling some fifty yards off but never saw one. Their nests, or " houses," as the natives call them, are very poorly constructed, and display none of the tasteful architecture of many birds and even insects. It was difficult to ascertain exactly the opinion of the natives regarding this Darwinian approach to man, but they were agreed in calling him a fool for sitting out in the rain, with his arms over his head, when he had a house to go into for shelter.

The trying nature of the travel in these districts began to tell upon Livingstone. Plunging into mud-holes and crossing vegetable bridges, the frequent wettings and the bad water, produced symptoms of cholera and, worse perhaps than that, ulcers in the feet. To an energetic and

10

earnest man, the delay of six months caused by these ailments must have been extremely trying. The despatch already quoted was written during the time of his enforced idleness at Bambarre. It appears that, at this time, there was a sort of California fever, not for gold, but for ivory, in this district, and the party were overtaken by no less than 600 armed men in search of tusks. It is to these people Livingstone alludes in this passage:—" I had already, in this journey, two severe lessons that travelling in an unhealthy climate in the rainy season is killing work. By getting drenched to the skin once too often in Marunga, I had pneumonia, the illness to which I have referred, and that was worse than ten fevers—that is fevers treated by our medicine and not by the dirt supplied to Bishop Mackenzie at the Cape as the same. Besides being unwilling to bear the new comers company, I feared that by further exposure in the rains the weakness might result in something worse." He finally went into winter quarters on the 7th of February. He was without medicine, and yet he says, in his quiet uncomplaining fashion, that rest, shelter, boiling all the water he used, and a new potato found among the natives, acted as restoratives and he was soon all right. Meanwhile the rains continued on into July, in which month fifty-eight inches fell. The mud from the clay soil was, to use Livingstone's expressive word, "awful," and even the ardent seekers after ivory were laid up. The next trouble was that, when ready to start, he could not induce his attendants to shift their quarters. During these months they had been lodged by slave-women whose husbands were engaged in the ivory trade, and they were not disposed to leave their comfortable resting places. Some of them pretended to be afraid of entering a canoe, so Livingstone forbore to buy one. Others simulated a fear of the neighbouring peoples who, they were sure, were cannibals. Like the guests invited to the marriage feast in the Gospel, "they all, with one consent, began to make excuse." At last, with that iron strength of purpose which had carried him through thirty years of labour in Africa, the brave man started forth with only three attendants. He took a north-westerly direction by mistake, not knowing that the river flowed west by south; but, as he plaintively remarked, "no one could tell me anything about it." They had not gone far when, from two causes, his expedition was temporarily suspended. Muhamad's party had penetrated further in the forest than Livingstone, and had met with hostile demonstrations from Balegga who dwelt in the mountains. In addition to this, the trading party found that some of the rivers were not fordable, and that it was very difficult to find means of crossing them. This was not in itself a promising prospect, but Livingstone's perseverance might have overcome the obstacles which daunted Muhamad, but for the ulcerous sores on his feet. Wading in the mud had done its work, and the disabled explorer limped back to Bambarre, to abide there during half-a-year's enforced rest. The ulcers were so painful as to prevent sleep, and if he ventured to put his foot to the ground, a discharge of matter, mingled with blood, immediately took place. These sores Livingstone supposes to be allied to fevers, and he states that he has often heard the wailing of poor slaves who were afflicted with ulcers that had eaten even to the bone. During the time he had been away the traveller had lived in "what may be called the Tipperary of Manyema," the country, as he was informed, of cannibalism, and this is what he has to say about them :—"They are certainly a bloody people among themselves. But they are very far from being in appearance like the ugly negroes on the West Coast. Finely formed heads are common, and generally the men and women are vastly superior to the slaves of Zanzibar and elsewhere. We must go deeper than phrenology to account for their low moral tone. If they are cannibals they are not ostentatiously so. The neighbouring tribes all assert that they are man-eaters, and they themselves laughingly admit the charge. But they like to impose on the credulous, and they showed the skull of a recent victim to horrify one of my people. I found it to be the skull of a gorilla, or soko—the first I knew of its existence here—and this they do eat. If I had believed a tenth of what I heard from traders, I might never have entered the country. Their people told tales with shocking circumstantiality, as if of eye-witnesses, that could not be committed to paper, or even spoken about beneath the breath. Indeed, one wishes them to vanish from memory. But fortunately I was never frightened in infancy with 'bogie,' and am not liable to attacks of what may almost be called ' bogie-phobia ;'

for the patient, in a paroxysm, believes everything horrible, if only it be ascribed to the possessor of a black skin."

Yet Livingstone was not satisfied after all, as to the
truth or falsehood of the charge of cannibalism. He had
offered goods sufficient to tempt any of them to take him
to see a cannibal feast, without success. On the whole,
he was disposed to return a verdict of "not proven." When
intelligence of the Young Search Expedition reached
him, he despatched a note to the Foreign Secretary in reference to Moosa and the Johanna men. We are perhaps
anticipating events, but it may be as well to give Livingstone's opinion of these fellows before continuing the
narrative. He expresses some surprise that the story had
obtained any credence. "Had," he continues, "the low tone
of morality among the East African Mohammedans been
known, Moosa's tale would have received but little attention. Moosa is perhaps a little better than the average
low class Moslem, but all are notorious for falsehood and
heartlessness." He then proceeds to give instances of the
unfeeling character of these men, and contrasts their degraded moral character with the truthful and humane
features in the character of Makololo. "All my difficulties," he says, in another place, "have arisen from having
low-class Moslems, or those who had been so before they
were captured. Even the better class cannot be trusted."

As soon as Livingstone was able to leave Bambarre, he
started again for the Lualaba, following amidst many
difficulties, the course of that noble, but tortuous river,
until it emptied itself into the long and narrow lake of

Kamolondo (or Ulenge). During its course the river varies from one to three miles in breadth. From that point, he traced it back again, with his wonted pertinacity of purpose, in a southerly direction, to the point where he had seen it issue from lake Moero. Of the Moero valley, Livingstone speaks in glowing terms. Shut in on all sides by mountains, clad in all the rich colouring of tropical vegetation, this lovely lake discharges its waters through a deep gorge, torn through the bosom of the lofty hills. The vast volume of water rushes impetuously through the chasm with the roar of a cataract, until it reaches an ampler and deeper bed in which it flows by many a sinuous bend to almost every point of the compass, to the lake of Kamalondo. It was at this time, that Livingstone gave the Lualaba the name of Webb's river, in honour of his old friend, to distinguish it from other streams bearing the same name. To the south-west of Kamalondo he found another lake of considerable size, called by the natives Chebungo. To this water the name was given of Lake Lincoln, in honour of the President of the United States, whose emancipation proclamation had struck Livingstone with profound admiration.

Again entering Webb's river from the south-west end, a little above Kamalondo, is another large river Lufira. The streams, however, were so numerous, that Livingstone's map could not indicate any but the chief and most important ones. Following the Lualaba through all its curves to 4° S., he came to another large lake called the Unknown Lake. This was the furthermost point, and

he was obliged to return by a toilsome journey to Ujiji of
600 miles.    The cause of this abrupt termination of the
expedition was, first, continued ill-health, but chiefly the
rascally conduct of his attendants.    In the first place,
Ludha had deceived him by sending Banian slaves instead
of Zanzibar freemen.    The leaders of these men, Shereef
and Awathe were extortioners to begin with, and the entire gang did all they could to embarrass Livingstone,
impede his progress, and baffle his designs.    It was the
lies which these men persistently and positively told, that
first prejudiced the traveller against Dr. Kirk, and prepared him to accept any story told against the Consul.    The
Banians swore that the latter had told them to force Livingstone back, and on no account to go forward.    By working
on their fears, aided materially by the efforts of his friend
Muhamad Bogharit, he had forced them to proceed; but
had it not been for the ivory-trader, "they would have
gained their point by sheer brazen-faced falsehood."    The
last are Livingstone's words; yet, it would appear from
the lately published letter to Mr. John Livingstone, written in 1872, that by some means or other, the doctor had
been persuaded to believe the "falsehood" by that time.
These men were fearful cowards; they were constantly
quaking with fear lest they should be killed and eaten by
the Manyema.    At length, as we have already seen, they
refused to go on from Bambarre, and left the traveller with
only three attendants.    They told the most outrageous
falsehoods, and aided by the Arabs, poisoned the minds of
the natives by insinuating that Livingstone "wanted nei-

ther ivory nor slaves, but a canoe to kill Manyema." By slanders like this the Arabs succeeded in getting nine canoes, while Livingstone could not purchase one. " But four days below this part," he proceeds to say, " narrows occur in which the mighty river is compressed by rocks, which jut in, not opposite to each other, but alternately ; and the water, rushing round the promontories, forms terrible whirlpools which overturned one of the canoes, and so terrified the whole party that by deceit preceded me, that they returned without ever thinking of dragging the canoes past the difficulty. This I should have done to gain the confluence of the Lomame, some fifty miles below, and thence ascend through Lake Lincoln to the ancient fountains beyond the copper mines of Katanga ; and this would nearly finish my geographical work. But it was so probable that the dyke which forms the narrows would be prolonged across the country into Lomame, that I had to turn towards this great river considerably above the narrows ; and where the distance between the Lualaba and Lomame is about eighty miles."

At this time, a friend named Dugambe was on his way from Ujiji, with a large armed caravan, and nine under-traders with their people. For him, therefore, Livingstone waited three months in the hope of getting some reliable freemen in the room of the faithless Banians, and also a canoe. Dugambe appeared to be a gentleman, and the doctor offered him £400 for ten men and a canoe, and afterwards all the goods he supposed he had at Ujiji, so as to enable him to finish his work. His first words were,

" Why your own slaves are your greatest enemies.   I hear everywhere how they have baffled you."   He closed the bargain with Livingstone provisionally, but required a few days to consult his associates.   Then occurred an event which precipitated the return of the expedition ; we give the traveller's own account of it :—

" Two days afterwards, or on the 13th of June, a massacre was perpetrated which filled me with such intolerable loathing that I resolved to yield to the Banian slaves, return to Ujiji, get men from the coast, and try to finish the rest of [my work by going outside the area of Ujijian bloodshed, instead of vainly trying from its interior outwards.

" Dugambe's people built their huts on the right bank of the Lualaba, at a market place called Nyanwe.   On hearing that the head slave of a trader at Ujiji had, in order to get canoes cheap, 'mixed blood' with the head men of the Bagenya on the left bank, they were disgusted with his assurance, and resolved to punish him, and make an impression in the country in favour of their own greatness by an assault on the market people, and on all the Bagenya who had dared to make friendship with any but themselves. Tagamalo, the principal undertaker of Dugambe's party, was the perpetrator.   The market was attended every fourth day by between 2,000 and 3,000 people.   It was held on a large slope of land which, down at the river, ended in a creek capable of containing between fifty and sixty large canoes.   The majority of the market people were women many of them very pretty.   The people west of the river brought fish, salt, pepper, oil, grass-cloth, iron, fowls, goats, sheep, pigs, in great numbers to exchange with those east of the river for cassava, grain, potatoes and other farinaceous products. They have a strong sense of natural justice, and all unite in forcing each other to fair dealing. At first my presence made them all afraid, but wishing to gain their confidence, which my enemies tried to undermine or prevent, I went among them frequently, and seeing no harm in me became very gracious; the bargaining was the finest acting I ever saw. I understand but few of the words that flew off the glib tongues of the women, but their gestures spoke plainly. I took sketches of the fifteen varieties of fish brought in, to compare them with those of the Nile farther down, and all were eager to tell their names. But on the date referred to I had left the market only a minute or two when three men whom I had seen with guns, and felt inclined to reprove them for bringing them into the market place, but had refrained by attributing it to ignorance in new comers, began to fire into the dense crowd around them. Another party, down at the canoes, rained their balls on the panic-struck multitude that rushed into these vessels. All threw away their goods, the men forgot their paddles, the canoes were jammed in the creek and could not be got out quick enough, so many men and women sprung into the water. The women of the left bank are expert divers for oysters, and a long line of heads showed a crowd striking out for an island half a mile off; to gain it they had to turn the left shoulder against a current of between a mile and a half to two miles an hour. Had they gone diagonally with the current, though that would have been a distance of three miles, many of them would have gained the shore. It was horrible to see one head after another disappear, some calmly, others throwing their arms high up towards the Great Father of all, and going down. Some of the men who got canoes out of the crowd paddled quick with hands and arms, to help their friends; three took people in till they all sank together. One man had clearly lost his head, for he paddled a canoe which would have held fifty people straight up stream nowhere. The Arabs estimated the loss at between four and five hundred souls. Dugambe sent out some of his men in one of the thirty canoes which the owners in their fright could not extricate, to save the sinking. One lady refused to be taken on board because she thought that she was to be made a slave; but he rescued twenty-one, and of his own accord sent them the next day home. Many escaped and came to me, and were restored to their friends. When the firing began on the terror-stricken crowd at the canoes, Tagamalo's band began their assault on the people on the west of the river, and continued the fire all day. I counted seventeen villages in flames, and next day six. Dugambe's power over the underlings is limited, but he ordered them to cease shooting. Those in the market were so reckless they shot two of their own number. Tagamalo's crew came back next day in canoes, shouting and firing off their guns as if believing that they were worthy of renown.

"The next day, about twenty head-men fled from the

west bank and came to my house. There was no occasion now to tell them that the English had no desire for human blood. They begged hard that I should go over with them and settle with them, and arrange where the new dwellings of each should be. I was so ashamed of the bloody Moslem company in which I found myself that I was unable to look at the Manyema. I confessed my grief and shame, and was entreated, if I must go, not to leave them now. Dugambe spoke kindly to them and would protect them as well as he could against his own people; but when I went to Tagamalo to ask back the wives and daughters of some of the head-men, he always ran off and hid himself.

"This massacre was the most terrible scene I ever saw. I cannot describe my feelings, and am thankful that I did not give way to them, but by Dugambe's advice avoided a bloody feud with men who, for the time, seemed turned into demons. The whole transaction was the more deplorable, inasmuch as we have always heard from the Manyema that though the men of the districts may be engaged in actual hostilities, the women pass from one market-place to another with their wares, unmolested. The change has come only with these alien blood-hounds, and all the bloodshed has taken place in order that captives might be seized where it could be done without danger, and in order that the slaving privileges of a petty sultan should produce abundant fruit. Heartsore, and greatly depressed in spirits by the many instances of 'man's inhumanity to man' I had unwillingly seen, I commenced the long, weary tramp to Ujiji, with the blazing sun right overhead. The mind acted on the body, and it is no over statement to say, that almost every step of between four and five hundred miles was in pain. I felt as if dying on my feet, and I came very near death in a more summary way. It is within the area of bloodshed that danger alone occurs. I could not induce · my Moslem slaves to venture outside that area or sphere. They knew better than I did. ' Was Mohammed not the greatest of all, and their prophet ?'" The danger to which Livingstone refers arose in this way. They were about half way back to Bambarre, at a place where he had formerly seen a party of young men compelled to carry a trader's ivory. When Livingstone arrived they threw down the tusks and refused to take them any farther. They were compelled to take the ivory up again and they did, but, after a short time, they cast it into a dense mass of vegetation. On arriving at the next stage, the trader sent back some men to demand the stolen ivory. The elders denied the theft and were fired upon; five men were killed, and eleven women and children captured, with twenty-five goats. The young men then gathered the ivory and carried it after the·trader some twenty miles. He asserted that three tusks were missing, and went off carrying the captives and goats with him. By way of revenge, the young men waylaid Dugambe's party as he passed shortly after and killed one of his men. On his return journey Livingstone's expedition passed another camp of Ujijian traders, who begged to be allowed to join

their party to his.    Amongst them were seventeen Manyema who had volunteered to carry ivory for the trader
to Ujiji, and goods back again.    They were, we are told,
the first Manyema in modern times who had gone fifty
miles from home.    The entire caravan now consisted of
eighty souls, and had the general appearance of an ordinary trading party.    On arriving at the locality where
the five men had been shot, the maltreated men, now
burning for revenge, remembered the glaring dress made
of red blankets, and naturally tried to kill the man who
had murdered their relatives.    They would hold no parley,
but attacked Livingstone from the depths of a forest
through which he had to pass.    Two men near him were
slain ; a large spear lunged past close behind ; another
missed him by a foot, just in front.    Coming to a small
cleared spot, he found that fire had been applied to one of
the immense trees.    He heard the fire crack ; the fire had
eaten through, but he felt there was no danger, till it
appeared to be coming right down upon him.    He ran
a few paces back, and the tree came to the ground only
one yard off, broke in several lengths, and covered Livingstone with a cloud of dust.    His attendants ran back, ex-
claiming, " Peace, peace! you will finish your work in
spite of these people, and in spite of everything."    In
reference to his preservation from death, Livingstone
says, " I, too, took it as an omen of good, that I had
three narrow escapes from death in one day.    The Manyema are expert in throwing the spear, and as I had
a glance of him whose spear missed by less than an inch

behind, and he was not ten yards off, I was saved clearly by the good hand of the Almighty Preserver of men. I can say this devoutly now, but in running the terrible gauntlet for five weary hours, among furies all eager to signalize themselves by slaying one they sincerely believed to have been guilty of a horrid outrage, no elevated sentiments entered the mind. The excitement gave way to overpowering weariness, and I felt as I suppose soldiers do on the field of battle—not courageous, but perfectly indifferent whether I were killed or not."

Soon after the head man of the next group of villages approached Livingstone unarmed, and an explanation followed. He desired the traveller to lend him his people, who had guns, in return for which he offered ten goats in place of three Livingstone had lost. An explanation of the mistake made by the tribe followed, and the chief, when he understood the whole case, admitted that the doctor's joining in his ancient feud would only make matters worse. Livingstone adds: "Indeed, my old Highland blood had been roused by the wrongs which his foes had suffered, and all through I could not help sympathizing with them, though I was the especial object of their revenge."

On the 30th of October, Livingstone wrote a long letter of complaint to Dr. Kirk, in which he speaks bitterly of the Banian slaves, whose treachery and extortion had prevented him from completing his work. In a postcript to this communication he says: "Like the man who was tempted to despair when he broke the photograph of his wife, I feel inclined to relinquish hope of ever getting help from Zanzibar to finish the little work I have still to do. I wanted men, not slaves, and free men are abundant at Zanzibar; but if the matter is committed to Ludha, instead of an energetic Arab, with some little superintendence by your dragoman or others, I may wait twenty years, and your slaves feast and fail."

On the 10th of November, 1871, within two weeks of Livingstone's arrival at Ujiji, Stanley arrived with the *Herald* expedition, and shook hands with the long suffering explorer. The sight of the American correspondent must have been as balm to the wounded spirit of Livingstone, and he welcomed his deliverer from hunger and poverty, with a heartiness and cordiality of the sincerest kind. Stanley had brought food of a nourishing kind, medicines, cloth, and beads, the currency of the interior. After spending a few days in conversation, Stanley imparting information about the stirring events of the outside world, and Livingstone narrating the story of his discoveries, and the trials and dangers amid which they were made, the correspondent proposed that they should together explore the north end of Tanganyika—an offer which Livingstone gladly accepted. On the 20th of November, therefore, ten days after Stanley's arrival, they started forth together. Lake Tanganyika it will be remembered is connected with the Albert Nyanza, and may be called Speke and Baker's Nile. According to Livingstone's theory this line of drainage is not the main line of the great river of Egypt, since it takes its rise far to the north of Livingstone's water-course, which, beginning with the Chambezi, flows under different names through large lakes, to form the main trunk of the White Nile. Accordingly, when asked by Stanley if he had explored the head of Tanganyika, he said he had not ; " he had not thought it of as much importance as the central line of drainage; besides, when he proposed to do it, before leaving for Manyema, the Wajiji had shown such a disposition to fleece him, that he had desisted from the attempt." Stanley explained to him, that however satisfied he might be in his own mind, geographers at home attached great importance to the lake in question, and would not be satisfied until it was thoroughly explored. He further suggested that as Livingstone was about leaving the lake, and might not visit it again, he might take advantage of Stanley's offer of putting himself, men and effects of the expedition at his disposal. On the 20th, therefore, as we have already stated, Livingstone and " our own correspondent" started with twenty picked men of the *Herald* party. The Arabs had warned them that the Warundi were hostile, and would give some trouble; the party, notwithstanding, hugged their shore closely, and even encamped in the country at night. Once they were compelled to fly at dead of night, when they found they were being surrounded on the land side, and once they were stoned. Stanley, it is plain, would like to have peppered them as they deserved, but Livingstone would permit no reprisals. No heed, therefore, was paid to them, and the

11

party made its way along the coast till they arrived at
the village of Mokamba, one of the chiefs of the Usige.
Mokamba was at war with another chief who lived on
the left bank of the Rusizi, a river whose course it was
of essential importance to explore. As far as the lake
itself, they found it for all practical purposes, fathomless.
Stanley, perhaps, entertains an exaggerated notion of its
depth, placing it at three thousand feet. For this estimate
he appears to have no other warrant than the soundings
taken by himself and Livingstone. In his address before
the British Association, he records their ascertained acts
at that date: and it will be at once apparent how much
remains to be done, in order to supplement the accurate
observations of Livingstone :—

"Only two miles from shore I sounded, and though I
let down 620 feet of line I found no bottom. Livingstone
sounded when crossing the Tanganyika from the westward, and found no bottom with 1,800 feet of line. The
mountains around the northern half of the Tanganyika
fold around so close, with no avenue whatever for the escape of waters, save the narrow valleys and ravines which
admit rivers and streams into the lake, that were it possible to force the water into a higher altitude of 500 feet
above its present level, its dimensions would not be increased very considerably. The valley of the Malagarazi
would then be a narrow deep arm of the lake, and the
Rusizi would be a northern arm, crooked and tortuous, of
sixty or seventy miles in length. The evening before we
saw the Rusizi, a freedman of Zanzibar was asked which

way the river ran—out of the lake or into it? The man swore that he had been on the river but the day before, and that it ran out of the lake. Here was an announcement calculated to shake the most sceptical. I thought the news too good to be true. I should certainly have preferred that the river ran out of the lake into either the Victoria or the Albert. The night we heard this announcement, made so earnestly, Livingstone and myself sat up very late, speculating as to where it went. We resolved, if it flowed into the Victoria Nyanza, to proceed with it to that lake, and then strike south to Unyanyembe, and, if it flowed into the Albert lake, to proceed into the Albert, and cruise all around it, in the hope of meeting Baker."

The exploration of the Rusizi was attended with difficulties, the tribes at both banks being at war with each other. King Mokamba, who appears to have behaved very kindly to the travellers, advised them to proceed to the village of his brother, Rubinga, in Mugehawa, by night. They did so, arriving at the residence of the brother, (who was the principal chief of the Usige,) early in the morning. They immediately proceeded to the mouth of the river. A short row brought them to what appeared to be a marsh or brake of cane and papyrus, through which they saw canoes which had preceded them, alternately disappearing and reappearing. Some stout pulling brought them at length into the principal mouth of the river, which unquestionably flowed *into* the lake. The stream gradually broadened into lagoons on either side. Its exit they discovered to be an alluvial plain some twelve miles wide, which gradually narrows to a point, on either side of which is a range of mountains, stretching on the one side to the west, and on the other to the east. The former breaks off precipitately with a sharp inclination to the north-west ; while the latter first inclines westward after leaving the bank and divides into numerous spurs—"a perfect jumble of mountains." Stanley's description of the chief Rubinga, whom they visited at Mugehawa, is worth quoting. It appears that he is a great traveller. Born in the Mundi country, he had been at Karagwa and Ruanda, and came to Usige, where he was now the principal chief, when a young man. He took great interest in the solution of geographical questions, and entered with readiness into a discussion about the moot points yet to be decided.

From the information received from Rubinga, Mr. Stanley, it will be seen, forms his own conclusions:—

"Briefly, he said that the Rusizi rose from the Lake Kivo, a lake fifteen miles in length, and about eight in breadth. Kwansibura was the chief of the district in north-eastern Urundi, which gives its name to the lake. Through a gap in a mountain the river Rusizi escaped out of Lake Kivo. On leaving Kivo Lake, it is called Kwangeregere. It then runs through the district of Unyambungu, and becomes known as the Rusizi or Lusizi. A day's march from Mugihewa, or say twenty miles north of the mouth, it is joined by the Luanda or Ruanda, flowing from a north-westerly direction, from which I gather that the river Luanda is called after the name of the country—

Ruanda, said to be famous for its copper mines.    Besides
the Luanda there are seventeen other streams which con-
tribute to Rusizi.    Usige, a district of Urundi occupying
the head of the lake, extends two marches to the north,
or 30 miles ; after which comes what is called Urundi
Proper, for another two days' march; and directly north
of that is Ruanda, a very large country, almost equal in
size to Urundi.    Rubinga had been six days to the northward.  There were some in his tribe who had gone further,
but from no one could we obtain any intelligence of a lake
or of a large body of water, such as the Albert Nyanza,
being to the north.    Sir Samuel Baker has sketched the
lake as being within one degree north of Tanganyika;
but it is obvious that its length is not so great as it is
represented, though it might extend thirty to forty miles
south of Vacobia.    Ruanda, as represented to us by Rubinga, Mokamba, chiefs of Usige, and their elders, is an
exceedingly mountainous country, with extensive copper
mines.    It occupies that whole district north of Urundi
Proper, between Mutumbi on the west and Urundi on the
east, and Itara on the north-east.   Of the countries lying
north of Ruanda, we could obtain no information.    West
of Urundi is the extreme frontier of Manyema, which
even here has been heard of.   In returning to Ujiji after
the satisfactory solution of the River Rusizi, we coasted
down the western shore of the Tanganyika, and came to
Uvira at noon on the following day.  We were shown the
sandy beach on which the canoes of Burton and Speke
had rested.    Above, a little south of this, rises the lofty

peak of Samburizi, fully 4,500 feet above the level of the lake. Mruti, the chief of Uvira, still lives in the village he occupied when Burton and Speke visited his dominions. A day's march, or fifteen miles south of this, Uvira narrows down to the alluvial plains formed by the numerous streams which dash down the slopes of the western range, while the mountainous country is known as Ubembe, the land of the cannibals, who seldom visit the canoes of the traders. South of Uvira is Usansi, peopled by a race extremely cannibalistic in its taste, as the doctor and myself had very good reason to know. I think if we had had a few sick or old men among our party, we could have disposed of them to advantage, or we might have exchanged them for vegetables, which would have been most welcome to us. From Usansi we struck off across the lake, and rowing all night, at dawn we arrived at a port in Southern Urundi. Three days afterwards we were welcomed by the Arab traders of Ujiji, as we once more set foot on the beach near that bunder. We have thus coasted around the northern half of the Tanganyika, and I might inform you of other tribes who dwell on its shores; but the principal subject of my paper was to show you how we settled that vexed question: ' Was the Rusizi an effluent or an influent ?' There is, then, nothing to be said on that point."

Livingstone and Stanley arrived at Ujiji on the 18th of December, 1871, and remained there until the 27th. The importance of the discovery thus made, in an attempt to solve the Nile mystery, is considerable. Everywhere the travellers had been told that this river, the Rusizi, flowed *out* of Lake Tanganyika, into the Victoria Nyanza. Livingstone and Stanley found, beyond question, that it flowed *into* the former lake. As Stanley observes, in one of his *Herald* letters :—

"There could be no mistake. Dr. Livingstone and myself had ascended it, had felt the force of the strong inflowing current—the Rusizi was an influent, as much so as the Malagarazi, the Linche, and Rugufu, but, with its banks full, it can only be considered as ranking third among the rivers flowing into the Tanganyika. Though rapid, it is extremely shallow; it has three mouths, up which an ordinary ship's boat, loaded, might in vain attempt to ascend. Burton and Speke, though they ascended to within six hours' journey by canoe from the Rusizi, were compelled to turn back by the cowardice of the boatmen. Had they ascended to Meuta's capital, they could easily have seen the head of the lake. Usige is but a district of Wumdi, governed by several small chiefs, who owe obedience to Mwezi, the great King of Wumdi."

In the same letter, we are again confronted with the doubts which yet hang upon the skirts of geographical certainty in this portion of the Nile exploration :—

"Though the Rusizi river can no longer be a subject of curiosity to geographers—and we are certain that there is no connection between Tanganyika and Baker's Lake, or the Albert Nyanza—it is not yet certain that there is no connection between Tanganyika and the Nile river. The western coast has not all been explored; and there is reason to suppose that a river runs out of Tanganyika through the deep caverns of Kabogo Mountain, far underground, and out on the western side of Kabogo, into the Lualaba, or the Nile. Livingstone has seen the river about forty miles or so west of Kabogo, (about forty yards broad at that place,) but he does not know that it runs out of the mountain."

Altogether, twenty-eight days were spent in this journey, nine of which were devoted at the head of Tanganyika, in exploring the islands and the many bays which indent its shores. Three hundred miles by water had been traversed during this fruitful exploration or " picnic" as Livingstone called it.

The Christmas of 1871 was spent quietly at Ujiji, and, during the breathing-time thus afforded, Mr. Stanley appears to have urged the doctor to give up Nile exploration for the time, and revisit his home for rest and recuperation. Livingstone admitted at once that he longed to return home and see his children; but he felt that his undertaking was not complete. If his servants had only been trustworthy and courageous, and if that massacre had not taken place, " a little month " would have seen his task accomplished. Whether we ought now to regret that he did not accept Mr. Stanley's generous offer to escort him in comfort to the coast, who shall say?

On the 27th of December Dr. Livingstone and Stanley again left Ujiji, their ultimate destination being Unyanyembe, where the former expected to find his stores from Zanzibar, which had been on the road since November,

1870. The escort was the *Herald* party, composed of forty Wauguana soldiers, well armed. Mr. Stanley was fully sensible of the responsible task he had undertaken, and he accordingly mapped out the route of travel and provided for the mode of it with anxious care. Nothing illustrates better the sterling mettle of the man than the prescience he showed in providing against all contingencies, knowing, as he did, that he had Livingstone's life and safety on his hands.

The first stage of the journey was a seven days' trip along the eastern shore of Tanganyika, southward to Urimba, by water. The main body of their attendants formed a shore party which passed through the desolate Ukawendi country. The boat containing Livingstone and Stanley entered a number of bays, the finest and most picturesque of which was Sigunga, a beautiful harbour, sheltered by an island at its mouth, and nestling at the base of green and tree-clad hills which gradually sloped upwards from its shores. At Urimba they were compelled to wait three days for the land party—an interval spent by Stanley principally in hunting wild animals. Before leaving this place the American had a renewed attack of fever. It was on the 7th January, 1872, that they finally left Tanganyika, and bent their steps eastward. The Kawendi woods, through which they now marched for about ten days, formed the most trying portion of the journey. No supplies could be got, and the expedition suffered extremely from famine as well as fever. The woods and the tall tangled grass made the march extremely trying; Livingstone, however, as Stanley says in his letter, "tramped it on foot like a man of iron." Besides the difficulties of the journey on a level, they were obliged to cross a number of ridges parallel to the lake and to each other; and so to Mount Magdala, the isolated peak of which was observed towards the close of this stage.   Notwithstanding the toilsome character of the journey, Stanley appears to have enjoyed the luxuriance of the Ukawendi district, which he describes as singularly beautiful and attractive.   The next thirty-two days were spent in Unkonongo, first eastward and then northward. Before commencing this tramp they halted for a few days to recruit their strength at Mrera or Imrera, the old camping ground of Stanley during his western journey. During this stage Stanley was frequently troubled by the recurrence of fever.   On the whole, however, the journey was a comfortable and pleasant one; they shot abundance of game, and on one occasion obtained 719 lbs. of meat from two zebras.   After traversing the Unkonongo country, five days brought them to Unyanyembe, "where," Stanley writes, "we arrived without any adventure of any kind, except killing zebras, buffaloes, and giraffes, after fifty-four days' travel.

This was on the 18th February, 1872, and Stanley remained with Livingstone for nearly a month, finally taking what proved to be a last farewell of the great explorer on the 14th of March.   They had travelled nearly 800 miles, and Stanley had learned to be strongly and even passionately attached to Livingstone.   This should be borne in mind in reading the words of impatience the correspondent uttered when any of Livingstone's geographical conclusions or the soundness of any of his judgments was impugned. The doctor spent much of the interval during which they still sojourned together in writing despatches to the Foreign Office and letters to his relatives and friends; also in completing his immense journal of travel. This last he sealed up and committed to Stanley, to be delivered to his daughter. At length the time of parting arrived. Stanley turned over to Livingstone a valuable supply of stores of all descriptions—cloths, cottons, beads, wire, fire-arms, ammunition, medicines, tea, flour, crackers, and an infinite variety of useful commodities of all sorts. The moment of separation must have powerfully affected both the men. The last scene seems to have been painful in the extreme. Livingstone again expressed his gratitude in brief but earnest language; his deliverer breathed a prayer that God would bring back to them his dear friend. One single word, too often lightly spoken, but uttered now from the depths of two brave hearts—"FAREWELL;" and Stanley hurried away lest his emotion should unman him utterly. It is unnecessary to follow the correspondent in his journey homeward. He reached Zanzibar in safety on the 7th of May, and thence sailed for England, *via* Seychelles. . He delivered Livingstone's despatches at the Foreign Office on the 1st of August. The mortality in Stanley's party was thus summed up at Unyanyembe:—" On my arrival I found that the Englishman, Shaw, whom I had turned

back as useless, had, about a month after his return, succumbed to the climate of the interior, and had died, as
well as two Wauguana of the expedition, who had been
left behind sick.  Thus, during less than twelve months,
William Lawrence Farquhar, of Leith, Scotland, and John
William Shaw, of London, England, the two white men I
had engaged to assist me, had died ; also eight baggage-
carriers and eight soldiers of the expedition had died."

Before leaving Zanzibar, Mr. Stanley despatched, as
Livingstone had requested, a party of reliable freemen,
fifty-seven in number, to carry his supplies and stores
westward from Unyanyembe.  These attendants reached
their destination about five months after, and with the
five old and faithful servants who had shared his fortunes
from 1866, swelled the party to sixty-two.  Amongst the
letters sent by Stanley was one of thanks to Mr. Bennett,
jr.  We insert some extracts from it, which will serve to
show that, notwithstanding Livingstone's cold and im-
passive manner, he had a warm and affectionate heart :—

Ujiji or Tanganyika, East Africa,<br>
November, 1871.

James Gordon Bennett, Esq., Junior,

My Dear Sir,—It is in general somewhat difficult to
write to one we have never seen, it feels so much like
addressing an abstract idea ; but the presence of your re-
presentative, Mr. H. M. Stanley, in this distant region
takes away the strangeness I should otherwise have felt

and in writing to thank you for the extreme kindness that prompted you to send him, I feel quite at home. If I explain the forlorn condition in which he found me, you will easily perceive that I have good reason to use very strong expressions of gratitude. I came to Ujiji after a tramp of between 400 and 500 miles beneath a blazing vertical sun, having been baffled, worried, defeated and forced to return, when almost in sight of the end of the geographical part of my mission, by a number of half-caste Moslem slaves sent to me from Zanzibar instead of men. The sore heart made still sorer by the truly woeful sights I had seen of " man's inhumanity to man " reacted on the bodily frame, and depressed it beyond measure—I thought that I was dying on my feet. It is not too much to say that almost every step of the weary sultry way was in pain, and I reached Ujiji a mere ruckle of bones. Here I found that some £500 worth of goods I had ordered from Zanzibar had unaccountably been entrusted to a drunken half-caste Moslem tailor, who, after squandering them for sixteen months in the way to Ujiji, finished up by selling off all that remained, for slaves and ivory for himself. He had " divined " on the Koran, and was informed that I was dead. He had also written to the Governor of Unyanyembe that he had sent slaves after me to Manyuema, who returned and reported my decease, and begged permission to sell off the few goods that his drunken appetite had spared.

He, however, knew perfectly well from men who had seen me, that I was alive and waiting for the goods and men ;

but as for morality, he is evidently an idiot, and there being no law here except that of the dagger or musket, I had to sit down in great weakness, destitute of everything save a few barter cloths and beads which I had taken the precaution to leave here in case of extreme need. The near prospect of beggary among Ujijians made me miserable. I could not despair, because I laughed so much at a friend who, on reaching the mouth of the Zambezi, said that he was tempted to despair on breaking the photograph of his wife. We could have no success after that. Afterwards the idea of despair had to me such a strong smack of the ludicrous that it was out of the question.

Well, when I had got to about the lowest verge, vague rumours of an English visitor reached me. I thought of myself as the man who went down from Jerusalem to Jericho; but neither priest, Levite, nor Samaritan could possibly pass my way. Yet the good Samaritan was close at hand, and one of my people rushed up at the top of his speed, and in great excitement gasped out, "An Englishman coming! I see him!" and off he darted to meet him. An American flag, the first ever seen in these parts, at the head of a caravan, told me the nationality of the stranger.

I am as cold and undemonstrative as we islanders are usually reputed to be; but your kindness made my frame thrill. It was, indeed, overwhelming, and I said in my soul, "Let the richest blessings descend on you and yours!"

The news Mr. Stanley had to tell was thrilling    *    *
I had been absent without news from home for years,

save what I could glean from a few *Saturday Reviews* and *Punch*, of 1868. The appetite revived, and in a week I began to feel strong again. Mr. Stanley brought a most kind and encouraging despatch from Lord Clarendon, (whose loss I sincerely deplore,) the first I have received from the Foreign Office since 1866, and information that the British Government had kindly sent £1000 stg. to my aid. Up to his arrival I was not aware of any pecuniary aid. I came unsalaried, but this want is happily repaired, and I am anxious that you and all my friends should know that, though uncheered by letter, I have stuck to the task which my friend, Sir Roderick Murchison, set me, with "John Bullish" tenacity, believing that all would come right at last.

The water-shed of South Central Africa is over seven hundred miles in length. The fountains thereon are almost innumerable, that is, it would take a man's lifetime to count them. From the water-shed they converge into four large rivers, and these again into two mighty streams in the great Nile Valley, which begins in ten degrees to twelve degrees, south latitude. It was long ere light dawned on the ancient problem, and gave me a clear idea of the drainage. I had to feel my way, and every step of the way was, generally, groping in the dark, for who cared where the rivers ran? "We drank our fill and let the rest run by."

The Portuguese who visited Cazembe asked for slaves and ivory, and heard of nothing else. I asked about the waters, questioned and cross-questioned, until I was

almost afraid of being set down as afflicted with hydrocephalus.

My last work, in which I have been greatly hindered
from want of suitable attendants, was following the central line of drainage down through the country of the
cannibals, called Manyuema, or shortly, Manyema. This
line of drainage has four large lakes in it. The fourth
I was near when obliged to turn. It is from one to three
miles broad, and never can be reached at any point, or at
any time of the year. Two western drains, the Lufira or.
Bartle Frere's River, flow into it at Lake Kamolondo.
There the great river Lomame flows through Lake Lincoln
into it too, and seems to form the western arm of the
Nile on which Petherick traded.

Now, I knew about six hundred miles of the watershed, and unfortunately the seventh hundred is the most
interesting of the whole; for in it, if I am not mistaken,
four fountains arise from an earthen mound, and the last
of the four becomes, at no great distance off, a great river.
Two of these run north to Egypt, Lufira, and Lomame, and
two more run south into inner Ethiopia, as the Leanbaye
or Upper Zambezi, and the Kaful. Are not these the
sources of the Nile, mentioned by the Secretary of Minerva, in the City of Sais, to Herodotus? I have heard of
them so often and at great distances off, that I cannot
doubt their existence, and in spite of the sore longing for
home that seizes me every time I think of my family, I
wish to finish up by their re-discovery.

Five hundred pounds sterling worth of goods have again

unaccountably been entrusted to slaves, and have been over a year on the way, instead of four months. I must go where they lie at your expense, ere I can put the natural completion to my work.

And if my disclosures regarding the terrible Ujijian slavery should tend to the suppression of the East Coast slave trade, I shall regard that as a greater matter far than the discovery of all the Nile sources together. Now that you have done with domestic slavery for ever, lend us your powerful aid towards this great object. This fine country is blighted, as with a curse from above, in order that the slavery privileges of the petty Sultan of Zanzibar may not be infringed, and the rights of the Crown of Portugal, which are mythical, should be kept in abeyance till some future time, when Africa will become another India to Portuguese slave traders.

I conclude by again thanking you most cordially for your great generosity, and am,

Gratefully yours,

DAVID LIVINGSTONE.

As our readers are aware, the stirring appeals of Livingstone in this and other letters moved the British Government to action, and Sir Bartle Frere was sent to negotiate a treaty with the Sultan of Zanzibar for the suppression of the slave trade. The mission was, to a large extent, successful ; but whether the traffic will be extinguished without a display of force on the part of Britain is problematical. The allusion in Livingstone's letter to Hero-

12

dotus' account of the sources of the Nile tempts us to quote the passage as translated by Cary. It used to be the fashion to discredit the authority of "the father of history," and to regard him merely as a credulous collector of surmise, gossip, and fable—a sort of early Greek Münchausen. Singularly enough, modern geographical research has tended, in every instance, to confirm the statements of Herodotus, and his authority stands, therefore, proportionally high. It will be seen that Herodotus' information about the fountains of the Nile, and Livingstone's agree almost exactly :—

"With respect to the sources of the Nile, no man, of all the Egyptians, Libyans, or Grecians, with whom I have conversed, ever pretended to know anything, except the registrar (*grammatistes*) of Minerva's treasury at Sais, in Egypt. He indeed seemed to be trifling with me, (i.e. I could hardly believe him,) when he said he knew perfectly well; his account was as follows : 'That there are two mountains rising into a sharp peak, situated between the City of Syene, in Thebais and Elephantine. The names of these mountains are, the one Crophi, the other Mophi ; that the sources of the Nile, which are bottomless, flow from between these mountains, and that half of the water flows over Egypt, and to the North, and the other over Ethiopia and the South. That the fountains of the Nile are bottomless,' he said, 'Psamittichus, king of Egypt, proved by experiment, for having caused a line to be twisted many thousand fathoms in length, he let it down, but could not find a bottom.' Such, then, was the opinion

the registrar gave, if indeed he spoke the real truth [mark
the incredulity of Herodotus, whom people supposed to
be so gullible]; *proving*, in my opinion, that there are
strong whirlpools and an eddy here, so that the water
beating against the rocks, a sounding line, when let down
cannot reach the bottom.  I was unable to learn anything
from anyone else.  But this much I learnt by carrying
my researches as far as possible, having gone and made
my own observations as far as Elephantine, and beyond
that obtaining information from hearsay.  As one ascends
the river, above the city of Elephantine, the country is
steep; here, therefore, it is necessary to attach a rope on
both sides of a boat, as one does with an ox and a plough,
and so proceed ; but if the rope should happen to break, the
boat is carried by the force of the stream. [He evidently refers
here to the so-called cataracts of the Nile above Syene and
the Island Elephantine.]  This kind of country lasts for a
four days' passage, and the Nile here winds as much as
Mæander.  There are twelve schæni, which it is necessary to sail through in this manner; and after that you
come to a level plain, where the Nile flows round an
island; its name is Tachompso.  Ethiopians inhabit the
country immediately above Elephantine, and one-half of
the island ; the other half is inhabited by Egyptians.
Near to this Island lies a vast lake, on the borders of
which Ethiopian nomades dwell.  After sailing through
this lake you will come to the channel of the Nile, which
flows into it, then you will have to land and travel forty
days by the side of the river, for sharp rocks rise in the

Nile, and there are many sunken ones, through which it is not possible to navigate a boat. Having passed this country in the forty days you must go on board another boat, and sail for twelve days; and then you will arrive at a large city called Meröe, this city is said to be the capital of all Ethiopia. [The country formed the greater part of the modern Nubia and Senaar.] The inhabitants worship no other gods than Jupiter and Bacchus: but these they honour with great magnificence. They have also an oracle of Jupiter; and they make war whenever that god bids them by an oracular warning, and against whatever country he bids them. Sailing from this city, you will arrive in the country of the Automoli, in a space of time equal to that which you took in coming from Elephantine to the capital of the Ethiopians. These Automoli are called by the name of Asmach, which in the language of Greece, signifies ' those that stand at the left hand of the king.' These, to the number of two hunc'red and forty thousand of the Egyptian war tribe, revolted to the Ethiopians on the following occasion. In the reign of King Psammitichus, garrisons were stationed at Elephantine, against the Ethiopians, and another at the Pelusian Daphnæ against the Arabians and Syrians, and another at Marea against Libya; and even in my time garrisons of the Persians are stationed in the same places as they were in the time of Psammitichus, for they maintain guards at Elephantine and Daphnæ. Now, these Egyptians, after they had been on duty three years, were not relieved; therefore, having consulted together and come to an unanimous resolution, they all revolted from Psammitichus and went to Ethiopia. Psammitichus, hearing of this, pursued them; and when he overtook them he entreated them, by many arguments, and adjured them not to forsake the gods of their fathers, and their children and wives. These men, when they arrived in Ethiopia, offered their services to the King of the Ethiopians, who made them the following recompense. There were certain Ethiopians disaffected towards him; these he bade them expel, and take possession of their land. By the settlement of these men among the Ethiopians, the Ethiopians became more civilized, and learned the manners of the Egyptians.

"Now, for a voyage and land journey of four months, the Nile is known, in addition to the part of the stream that is in Egypt; for, upon computation, so many months are known to be spent by a person who travels from Elephantine to Automoli. This river flows from the west and the setting of the sun, but beyond this no one is able to speak with certainty, for the rest of the country is desert by reason of the excessive heat. But I have heard the following account from certain Cyrenæans, who say that they went to the oracle of Ammon, and had a conversation with Etearchus, King of the Ammonians, and that, among other subjects, they happened to discourse about the Nile—that nobody knew its sources; whereupon Etearchus said that certain Nasimonians once came to him—this nation is in Libya, and inhabits the Syrtes, and the country for no great distance eastward of the

Syrtes—and that when these Nasimonians arrived, and were asked if they could give any further information touching the deserts of Libya, they answered that there were some daring youths amongst them, sons of powerful men; and that they, having reached man's estate, formed many other extravagant plans and, moreover, chose five of their number, by lot, to explore the deserts of Libya, to see if they could make any further discovery than those who had penetrated the farthest. (For, as respects the parts of Lybia along the Northern Sea, beginning from Egypt to the promontory of Solois, where is the extremity of Libya, Libyans and various nations of Lybians reach all along it, except those parts which are occupied by Grecians and Phœnicians; but as respects the parts above the sea, in the upper parts Lybia is infested by wild beasts; and all beyond that is sand, dreadfully short of water and utterly desolate.) *They further related* that when the young men deputed by their companions set out, well furnished with water and provisions, they passed first through the inhabited country, and, having traversed this, they came to the region infested by wild beasts, and after this they crossed the desert, making their way towards the west; and, when they had traversed much sandy ground, during a journey of many days, they at length saw some trees growing in a plain, and that they approached and began to gather the fruit that grew on the trees. While they were gathering, some dimunitive men, less than men of middle stature, came up, and having seized them carried them away; and that the Nasimo-

nians did not at all understand their language, nor those
who carried them off the language of the Nasamonians.
However, they conducted them through vast morasses,
and when they had passed these they came to a city in
which all the inhabitants were of the same size as their
conductors, and black in colour; and by the city flowed a
great river running from the west to the east, and that
crocodiles were seen in it. Thus far I have set  rth the
account of Etearchus the Ammonian, to which may be
added—as the Cyrenæans assured me—that he said the
Nasimonians all returned safe to their own country, and
that the men whom they came to were all necromancers.
Etearchus also conjectured *that this river which flows by
their city is the Nile,* and reason so evinces; for the Nile
flows from Libya and intersects it in the middle; and (as
I conjecture, inferring things unknown from things known)
it sets out-from a point corresponding with the Ister
(Danube). For the Ister, beginning from the Celts and
the city of Pyrene, divides Europe in its course, but the
Celts are beyond the pillars of Hercules (Gibralter), and
border on the territories of the Cynesians, who lie in the
extremity of Europe to the westward, and the Ister termi-
nates by flowing through all Europe into the Euxine
(Black) Sea, where a Milesian colony is settled in Istria.
Now the Ister, as it flows through a well-peopled country,
is generally known, but no one is able to speak about the
sources of the Nile because Libya, through which it flows,
is uninhabited and desolate. Respecting this stream
therefore, as far as I was able to reach by inquiry, I have

IMAGE EVALUATION
TEST TARGET (MT-3)

6"

Photographic
Sciences
Corporation

23 WEST MAIN STREET
WEBSTER, N.Y. 14580
(716) 872-4503

already spoken.   It, however, discharges itself into Egypt (an ascertained fact on which the old historian plants himself as upon sure ground), and Egypt lies as near as may be opposite to the mountains of Cilicia, from whence to Sinope, on the Euxine Sea, is a five days' journey in a straight line to an active man; and Sinope is opposite to the Ister, where it discharges itself into the sea.   So I think that the Nile, traversing the whole of Libya may be properly compared with the Ister.   Such then is the account that I am able to give respecting the Nile."—Book II. (*Euterpe*) 28–35.

This fanciful comparison of the Nile with the Danube, and some of the obvious errors into which Herodotus fell, were the result partly of his limited knowledge, but mainly of the vicious geographical theory prevalent in his time. Making every allowance for the difficulties the Greek historian had to encounter, the extent and accuracy of his information is very surprising.   We have already seen that Livingstone cites the passage we have quoted, as confirming the universal opinion of native tribes widely separated from each other; a comparison has been made of the account given by the historian with the theory almost demonstrated by the missionary-explorer, by the Rector of Stone: "Herodotus speaks of two peaked mountains, between which lie the sources of the river; Livingstone, of an earthen mound and four fountains, as the source of the river.   Herodotus writes, that one-half of the water flows north into Egypt; Livingstone, two of these run north to Egypt—Lufira and Lomame.   Herodotus again, the other half flows into Ethiopia; Livingstone, and two run south into Inner Ethiopia, as the Liambe or Upper Zambesi, and the Kaful. Again, the father of history is confirmed by modern research, and the information which the great doctor has obtained almost in the immediate neighbourhood of the object of his ambition, shows how carefully the curious old traveller of 2,300 years ago, must have pursued his inquiries and recorded the results, although he puts it upon record that he thought the man of letters or notary was joking with him."

As nearly all the information we as yet possess of Livingstone's movements during the last year and a half of his life is contained in his letters and despatches, we shall proceed to give these, so far as they are accessible, in chronological order. The first was transmitted by Mr. Stanley, and addressed to Earl Granville. It will be observed that it principally relates to the manner in which he was treated by the Banian slaves :—

UNYANYEMBE, near the Kazeh of Speke,

Feb. 20, 1852.

MY LORD,—My letters to and from the coast have been so frequently destroyed by those whose interest and cupidity lead them to hate correspondence, as likely to expose their slaving, that I had nearly lost all heart to write, but being assured that this packet will be taken safe home by Mr. Stanley, I add a fifth letter to four already penned, the pleasure of believing that this will really come into your Lordship's hands, overpowering the consciousness of having been much too prolix.

The subject to which I beg to draw your attention is the part which the Banians of Zanzibar, who are protected British subjects, play in carrying on the slave trade in Central Africa, especially in Manyema, the country west of the Ujiji ; together with a proposition which I have very much at heart—the possibility of encouraging the native Christians of English settlements on the West Coast of Africa to remove, by voluntary emigration, to a healthy spot on this side the continent.

The Banian British subjects have long been and are now the chief propagators of the Zanzibar slave trade ; their money, and often their muskets, gunpowder, balls, flints, beads, brass wire and calico, are annually advanced to the Arabs at enormous interest, for the murderous work of slaving, of the nature of which every Banian is fully aware. Having mixed much with the Arabs in the interior, I soon learned that the whole system, which is called "butchee" or Banian trading, is simply marauding and murdering by the Arabs, at the instigation and by the aid of our Indian fellow-subjects. The cunning Indians secure nearly all the profits of the caravans they send inland, and very adroitly let the odium of slavery rest on their Arab agents. As a rule, very few Arabs could proceed on a trading expedition unless supplied by the Banians with arms, ammunition, and goods. Slaves are not bought in the countries to which the Banian agents proceed—indeed, it is a mistake to call the system of Ujiji slave "trade"

at all; the captives are not traded for, but murdered for,
and the gangs that are dragged coastwards to enrich the
Banians are usually not slaves, but captive free people.
A sultan, anxious to do justly rather than pocket head-
money, would proclaim them all free as soon as they
reached his territory.

Let me give an instance or two to illustrate the trade of
our Indian fellow-subjects. My friend Muhamad Bogharib
sent out a large party of his people far down the great river
Lualaba to trade for ivory about the middle of 1871. He
is one of the best of the traders, a native of Zanzibar, and
not one of the mainlanders, who are lower types of man.
The best men have, however, often the worst attendants.
This party was headed by one Hassani, and he, with two
other head men, advanced to the people of Nyangwe
twenty-five copper bracelets to be paid for in ivory on their
return. The rings were worth about five shillings at Ujiji,
and it being well known that the Nyangwe people had
no ivory, the advance was a mere trap; for, on returning
and demanding payment in ivory in vain, they began an
assault which continued for three days. All the villages
of a large district were robbed, some burned, many men
killed, and about one hundred and fifty captives secured.

On going subsequently into Southern Manyuema I met
the poorest of the above-mentioned head men, who had
only been able to advance five of the twenty-five bracelets, and he told me he had bought ten tusks with part
of the captives; and having received information at the
village where I found him, about two more tusks, he was

waiting for eight other captives from Muhamad's camp to
purchase them.  I had now got into terms of friendship
with all the respectable traders of that quarter, and they
gave information with unrestrained freedom ; and all I
state may be relied on.  On asking Muhamad himself
afterwards, near Ujiji, the proper name of Muhamad Nassur, the Indian who conspired with Shereef, to interpose
his own trade speculation between Dr. Kirk and me, and
defray all his expenses out of my goods, he promptly replied, "This Muhamad Nassur is the man from whom I
borrowed all the money and goods for this journey."

I will not refer to the horrid and senseless massacre which
I unwillingly witnessed at Nyangwe, in which the Arabs
themselves computed the loss of life at between three hundred and four hundred souls.  It pained me sorely to let
the mind dwell long enough on it to pen the short account
I gave, but I mention it again to point out that the chief
perpetrator, Tagamolo, received all his guns and gunpowder from Ludha Damji, the richest Banian and chief slave-
trader of Zanzibar.  He has had the cunning to conceal
his actual participation in slaving, but there is not an Arab
in the country who would hesitate a moment to point out
that, but for the money of Ludha Damji and other Banians
who borrow from him, slaving, especially in these
more distant countries, would instantly cease.  It is not
to be overlooked that most other trades as well as slaving
is carried on by Banians ; the custom-house and revenue
are entirely in their hands ; the so-called governors are
their trade agents ; Syde bin Salem Buraschid, the thievish

governor here, is merely a trade agent of Ludha, and honesty having been no part of his qualifications for the office, the most shameless transactions of other Banian agents are all smoothed over by him.  A common way he has of concealing crimes is to place delinquents in villages adjacent to this, and when they are inquired for by the Sultan he reports that they are sick.  It was no secret that all the Banians looked with disfavour on my explorations and disclosures as likely to injure one great source of their wealth.  Knowing this, it almost took away my breath when I heard that the great but covert slave-trader, Ludha Damji, had been requested to forward supplies and men to me.  This and similar applications must have appeared to Ludha so ludicrous that he probably an" swered with his tongue in his cheek.  His help was all faithfully directed towards securing my failure.  I am extremely unwilling to appear as [if making a wail on my own account, or as if trying to excite commiseration.  I am greatly more elated by the unexpected kindness of unknown friends and the liberality and sympathy of Her Majesty's government, than cast down by losses and obstacles.  But I have a purpose in view in mentioning mishaps.

Before leaving Zanzibar in 1866, I paid for and dispatched a stock of goods to be placed in depot at Ujiji ; the Banyamwezi porters, or pagazi, as usual, brought them honestly to this governor or Banian agent, the same who plundered Burton and Speke pretty freely ; and he placed my goods in charge of his own slave, Musa bin Saloom, who, about midway between this and Ujiji, stopped the caravan ten days while he plundered as much as he chose, and went off to buy ivory for his owner, Karague. Saloom has been kept out of the way ever since; the dregs of the stores left by this slave are the only supplies I have received since 1866. Another stock of goods was despatched from Zanzibar in 1868, but the whole was devoured at this place and the letters destroyed, so that I should know nothing about them. Another large supply, sent through Ludha and his slaves in 1869-1870, came to Ujiji, and, except a few pounds of worthless beads out of 700 pounds of fine dear beads, all were sold off for slaves and ivory by the persons selected by Ludha Damji. I refer to these wholesale losses because, though well known to Ludha and all the Banians, the statement was made in the House of Lords (I suppose on the strength of Ludha's plausible fables) that all my wants had been supplied.

By coming back in a roundabout route of 300 miles from Ujiji, I did find two days ago a good quantity of supplies, the remains of what had been sent from Zanzibar, sixteen months ago, Ludha had again been employed, and the slaves he selected began by loitering at Bagomoyo, opposite Zanzibar, for nearly four months. A war here, which is still going on, gave them a good excuse for going no further. The head men were thieves, and had I not returned and seized what remained, I should again have lost all. All the Banian slaves who have been sent by Ludha and other Banians were full of the idea that

they were not to follow but force me back. I cannot say
that I am altogether free from chagrin in view of the
worry, thwarting, baffling, which the Banians and their
slaves have inflicted. Common traders procure supplies
of merchandise from the coast, and send loads of ivory
down by the same pagazi or carriers we employ, without
any loss. But the Banians and their agents are not their
enemies. I have lost more than two years in time, have
been burdened with 1,800 miles of tramping, and how
much waste of money I cannot say, through my affairs
having been committed to Banians and slaves who are not
men. I have adhered, in spite of losses, with a sort of
John Bullish tenacity to my task, and while bearing misfortune in as manly a way as possible, it strikes me that
it is well that I have been brought face to face with the
Banian system that inflicts enormous evils on Central
Africa. Gentlemen in India who see only the wealth
brought to Bombay and Cutch, and know that the religion of the Banians does not allow them to harm a fly,
very naturally conclude that all Cutchees may safely be
entrusted with the possession of slaves. But I have been
forced to see that those who shrink from killing a flea or
mosquito are virtually the worst cannibals in all Africa.
The Manyema cannibals, among whom I spent nearly two
years, are innocent compared with our protected Banian fellow-subjects. By their Arab agents they compass the destruction of more human lives in one year than the Manyema
do for their fleshpots in ten: and could the Indian gentlemen
who oppose the anti-slave-trade policy of the Foreign Of-

fice, but witness the horrid deeds done by the Banian agents, they would be foremost in decreeing that every Cutchee found guilty of direct or indirect slaving should forthwith be shipped back to India, if not to the Andaman Islands.

The Banians, having complete possession of the Custom House and revenue of Zanzibar, enjoy ample opportunity to aid and conceal the slave trade and all fraudulent trans-actions committed by their agents.   It would be good policy to recommend the Sultan, as he cannot trust his Moslem subjects, to place his income from all sources in the hands of an English or American merchant of known uprightness.   He would be a check on the slave trade, a benefit to the Sultan, and an aid to lawful com-merce.

But by far the most beneficial measure that could be introduced into Eastern Africa would be the moral ele-ment, which has worked so beneficially in suppressing the slave trade around all the English settlements of the West Coast.   The Banians seem to have no religion worthy of the name, and among Mahommedans religion and morality are completely disjoined.   Different opinions have been expressed as to the success of Christian missionaries, and gentlemen who judge by the riff-raff that follow Indian camps speak very unfavourably, from an impression that the drunkards who profess to be of "master's caste and drink brandy" are average specimens of Christian converts. But the comprehensive report of Colonel Ord, presented to Parliament (1865), contains no such mistake.   He states

that while the presence of the squadron has had some
share in suppressing the slave trade, the result is mainly
due to the existence of the settlements.  This is supported
by the fact that, even in those least visited by men-of-
war, it has been as effectually suppressed as in those which
have been their most constant resort.  The moral element
which has proved beneficial to all round the settlements
is mainly due to the teaching of missionaries.  I would
carefully avoid anything like boasting over the benevolent
efforts of our countrymen, but here their good influences
are totally unknown.  No attempt has ever been made by
the Mahommedans in East Africa to propagate their faith,
and their trade intercourse has only made the natives
more avaricious than themselves.  The fines levied on all
traders are nearly prohibitive, and nothing is given in return.  Mr. Stanley was mulcted of 1,600 yards of superior
calico between the sea and Ujiji, and we made a détour of
300 miles to avoid similar spoliation among people accustomed to Arabs.  It has been said that Moslems would be
better missionaries than Christians, because they would
allow polygamy; but nowhere have the Christians been
loaded with the contempt the Arabs have to endure in
addition to being plundered.  To "honga" originally
meant to make friends.  It does so now in all the more
central countries, and presents are exchanged at the ceremony, the natives usually giving the largest amount;
but on routes much frequented by Arabs it has come to
mean not "black-mail," but forced contributions impu-
dently demanded, and neither service nor food returned.
13

If the native Christians of one or more of the English
settlements on the West Coast, which have fully accomplished the objects of their establishment in suppressing
the slave trade, could be induced by voluntary emigration to remove to some healthy spot on the East Coast,
they would in time frown down the duplicity which prevails so much in all classes, that no slave treaty can bind
them.   Slaves purchase their freedom in Cuba and return
to unhealthy Lagos to settle as petty traders.  Men of the
same enterprising class who have been imbued with the
moral atmosphere of our settlements, would be of incalculable value in developing lawful commerce.  Mombas is
ours already; we left it, but never ceded it.  The mainland opposite Zanzibar is much more healthy than the
island, and the Sultan gives as much land as can be cultivated to any one who asks.  No native right is interfered
with by the gift.  All that would be required would be
an able, influential man to begin and lead the movement;
the officials already in office could have passages in men-
of-war.  The only additional cost to what is at present
incurred would be a part of the passage money on loan
and small rations and house rent, both of which are very
cheap, for half a year.  It would be well to prevent Europeans, even as missionaries, from entering the settlement
till it was well established.

Many English in new climates reveal themselves to be
born fools, and then blame some one for having advised
them, or lay their own excesses to the door of African
fever.  That disease is in all conscience bad enough, but

medical men are fully aware that frequently it is not fever, but folly that kills. Brandy, black women, and lazy inactivity are worse than the climate. A settlement once fairly established and reputed safe will not long lack religious teachers, and it will then escape the heavy burden of being a scene for martyrdom.

If the Sultan of Zanzibar were relieved from the heavy subsidy to the ruler of Muscat, he would, for the relief granted, readily concede all that one or two transferred English settlements would require. The English name, now respected in all the interior, would be a sort of safeguard to petty traders, while gradually supplanting the unscrupulous Banians who abuse it. And lawful trade would, by the aid of English and American merchants, be exalted to a position it has never held since Banians and Moslems emigrated to Africa. It is true that Lord Canning did ordain that the annual subsidy should be paid by Zanzibar to Muscat. But a statesman of his eminence never could have contemplated it as an indefinite aid to eager slave traders, while non-payment might be used to root out the wretched traffic. If, in addition to the relief suggested, the Sultan of Zanzibar were guaranteed protection from his relations and others in Muscat, he would feel it to be his interest to observe a treaty to suppress slaving all along his coast.

I am thankful in now reporting myself well supplied with stores, ample enough to make a feasible finish-up of the geographical portion of my mission. This is due partly to the goods I seized two days ago from the slaves, who have been feasting on them for the last sixteen months, but chiefly to a large assortment of the best barter articles presented by Henry M. Stanley, who, as I have already informed your Lordship, was kindly sent by James Gordon Bennett, jr., of New York, and who bravely persisted, in the teeth of the most serious obstacles, till he found me at Ujiji, shortly, or one month, after my return from Manyema, ill and destitute. It will readily be believed that I feel deeply grateful for this disinterested and unlooked-for kindness. The supplies I seized two days ago, after a return march of 300 miles, laid on me by the slaves in charge refusing to accompany Mr. Stanley to Ujiji, were part of those sent off in the end of October, 1870, at the instance of Her Majesty's government, and are virtually the only stores worthy of the name that came to hand, besides those despatched by Dr. Seward and myself in 1866. And all in consequence of Ludha and Banian slaves having unwittingly been employed to forward an expedition opposed to their slaving interests. It was no doubt amiable in Dr. Kirk to believe the polite Banians in asserting that they would send stores off at once, and again that my wants had all been supplied ; but it would have been better to have dropped the money into Zanzibar harbour than trust it in their hands, because the whole population has witnessed the open plunder of English property, and the delinquents are screened from justice by Banian agents. The slaves need no more than a hint to plunder and baffle. Shereef and all the Banian slaves who acted in accordance with the views of their

masters are now at Ujiji and Unyanyembe by the conni-
vance of the governor, or rather, Banian trade agent,
Syde bin Salem Buraschid, who, when the wholesale plunder by Shereef became known, wrote to me that he (the
governor) had no hand in it. I never said he had.

However, though sorely knocked up, ill and dejected,
on arriving at Ujiji, I am now completely recovered in
health and spirits. I need no more goods, but I draw on
Her Majesty's government, in order that Mr. Stanley may
employ and send off fifty free men, but no slaves, from
Zanzibar. I need none but them, and have asked Seyed
Burghash to give me a good, honest head man, with a
character that may be inquired into. I expect them
about the end of June, and after all the delay I have endured, feel quite exhilarated at the prospect of doing my
work.

Geographers will be interested to know the plan I propose to follow. I shall at present avoid Ujiji, and go
about south-west from this to Fipa, which is east of and
near the south end of Tanganyika; then round the same
south end, only touching it again at Pambette; thence
resuming the south-west course, to cross the Chambeze
and proceed along the southern shores of Lake Bangweolo,
which being in 12 degrees south, the course will be due
west to the ancient fountains of Herodotus. From them
it is about ten days north to Katanga, the copper mines
of which have been worked for ages. The Malachite ore
is described as so abundant that it can only be mentioned
by the coal-heavers' phrase, "practically inexhaustible."

About ten days north-east of Katanga very extensive under-ground rock excavations deserve attention as very ancient, the natives ascribing their formation to the Deity alone.  They are remarkable for all having water laid on in running streams, and the inhabitants of large districts can all take refuge in them in case of invasion.  Returning from them to Katanga, twelve days north-northwest, take to the southern end of Lake Lincoln.  I wish to go down through it to the Lomani, and into Webb's Lualaba and home.  I was mistaken in the information that a waterfall existed between Tanganyika and Albert Nyanza.  Tanganyika is of no interest except in a very remote degree in connection with the sources of the Nile.  But what if I am mistaken, too, about the ancient fountain?  Then we shall see.  I know the rivers they are said to form—two north and two south; and in battling down the central line of drainage the enormous amount of westing caused me to feel at times as if running my head against a stone wall.  It might, after all, be the Congo; and who would care to run the risk of being put into a cannibal pot and converted into a black man for anything less than the grand old Nile?  But when I found that Lualaba forsook its westing and received through Kamolondo, Bartle Frere's great river, and that afterwards, further down, it takes in Young's great stream through Lake Lincoln, I ventured to think I was on the right track.

Two great rivers arise somewhere on the western end of the watershed and flow north—to Egypt (?).  Two other large rivers rise in the same quarter and flow south,

as the Zambesi or Lambai, and the ⸢Kafue into Inner
Ethiopia. Yet I speak with diffidence, for I have no
affinity with an untravelled would-be geographer, who
used to swear to the fancies he collected from slaves till
he became blue in the face.

I know about six hundred miles of the watershed pretty
fairly. I turn to the seventh hundred miles, with pleasure
and hope. I want no companion now, though discovery
means hard work. Some can make what they call theoretical discoveries by dreaming. I should like to offer a
prize for an explanation of the correlation of the structure
and economy of the watershed with the structure and
economy of the great lacustrine rivers in the production
of the phenomena of the Nile. The prize cannot be un-
dervalued by competitors even who may only have
dreamed of what has given me very great trouble, though
they may have hit on the division of labour in dreaming,
and each discovered one or two hundred miles. In the
actual discovery so far, I went two years and six months
without once tasting tea, coffee, or sugar; and except at
Ujiji, have fed on buffaloes, rhinoceros, elephants, hippopotami, and cattle of that sort, and have come to believe
that English roast beef and plum pudding must be the
real genuine theobroma, the food of the gods, and I offer
to all successful competitors a glorious feast of beefsteak
and stout. No competition will be allowed after I have
published my own explanation, on pain of immediate execution, without benefit of clergy!

I send home my journal by Mr. Stanley, sealed, to my

daughter Agnes. It is one of Lett's large folio diaries, and is full except a few (five) pages reserved for altitudes which I cannot at present copy. It contains a few private memoranda for my family alone, and I adopt this course in order to secure it from risk in my concluding trip.

Trusting that your Lordship will award me your approbation and sanction to a little longer delay, I have, &c.,

DAVID LIVINGSTONE,<br>
Her Majesty's Consul, Inner Africa.

In order to complete the official letters, we may insert here, though slightly out of its chronological place, the following interesting letter to Earl Granville. It was published in the London papers of October 22nd:—

UNYANYEMBE, July 1st, 1872.

MY LORD,—It is necessary to recall to memory that I was subjected to very great inconvenience by the employment of slaves instead of freemen. It caused me the loss of quite two years of time, inflicted 1,800 or 2,000 miles of useless marching, imminent risk of violent death four several times, and how much money I cannot tell. Certain Banians, Indian British subjects, headed by one Ludha Damji, seemed to have palmed off their slaves on us at more than double freemen's pay, and all the slaves were imbued with the idea that they were not to follow but to force me back. By the money and goods of these Banians nearly all the slave trade of this region is carried on. They employed dishonest agents to conduct the caravans, and that has led to my being plundered four several times. No trader is thus robbed. I sent a complaint of this to Dr. Kirk, and in my letter of the 14th of November last, I enclosed a copy in the hope that, if necessary, his hands might be strengthened by the Foreign Office in administering justice; and I was in hopes that he would take action in the matter promptly, because the Banians and their dishonest agent Shereef, placed a private trade speculation between Dr. Kirk and me, and we were unwittingly led into employing slaves, though we all objected to Captain Fraser doing the same on his sugar estate. I regret very much to hear incidentally that Dr. Kirk viewed my formal complaint against the Banians as a covert attack upon himself. If I had foreseen this I should certainly have borne all my losses in silence. I never had any difference with him, though we were together for years, and I had no intention to give offence now, but the public interest taken in this expedition enforces publicity as to the obstacles that prevented its work being accomplished years ago. I represented the Banians and their agents as the cause of all my losses, and that the governor here is their chief trade agent. This receives confirmation from the fact that Shereef and all the first gang of slaves are living comfortably with him at a village about twelve miles distant from the spot at which I write. Having, as I mentioned in my above letter, abundant supplies to enable me in a short time to make a feasible finish-up of my work, and the first and second gangs of slaves having proved so very unsatisfactory,

I felt extremely anxious that no more should come, and requested Mr. Stanley to hire fifty freemen at Zanzibar, and should he meet the party of slaves coming, by all means to send them back. No matter what expense had been incurred. I would cheerfully pay it all. I had no idea that this would lead to the stoppage of an English expedition sent in the utmost kindness to my aid. I am really and truly profoundly grateful for the generous effort of my noble countrymen, and deeply regret that my precaution against another expedition of slaves should have damped the self-denying zeal of gentlemen who have not a particle of the slave spirit in them. As I shall now explain, but little good could have been done in the direction in which I propose to go; but had we a telegraph, or even a penny post, I should have advised Dr. Kirk in another direction that would have pleased the Council. A war has been going on here for the last twelve months. It resembles one of our own Caffre wars in miniature, but it enriches no one. All trade is stopped, and there is a general lawlessness all over the country. I propose to avoid this confusion by going southwards to Fipa, then round the south end of Tanganyika, and, crossing the Chambezi, proceed west along the shore of the Lake Bangweolo, being then in latitude 12 degrees south I wish to go straight west to the ancient fountains reported at the end of the watershed, then turn north to the copper mines of Katanga, which are only about ten days south-west of the underground excavations. Returning thence to Katanga, twelve days south-west leads to the head of Lake Lincoln.  Arrived there, I shall devoutly thank Providence, and retire along Lake Kamolondo towards Ujiji and home.  By this trip I hope to make up for the loss of ground caused by the slaves.

If I retired now, as I wish with all my heart I could do with honour, I should be conscious of having left the discovery of the sources unfinished, and that soon some one else would come and show the hollowness of my claim; and worse by far than that, the Banians and their agents, who I believe conspired to baffle me, would virtually have success in their design.  I already know many of the people among whom I go as quite friendly, because I travelled extensively in that quarter in eliminating the error into which I was led by the Chambezi being called by the Portuguese and others, the Zambesi.  I should like very much to visit the Basango, who are near my route, but I restrict myself to six or eight months more sustained exertions.

Five generations ago a white man came to the Highlands of Basango, which are in a line east of the watershed.  He had six attendants, who all died, and eventually their head man, Charura, was elected chief by the Basango.  In the third generation he had sixty ablebodied spearmen as lineal descendants.  This implies an equal number of the other sex.  They are very light in colour, and easily known, as no one is allowed to wear coral beads such as Charura brought except the royal family.  A book he brought was lost only lately.  The interest of the case lies in its connection with Mr. Darwin's celebrated theory on the " Origin of Species," for it shows that an improved variety, as we whites modestly call ourselves, is not so liable to be swamped by numbers, as some have thought.

Two Magitu chiefs live near the route. I would fain call and obtain immunity for Englishmen such as has been awarded to the Arabs of Seyed Majid, but I am at present much too rich to go among thieves. At other times, when I have called I have gone safely, because, to use a Scotch proverb, " No one can take the breeks off a Highlander."

With ordinary success I hope to be back at Ujiji eight months hence. If any one doubts the wisdom of my decision, or suspects me of want of love to my family in making this final trip, I can confidently appeal for approbation to the Council of the Royal Geographical Society as thoroughly understanding the subject.

Had it been possible for me to know of the coming of the late Search Expedition, I should certainly have made use of it as a branch expedition to explore Lake Victoria, for which the naval officers selected were, no doubt, perfectly adapted. The skeleton of a boat left here by Mr. Stanley would have served their purpose, and they would have had all the merit of independent exploration and success.

I travelled for a considerable time in company with three intelligent Suabelli, who had lived three, six, and nine years respectively in the country east of the Victoria Lake, there called Okara, but on this side Urkara. They described three or four lakes only, one of which sends its waters to the north. Okara seems to be Lake Victoria proper. About its middle it gives off an arm eastward, called Kidette, in which many weirs are set and many fish caught. It is three days in length by canoe, and joins Lake Kavirondo, which may not deserve to be called a lake, but only an arm of Okara. Very dark people live on it and have cattle. The Masiri are further east. To the south-east of Kavirondo stands Lake Neibash, or Neybash. They travelled along its southern bank for three days, and thence saw Mount Kimanjaro, also in the south-east. It had no outlet away far to the north of Kavirondo. They described Lake Baringo (not Bahrugo). A river, or rivulet, called Ngare-na-Rogwa, flows into it from the south or south-east. Its name signifies that it is brackish. Baringo gives forth a river to the north-east, called Ngardabash. The land east and west of Baringo is called Burnkinegge, and Gallahs, with camels and horses, are reported, but my informants did not see them. I give their information only for what it may be worth. Their object was plunder, and they could scarcely be mistaken as to the number of lakes, where we suppose there is only one. Okara, or Lake Victoria proper, is the largest, and has many very large islands in it. I have not the faintest wish to go near it, either now or at any future time. In performing my one work I desire to do it well, and I think that I may lay claim to some perseverance. Yet, if ordered to go anywhere else, I should certainly plead "severe indisposition, or urgent private affairs." I have been reported as living among the Arabs as one of themselves, that only means that I am on good terms with them all. They often call me the " Christian," and I never swerved from that character in any one respect.

An original plan of getting the longitude, which I submitted to Sir Thomas Maclear, of the Royal Observatory at the Cape, gives 27 degrees east as the longitude of the great river Lualaba, in latitude 4 degs., 9 south. It runs between 26 deg. to 27 degs. east, and is, therefore, not so far west as my reckoning, carried on without watch, through dense forests and gigantic grasses, made it. It is thus less likely to be the Congo, and I ought to meet Baker on it. In reference to the ancient fountains, I already know the four rivers that unquestionably do arise near or on the western end of the watershed. Mr. Oswell and I were told about 1851 that the Kafue and Liambai (Upper Zambesi) arose at one spot, though we were then some 300 miles distant. The two rivers Lomame and Lufira come from the same quarter. The only point that remains doubtful is the distance of their fountain-heads, and this I am very anxious to ascertain. I send astronomical observations and a sketch map to Sir Thomas Maclear by a native. The map is very imperfect from want of convenience for tracing, and no position is to be considered settled or published until it is circulated at the observatory. There is a good deal of risk in so doing, but not so much danger as if I entrusted it to my friend, the governor. A former sketch map, a multitude of astronomical observations, and nearly all my letters, have disappeared here; but it is better that they run the risk in the hand of a native than go with one over waters innumerable. The fear of losing my journal altogether led me to entrust it to Mr. Stanley to be kept by my daughter till I return, and I hope it has arrived safely. I am waiting here only till my fifty men arrive.

In conclusion, let me beg your Lordship to offer my very warmest thanks to the Council and Fellows of the Royal Geographical Society, and to all who kindly contributed in any way towards securing my safety. I really feel that no one in this world ought to be more deeply grateful than your obedient servant,

DAVID LIVINGSTONE.

The following letter to Sir Bartle Frere bears the same date as this last despatch :—

UNYANYEMBE, July 1st, 1872.

MY DEAR SIR BARTLE,—I embrace the opportunity of a native going to the coast to send a sketch-map and a number of astronomical observations towards the Cape Observatory ; copies of the same were sent long ago (1869), but disappeared at this place of the " longnebbed " name, and almost everything else sent subsequently vanished in the same way. I am now between two fires or dangers ; for if I take up my journal, map, and observations with me in my concluding trip I am afraid that in crossing rivers and lakes they would be injured or lost. There is a danger, too, of losing them between this and the coast; but the last is the homeward route. I entrusted my journal to Mr. Stanley for like reasons; and now I have but a short trip in prospect to make a feasible finish-up of my work. It is to go round south about all the sources, while actually shaping my course towards the ancient fountains. I perpetrated a heavy joke at the geographers by offering a prize for the best explanation of the structure and economy of the watershed, in correlation with the great lakes and lacustrine rivers, in producing the phenomena of the Nile; and now they will turn the laugh against me if I have to put in fountains which have no existence. The rivers that rise near the west end of the watershed I know, and they give me good hopes that the reports I have heard so often are true. I have a copy of Ptolemy's map with me, copied by a young lady at Bombay. It does not contain the fountains referred to, but it contains the *Montes Lunæ*, and as I found the springs of the Nile rising at the base of certain hills on the watershed in Ptolemy's latitude, I am bracing myself up to call every one who won't believe in his *Lunæ Montes*, a Philistine. After Katanga copper mines, which are eight days north of the fountains, I go ten days north-east to extensive underground excavations, used as places of retreat and safety. One I came near, but was refused an entrance. It was sufficient to receive the inhabitants of a large district with all their gear. A burrowing race seems to have inhabited Africa at a very remote period. Big feet are the only sculpture I have seen, and they are like the footprints of Adam on the mountain in Ceylon. Returning to Katanga, I propose to go twelve

days north-northwest to the head of Lake Lincoln, and
then turn back along Lake Kamalondo homeward.   The
Banians and their agents have hindered us greatly by
palming off their slaves on Dr. Kirk and me as free men.
If I can but make this short trip successfully, I shall frus-
trate their design of baffling all my progress.   I complained
to Kirk against them, and he, unfortunately, took it as a
covert attack on himself, which was never my intention,
and makes me sorry.   I think that the delinquents should
be punished.   In fear of a third batch of slaves being imposed on us, I desired Stanley, if he met any such, to turn
them back, no matter how much he had expended on them.
This led to the resignation of the naval officers in charge.
I had not the remotest suspicion that a Search Expedition
was coming, and am very much grieved to think that I
may appear ungrateful.   On the contrary, I feel extremely
thankful, and from the bottom of my heart thank you and
all concerned for your very great kindness and generosity.
I wish they had thought of Lake Victoria when not needed
here.

By an original and perhaps absurd plan, I tried to get
a longitude for the great central line of drainage out of a
dead chronometer.   I have submitted it to Sir Thomas
Maclear.   He is used to strange things.   Ladies have come
asking to have their futures told them by the stars.   My
horoscope tells me that in latitude 49 deg. south the Lualaba runs between 26 and 27 deg. east.  Never mind about
the truth of it; it makes this great river less likely to be
the Congo.   Surely I may joke about it when others get
14

angry when they talk about Inner Africa, which they never saw. In a speech of yours reported in an *Overland Mail* that came to hand yesterday, you say, if I read it right, that the government have given £300 to my daughters. I read it over and over again to be sure, for it seemed too good news to be true. If there is no mistake, my blessing upon them. I have only been trying to do my duty like a Briton, and I take it as extremely kind that me and mine have been remembered by Her Majesty's Ministers.

I am distressed at hearing no tidings of Sir Roderick, except that he had been ill. It awakens fears for the dearest friend in life.

With kind saluations to Lady and Miss Frere, I am, affectionately yours,

DAVID LIVINGSTONE.

Next in order follow his letters to Mr. Bennett, of the *Herald*. These contain a vast amount of information concerning Africa, and a luminous exposition of the miseries inflicted by the slave trade. The second letter was only given to the world a few months ago, having been found amongst the doctor's papers after his decease :

SOUTH-EASTERN CENTRAL AFRICA,

February, 1872.

MY DEAR SIR,—I wish to say a little about the slave trade in Eastern Africa. It is not a very inviting subject, and to some I may appear as supposing your readers to be

very much akin to the old lady who relished her paper
for neither births, deaths, nor marriages, but for good racy,
bloody murders.   I am, however, far from fond of the horrible—often wish I could forget the scenes I have seen,
and certainly never try to inflict on others the sorrow
which, being a witness of "man's inhumanity to man,"
has often entailed on myself.

Some of your readers know that about five years ago I
undertook, at the instigation of my very dear old friend, Sir
Roderick Murchison, Bart., the task of examining the
water shed of South Central Africa.   The work had a
charm for my mind, because the dividing line between
North and South was unknown, and a fit object for exploration.   Having a work in hand, I at first recommended
another for the task ; but, on his declining to go without a
handsome salary, and something to fall back on afterwards, I agreed to go myself, and was encouraged by Sir
Roderick saying, in his warm jovial manner, "You will be
the real discoverer of the sources of the Nile,"   I thought
that two years would be sufficient to go from the coast
inland across the head of Lake Nyassa to the watershed,
wherever that might be, and, after examination, try to
begin a benevolent mission with some tribe on the slopes
reaching towards the coast.   Had I known all the time,
toil, hunger, hardships, and worry involved in that precious water-parting, I might have preferred having my
head shaved, and a blister put on it, to grappling with
my good old friend's task.   But, having taken up the
burden, I could not bear to be beaten by it.   I shall tell

you a little about the progress made by-and-by. At present, let me give you a glimpse of the slave trade with which the search and discovery of most of the Nile fountains has brought me face to face. The whole traffic, whether on land or ocean, is a gross outrage on the common law of mankind. It is carried on from age to age, and, in addition to the untold evil it inflicts, it presents almost insurmountable obstacles to intercourse between the different portions of the human family. This open sore in the world is partly owing to human cupidity, and partly to ignorance among the more civilized of mankind, of the blight which lights chiefly on the more degraded. Piracy on the high seas was once as common as slave-trading is now. But as it became thoroughly known, the whole civilized world rose against it. In now trying to make the Eastern African slave trade better known to Americans, I indulge the hope that I am aiding on, though in a small degree, the good time coming yet, when slavery as well as piracy shall be chased from the world.

Many have but a faint idea of the evils that trading in slaves inflicts on the victims and on the authors of the atrocities. Most people imagine that negroes, after being brutalized by a long course of servitude, with but few of the ameliorating influences that elevate more favoured races, are fair average specimens of the African man.

Our ideas are derived from the slaves of the West Coast, who have for ages been subjected to domestic bondage and all the depressing agencies of a most unhealthy climate. These have told most injuriously on their physical frames, while fraud and trade rum have ruined their moral natures.

Not to discriminate the difference, is monstrous injustice to the main body of the population, living free in the interior, under their own chiefs and laws, cultivating their own farms, catching the fish of their own rivers, or fighting bravely with the grand old denizens of the forests, which in more recent continents can only be reached in rocky strata or under perennial ice.

Winwoode Reade hit the truth when he said the ancient Egyptian, with his large round black eyes, full luscious lips, and somewhat depressed nose, is far nearer the typical negro than the West Coast African, who has been debased by the unhealthy land he lives in.

Slaves generally—and especially those on the West Coast, at Zanzibar and elsewhere—are extremely ugly.  I have no prejudice against their colour; indeed, any one who lives long among them forgets that they are black, and feels they are just fellow-men.  But the low retreating foreheads, prognathous jaws, lark heels, and other physical peculiarities common among slaves and West Coast negroes, always awaken the same feelings of aversion, as those with which we view specimens of the "Bill Sykes" and " bruiser" class in England.

I would not utter a syllable calculated to press down either class more deeply in the mire in which they are already sunk.  But I wish to point out that these are not typical Africans, any more than typical Englishmen, and that the natives of nearly all the high lands of the interior of the continent are, as a rule, fair average specimens of humanity.

I happened to be present when all the head men of the great chief Insama, who lives west of the south end of Tanganyika, had come together to make peace with certain Arabs who had burned their chief town, and I am certain one could not see more finely-formed intellectual heads in any assembly in London or Paris, and the faces and forms corresponded with the finely-shaped heads.

Insama himself had been a sort of Napoleon for fighting and conquering in his younger days, was exactly like the ancient Assyrians sculptured on the Nineveh marbles, as Nimrod and others; he showed himself to be one of ourselves by habitually indulging in copious potations of beer, called *pombe*, and had become what Nathaniel Hawthorne called "bulbous," below the ribs.

I don't know where the phrase "bloated aristocracy" arose. It must be American, for I have had glimpses of a good many English noblemen, and Insama was the only specimen of a bloated aristocrat on whom I ever set my eyes.

Many of the women were very pretty, and, like all ladies, would have been much prettier if they had only let themselves alone. Fortunately, the dears could not change their charming black eyes, beautiful foreheads, nicely rounded limbs, well-shaped forms, and small hands and feet. But they must adorn themselves; and this they do —oh, the hussies!—by filing their splendid teeth to points like cat's teeth. It was distressing, for it made their

smile, which has generally so much power over us great
he-donkeys, rather crocodile-like. Ornaments are scarce.
What would our ladies do, if they had none, but pout and
lecture us on "women's rights"? But these specimens of
the fair sex make shift by adorning their fine warm brown
skins, tattooing them with various pretty devices without
colours, that, besides purposes of beauty, serve the heraldic
uses of our Highland tartans. They are not black, but of
a light warm brown colour, and so very *sisterish*—if I
may use the new coinage—it feels an injury done to one's
self to see a bit of grass stuck through the cartilage of the
nose, so as to bulge out the *alæ nasi* (wings of the nose
of anatomists). Cazembe's Queen—a Ngombe, Moari by
name—would be esteemed a real beauty either in London,
Paris, or New York; and yet she had a small hole through
the cartilage near the tip of her fine slightly aquiline nose.
But she had only filed one side of the two fronts of her superb snow-white teeth; and then what a laugh she had!
Let those who wish to know, go and see her carried to
her farm in her pony phæton, which is a sort of throne
fastened on two very long poles, and carried by twelve
stalwart citizens. If they take *Punch's* motto for Cazembe,
"Niggers don't require to be shot here," as their own,
they may show themselves to be men; but, whether they
do or not, Cazembe will show himself a man of sterling
good sense.

Now these people, so like ourselves externally, have
genuine human souls. Rua, a very large section of country north and west of Cazembe's, but still in the same

inland region, is peopled by men very like those of Insama and Cazembe.

An Arab, Said Bin Habib, went to trade in Rua two years ago, and, as the Arabs usually do where the natives have no guns, Said Bin Habib's elder brother carried matters with a high hand. The Rua men observed that the elder brother slept in a white tent, and, pitching their spears into it by night, killed him. As Moslems never forgive blood, the younger brother forthwith ran amuck at all indiscriminately, in a large district.

Let it not be supposed that any of these people are like the American Indians—insatiable, bloodthirsty savages, who will not be reclaimed or enter into terms of lasting friendship with fair-dealing strangers.

Had the actual murderers been demanded, and a little time been granted, I feel morally certain, from many other instances among tribes who, like the Ba Rue, have not been spoiled by Arab traders, they would have all been given up. The chiefs of the country would, first of all, have specified the crime of which the elder brother was guilty, and who had been led to avenge it. It is very likely that they would stipulate that no other should be punished but the actual perpetrator. Domestic slaves, acting under his orders, would be considered free from blame. I know of nothing that distinguishes the uncontaminated Africans from other degraded peoples more than their entire reasonableness and good sense. It is different after they have had wives, children, and relatives kidnapped; but that is more than human nature, civilized or savage, can bear.

In the case in question, indiscriminate slaughter, capture, and plunder took place. A very large number of very fine young men were captured and secured in chains and wooden yokes. I came near the party of Said Bin Habib close to a point where a huge rent in the mountains of Rua allows the escape of the great River Lualaba out of Lake Moero. And here I had for the first time an opportunity of observing the difference between slaves and freemen made captives. When fairly across Lualaba, Said thought his captives safe, and got rid of the trouble of attending to and watching the chained gangs by taking off both chains and yokes. All declared their joy and perfect willingness to follow Said to the end of the world or elsewhere, but next morning twenty-two made clear off to the mountains. Many more, on seeing the broad Lualaba roll between them and the homes of their infancy, lost all heart, and in three days eight of them died. They had no complaint but pain in the heart, and they pointed out its seat correctly, though many believe that the heart is situated underneath the top of the sternum or breastbone. This to me was the most startling death I ever saw. They evidently died of broken-heartedness, and the Arabs wondered, "seeing they had plenty to eat." I saw others perish, particularly a very fine boy of ten or twelve years of age. When asked where he felt ill, he put his hand correctly and exactly over the heart. He was kindly carried, and as he breathed out his soul was laid gently on the side of the path. The captors were not unusually cruel. They were callous—slaving had hardened their hearts.

When Said, who was an old friend of mine, crossed the Lualaba, he heard that I was in a village where a company of slave traders had been furiously assaulted for three days by justly incensed Mabemba. I would not fight, nor allow my people to fire if I saw them, because the Mabemba had been especially kind to me. Said sent a party of his own people to invite me to leave the village by night, and come to him. He showed himself the opposite of hard-hearted; but slaving "hardens all within, and petrifies the feelings." It is bad for the victims, and ill for the victimizers.

I once saw a party of twelve who had been slaves in their own country—Lunda or Londa, of which Cazembe is chief or general. They were loaded with large, heavy wooden yokes, which are forked trees about three inches in diameter and seven or eight feet long. The neck is inserted in the fork, and an iron bar driven in across from one end of the fork to the other, and riveted; the other end is tied at night to a tree, or to the ceiling of a hut and the neck being firm in the fork, the slave is held off from unloosing it. It is excessively troublesome to the wearer, and when marching two yokes are tied together by their free ends, and loads put on the slaves' heads besides. Women, having in addition to the yoke and load a child on the back, have said to me on passing, " They are killing me; if they would take off the yoke I could manage the load and child, but I shall die with three loads." One who spoke thus did die, and the poor little girl, her child, perished of starvation. I interceded for some; but, when unyoked, off they bounded into the long grass, and I was gently blamed for not caring to preserve the owner's property. After a day's march under a broiling vertical sun, with yokes and heavy loads, the strongest are exhausted. The party of twelve above mentioned were sitting singing and laughing. "Hallo!" said I, "these fellows take to it kindly; this must be the class for whom philosophers say slavery is the natural state;" and I went and asked the cause of their mirth. I had to ask the aid of their owner as to the meaning of the word *rukha*, which usually means to fly or to leap. They were using it to express the idea of haunting, as a ghost, and inflicting disease and death; and the song was: "Yes, we are going away to Manga (abroad, or white man's land) with yokes on our necks; but we shall have no yokes in death, and we shall return to haunt and kill you." The chorus then struck in with the name of the man who had sold each of them, and then followed the general laugh, in which at first I saw no bitterness. Perembe, an old man at least 104 years, had been one of the sellers. In accordance with African belief, they have no doubt of being soon able, by ghost power, to kill even him. Their refrain might be rendered,

> Oh, oh, oh!
> Bird of freedom, oh!
> You sold me, oh, oh, oh!
> I shall haunt you, oh, oh, oh!

The laughter told not of mirth, but of the tears of such as

were oppressed, and they had no comforter.  " He that is higher than the highest regardeth."

About north-east of Rua we have a very large country, called Manyuema, but by the Arabs it is shortened into Manyema.  It is but recently known.  The reputation which the Manyuema enjoyed of being cannibals, prevented the half-caste Arab traders from venturing among them.

The circumstantial details of the practices of the men-eaters given by neighbouring tribes were confirmed by two Arabs, who two years ago went as far as Bambarre, and secured the protection and friendship of Moenekuss —lord of the light-gray parrot with scarlet tail—who was a very superior man.

The minute details of cannibal orgies given by the Arabs' attendants erred through sheer excess of the shocking. Had I believed a tenth part of what I was told I might never have ventured into Manyuema ; but, fortunately, my mother never frightened me with " Bogie" and stuff of that sort, and I am not liable to fits of bogiephobia, in which disease the poor patient believes everything awful if only it is attributed to the owner of a black skin.  I have heard that the complaint was epidemic lately in Jamaica, and the planters' mothers have much to answer for.  I hope that the disease may never spread in the United States.  The people there are believed to be inoculated with common sense.

But why go among the cannibals at all ?  Was it not like joining the Alpine Club in order to be lauded if you don't break your neck where your neck ought to be broken ?  This makes me turn back to the watershed, as I promised.

It is a broad belt of tree-covered upland, some 700 miles in length from west to east. The general altitude is between 4,000 and 5,000 feet above the sea, and mountains stand on it at various points, which are between 6,000 and 7,000 feet above the ocean level. On this watershed springs arise which are well nigh innumerable—that is, it would take half a man's lifetime to count them. These springs join each other and form brooks, which again converge and become rivers, or say streams, of twenty, forty, or eighty yards, that never dry.  All flow towards the centre of an immense valley, which I believe to be the Valley of the Nile.

In this trough we have at first three large rivers. Then all unite into one enormous lacustrine river, the central line of drainage, which I name Webb's Lualaba. In this great valley there are five great lakes.  One near the upper end is called Lake Bemba, or, more properly, Bangweolo, but it is not a source of the Nile, for no large river begins in a lake.  It is supplied by a river called Chambezi, and several others, which may be considered sources; and out of it flows the large river Luapula, which enters Lake Moero and comes out as the great lake river Lualaba to form Lake Kamolondo. West of Kamolondo, but still in the great valley, lies Lake Lincoln, which I named as my little tribute of love to  the great and good man America enjoyed for some time and lost.

One of the three great rivers I mentioned—Bartle Frere's, or Lufira—falls into Kamolondo, and Lake Lincoln becomes a lacustrine river, and it, too, joins the central line of drainage, but lower down, and all three united form the fifth lake, which the slaves sent to me instead of men forced me, to my great grief, to leave as the "unknown lake." By my reckoning—the chronometers being all dead—it is five degrees of longitude west of Speke's position of Ujiji; this makes it probable that the great lacustrine river in the valley is the western branch—or Petherick's Nile—the Bahar Ghazal, and not the eastern branch, which Speke, Grant, and Baker believed to be the river of Egypt. If correct, this would make it the Nile only after all the Bahar Ghazal enters the eastern arm.

But though I found the watershed between 10 deg. and 12 deg. south—that is, a long way further up the valley than any one had dreamed—and saw the streams of some 600 miles of it converging into the centre of the great valley, no one knew where it went after that departure out of Lake Moero. Some conjectured that it went into Tanganyika, but I saw that to do so it must run up hill. Others imagined that it might flow into the Atlantic. It was to find out where it actually did go that took me into Manyuema. I could get no information from traders outside, and no light could be obtained from the Manyuema within—they never travel, and it was so of old. They consist of petty headmanships, and each brings his grievance from some old feud, which is worse than our old Highland ancestors. Every head man of a hamlet

would like to see every other ruling blockhead slain. .But
all were kii : to strangers; and, though terrible fellows
among themselves, with their large spears and huge
wooden shields, they were never known to injure foreigners,
till slavers tried the effects of gunshot upon them and
captured their women and children.

As I could get no geographical information from them,
I had to feel my way, and grope in the interminable forests
and prairies, and three times took the wrong direction,
going northerly, not knowing that the great river makes
immense sweeps to the west and south-west.    It seemed
as if I were running my head against a stone wall.    It
might after all turn out to be the Congo; and who would
risk being eaten and converted into black man for it ?    I
had serious doubts, but stuck to it like a Briton; and at
last found that the mighty river left its westing and flowed
right away to the north.    The two great western drains,
the Lufira and Lomame, running north-east before joining
the central or main stream—Webb's Lualaba—told that
the western side of the great valley was high, like the
eastern ; and as this main is reported to go into large
reedy lakes, it can scarcely be aught else but the western
arm of the Nile. But, besides all this—in which it is quite
possible I may be mistaken—we have two fountains on
probably the seventh hundred mile of the watershed,
giving rise to two rivers—the Liambai, or Upper Zambezi,
and the Kafue, which flow into Inner Ethiopia ; and two
fountains are reported to rise in the same quarter, forming
Lufira and Lomame, which flow, as we have seen to the

north.  These four full-grown gushing fountains, rising so near each other, and giving origin to four large rivers, answer, in a certain degree, to the description given of the unfathomable fountains of the Nile, by the secretary of Minerva, in the city of Sais in Egypt, to the father of all travellers, Herodotus.  But I have to confess that it is a little presumptuous in me to put this forward in Central Africa, and without a single book of reference, on the dim recollection of reading the ancient historian in boyhood.  The waters are said to well up from an unfathomable depth, and then part, half north to Egypt and half south to-Inner Ethiopia.  Now I have heard of the fountains afore-mentioned so often I cannot doubt their existence, and I wish to clear up the point in my concluding trip. I am not to be considered as speaking without hesitation, but prepared, if I see reason, to confess myself wrong.  No one would like to be considered a disciple of the testy old would-be geographer, who wrote "Inner Africa Laid Open," and swore to his fancies till he became blue in the face.

The work would all have been finished long ago had the matter of supplies of men and goods not been entrusted by mistake to Banians and their slaves, whose efforts were all faithfully directed towards my failure.

These Banians are protected English subjects, and by their money, their muskets, their ammunition, the East African Moslem slave trade is mainly carried on.  The cunning East Indian secure most of the profits of the

slave trade, and adroitly let the odium rest on their Arab
agents.

The Banians will not harm a flea or a mosquito, but my
progress in geography has led me to the discovery that they
are by far the worst cannibals in all Africa. They compass, by means of Arab agents, the destruction of more
human lives for gain in one year than the Manyuema do
for their flesh-pots in ten.

The matter of supplies and men was unwittingly committed to these, our Indian fellow-subjects, who hate to
see me in their slave market, and dread my disclosures on
the infamous part they play. The slaves were all imbued
with the idea that they were not to follow but force me
back; and after rioting on my goods for sixteen months
on the way, instead of three, the whole remaining stock
was sold off for slaves and ivory.

Some of the slaves who came to Manyuema so baffled
and worried me, that I had to return between 500 and
600 miles.

The only [help I have received, except half a supply
which I despatched from Zanzibar in 1866, has been from
Mr. Stanley, your travelling correspondent, and certain remains of stores which I seized from the slaves sent from
Zanzibar seventeen months ago, and I had to come back
300 miles to effect the seizure.

I wait here—Unyanyembe—only till Mr. Stanley can
send me fifty free men from the coast, and then I proceed
to finish up the geographical part of my mission.

I come back to the slavery question, and if I am per-
15

mitted in any way to promote its suppression, I shall not grudge the toil and time I have spent. It would be better to lessen human woe than discover the sources of the Nile.

When parties leave Ujiji to go westwards into Manyuema, the question asked is not what goods they have, but how many guns and kegs of gunpowder. If they have 200 or 300 muskets, and ammunition in proportion, they think success is certain.

No traders having ever before entered Manyuema, the value of ivory was quite unknown. Indeed, the tusks were left in the forests, with the other bones, where the animals had been slain; many were rotten, others were gnawed by a rodent animal to sharpen his teeth, as London rats do on leaden pipes.

If civilly treated, the people went into the forests to spots where they knew elephants had been killed either by traps or spears, and brought the tusks for a few copper bracelets. I have seen parties return with so much ivory that they carried it by three relays of hundreds of slaves. But even this did not satisfy human greed.

The Manyuema were found to be terrified by the report of guns; some, I know, believed them to be supernatural, for when the effect of a musket ball was shown on a goat, they looked up to the clouds, and offered to bring ivory to buy the charm by which the lightning was drawn down. When a village was assaulted, the men fled in terror, and the women and children were captured.

Many of the Manyuema women, especially far down

the Lualaba, are very light coloured and lovely. It was common to hear the Zanzibar slaves—whose faces resemble the features of London door-knockers, which some atrocious ironfounder thought were like those of lions—say to each other, "Oh, if we had Manyuema wives, what pretty children we should get!"

Manyuema men and women were all vastly superior to the slaves, who evidently felt the inferiority they had acquired by wallowing in the mire of bondage. Many of the men were tall, strapping fellows, with but little of what we think distinctive of the negro about them. If one relied on the teachings of phrenology, the Manyuema men would take a high place in the human family. They felt their superiority, and often said truly, "Were it not for fire-arms, not one of the strangers would ever leave our country."

If a comparison were instituted, and Manyuema, taken at random, placed opposite, say, the members of the Anthropological Society of London, clad like them in kilts of grass cloth, I should like to take my place alongside the Manyuema, on the principle of preferring the company of my betters; the philosophers would look woefully scraggy. But though the "inferior race," as we compassionately call them, have finely-formed heads, and often handsome features, they are undoubtedly cannibals. It was more difficult to ascertain this than may be imagined. Some think that they can detect the gnawings of our cannibal ancestry on fossil bones, though the canine teeth of dogs are pretty much like the human.

For many a month all the evidence I could collect amounted only to what would lead a Scotch jury to give a verdict of "not proven." This arose partly from the fellows being fond of a joke, and they like to horrify any one who seemed credulous. They led one of my people, who believed all they said, to see the skull of a recent human victim, and he invited me in triumph. I found it to be the skull of a gorilla—here called a Soko—and for the first time I became aware of the existence of the animal there.

The country abounds in food of all kind, and the rich soil raises everything planted in great luxuriance. A friend of mine tried rice, and in between three and four months it yielded one hundred and twenty fold; three measures of seed yielded three hundred and sixty measures. Maize is so abundant that I have seen forty-five loads, each about sixty pounds, given for a single goat. The "maize-dura"—or *holcus sorghum Tennisetum cassava*—sweet potatoes, and yams, furnished in no stinted measure the farinaceous ingredients of diet; the palm oil, the ground nuts, and the forest tree afford the fatty materials of food; bananas and plantains, in great profusion, and the sugar-cane yields saccharine; the palm toddy, beer of bananas, tobacco and bange, *canabis sativa*, form the luxuries of life; and the villages swarm with goats, sheep, dogs, pigs, and fowls; while the elephants, buffaloes, zebras, and sokos, or gorillas, yield to the expert hunter plenty of nitrogenous ingredients of human food. It was puzzling to see why they should be cannibals.

New Zealanders, we were told, were cannibals because they had killed all their gigantic birds (moa, &c.), and they were converted from the man-eating persuasion by the introduction of pigs. But the Manyuema have plenty of pigs and other domestic animals, and yet they are cannibals. Into the reasons of their cannibalism I do not enter. They say that human flesh is not equal to that of goats or pigs; it is saltish, and makes them dream of the dead. Why fine-looking men like them should be so low in the moral scale can only be attributed to the non-introduction of that religion which makes those distinctions among men which phrenology and other ologies cannot explain.

The religion of Christ is unquestionably the best for man. I refer to it not as the Protestant, the Catholic, the Greek, or any order, but to the comprehensive faith which has spread more widely over the world than most people imagine, and whose votaries, of whatever name, are better men than any outside the pale. We have, no doubt, grievous faults, but these, as in Paris, are owing to the want of religion.

Christians generally are better than the heathens, but often don't know it, and they are all immeasurably better than they believe each other to be.

The Manyuema women, especially far down the Lualaba, are very pretty and very industrious. The market is with them a great institution, and they work hard and carry far, in order to have something to sell.

Markets are established about ten or fifteen miles apart. There those who raise cassava, maize, grain, and sweet

potatoes, exchange them for oil, salt, pepper, fish, and other
relishes; fowls, also pigs, goats, grass cloth, mats, and other
articles change hands.

All are dressed in their best—gaudy-coloured, many-
folded kilts, that reach from the waist to the knee.
When 2,000 or 3,000 are together they enforce justice,
though chiefly women, and they are so eager traders, that
they set off in companies by night, and begin to run as
soon as they come within the hum arising from hundreds
of voices. To haggle, and joke, and laugh, and cheat,
seems to be the dearest enjoyment of their life. They
confer great benefits upon each other.

The Bayenza women are expert divers for oysters, and
they barter them and fish for farinaceous food with the
women on the east of the Lualaba, who prefer cultivating
'he soil to fishing. The Manyuema have always told us
that women going to market were never molested. When
the men of two districts are engaged in actual hostilities,
the women passed through from one market to another un-
harmed; to take their goods, even in war, was a thing
not to be done. But at these market-women the half-
castes directed their guns. Two cases that came under my
own observation were so sickening, that I cannot allow
the mind to dwell upon or write about them. Many of
both sexes were killed, but the women and children chiefly
were made captives. No matter how much ivory they
obtained, these " Nigger Moslems " must have slaves, and
they assaulted the markets and villages, and made captives chiefly, as it appeared to me, because, as the men ran

off at the report of guns, they could do it without danger.
I had no idea before how bloodthirsty men can be when
they can pour out the blood of fellow-men in safety. And
all this carnage is going on in Manyuema at the very time
I write. It is the Banians, our protected Indian fellow-
subjects, that indirectly do it all. We have conceded to
the Sultan of Zanzibar the right, which is not ours to
give, of a certain amount of slave trading, and that amount
has been from 12,000 to 20,000 a year. As we have seen,
these are not traded for, but murdered for. They are not
slaves, but free people made captive. A Sultan with a
sense of justice would, instead of taking head-money, declare they were all free as soon as they touched his territory. But the Banians have the custom-house and all the
Sultan's revenue entirely in their hands. He cannot
trust his Mahometan subjects, even of the better class,
to farm his income, because, as they themselves say, he
would get nothing in return but a crop of lies. The Banians naturally work the custom-house so as to screen their
own slaving agents ; and so long as they have the power
to promote it, their atrocious system of slaving will never
cease. For the sake of lawful commerce, it would be poli-
tic to insist that the Sultan's revenue by the custom-house
should be placed in the hands of an English or American
merchant of known reputation and uprightness. By this
arrangement the Sultan would be largely benefited, legal
commerce would be exalted to a position it has never held
since Banians and Moslems emigrated into Eastern Africa,

and Christianity, to which the slave trade is an insurmountable barrier, would find an open door.

DAVID LIVINGSTONE.

James Gordon Bennett, Esq.

The other letter was published in the English papers, on the 11th of April, 1874, with the following prefatory note :—

"Among Dr. Livingstone's papers received at the Foreign Office was found a letter addressed to Mr. James Gordon Bennett, the proprietor of the New York *Herald*. Lord Tenderden has forwarded the letter to the London office of the New York *Herald*, and a copy thereof has been courteously sent to us by the London manager."

FROM UNYANYEMBE, South-eastern Africa,

April 9th, 1872.

JAMES GORDON BENNETT, Esq.:—

MY DEAR SIR,—When endeavouring to give you some idea of the slave trade, and its attendant evils in this country, it was necessary to keep far within the truth in order not to be thought guilty of exaggeration. But in sober seriousness the subject does not admit of being overdrawn. To exaggerate its enormities is a simple impossibility, and the accounts given by Sir S. Baker of the atrocious proceedings of the White Nile slave traders tally exactly with my own observations of the traffic in the hands of the Arabs and half-caste Portuguese further south. The sights I have seen, though common incidents of the so-called trade, are so terribly nauseous that I always strive to drive them from memory; and in cases of other disagreeable recollections I can in time succeed in consigning them to oblivion. These slaving scenes, however, come back unbidden and unwelcome, and sometimes make me start up at dead of the night horrified by their vividness. To some this may appear weak and unphilosophical, since it is alleged that the whole human family has passed through slavery as one of the stages of development from the lowest state of bestiality, cannibalism, stone, bronze, iron ages. Idolatry and slavery, it is said, are portions of the ascending education of mankind. The propagators of these views have many interesting facts in their favour, and every educated man receives new facts gladly, though he may not be able to explain them or reconcile them to other facts previously known. He hopes that they may yet be proved to be portions of light from above. One must admire the industry of many ardent searchers after scientific truth—men really noble in their life-long aims—following truth wherever that may lead; and it must be conceded that real investigators are by no means bigoted. If our stupid human race still needs the outrageous schooling of slavery and the slave trade, it is in a bad way still, and one might almost vote for allowing it to die out. It may have been want of charity on my part, but I was so frequently asked when in England, " Would these Africans work for one ?" "Yes, if you could pay them." This answer produced such a palpable lengthening of visage that I suspected my questioners had been

speculating on getting them to work for nothing—in fact,
be slave-owners. I fear that a portion at least of the
sympathy in England for what simple folk called the
"Southern cause" was a lurking liking to be slave-owners
themselves. One Englishman at least tried to put his
theory of getting the inferior race to work for nothing
into practice. He was brother to a member of Parliament
for a large and rich constituency, and when his mother
died she left him £2,000. With this he bought a waggon
and oxen at the Cape of Good Hope, and an outfit composed chiefly of *paper mâché* snuff boxes, each of which
had a looking-glass outside and another inside the lid;
these, he concluded, were the "sinews of war." He made
his way to my mission station, more than 1,000 miles inland, and then he found that his snuff boxes would not
even buy food. On asking the reason for investing in that
trash, he replied, that in reading a book of travels he saw
that the natives were fond of peering into looking-glasses
and liked snuff, and he thought that he might obtain ivory
in abundance for these luxuries. I gathered from his
conversation that he had even speculated on being made
a chief. He said that he knew a young man who had so
speculated, and I took it to be himself. We supported him
for about a couple of months, but our stores were fast
drawing to a close. We were then recently married, and
the young housekeeper could not bear to appear inhospitable to a fellow-countryman. I relieved her by feeling an
inward call to visit another tribe. "Oh!" said our depend-
ant, "I shall go too." "You had better not," was the reply,

and no reason assigned. He civilly left some scores of his
snuff boxes, but I could never use them either. He frequently reiterated, "People think these blacks stupid and
ignorant, but, by George, they would sell any Englishman." We surely have but few men of such a silly type
as this.

I may now give an idea of the state of supreme bliss for
the attainment of which all the atrocities of the so-called
Arabs are committed in Central Africa. In conversing
with a half-caste Arab prince he advanced the opinion,
which I believe is general among them, that all women
were utterly and irretrievably bad. I admitted that some
were no better than they should be, but the majority were
unmistakably good and trustworthy. He insisted that the
reason why we English allowed our wives so much liberty,
was because we did not know them so well as Arabs did.
"No, no," he added, "No woman can be good. No Arab
woman, no English woman can be good. All must be bad."
And then he praised his own and countrymen's wisdom
and cunning in keeping their wives from seeing other men.
A rough joke as to making themselves turnkeys, or, like
the inferior animals, bulls over herds, turned the edge of
his invectives, and he ended by an invitation to his harem,
to show that he could be as liberal as the English. Captain
S., of Her Majesty's corvette——, accepted the invitation
also, to be made everlasting friends by eating bread with
the prince's imprisoned wives. The prince's mother, a
stout lady of about forty-five, came first into the room
where we sat with her son. When young she must have

been very pretty, and she still retained many of her former good looks. She shook hands, inquired for our welfare, and to please us, sat on a chair, though it would have been more agreeable for her to squat on a mat. She then asked the captain if he knew AdmiralWyvil who formerly, as commodore, commanded the Cape station. It turned out that many years before, an English ship was wrecked at the island on which she lived, and this good lady had received all the lady passengers into her house and lodged them courteously. The admiral had called to thank her, and gave her a written testimonial acknowledging her kindness. She now wished to write to him for old acquaintance sake, and the captain promised to convey the letter.

She did not seem to confirm her son's low opinion of women. A red cloth screen was lifted from a door in front of where we sat, and the prince's chief wife entered, in gorgeous apparel. She came forward with a pretty jaunty step, and with a pleasant smile held out a neat little sweet-cake, off which we each broke a morsel and ate it. She had a fine, frank address, and talked and looked just as a fair English lady does who wishes her husband's friends to feel themselves perfectly at home. Her large, beautiful, jet-black eyes riveted the attention for some time before we could notice the adornments, on which great care had evidently been bestowed. Her head was crowned with a tall scarlet hat of nearly the same shape as that of the Jewish high priest or that of some of the lower ranks of Catholic clergymen. A tight-fitting red jacket, profusely

ny of her for-
d for our wel-
it would have
int. She then
who formerly,
n. It turned
p was wrecked
good lady had
use and lodged
l to thank her,
owledging her
him for old ac-
to convey the

low opinion of
a door in front
wife entered, in
a pretty jaunty
eat little sweet-
d ate it. She
oked just as a
sband's friends
large, beautiful,
me time before
great care had
rowned with a
as that of the
lower ranks of
cket, profusely

docked with gold lace, reached to the waist, and allowed
about a finger's breadth of the skin to appear between it
and the upper edge of the skirt, which was of white Indian
muslin, dotted over with tamborine spots of crimson silk.
The drawers came nearly to the ankles, on which were
thick silver bangles, and the feet were shod with greenish
yellow slippers, turned up at the toes and roomy enough
to make it probable she had neither corns nor bunions.
Around her neck were many gold and silver chains, and
she had earrings, not only in the lobes of the ears but
others in holes made all round the rims. Gold and silver
bracelets of pretty Indian workmanship decked the arms,
and rings of the same material, set with precious stones,
graced every finger and each thumb. A lady alone could
describe the rich and rare attire; so I leave it. The only
flaw in the get-up was short hair. It is so kept for the
convenience of drying soon after the bath. To our
Northern eyes it had a tinge too much of the masculine.

While talking with this, the chief lady of the harem, a
second entered and performed the ceremony of breaking
bread too. She was quite as gayly dressed, about eighteen
years of age, of perfect form and taller than the chief lady.
Her short hair was oiled and smoothed down and a little
curl cultivated in front of each ear. This was pleasantly
feminine. She spoke little, but her really resplendent eyes
did all save talk. They were of a brown shade and
lustrous. Like the "een of Jeanie Deans, filled wi' tears,
they glanced like lamour beads." ("Lamour," Scotice for
amber.) The lectures of Mr. Hancock, at Charing Cross

Hospital, London, long ago, have made me look critically, on eyes ever since.  A third lady entered and broke bread also.  She was plain as compared with her sister houris, but the child of the chief man of those parts. Her complexion was fair brunette.

The prince remarked that he had only three wives, though his rank entitled him to twelve.  The mother of the prince had just before this earnestly begged a gentleman to remonstrate with him because he was ruining himself by devotion to three!  A dark slave woman, dressed like but less gaudily than her superiors, now entered with a tray and tumblers of sweet sherbet.  Having drank thereof, flowers were presented, and then beetle nut for chewing.  The head lady wrapped up enough for a quid in a leaf and handed it to each of us, and to please her we chewed a little.  It is slightly bitter and astringent, and, like the Kola nut of West Africa, was probably introduced as a tonic and preventive of fever.  The lady superior mixed lime with her own and sisters' good large quids.  This made the saliva flow freely, and, it being of a brick-red colour, stained their pretty teeth and lips, and by no means improved their looks.  It was the fashion, and to them nothing uncomely, when they squirted the red saliva quite artistically all over the floor. On asking the reason why the mother took no lime in her quid, and kept her teeth quite white, she replied that the reason was she had been on a pilgrimage to Mecca, and was a Hadjee.  The whole scene of the visit was like a gorgeous picture.  The ladies had tried to please us and

look critically,
red and broke
rith her sister
of those parts.

y three wives,
The mother of
egged a gentle-
le was ruining
slave woman,
superiors, now
sherbet. Hav-
and then beetle
l up enough for
is, and to please
tter and astrin-
frica, was prob-
e of fever. The
nd sisters' good
reely, and, it be-
retty teeth and
s. It was the
ly, when they
l over the floor.
k no lime in her
replied that the
to Mecca, and
visit was like a
o please us and

were thoroughly successful. We were delighted with the sight of the life in a harem; but whether from want of wit or wisdom or something else, I should still vote for the one wife system. Having tried it for some eighteen years, I would not exchange a monogamic harem, with some merry, laughing, noisy children, for any polygamous gathering in Africa or the world.

It scarcely belongs to the picture which I have attempted to draw as favourably as possible in order to show the supreme good for the sake of the possible attainment of which the half-caste Arabs perpetrate all the atrocities of the slave trade; but a short time after this visit the prince fled on board our steamer for protection from creditors. He was misled by one calling himself Colonel Abco, who went about the world saying he was a persecuted Christian.

At a spot some eighty miles south-west of the south end of Tanganyika stands the stockaded village of the chief Chitimbwa. A war had commenced between a party of Arabs, numbering 600 guns, and the chief of the district situated west of Chitimbwa, while I was at the south end of the lake. The Arabs hearing that an Englishman was in the country, naturally inquired where he was, and the natives, fearing that mischief was intended, denied positively that they had ever seen him. They then strongly advised me to take refuge on an uninhabited island; but not explaining their reasons, I am sorry to think that I suspected them of a design to make me a prisoner, which they could easily have done by removing the canoes—the island being a mile from the land. They afterwards told me how nicely they had cheated the Arabs and saved me from harm.

The end of the lake is a deep cup-shaped cavity with sides running sheer down in some parts, 2,000 feet into the water. The rocks of red clay schist, crop out among the sylvan vegetation, and here and there pretty cascades leap down the precipices, forming a landscape of surpassing beauty. Herds of elephants, buffaloes, and antelopes enliven the scene, and, with the stockaded villages embowered in palms along the shores of the peaceful water, realize the idea of Xenophon's Paradise. When about to leave the village of Mbette or Pambette, down there, and climb up the steep path by which we had descended, the wife of the chief came forward and said to her husband and the crowd looking at us packing up our things, "Why do you allow this man to go away? He will certainly fall into the hands of the Mazitu (here called Batuba), and you know it and are silent." On inquiry it appeared certain that these marauders were then actually plundering the villages up above the precipices at the foot of which we sat. We waited six days, and the villagers kept watch on an ant-hill outside the stockade, all the time looking up for the enemy. When we did at last ascend we saw the well-known lines of march of the Mazitu—straight as arrows through the country, without any regard to the native paths, and in the details of their plundering, for in this case there was no bloodshed. We found that the really benevolent lady had possessed accurate information. On going thence round the end of the lake, we came to the village of Karambo, at the confluence of a large river, and the head man refused us a passage across, " Because," said he, " the Arabs have been fighting with the people west of us; and two of their people have since been killed, though only in search of ivory. You wish to go round by the west of the lake, and the people may suppose that you are Arabs, and I dare not allow you to run the risk of being killed by mistake." On seeming to disbelieve, Karambo drew his finger across his throat, and said, "If at any time you discover that I have spoken falsely, I give you leave to cut my throat." That same afternoon two Arab slaves came to the village in search of ivory and confirmed every word Karambo had spoken.

Unable to go north west we turned off to go due south 150 miles or so ; then proceed west till past the disturbed district, and again resume our northing. But on going some sixty miles we heard that the Arab camp was twenty miles further south, and we went to hear the news. The reception was extremely kind, for this party consisted of gentlemen from Zanzibar, and of a very different stamp from the murderers we afterwards saw in Manyuema. They were afraid that the chief with whom they had been fighting might flee southwards, and that in going that way I might fall into his hands. Being now recovered I could readily believe them, and they, being eager ivory traders as readily believed me when I asserted that a continuance of hostilities meant shutting up the ivory market. No one, would like to sell if he stood a chance of being shot. Peace,

16

therefore, was to be made ; but the process of "mixing blood," forming a matrimonial alliance with the chief's daughter, &c., required three and a half months, and during long intervals of that time I remained at Chitimbwa's. The stockade was situated by a rivulet, and had a dense grove of high, damp-loving trees round a spring on one side, and open country, pretty well cultivated, on the other. It was cold, and over 4,700 feet above the sea, with a good deal of forest land and ranges of hills in the distance. The Arabs were on the west side of the stockade, and one of Chitimbwa's wives at once vacated her house on the east side for my convenience. Chitimbwa was an elderly man, with gray hair and beard, and of quiet, self-possessed manners. He had five wives, and my hut being one of the circle which their houses formed, and I often sat reading or writing outside, I had a good opportunity of seeing the domestic life in this Central African harem without appearing to be prying. The chief wife, the mother of Chitimbwa's son and heir, was somewhat aged, but was the matron in authority over the establishment. The rest were young, with fine shapes, pleasant countenances, and nothing of the West Coast African about them. Three of them had each a child, making, with the eldest son, a family of four children to Chitimbwa. The matron seemed to reverence her husband, for when she saw him approaching she invariably went out of the way and knelt down till he passed. It was the time of year for planting and weeding the plantations, and the regular routine work of all the families in the town was nearly as follows :—Between three and four o'clock in the morning, when the howling of the hyenas and growling of the lions or leopards told that they had spent the night fasting, the first human sounds heard were those of the good wives knocking off the red coals from the ends of the sticks in the fire, and raising up a blaze to which young and old crowded for warmth from the cold, which at this time is the most intense of the twenty-four hours. Some Psang smoker lights his pipe, and makes the place ring with his nasty screaming, stridulous coughing. Then the cocks begin to crow (about four A.M.) and the women call to each other to make ready to march. They go off to their gardens in companies, and keep up a brisk, loud conversation, with a view to frighten away any lion or buffalo that may not yet have retired, and for this the human voice is believed to be efficacious. The gardens or plantations, are usually a couple of miles from the village. This is often for the purpose of securing safety for the crops from their own goats or cattle, but more frequently for the sake of the black, loamy soil near the banks of rivulets. This they prefer for maize and dura (*holcus sorghum*), while for a small species of millet, called mileza, they select a patch in the forest which they manure by burning the branches of trees. The distance which the good wives willingly go to get the soil best adapted for different plants makes their arrival just about dawn. Fire has been brought from home, a little pot is set on with beans or pulse, something that requires long simmering—and the whole family begins to work at what seems to give them real pleasure. The husband, who had

marched in front of each little squad with a spear and
little axe over his shoulder, at once begins to cut off all the
sprouts on the stumps left in clearing the ground.  All
bushes also fall to his share, and all the branches of tall
trees too hɪ·d to be cut down are filed round the root, to
be fired when dry.  He must also cut branches to make
a low fence round the plantations, for few wild beasts
like to cross over anything having the appearance of human workmanship.  The wart hog having a great weakness for ground nuts, otherwise called pignuts (*Arachis
hypogæa*), must be circamvented by a series of pitfalls, or
a deep ditch and earthen dyke all round the nut plot.  If
any other animal has made free with the food of the family,
papa carefully examines the trail of the intruder, makes a
deep pitfall in 'it, covers it carefully over, and every day
it is a most interesting matter to see whether the thief has
been taken for the pot.  The mother works away vigorously with her hoe, often adding new patches of virgin
land to that already under cultivation.  The children help
by removing the weeds and grass which she has uprooted
into heaps to be dried and burned.  They seem to know
and watch every plant in the field,    It is all their own ;
no one is stinted as to the land he may cultivate ; the
more they plant the more they have to eat and to spare.
In some parts of Africa the labour falls almost exclusively
on the women, and the males are represented as atrociously
cruel to them.  It was not so here, nor is it so in Central
Africa generally ; indeed, the women have often decidedly
the upper hand.  The clearances by law and custom were

the work of the men; the weeding was the work of the whole family and so was the reaping.

When the grain is dry it is pounded in a large wooden mortar to separate the scales from the seed; a dexterous toss of the hand drives all the chaff to one corner of the vessel. This is lifted out, and then the dust is tossed out by another peculiar up and down half horizontal motion of the vessel—difficult to describe or to do—which leaves the grain quite clean. It is then ground into fine meal by a horizontal motion of the upper millstone, to which the whole weight is applied, and at each stroke the flour is shoved off the farther end of the nether millstone. The flour is finished late in the afternoon, at the time maidens go forth to draw water. The lady poises a huge earthen pot on her head, fills it full at the rivulet, and though containing ten or twelve gallons, balances it on her head, and without lifting up her hand, walks jauntily home. They have meat, but seldom make relishes for the porridge, into which the flower is cooked of the leaves of certain wild and cultivated plants; or they roast some ground nuts, grind them fine and make a curry. They seem to know that only matter such as the nuts contain is requisite to modify their otherwise farinaceous food, and some even grind a handful of castor oil nuts with the grain for the same purpose. The husband having employed himself in the afternoon in making mats for sleeping on, in preparing skins for clothing, or in making new handles for hoes, or cutting out wooden bowls, joins the family in the evening, and all partake abundantly of the chief meal of the day before going off to sleep.  They have considerable skill in agriculture, and great shrewdness in selecting the soils proper for different kinds of produce.  When Bishop Mackenzie witnessed their operations in the field, he said to me, "When I was in England, and spoke in public meetings about our mission, I mentioned that among other things that I mean to teach them agriculture, but I now see that the Africans know a great deal more than I do."  One of his associates, earnestly desiring to benefit the people to whom he was going, took lessons in basket making before he left England, but the specimens of native workmanship he met with everywhere led him to conclude that he had better say nothing about his acquisition.  In fact, he could "not hold a candle to them."

The following is as fair an example of every-day life of the majority of the people in Central Africa as I can give —it as truly represents surface life in an African village as the other case does the surface condition in an Arab harem.  In other parts the people appear to travellers in much worse light.  The tribes lying more towards the east coast, who have been much visited by Arab slavers, are said to be in a state of chronic warfare—the men always ready to rob and plunder, and the women scarcely ever cultivating enough of food for the year.  That is the condition to which all Arab slaving tends.  Captain Speke revealed a state of savageism and brutality in Uganda, of which I have no experience.  The murdering by wholesale of the chief Mteza, or Mtesa, would not be tolerated among the tribes I have visited.  The slaughter of head men's daughters would, elsewhere than in Uganda, insure speedy assassination. I have no reason to suppose that Speke was mistaken in his statement as to the numbers of women led away to execution, though the most intelligent of 200 Biganda Mteza's people now here assert that many were led away to become field labourers, and one seen by Grant with her hoe on her head seems to countenance the idea. But their statements are of small account as compared with those of Speke and Grant, for they now all know that cold-blooded murder like that of Mteza is detested by all civilized tribes, and they naturally wish to smooth the matter over. The remedy open to all other tribes in Central Africa is desertion. The tyrant soon finds himself powerless. His people have quietly removed to other chiefs, and never return. The tribes subjected by the Makololo had hard times of it, but nothing like the butchery of Mteza. A large body went off to the north. Another sent to Zette refused to return, and absent with me to the Shire for medicine, for the chief did the same thing. When the chief died the tribe broke up and scattered. Mteza seems to be an unwhipped fool. We all know rich men who would have been much better fellows if they had ever got bloody noses and sound thrashings at school. The 200 of his people here have been detained many months, and have become thoroughly used to the country, but not one of them wishes to remain. The apparent willingness to be trampled in the dust by Mteza is surprising.

The whole of my experience in Central Africa says that

the negroes, not yet spoiled by contact with the slave trade, are distinguished for friendliness and good sound sense. Some can be guilty of great wickedness, and seem to think little about it; others perform actions as unmistakably good with no great self-complacency; and if one catalogued all the good deeds or all the bad ones he came across he might think the men extremely good or excessively bad, instead of calling them, like ourselves, curious compounds of good and evil. In one point they are remarkable—they are honest. Even among the cannibal Manyuema a slave trader at Bambarre and I had to send our goats and fowls up to the Manyuema village to prevent their being all stolen by my friend's own slaves. Another wide-spread trait of character is a trusting disposition. The central African tribes are the antipodes to some of the North American Indians, and very unlike many of their own countrymen who have come into contact with Mohammedans and Portuguese and Dutch Christians. They at once perceive the superiority of the strangers in power of mischief, and readily listen to and ponder over friendly advice. After the cruel massacre of Nyangue, which I unfortunately witnessed, fourteen chiefs, whose villages had been destroyed, and many of them killed, fled to my house and begged me to make peace for them with the Arabs, and then come over to their side of the river Lualaba, divide their country anew, and point out where each should build a new village and cultivate other plantations. The peace was easily made, for the Arabs had no excuse for their senseless murders, and each blamed the other for the guilt. Both parties pressed me to remain at the peace-making ceremonies, and had I not known the African trusting disposition, might have set down the native appeal to great personal influence. All I had in my favour was common decency and fairness of behaviour, and perhaps a little credit for goodness awarded by the Zanzibar slaves. The Manyuema could easily see that the Arab religion was disjoined from morality. Their immorality in fact has always proved an effectual barrier to the spread of Islam in Eastern Africa.

It is a sad pity that our good "Bishop of Central Africa," albeit ordained in Westminster Abbey, preferred the advice of a colonel in the army to remain at Zanzibar, rather than proceed into his diocese and take advantage of the friendliness of the still unspoiled interior tribes, to spread our faith. The Catholic missionaries lately sent from England to Maryland to convert the negroes might have obtained the advice of half a dozen of army colonels to remain at New York, or even at London. But the answer, if they have any Irish blood in them, might have been, "Take your advice and yourselves off to the battle of Dorking; we will fight our own fight." The Venerable Archbishop of Baltimore told these brethren that they would get "chills and fever," but he did not add, "when you do get the shivers, then take to your heels, my hearties." When any of the missionaries at Zanzibar get "chills and fever," they have a nice pleasure trip in a man-of-war to the Seychelles Islands. The good men deserve it, of course, and no one would grudge to save their precious lives.   But human nature is frail.   Zanzibar is much more unhealthy than the mainland, and the Government, by placing men-of-war at the disposal of these brethren, though meaning to help them in their work, virtually aids them to keep out of it.   Some eight years have rolled on, and good, Christian people have contributed their money annually for Central Africa, and the Central African diocese is occupied by the lord of all evil.   It is with a sore heart I say it, but recent events have shown that those who have so long been playing at being missionaries and peeping across from the sickly island to their diocese in the main land with telescopes might have been turned to far better account.

It may seem hard to say so, but sitting up here in Unyanyembe in weariness waiting for Mr. Stanley to send men from the coast, two full months' march of 500 miles distant, and all Central Africa behind me, the thought will rise up that the Church of England and universities have, in intention at least, provided the Gospel for the perishing population, and why does it not come ?  If I might address those who hold back, I should say : " Come on, brethren ; you have no idea how brave you are till you try.   The real heathen who are waiting for you have many faults, but also much that you can esteem and love."  The Arabs never saw mothers selling their offspring, nor have I, though one authority made a broad statement to that effect, a nice setting to a nice little story about " a mother bear."   He may have seen an infant sold who had the misfortune to cut its upper teeth before the under, because it was called unlucky and likely to bring death into the family; but the general declaration from an isolated fact is like the assertion of the Frenchman who thought the English so partial to suicide in November you might see them swinging on trees along the highway. We have had foundlings among us, but that does not mean that English mothers are no better than she-bears. If you go into other men's labours you need not tell at home who reared the converts you have secured, but you will feel awfully uncomfortable, even in heaven, till you have made abject apologies to your brethren who, like yourselves, are heavenward bound.

Let no one under-estimate the difficulties that must be encountered in beginning a mission in a new country. The belt of forest that lies round the island near the coast of Madagascar involved almost certain death to the brave pioneers who passed through to the highlands in the interior, without knowing that at a certain season it might be traversed in safety. But the London Missionary Society braved it, at a great loss in men and money, and the result is missionary success, which men of minor pluck may well envy. This continent must be civilized from within outwards, the missionaries who will undertake the work must possess a good deal of the Robinson Crusoe spirit. Men have felt perfectly willing to sacrifice everything, even their lives, for the sake of the Gospel, before they left home; but as in one gallant officer's case I witnessed, he tempted to despair on breaking the photograph

of his wife ! or feel it to be an excruciating hardship to be
without sugar for the tea. The boys who, on reading
Captain Mayne Reid's books, would like to be "castaways,"
have the ring of the true missionary metal.

Speke was delighted with the central countries he
passed through as most inviting for Christian missions—
Karagwee, for instance, with the intelligent and friendly
chief Rumanyiki (spelled by him Rumanika) and Buganda
(by the Arabs called Uganda), with a teeming and polite
population under the vain, cruel, but friendly Mtesa. This
chief is the first that the Arabs have attempted to convert in Eastern Africa. Ghamees-bin-Abdullah, a very
good man lately killed here, taught Mtesa to read Suaheli
in Arab characters, and his pupil gave him about 500
young slaves and an enormous amount of ivory. Ghamees
was a Muscat Arab, and, like his class, was brave, honourable and really kind-hearted. The country-born or mainlanders, being mostly of slave mothers, have, in general,
neither honour, honesty, nor zeal. As marauders they are
energetic enough, and, like the interior Dutch boers of
South Africa, very brave, where the natives have no guns.
A few slaves are operated on, taught a few prayers from
the Koran in Arabic, in order to be "clean" as butchers
in slaughtering animals for their masters, and are then
dressed in long calico nightgowns and tight fitting cotton
caps. This is all the conversion that the system requires,
and they become perverse liars and as unmitigated
cowards as their masters. Their dress makes them all
appear like great coarse women in their nightgowns.

When they come near danger the first thought of master and man is who can run fastest. The gowns are all tucked up ready for flight, and, as poor Ghamees-bin-Abdullah found with his eighty armed slaves, not a single bondman stands by his master.

The whole of this upland region, being between 3,500 and 4,000 feet above the sea, is comparatively cold. The minimum temperature here in the dry season (our winter) is from 54 degrees to 62 degrees Fahrenheit, the maximum 74 degrees, but it does not promise entire immunity from fever. Here that takes the place of our colds and consumptions, and is not so fatal if you are not lazy or compelled to lead a sedentary life. The land is undulating, being, at the crests of the Twaveslow Hills, covered with bushes and trees, and showing here and there rounded, outcropping masses of the light gray granite, the general rock of the country. At the bottom of the troughs of the earthen billows, springs are numerous. The grass is short, and cattle thrive on it and are abundant. Grasses, which in the hot lowlands attain a height of five or six feet, here appear only one or two feet high. Wheat and rice are successfully cultivated, and require only about three months to come to maturity. By following the Arab advice as to the proper seasons for cultivation, a missionary could soon render himself independent of foreign supplies. Coffee grows wild in Karagew, and is cultivated by the Manyuema. Sugar cane is cultivated everywhere. When laid up among the cannibals by irritable, eating ulcers on the feet, I had sugar cane pounded in the common

country wooden mortar and the juice wrung out by the
hands.   When boiled thick it served well as sugar ; but I
had no time to correct the latent acidity, and it soon
spoiled.   I had onions and radishes in abundance, though
the country is so hot and low lying.  The Arabs here have
oranges, lemons, guavas, mangoes, pomegranates, pepows,
sweetsops, onions, pumpkins, watermelons, and some begin
to grow the grape-vine.  I believe that all European vegetables would prosper if care were taken to select the proper seasons for sowing, and the seeds were brought in
brown paper parcels hung up in the cabin of the ship and
never exposed to the direct rays of the sun, or soldered in
tins or confined in boxes.  All very clever contrivances
for travellers' convenience ought to be shunned.  In
general they are heavy, burdensome trash, which any one
who has learned to use his eyes and ears finds to be intolerable nuisances.   The only articles essentially necessary
for a missionary of the Robinson Crusoe type that strikes
me at present are a few light tools, a few books, clothes,
soap, and shoes.  I mention soap because I have not met
the plant with the ashes of which my wife made soap in
the South.  Four suits of strong gray tweed served me
comfortably for five years, and might have worn longer,
for I saw Arabs who bought them from my people wearing them long after I had discarded them.  An energetic
man, who liked labour, would soon surround himself with
comforts at a comparatively small expense, and he would
soon find that he had expatriated himself for a noble and
soul-satisfying object.

Having now been some six years out of the world, and most of my friends having apparently determined by their silence to impress me with the truth of the adage, "Out of sight out of mind," the dark scenes of the slave trade had a most distressing and depressing influence. The power of the Prince of Darkness seemed enormous. It was only with a heavy heart I said, "Thy kingdom come!" In one point of view the evils that brood over this beautiful country are insuperable. When I dropped among the Makololo and others in the Central region, I saw a fair prospect of the regeneration of Africa. More could have been done in the Makololo country than was done by St. Patrick in Ireland. But I did not know that I was surrounded by the Portuguese slave trade—a blight like a curse from heaven that proved a barrier to all improvement. Now I am not so hopeful. I don't know how the wrong will become right. But the great and loving Father of all knows, and He will do it according to His infinite wisdom.

A batch of New York *Herald* newspapers of 1871 has lately made the horizon clear up a little. Commercial enterprise, it seems, is daily bringing people geographically remote into close connection. The tendency of heathenism is towards isolation. In the Manyuema country it keeps the inhabitants of one village apart from every other, except as was the case with our remote ancestors, when they went to fight. The head man of a hamlet of half a dozen houses walks unarmed around his plantation, with a long staff, carrying some potent charm on each end, and rejoicing in being called "Mologhwe," chief, or, say, "Free and sovereign citizen," and would be glad to see every other ruling blockhead slain. When we got a guide to conduct us through the dense dark forests that often lie between districts, he and others went on cheerily enough till within a few miles of the next human habitations, and nothing could induce them to go further for fear, they said, of being killed and eaten. Kindly inviting us to lodge at their villages on our return, they departed homewards. Are there not vestiges of similar heathenism that linger in the passport system, in certain tariffs, and even in religious sectarian differences? Crotchety Christians seem not to know that the followers of Jesus, of whatever name, are incomparably superior in morality to Moslems, Budhists, Brahmins or any other pagans. Morbid zeal to appear impartial sometimes leads to the assertion that the morality of the Koran is nearly equal to the morality of the Gospel. It is conceded that at one time Mahomet acted as a reformer in relation to idolatry; but his orders to murder Christians are the "dead flies in the apothecary's ointment," and even the prophet was so ashamed of the immoral injuctions that he put the blame on the Angel Gabriel, and his followers continue to do the same. We are enjoined to be humble, and without doubt there is reason for a sober estimate of ourselves. Yet, look at the Suez Canal, the Pacific Railroad, the railways in India and Western Asia, the Mount Cenis Tunnel, the proposed Euphrates Railway and Canal of Panama; telegraphic lines everywhere, and steamships on every sea,—all the work of Christians, and all combining to make the world one.   The descendants of the Galileans are breaking down national prejudices faster than St. Francis Xavier, or the most devoted professional missionaries.   The influences brought to bear by one nation on another, though sometimes for evil, are mainly for good. The freedom of the slaves of the United States must tell towards the deliverance of 8,000,000 of bondsmen in Brazil, and something must result of good to this trodden-down, scattered, and peeled Africa, so that it shall not always remain the waste place of the world.

I look towards benevolent statesmen and the public press as more likely to stop this East Coast slave trade than any other agency.   Statesmen have for many years appeared to me as missionaries of the first water. Formerly I took them to be what some still consider them, as anxious only for place and power; gentlemen, perhaps, but not over scrupulous as to the means employed to gain their own selfish ends.   I forbear mentioning the names of the living, but circumstances led to a more accurate knowledge of several—the good Lord Palmerston, for instance, who gave me a widely different impression.   For fourteen years he laboured unweariedly at what was really doing good on a large scale—the suppression of the slave trade on the West Coast of Africa.   This climate has deprived me completely of all taste for politics; so I think I can give an unbiased opinion that the great English statesmen, of my time at least, have followed as their chief aim the doing good on a large scale.   Their un-

17

wearied toil, and apparently sincere desire, to do only what was right, inspired me with profound respect, and I shall revere Lords Palmerston, Clarendon, and President Lincoln for their goodness as long as I live. The work of the Joint High Commission shows that America has statesmen of the same noble character. Let our race continue to pursue the wise Christian course now so fairly begun, and let the low cunning, the smartness to hoodwink each other, in which old diplomatists gloried, go the dogs. It is refreshing to hear of the royal honours showered down on Mr. Seward in recognition of his great work in connection with Mr. Lincoln. Dare we call to remembrance that when English statesmen laboured hard for the suppression of the slave trade, on the West Coast of Africa, they were often sorely thwarted by Southern pro-slavery men in possession of your government. The Western slave trade is happily finished, and now that you have got rid of the incubus of slavery, it is confidently hoped that the present holders of office will aid in suppressing the infamous breaches of the common law of mankind that still darken this Eastern Coast. If the Khedive, with his Lieutenant Baker, stops the Nile slave traffic, he will have fairly earned the title of a benefactor of humanity. All I can add in my loneliness is, may Heaven's rich blessing come down on every one—American, English or Turk—who will help to heal the open sore of the world.

This interesting letter, which, as we have stated, was found amongst Livingstone's papers after his death, was not published for two years after it was written. It is, on the whole, the most valuable and instructive of the entire series. The information given of the country, of the habits and disposition of the natives, of the obstacles in the way of civilization in Central Africa, appears in a more graphic and compact form than elsewhere. We may now give the doctor's letters to his brother, Mr. John Livingstone, of Listowel, Ontario. The latter is, as it were, a link connecting and associating Canada with the great African explorer.

It will be seen that these two letters bear dates five years apart.

STEAMSHIP THULE, at Sea, January 12, 1866.

MY DEAR BROTHER,—The last letter I got from you, with the enclosure of money, I forwarded at once to Janet, with a request that she would send a kind answer to you in return. I was unable to write myself at the time, and, though I have been three months at Bombay, I had the same excuse; and only now, when on my way to Zanzibar, have I leisure to give you a "screed," and I fear it may be the last for a good while to come. The vessel in which I sail was one of Sherrard Osborne's late Chinese fleet, and it is now going as a present from the Bombay government to the Sultan of Zanzibar. I am to have the honour of making the formal presentation, and I value it, because it will give me a little lift up in the eyes of the Sultan's people, and probably prevent them from any open opposition to my progress. She is very gorgeously got up. The fleet by the way (with this exception) still lies rotting at Bombay. Our government let themselves in for a very large amount, by placing an embargo on the sale of vessels which might possibly have gone to the Confederates as *Alabamas*. For this an offer of £9,000 was made ; now it went for £3,000, and all the difference comes out of John Bull's pocket. Here where they could not act fairly to the United States they did it even at a great sacrifice.

The Sultan of Zanzibar visited the Governor of Bombay while I was there. He was very gracious, and gave me a firman to all his people, and an order to one of his captains to carry some tame buffaloes across. These are to be used as an experiment with the tsetze, and if they withstand the poison of that pest we shall have done something to open Africa. At present they have no beast of burden in the country, and this is so like the wild ones which live in the very *habitat* of the tsetze that I have good hopes of success.

My party consists of thirteen Sepoys of the old East India Company's Marine Battalion. They have been accustomed to rough it on board ship. (This one is kicking about now in a way that might make " a grumphy grew.") They are likely enough fellows. I have also nine boys who were recaptured, and have been taught trades and other things at a government school near Bombay. They know a little of their native tongues still. These, with two mules and a little dog named Titani, constitute the party. I had many offers of service from Europeans, but have invariably declined them. Unless a man has been tried, he may become a nuisance, and entail the burden on the leader of being " a servant of servants " to his brethren. I proposed to go due west from the river Rovuma or Livuma, then turn north after reaching the middle of the continent. The objects are partly geographical, and partly to open the country to better influences than have prevailed for ages. I anticipate great good from the abolition of slavery in the States. The Spaniards and Portuguese are quaking in their shoes, in expectation that the new-born zeal of the Americans will be hot. My book will not tend to allay the perturbation of the Portuguese. It has been favourably reviewed in the *Athenæum* and *Saturday Review*, so I can go away with a light heart.

A nasty spirit is abroad in England, which may, if unchecked, lead to a war of races. We were very much bamboozled by the Southerners, and our own newspapers. " They were the true gentlemen;" the benevolent harpies who prevented the negro race from utter annihilation; and the contempt they laboured to diffuse has received a great accession in strength by the late Jamaica outburst. That fellow Hobbs must have been steeped full of that nasty race prejudice, and nothing could be more disgusting than his mad ferocity when overcharged with a frenzied " funk." I don't suppose we have another case in history in which a man was hung for giving a fiendish look at the forty-seventh lash. I would have given one at the first. I think it will be found a wise dispensation of Providence that has allotted the elevation of so many freedmen to the Americans. They go at these things with wonderful ardour. The United States Christian Commission and Freedmen's Bureau seem to be admirable institutions, showing true Christian zeal and wisdom, while, unfortunately, the countrymen of Clarkson and Wilberforce are becoming imbued with prejudices and hatred, which found no place in their noble breasts.

A Baron Vander Decken went up the river Juba, which is just on the Equator, a few months ago, in two steamers, built at his own expense. When about three hundred miles from the sea he knocked two holes in the bottom of one—the other he had already lost. Then went ashore with his doctor. The vessel was forthwith attacked by a large body of natives, and several of the baron's people killed. His lieutenant, an officer of the Prussian navy, left at night in a boat with some of the survivors and escaped to Zanzibar. From the way the letter was worded, the lieutenant seems to have "skedaddled," but this is probably owing to his imperfect English. Nothing is known of the baron and doctor, but it looks ill at present, for the natives would scarcely allow him to pass in safety, while going to attack the vessel.

My love to Sarah and all the children. Agnes is in Paris and doing well; Tom at Glasgow College, and Oswell at school; Anna Mary with her aunts at Hamilton.

Affectionately yours,

DAVID LIVINGSTONE.

P.S.—The baron and his doctor were killed by Somaulies, who are bigoted Mahommedans. The servants, who were

Mahommedans, were allowed to escape and came to Zanzibar, where I now am (29th January).  The officer who escaped seems to have acted wisely, and no blame can be fairly attributed.                              D. L.

TORONTO, CANADA, August 19, 1873.

The following is Dr. Livingstone's second letter to his brother, John Livingstone, residing at Listowel, Ontario, Canada.  It bore on the envelope, " This leaves Unyanyembe, March 14, 1872 ":—

UJIJI, Nov. 16, 1871.

MY DEAR BROTHER,—I received your welcome letter in February last, written when the cable news made you put off your suits of mourning.  This was the first intimation I had that a cable had been successfully laid in the deep Atlantic.

Very few letters have reached me for years, in consequence of my friends speculating where I should come out—on the West Coast, down the Nile, or elsewhere.

The watershed is a broad upland between 4,000 and 5,000 feet above the sea and some seventy miles long. The springs of the Nile that rise thereon are almost innumerable.  It would take the best part of a man's lifetime to count them.  One part—sixty-four miles of latitude—gave thirty-two springs from calf to waist deep, or one spring for every two miles.  A birdseye view of them would be like the vegetation of frost upon the window panes.  To ascertain that all of these fountains united with four great rivers in the upper part of the Nile valley was a work of time and much travel.

Many a weary foot I trod ere light dawned on the ancient problem. If I had left at the end of two years, for which my bare expenses was paid, I could have thrown very little more light on the country than the Portuguese, who, in their three slavery visits to Cazambe, asked for ivory and slaves and heard of nothing else. I asked about the waters; questioned and cross-questioned till I was really ashamed, and almost afraid of being set down as afflicted with hydrocephalus.

I went forward, backwards and sideways, feeling my way, and every step of the way I was generally groping in the dark, for who cared where the rivers ran?

Of these four rivers into which the springs of the Nile converge, the central one, called Lualaba, is the largest. It begins as the River Chambezi, which flows into the great Lake Bangweolo. On leaving it its name is changed from Chambezi to Luapula, and that enters Lake Moero. Coming out of it the name Lualaba is assumed, and it flows into a third lake, Kamolondo, which receives one of the four large drains mentioned above. It then flows on and makes two enormous bends to the west, which made me often fear that I was following the Congo instead of the Nile. It is from one to three miles broad, and can never be waded at any part or at any time of the year. Far down the valley it receives another of the four large rivers above mentioned, the Lockie or Lomani, which flows through what I have named Lake Lincoln, and then joins the central Lualaba.

We have, then, only two lines of drainage in the lower part of the great valley—that is, Tanganyika and Albert Lake, which are but one lake-river, or say, if you want to be pedantic, lacustrine river. These two form the eastern line. The Lualaba, which I call Webb's Lualaba, is then the western line, nearly as depicted by Ptolemy in the second century of our era. After the Lomani enters the Lualaba the fourth great lake in the central line of drainage is found; but this I have not yet seen, nor yet the link between the eastern and western mains.

At the top of Ptolemy's Loop the great central line goes down into large, reedy lakes, possibly those reported to Nero's centurion, and these form the western or Petherick's arm, which Speke and Grant and Baker believed to be the river Egypt. Neither can they be called the Nile until they unite. The lakes mentioned in the central line of drainage are by no means small. Lake Bangweolo, at the lowest estimate, is 150 miles long, and I tried to cross it and measure its breadth exactly. The first stage was to an inhabited island, twenty-four miles; the second stage could be seen from its highest point, or rather the tops of the trees upon it, evidently lifted up by mirage; the third stage, the main land, was said to be as far beyond; but my canoe men had stolen the canoe, and they got a hint that the real owners were in pursuit and got in a flurry to return home. Oh, that they would! but I had only my coverlet left to hire another craft, and the lake being four

hundred feet above the sea, it was very cold.  So I gave
in and went back, but I believe the breadth to be between
sixty and seventy miles.  Bangweolo, Moero and Kamolondo are looked on as one great riverine lake, and is one
of Ptolemy's.

The other is the Tanganyika, which I found steadily
flowing to the north.  This geographer's predecessors must
have gleaned their geography from men who visited the
very region.  The reason why the genuine geography was
rejected was the extreme modesty of modern map makers.
One idle person in London published a pamphlet which,
with killing modesty, he entitled, "Inner Africa Laid Open,"
and in the newspapers, even in the *Times*, rails at any one
who travels and dares to find the country different from
that drawn in his twaddle.  I am a great sinner in the poor
fellow's opinion, and the *Times* published his ravings even
when I was most unwisely believed to be dead.  Nobody
but Lord Brougham and I know what people will say after
we are gone.  The work of trying to follow the central
line of drainage down has taken me away from mails or
postage.

The Manyema are undoubtedly cannibals, but it was long
before I could get conclusive evidence thereon.  I was
sorely let and hindered by having half-caste Moslem attendants, unmitigated cowards and false as their prophet,
of whose religion they have only imbibed the fulsome pride.
They forced me back when almost within sight of the end
of my exploration, a distance of between four and five
hundred miles, under a blazing vertical sun.

So I gave
be between
nd Kamo-
and is one

nd steadily
essors must
visited the
graphy was
nap makers.
hlet which,
Laid Open,"
s at any one
fferent from
r in the poor
ravings even
d. Nobody
will say after
the central
bm mails or

t it was long
eon. I was
Moslem at-
eir prophet,
lsome pride.
t of the end
ur and five

I came here a mere ruckle of bones, terribly jaded in body and mind. The head man of my worthless Moslems remained here, and, as he had done from the coast, ran riot with the goods sent to me, drunk for a month at a time. He then divined on the Koran and found that I was dead, sold off all the goods that remained for slaves and ivory for himself, and I arrived to find myself destitute of everything except a few goods I left in case of need. Goods are the currency here, and I have to wait now till other goods and other men come from Zanzibar. When placed in charge of my supply of soap, brandy, opium and gunpowder from certain Banians (British subjects) he was fourteen months returning, all expenses being paid out of my stocks ; three months was ample, and he then remained here and sold off all. You call this smart, do you ? some do, if you don't. I think it moral idiocy.

Yours affectionately,

DAVID LIVINGSTONE.

Frequent allusion has been made, in the course of this work, to the enmity of the slave traders, and their continual efforts to baffle Livingstone by stealing his stores and destroying his letters. The subjoined letter, with an enclosure from Dr. David Livingstone to W. F. Stearns, Esq., dated Unyanyembe, March 13, 1872, was among the number brought to the coast by Mr. Stanley, the *Herald* correspondent. The package was forwarded, as directed, to Bombay, to the firm of Stearns, Hobart & Co., in which Mr. Stearns was a partner at the date of Dr. Livingstone's departure for the coast of Africa in 1866. Mr. Stearns, who is an American, and son of President Stearns, of Amherst College, is now engaged in business in New York, hence the letter and enclosure had to be re-directed to that city, where they arrived yesterday from Bombay.

The enclosure referred to in the letter is dated November, 1870, from Manyema, Central Africa. In it a special and friendly reference is made by Dr. Livingstone to the American Geographical Society, with a request that Mr. Stearns would communicate such extracts to that scientific body as he saw fit. Mr. Stearns has therefore withheld the enclosure from publication in order that he may first carry out the great traveller's commission to the American Society. Dr. Livingstone has been for many years a corresponding member of the American Geographical Society. He was about to be made an honorary member of the body six years ago; but, owing to the doubts of his being alive, this was not carred into effect.

UNYANYEMBE, i. e., SIXTY DAYS' SMART
MARCHING FROM THE EAST COAST,
AFRICA, March 13, 1872.

MY DEAR STEARNS,—I have written to you before, but my letters were destroyed, because I have been considered a spy on the slave traders. The enclosure was penned long ago, among the cannibals, when I had no paper. I gave you an idea of matters then, but my own knowledge has been increasing, and perhaps the enclosed statements do not tally exactly with what I have to say now, an

66. Mr. Stearns,
it Stearns, of Am-
is in New York,
re-directed to that
Bombay.
r is dated Novem-
:a. In it a special
Livingstone to the
, request that Mr.
icts to that scien-
ias therefore with-
order that he may
commission, to the
ias been for many
American Geogra-
made an honorary
but, owing to the
; carred into effect.

DAYS' SMART
E EAST COAST,
ch 13, 18/2.

n to you before, but
have been considered
iclosure was penned
I had no paper.
my own knowledge
enclosed statement
e to say now, and



much of which will be published in my despatches. I have to thank you very heartily for all your kindness to me in Bombay and afterwards. * * *

This goes to the coast by Henry M. Stanley, travelling correspondent of the New York *Herald*, sent by James Gordon Bennett, jr., to aid your servant, and he has done it right nobly.

Our consul believed the Banians, who are the chief slave traders by means of Arab agents, when they said they would forward supplies of goods and men to me. They sent slaves instead of men, and all the efforts of slaves and masters were faithfully directed to securing my failure. I was plundered shamelessly and forced back about five hundred miles from discovering the fifth great lake below the sources. But Mr. Stanley has supplied every want, and I now only need to re-discover the ancient fountains of Herodotus and retire.

The Agra and Masterman's bank broke. The receipt for £1,000 is in Mr. T——'s strong box, and he can draw out the deposit. All scientific expeditions are universally exempted from loss, even in time of war. Please tell them that I cannot enter into any creditor's arrangement; they must return the whole deposit and interest according to the rules agreed upon by all civilized people, and I hope they will act in accordance with what is manifestly right.

The buffaloes were killed for me; but the driver had a letter on his person, knowing that on its production his wages depended. This was the only one of forty sent.

The governor here, who is merely a low Banian trade agent, called by simple people the Great Sheikh Syde ben Salem, destroyed them and others to prevent evidence of plundering my goods going to the coast.

I have been among the Philistines, my dear fellow, but am now strong and well, and, thanks to the Americans, completely equipped for my concluding trip.  *  *  *
And believe me, ever truly yours,

DAVID LIVINGSTONE.

Nobody, at this late date, affects to doubt that Mr. Stanley really relieved Dr. Livingstone and spent several months in his company.   It was far otherwise, however, when the *Herald* expedition first returned.   Almost all the English journals and many American ones also were incredulous on the subject.   Mr. John Livingstone voluntarily came forward in Stanley's defence.   His letter, together with the remarks of the *Herald*, ought, therefore, to find a place here :—

We publish in the *Herald* to-day a letter from Hon. Charles Hale, Assistant and Acting Secretary of State, enclosing a communication from Mr. John Livingstone, of Listowel, Canada, the brother of Dr. David Livingstone, forwarded to the department through Mr. Freeman N. Blake, the United States Consul at Hamilton.   Mr. John Livingstone, while conveying to the *Herald* and to the leader of the Search Expedition, through that official source, his congratulations on the successful issue of the enterprise, takes occasion to express " the most implicit confidence in the statements " of both, and adds :—" I can assure you that Dr. Livingstone holds the American Government and people in the highest estimation, principally on account of the late abolition of slavery in the United States ; and I trust that his persistent efforts to check the nefarious traffic in slaves in Africa will be crowned with success." We presume that Mr. John Livingstone adopted this formal mode of forwarding his communication in view of the apparently stubborn unbelief of a small portion of the American press in the relief expedition and all relating to it, down to the point of incredulity in the existence of such a person as Mr. John Livingstone, of Listowel, Ontario, in the New Dominion. We are correspondingly grateful to that gentleman for the precaution he has taken to forestall the efforts of the enterprising journalists who have imposed upon themselves the duty of testing the genuineness of all the *Herald* correspondence on the subject, and who would doubtless have been speedily on his track to ascertain the authenticity of his letter had it reached us in the ordinary manner. As it comes back by the endorsement of the efficient Consul at Hamilton and the accomplished Assistant Secretary of State at Washington, we presume it will be accepted, as a sufficient proof that the brother of Dr. Livingstone in Canada unites with the son of the explorer in England, the British Foreign Office, the Royal Geographical Society, and Queen Victoria herself, in differing with the profound authorities who pronounce the

Livingstone letters forgeries, and deny that the doctor was ever discovered by Stanley at all.

When the *Herald* fitted out its Livingstone Search Expedition it had two objects in view:—First, to carry relief to the renowned explorer, in the confidence that the rumours of his death were unfounded, in the fear that he must be undergoing privations, and perhaps ill treatment in his unprotected condition, and in the conviction that it needed only energy and courage to follow the track he had pursued to find him, if living, or, in the sadder event, to obtain certain proof of his death; and second, to secure the credit and advantage that would assuredly follow success in such an enterprise. Any person who may be so disposed, is at liberty to reverse the order of these motives and to make the more selfish one predominate. We shall not quarrel with such critics, but shall be content to regard their judgment as the natural product of their minds. It is enough for us that in both instances our most sanguine anticipations have been realized. The assistance that was fortunate enough to reach Dr. Livingstone in the wilds of Africa arrived none too soon. It found him baffled, worried, defeated, a "mere ruckle of bones;" feeling as if he was dying on his feet, and with destitution in that inhospitable wilderness staring him in the face. It supplied his immediate necessities, enabled him to resume the work to which he has unselfishly devoted his life, left him in comparative ease and comfort, and secured the forwarding of supplies and help sufficient to insure him in the future against the disappointments and sufferings he had under-

gone in the past. We leave others to estimate the credit
due to the *Herald* for its share in the enterprise so well
carried to a successful issue by its faithful and daring
leader. The honour we covet finds happy expression in
Consul Blake's letter to Acting Secretary Hale — the
honour that can be justly claimed for "the expedition
instituted by American enterprise." The discovery of Dr.
Livingstone not only shows what individual American
spirit can accomplish, but proves the real power of the
American press. Independent American journalism will
hereafter occupy a higher position in the estimation of
foreign nations, and its usefulness, value, and intelligence
will no longer be measured by the standard of partisan
organs. Indications have already been given that the
lesson will have its effect upon our own journalists, in the
avowal of an independent position by some of our leading
political journals. The unfortunate bitterness of the Pre-
sidential campaign, it is true, temporarily checked this
commendable spirit; but now that the election is over,
there is a fair prospect that many of our best-conducted
newspapers will recognize the fact that the American press
has a higher and more patriotic mission to perform than
that of persuading foreigners that all our political parties
are corrupt, and all our public men debased and dishonest.
We regard the triumph of the Livingstone Expedition not
as the triumph of the *Herald* alone, but of the whole
American press, and not the least gratifying of its effects
is the impulse it has given to the promised improvement
in the character of American journalism.

18

There is one point, however, recalled to notice by Mr. John Livingstone, which, while it did not enter into any calculation of the probable issues of the *Herald* Search Expedition when the enterprise was set afoot, may prove one of its most important results. In all his letters—in those to the *Herald*, to the Royal Geographical Society, to the Foreign Office and to members of his family—Doctor Livingstone is earnest in his exhortations to the civilized world to stretch forth its strong arm over the suffering Africans, and snatch them from the horrors of slavery in the most hideous and revolting forms. "I trust," says his brother, "that his persistent efforts to check the nefarious traffic in slaves in Africa will be crowned with success." This Christian object is no doubt uppermost in the mind of the missionary and explorer, who, in his sorrowing over "man's inhumanity to man," awards a crown of honour to the American people for their abolition of slavery in the United States, without pausing to inquire how far the blacks owe their liberty to the uncertain chances of politics and war. The seed he planted in the letters sent home by the leader of the *Herald* Search Expedition has already borne some fruit, in moving the British Government to the more energetic action on the African coast recently announced in the Queen's speech to Parliament. But the subject will not be suffered to rest there. We have confidence that philanthropic men in all nations will soon take it up and make an effort to accomplish some practical work towards the uprooting of the inhuman system in the interior of Africa, as well as for its check on the coast.

There are indirect means, however, as well as direct means, by which slavery can be driven from the stronghold. The extension of trade into the regions travelled by Livingstone would do more than armies to remove the evil, and in this respect the Stanley expedition may have worked a good not anticipated for it. The success of one resolute, practical man, and the plain statement of his experience, will tempt adventure more than all the essays that could be written in a dozen years. Despite his energy and perseverance, Dr. Livingstone has been looked upon as a scientific explorer, and ordinary men, who would hesitate before they followed on the track he might indicate in search of profitable ventures, would strike out boldly in the path pointed out by such a traveller as Stanley. If Livingstone had remained in Africa two years longer unaided and unheard of, even if he had lived to return home, the good work now hoped for would at best have been so long delayed. But we even question whether the story he would then have had to tell would have worked any practical good in this important direction. The scientific features of his labours would have engrossed public attention, and the every-day facts would have been overlooked in admiration of the genius and devotion of the explorer. Stanley's successful expedition is of an entirely different character. He brings back information of the existence of a horrible traffic which is going on every day, and which can be stopped with comparative ease. He tells of riches in store for adventurers as tempting as the golden promises of the mines. He offers in his own person the proof that the land can be travelled in safety, and that the natives are harmless and tractable. We shall be mistaken if his experience and his story do not induce many of those bold spirits who are always ready to strike for fortune through difficult paths, to seek the wilds of Africa for their easily gathered treasures. Who shall say how soon commerce and civilization will stretch from the coast into the interior of the land in which Livingstone is to-day again shut out from the world, driving slavery before them more effectually than it could be scattered by armies? And who will deny that the "expedition instituted by American enterrpise" has happily tended to promote this practical result?

The following letter and enclosures, from Acting Secretary of State Hale, have been received at the office of the New York *Herald*. It will be recalled that Mr. John Livingstone stated to the *Herald* correspondent, who had called on him at his house in Canada, that he had taken the course indicated in the Acting Secretary of State's letter before he had any idea that a *Herald* attaché would visit him :—

DEPARTMENT OF STATE,<br>WASHINGTON, Sept. 7, 1872.

JAMES GORDON BENNETT, Esq., New York:—

SIR,—I enclose for your information copies of a despatch this day received from Mr. Freeman N. Blake, Consul of the United States at Hamilton, Canada, and of a letter addressed to him by Mr. John Livingstone, which accompanies the despatch.

An original letter (David Livingstone to John Livingstone) also accompanies the despatch, and is held by the Department subject to Mr. John Livingstone's expressed intention to ask its return.  I am, sir, your obedient servant,

CHARLES HALE, Acting Secretary.

LISTOWEL, August 24th, 1872.

F. N. BLAKE, Esq., United States Consul, Hamilton, Ontario :—

DEAR SIR,—Would you kindly oblige me by conveying in your official capacity to Mr. Bennett, proprietor of the New York *Herald*, and also to Mr. Stanley, the leader of the "*Herald's* Livingstone Search Expedition," my warmest congratulations on the successful issue of that expedition.

Having noticed a number of articles in the public press reflecting doubts on the veracity of Mr. Stanley and the *Herald*, I am glad to be able to say that I place the most implicit confidence in the statements of Mr. Stanley and the *Herald*.

I can also assure you that Dr. Livingstone holds the American Government and people in the highest estimation, principally on account of the late abolition of slavery in the United States, and I trust that his persistent efforts to check the nefarious traffic in slaves in Africa will be crowned with success.  I am yours respectfully,

JOHN LIVINGSTONE.

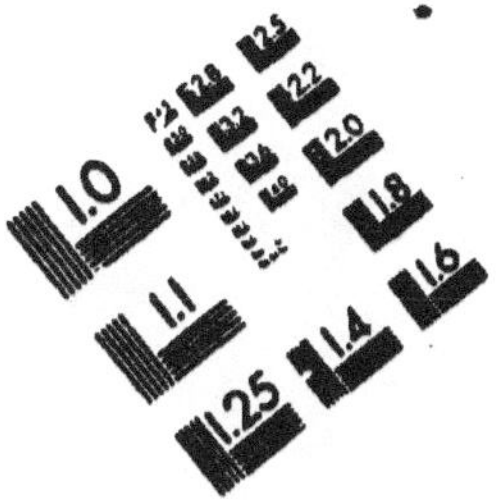

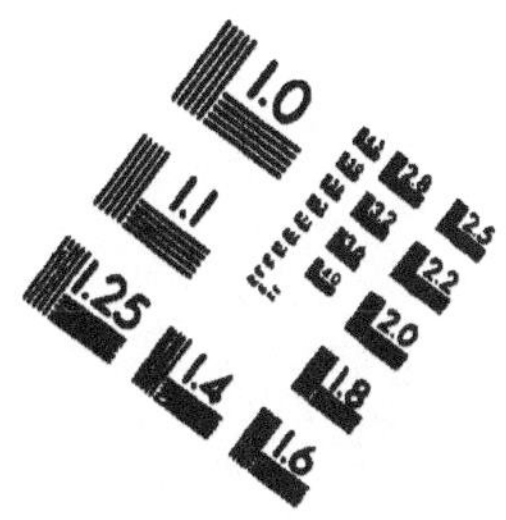

**IMAGE EVALUATION
TEST TARGET (MT-3)**

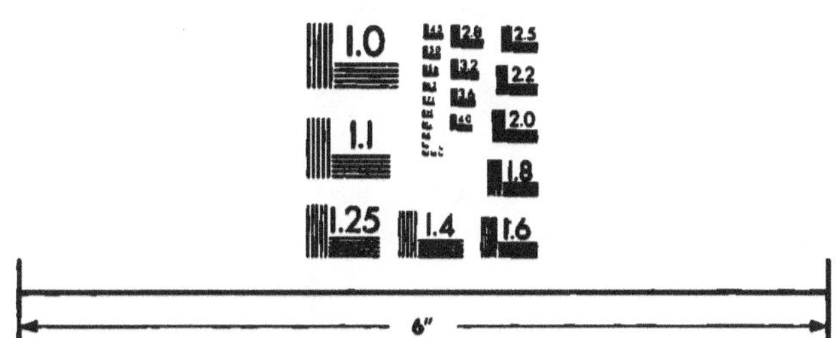

Photographic
Sciences
Corporation

23 WEST MAIN STREET
WEBSTER, N.Y. 14580
(716) 872-4503

UNITED STATES CONSULATE,
HAMILTON, Sept. 3rd, 1872.

HON. CHARLES HALE, Assistant Secretary of State :—

SIR,—I have the honour to enclose herewith a letter officially addressed to me by Mr. John Livingstone, of Listowel, Ontario, attesting his confidence in the statements recently published regarding his brother, Dr. David Livingstone, and conveying expressions of gratitude that the expedition instituted by American enterprise and private liberality succeeded in the discovery of his brother, and in furnishing aid to enable him to prosecute his work, when all other efforts for this object failed.

The public interest felt for the safety of this eminent explorer, and the success of his researches, prompt me most cheerfully to comply with the request in the only way I can properly do so—by transmitting the communication to the Department.

In the personal interview I had with Mr. John Livingstone he seemed desirous to authenticate the genuineness of Dr. Livingstone's despatches, by offering for examination the original letter enclosed herewith, which, in proper time, he would only claim again.  I am, sir, your obedient servant,

FREEMAN N. BLAKE,
United States Consul.


Sir Roderick Murchison was so warm and constant a friend of the great explorer, that it may not be amiss to insert such portions of the doctor's last letter as have been made public.   It possesses a melancholy interest, for before Stanley had discovered Livingstone,and months before the letter was written, Sir Roderick had breathed his last :—

UNYANYEMBE, March 13th, 1872.

MY DEAR SIR RODERICK,—        *        *        *

I have written you a long account of the worry, thwarting, and baffling I have endured in trying to work my way through the cannibal Manyuema down the central line of drainage—Webb's Lualaba; but it is not worth sending now.   I got one letter from you in February, 1870, the first I received from you since one dated 13th March, 1866, but I could not doubt that you had written oftener.   The loss of your letters has left me very much in the dark.   I did not know that I had a penny of income till Mr. Stanley came, and brought a mail he seized for me here, after it had been fourteen months on the way, and in it I saw the Royal Geographical Society's Report stated that £3,500 had been received for the East African Expedition, which I ventured to suppose means mine.   [*This is an error; no such sum was ever given. —Author.*]   I don't know where that money is, or if it really is for me; I wish to give my children a little, but I have to ask the Messrs. Coutts to inquire of you about it. I have been trusting to part of the price of my little steamer at Bombay, and determined, pay or no pay, to finish my work if I live.   The want of letters was bad; the want of goods was worse, and the only supplies that I virtually received were part of a stock I paid for, and with Dr. Seward, sent off from Zanzibar, in 1866, to be placed in depôt in Ujiji. They were plundered by the governor here, but I got a share; and it was a part of this share that I took the precaution to reserve at Ujiji, in case of extreme need, and found on my return lately. But for this I should have been in beggary; for a lot of goods sent off by ——, through a Banian slave-trader, called Ludha Damji, were all sold off at Ujiji by the drunken half-caste tailor, Shereef, to whom they were entrusted. He must have reported that he had delivered all, for the statement was made in the House of Lords that all my wants had been supplied. He divined on the Koran, and found that I was dead, and then invested all in slaves and ivory for himself. There being no law except that of the gun or dagger, I had to wait in misery till Mr. Stanley came and proved himself truly the good Samaritan.

Another lot of goods was entrusted to Ludha again, and he to slaves again with two free head men who were thieves. Mr. —— wrote on the 19th October, 1870, that they were all ready to leave, all impediments had been removed, and he remarked rather pleasantly, " that they were not perfect, but had expressed willingness to go;" and then they lay at Bagamoio three and a half months, and no one looked near them. Near the end of February they heard that the consul was coming, and started off two days before his arrival, not to look after them, but to look after the wild beasts along the Ujiji road, and show them to the captain of a man-of-war. Here they refused to go with Mr. Stanley to Ujiji, because of a war, which did not prevent him from going, nor him and me from coming, though it is still going on. I seized what remained of the goods after the slaves had feasted sixteen months. On the 18th ultimo one of the head men died of smallpox; the other, non-perfect head man, besides running riot on my goods, broke the lock and key of Mr. Stanley's store, and plundered his goods too.

Traders get their goods safely by the same carriers we employ; but all our slaves are deeply imbued with the idea that they are not to follow, but force me back. My expedition is looked on with disfavour by all the Banians, who are really and truly the great slave traders of the country. But for the goods, guns, ammunition, advanced by the Banians, no Arab who travels could go inland to slave. It is by their money that the slave trade is carried on. The wretched governor here—the same who plundered Burton and Speke pretty freely—is their trade agent; but simple people call him the "great Sheikh Syde ben Salem," &c. All my letters disappeared here. My sketches, maps, astronomical observations, &c., sent before cholera began, were never heard of beyond this. When Shereef sold off all my stores, except a few pounds of worthless beads, a little coffee and sugar, the governor wrote to me that he had no hand in it. I never said he had. I suppose that the Banians did not sit down and instruct their slaves to rob and baffle me; a mere hint would be sufficient, and then, when they reached me, they swore that the consul told them not to go with me—and he had paid them more than double freemen's pay. Had they been with me and mutinied, I should have blamed myself as partly the cause, from want of tact or something; but after they had been paid and fed for sixteen months, it was mortifying to find myself virtually without men. I have lost two full years of time, being burdened by one thousand eight hundred miles of extra tramp, and how much waste of money I cannot say, all through the matter of supplies and men being unwittingly committed to slave-dealing Banians and slaves. Mr. Webb sent nine packets and packages in the eleven months of his (Stanley's) trip. The sixteen months that elapsed from my last mail of November, 1872, included those eleven months, but Mr. Webb's messengers were not allowed to lie feasting at Bagamoio, in sight of the consulate, for three and a half months, as mine were. Nor were the Banian low cunning and duplicity instilled into their minds. —— may probably be able to explain it all.

* * * * * * * * *

Now I am all right. I have abundant supplies of all I need to finish my work. Some I seized from ——'s slaves, and Mr. Stanley gave me more; so I am thankful to say that I am now better off than when I got a share of what I sent off in 1866. I feel quite exhilarated by the prospect of starting back as soon as Mr. Stanley can send me fifty free men from the coast. Don't imagine, from my somewhat doleful tone, that I am trying to excite commiseration and pity. When Zanzibar failed me so miserably, I sat down at Ujiji only till I should become strong, and then work my way down to Mteza. I am now strong and well and thankful, and wish only to be let alone, to finish by the re-discovery of the ancient fountains. In ——'s letter he talks hazily about Tanganyika and my going home from being tired, and the work being finished by another. You remember that I recommended him for the task, and he would not accept it from you without a good salary, and some thing to fall back on afterwards. I went unsalaried; the sole hope I had was the statement in yours of March 13, 1866: "Do your work, and leave pecuniary matters to Young and me." I have been tired often, and began again. I have done it all on foot, except eight days' illness with pneumonia and the trip down Tanganyika. I could never bear the scorn the Portuguese endure in being carried when quite well. I am sorry to have to complain of any one; but the loss of time, useless tramps, and waste of money, are truly no faults of mine. If you share in ——'s idea that I must have been all this time trying if Tanganyika communicated with Albert Nyanza, I regret the destruction of my sketch maps and astronomical observations; but in a former case an imperfect sketch map was made the means of fleecing me, and in the lost maps I did my duty notwithstanding.

Tanganyika is of no importance in connection with the Nile, except in a very remote degree. The interesting and great valley lies altogether west of it. In that valley there are five great lakes and three large rivers—Bangweolo, Moero, Kamolondo, Lake Lincoln and another, which the slaves forced me to leave as the Unknown

Lake. The large rivers—Bartle Frere's, otherwise Lufira;
Webb's Lualaba—the central line of drainage; then Sir
Paraffin Young's Lualaba,* with its name further down
Lomame—all go into the central Webb's Lualaba; Bartle
Frere's through Lake Kamolondo; Young's (I have been
obliged to knight him to distinguish him from our friend
the man-of-war's man) Lualaba through Lake Lincoln,
and, as Lomame into Webb's, and four or five days beyond
the confluence into the Unknown Lake, which, from the
great westing I made, some 5° W. of Ujiji, must be part of
Petherick's branch. This is the interesting field. The correlation of the structure and economy of the watershed
with these great lakes and lacustrine rivers is the theme
of my prize. When you heard that the sources were
further south than any one dreamed, in the exuberance of
your kindly heart you were going to award something to
B——, F——, and A——, for having dreamed about it.
You had no idea that the watershed was seven hundred
miles long and the fountains innumerable. I smiled, of
course good naturedly, to think that you would need to
divide the seven hundred miles among the three, and
thereby show a great physiological discovery by your
friends—the division of labour in dreaming. I am much
more savage now than you, and any one who competes
after I have given my own explanation will be ordered
out for instant execution without benefit of clergy. I
doubt if there is an Upper Nile basin. I found it a gradual

---

* Sir Paraffin Young was a facetious term applied by Dr. Livingstone
to Mr. James Young of Kelly, the inventor of paraffine.

slope from the sources down, and I reached the altitude ascribed to Gondokoro. Mr. Stanley will tell you about what he saw of Tanganyika. I declined to examine it in 1869 because Ujijians wished to mulct me of the few goods I had, and there was no inducement to spend all in patching up Burton's failure rather than work out the great main line of drainage from the watershed.

I earnestly hope that you will be so far recovered when this reaches you as to live in comfort, though not in the untiring activity of your earlier years. The news of our dear Lady Murchison's departure filled me with sincere sorrow. Had I known that she kindly remembered me in her prayers it would have been a source of great encouragement. I often thought that Admiral Washington and Admiral Beaufort looked down from their abodes of bliss, to which she has gone, with approbation. Sir Francis's words to the Arctic explorers, that they "were going on discovery and not on survey," have been a guide to me, and I am in hopes that, in addition to discovery, my disclosures may lead to the suppression of the East Coast Slave Trade by Banian British subjects. If the good Lord of all grant me this, I shall never grudge the toil, time, and trouble I have endured. I pray that His blessing may descend on you according to your need, and am, &c.

(Signed)     DAVID LIVINGSTONE.

P.S.—Mr. Stanley will be at the Langham Place Hotel when this reaches you; attentions to him and James Gordon Bennett will gratify me. Agnes will keep my London box and my Journal, which I send home, sealed, by Mr. Stanley.                                    D. L.

The letters of Dr. Livingstone during his later years will have been completely given, so far as they are in the hands of the public, if we insert the text of the letter written by Dr. Livingstone to Mr. H. M. Stanley sometime before the great explorer's demise. Several passages which are omitted are of a confidential nature :—

### LAKE BANGWEOLO, SOUTH CENTRAL AFRICA.

MY DEAR STANLEY,—I wrote hurriedly to you when on the eve of starting for Unyanyembe, and the mind being occupied by all the little worries incidental to the starting of the caravan, I felt and I still feel that I had not expressed half the gratitude that wells up in my heart for all the kind services you have rendered to me. I am devoutly thankful to the loving Father also for helping you through all your manifold masika (rainy season) toils, and bringing you safely to Zanzibar, with your energies unimpaired, and with a desire to exert yourself to the utmost in securing all the men and goods needed for this my concluding trip.

I am perpetually reminded that I owe a great deal to you for the men you sent. With one exception, the party is working like a machine. I give my orders to Manwa Sera, and never need to repeat them. I parted with the Arab sent without any disagreement. He lost one of the new donkeys at Bagamoyo. I then put two strangers on the chain without fastening the free end, and they wisely walked off with the bridle, bits and all, then suffered a lazy Monbasian to leave the cocoa somewhere and got five dotis at Unyanyembe as ——. Well, no one either before or after that could get any good out of him. Added to this the Arab showed a disposition to get a second $500, supposing we should be one month over the year, though he could do nothing except through my native head man. I therefore let him go, and made Manwa Sera, Chowpereh, and Susi, heads of departments at $20, if they gave satisfaction. This they have tried faithfully to do, and hitherto have been quite a contrast to Bombay, who seemed to think that you ought to please him.

Majwara, the drummer, has behaved perfectly—but slow! slow! and keeps your fine silver teapot, spoons and knives as bright as if he were an English butler ; gets a cup of coffee at five A.M., or sooner, if I don't advise him to lie down again ; walks at the head of the caravan as drummer, this instrument being the African sign of peace as well as of war. He objected at first to the office because the drum had not been bought by either you or me. Some reasons are profound—this may be one of them.

The fruits, fish, pork, biscuit, fowl, have been selected far better than I could have done. No golden syrup could be found, or you would have sent some. The tea was very nicely secured. Your wish for joy of the plum pudding was fulfilled, though it would have been better had we been nearer to Chambezi, where we spent Christmas, to enjoy it.

I keep most of your handsome present of champagne for a special occasion. One rifle was injured at Bagamoyo; your other splendid rifle and revolver were all I could desire for efficiency. The fifteen-shooter cartridges are not satisfactory, but everything else gives so much satisfaction that I could not grumble though I were bilious. I thank you very much and sincerely for all your kind generosity.

The new Zanzibar donkey came—lean, leg-sore and stiff; so I left him with Sultan bin Ali. Your two country beasts were in capital condition. Another you left died with all the symptoms of tsetse poison fully developed. He had the run of all the patches of cultivation around us, and perfect liberty; but perished, the first of his species I had seen die like a tsetse-bitten ox. The larger country animal died from the same cause, but had none of the symptoms, except swelling of the mouth and nose and above the eyes. He rallied twice, but when we left the south end of the Tanganyika, where all was hot and dry, we suddenly mounted up into the rainy season of Urungu or Burungu, when the cold and wet acted as the natives told us in former years they would do on all our cattle that had the poison in their systems.

I had found long before we had done with the excessive heats in the mountains that flank Tanganyika, that riding in the sun is more trying to the system than marching on foot. The perspiration caused by tramping modifies the effects of the temperature somewhat, as wakefulness does that of extreme cold.

In the hurry of departure I neglected your advice to

buy others, but I was so overjoyed at having got the men, that the idea of being knocked up by marching found as little place in my mind as it does in that of a boy going home from school.

The Chambesi was crossed long ago by the Portuguese, who have thus the merit of its discovery in modern times. The similarity of names led to its being put down in maps as "Zambesi," (eastern branch), and I rather stupidly took the error as having some sort of authority. Hence my first crossing it was as fruitless as that of the the Portuguese. It took me full twenty-two months to eliminate this error. The Cazembe who was lately killed was the first to give me a hint that Chambesi was one of a chain of rivers and lakes which probably forms the Nile; but he did it in rather a bantering style that led me to go back to the head waters again, and see that it was not the mere "chaff" of a mighty potentate.

There is Omar Island in the middle of Bangweolo, with 183 degrees of sea horizon around. The natives slowly drawing the hand around, said "That is Zambezi, flowing all round this space, and forming Bangweolo, before it winds round that headland and changes its name to Luapula." That was the moment of discovery and not the mere crossing of a small river. The late Cazembe I found sensible and friendly. His empire has succumbed before a very small force of Arab slaves and Wanyamwezi.

Pereira, the first Portuguese who visited the Cazembe eighty years ago, said that he had 30,000 trained soldiers, sacrificed twenty human victims every day, and the streets

19

of his capital were watered daily. I thought my late friend had 30,000 diminished by 00's, and sacrificed five or six pots of pombe daily, but this may have been only a court scandal—the streets of his village were not made. So I was reminded of the famous couplet about the Scotch roads :—

> If you had seen these two roads before they were made,
> You'd lift your hands and bless Colonel Wade.

I have been the unfortunate means of demolishing two empires in Portuguese geography—the Cazembes and that of the Emperor Monomotopa. I found the last about ten days above Tette. He had too few men to make the show Cazembe did; but I learned from some decent mother-looking women attached to his court Zembere, that he had 100 wives! I have wondered ever since, and have been nearly dumb-founded with the idea of what a nuisance a man with 100 wives in England would be. It is awful to contemplate, and might be chosen as a theme for a young men's debating society.

I wish some one would visit Mtese or Uganda, without Bombay as an interpreter. He (Bombay) is by no means a sound author. The King of Dahomey suffered eclipse after a common-sense visit, and we seldom hear any more of his atrocities. The mightiest African potentate and the most dreadful cruelties told of Africans owe a vast deal to the teller.

You and I passed the islet Kassenge, where African mothers were said to sell their infants for a loin cloth each. This story was made to fit into another nice little story of "a mother bear" that refused to leave her young. A child that cuts its upper front teeth before the under is dreaded as unlucky, and is likely to bring death into the family. It is called an Arab child, and the first Arab who passes is asked to take it. I never saw a case, nor have the Arabs I have asked seen one either, but they have heard of its occurrence. The Kassenge story is, therefore, exactly like that of the Frenchman who asserted that the English were so fond of hanging themselves in November, you might see them swinging on trees along the road. He may have seen one; I never did. English and American mothers have been guilty of deserting infants; but who would turn up the whites of his eyes, and say, as our mothers at Kassenge did, these people are no better than, or not so good, as she-bears?

Three of the Burungu chiefs have died since my first visit, and the population all turned topsy-turvy as the result of the elections. They elect a sister's son instead of the heir apparent—the heathen!—because, say the sly dogs, the heir apparent may not be the heir real. New stockades had been built on new sites, cultivation on grass and forest lands necessarily small, and food could not be got for love or money. As I am of the old orthodox school, I disapprove of the election of chief magistrates everywhere. When ycu find a good man like General Grant why not call him Prince, as the Germans did their good man Bismarck, quintuple his salary, and live the rest of your days like Christians? You make the ladies think that your ranting at elections is perfect bliss; while if you caught them and forced them to vote only once, you would hear no more of women's rights. They, bless their dear hearts! would take to feeding the hungry, instead of palavering at public *omnium gatherums.*

It sent a glow through my frame to read in the *Herald* the kindness of the good kind-hearted souls in New York feeding the hungry people. Blessings on the donors.

This lake, so far as I have seen it, is surrounded by an extremely flat country, although all 4,000 feet above the level of the sea. When first discovered I was without paper, but borrowed a little from an Arab, and sent a short account home. I had so much trouble from attendants that I took only the barest necessaries. Yet no sooner was the discovery announced at the coast than the official description was forthwith sent to the Bombay Government, that "the lake is like Nyassa, Tanganyika and the Albert Nyanza, overhung by high mountains, sloping down to great plains, which during the rainy season become flooded, so that caravans march for days through water knee-deep seeking for higher ground on which to pass the night.

The only mountain slopes are ant-hills, some of them twenty feet high. They could scarcely be called high unless thought of as being built on the top of the 4,000 feet. These statements are equally opposed to the truth, as that Cazembe town is built on the banks of the Luapula.

People having a crotchet for map-making traced every step of the Portuguese slaving expeditions to Cazembe, and built the village in latitude 8 deg. 43 min. south.

That is in deep water, near the north end of Lake Moero, and over fifty miles from Luapula. I found it in latitude 9 deg. 37 min. south, and on the banks of a lagoon or loch, having no connection with the Luapula, which river, however, falls six or seven miles west of the village Moero.

Now, it is very unpleasant for me to expose any of these mis-statements, and so appear contradictious. But what am I to do? I was consulted by Sir Roderick Murchison as to this present expedition, and he recommended the writer of the above as a leader. Sir Roderick afterwards told me that the offer was declined unless a good salary and a good position to fall back upon were added, as Speke and Grant had in their pay and commission. He then urged the leadership on myself as soon as the work on which I was engaged should be published. My good, kind-hearted friend added, in a sort of pathetic strain: "You will be the real discoverer of the source of the Nile." I don't wish to boast of my good deeds, but I need not forget them.

*    *    *    *    *    *

Signed on envelope.          DR. LIVINGSTONE.

After Stanley's departure, Livingstone, it appears, left Unyanyembe, rounded the south end of Lake Tanganyika, travelled south to Lake Bemba or Bangweolo, and crossed it south to north. He then journeyed along the east side, returning north through the marshes to Ilala or Muilala. His object evidently was to complete the exploration in a southernly direction with a view to the discovery of the four fountains of which he had spoken in his letters. His last letter to Stanley, given in full above, was dated from Lake Bangweolo. Ill-health appears to have been the cause of his moving eastward and north to the Lobisa or Bisa country where he died. It is immediately south of Lake Tanganyika. Livingstone had suffered for several months from chronic dysentery; but though apparently despondent, and disposed to take a gloomy view of his chances for recovery, he had kept up bravely until the 1st of May, 1873. He had told his people that he intended to try to reach Zanzibar and England, and in the last entry in his diary, made April 27, he spoke sadly of home and his family. His hopes were greater than his strength, and this he finally felt on May 1, when he told his followers to build him a hut to die in. They built him a hut accordingly, and he laid himself down in it never to rise again alive. He suffered greatly for two or three days and died at midnight on the 4th of May.

The first detailed account of the doctor's death was telegraphed from Suez on the 28th of March, 1874, received in London on the 29th, and published in the New York *Herald* of the 30th. It was as follows :—

LONDON, March 29, 1874.

The steamer Malwa arrived off Suez at eleven o'clock on Saturday night, 28th inst., having on board Arthur Laing and Jacob Wainwright in charge of the remains of Doctor Livingstone. They reported that the great explorer had been ill with chronic dysentery several months.

He was well supplied with stores and medicines, but had a presentiment that the attack would prove fatal. He rode for a time on a donkey, and was then carried along by men. In this manner he arrived at Muilala, beyond Lake Bemba, in the Bisa country. Here he said, "Build me a hut to die in." A hut was accordingly built by his followers.

On the 1st of May, 1873, Livingstone was placed in bed. He suffered greatly, groaning from pain night and day. On the third day he said, " I feel very cold; put more grass over the hut." His followers could not speak or go near him. Kitumbo, Chief of the Bisa country, sent in flour and beans and behaved well towards the explorer's party.

On the fourth day Livingstone was insensible and died about midnight. Majawara, his servant, was present at the moment of his decease. The last entry in Livingstone's diary is under the date of April 27, 1873. He spoke much and sadly of his home and family. When he was first seized he told his followers that he intended to exchange everything for ivory and to give it to them, and then push on to Ujiji and Zanzibar and try to reach England.

The same day on which his death occurred his followers held a consultation on the subject of what was best to be done. The Nassick boys determined to preserve his remains. They were afraid to inform the chief of his death, and they secretly removed the body to another hut, and built a high fence around it to insure privacy. They then removed the entrails from the body and placed them in a tin box, which they buried inside of the fence, under a large tree.   Jacob Wainwright cut an inscription on the tree in the following words :—

**DR. LIVINGSTONE,**
**DIED**
**MAY 4, 1873.**

Wainwright then superscribed the name of the head man, Susa.  The body was preserved in salt, and dried under the sun during a space of twelve days.  When Kitumbo was informed of the death of the traveller he had drums beat and muskets fired in token of respect to his memory.  He allowed Livingstone's followers to remove the body, which was placed in a coffin of bark.  They then journeyed to Unyanyembe, in about six months, sending an advance party forward with information addressed to Livingstone's son.  This party met Cameron, who, on receipt of the news, sent back the bales of cloth and the powder which he was taking to Livingstone.

The body arrived at Unyanyembe in ten days after the advance party reached there.  The whole party rested there during a fortnight.

Messrs. Cameron, Murphy, and Dillon were there together, the latter very ill in health, blind, and with his mind affected.  He committed suicide at Kasakera, and was buried there.

At Unyanyembe, Livingstone's remains were placed in

another case of bark—one of smaller size, done up as a bale of merchandise, in order to deceive the natives, who objected to the passage of a corpse.  They were thus carried to Zanzibar.

Livingstone's clothing, papers and instruments accompanied the body.

When on his sick bed the doctor prayed much.  At Muilala he said: " I am going home; carry my remains to Zanzibar."

T. R. Webb, Esq,, United States Consul at Zanzibar, has received letters, through Murphy, from Dr. Livingstone, addressed to Mr. Stanley, which Consul Webb will deliver personally.

The only geographical news is as follows :—"After Stanley's departure Dr. Livingstone left Unyanyembe, rounded the south end of Lake Tanganyika, travelled south to Lake Bemba, or Bangweolo, and crossed it south to north. He then journeyed along the east side, returning north through the marshes to Muilala.  All his papers were sealed and addressed to the Secretary of State, in charge of Arthur Laing, a British merchant at Zanzibar.

Murphy and Cameron remain behind.

Before referring to the relief expeditions, to the second of which reference is made in the above telegram, we complete the narrative of Livingstone's last journey, as we find it in two documents, the one containing the substance of an interview between Mr. Stanley and Jacob Wainwright, one of the faithful servants who accompanied the body to England, and the other from Mr. F. Holmwood, of the British Consulate at Zanzibar :—

SOUTHAMPTON, April 15, 1874.

Among the passengers grouped around the gangway of the Malwa upon her arrival here to-day was Mr. Thomas Livingstone, eldest son of the doctor, and close by him stood a negro lad, apparently about eighteen years of age, dressed in a blue serge suit, with a field glass swung across his shoulder. This was Jacob Wainwright, Livingstone's faithful body servant, who had attended him in his last moments. He watched each arrival on board with eager gaze, and his eyes sparkled with joy as he recognized his old tutor, the Rev. Mr. Price, who had taught him, after his liberation from slavery, to read and write English in Bombay.

A group, consisting of Mr. Waller, Mr. Webb, Mr. Young and Mr. H. M. Stanley, was speedily formed round the boy, and, after each of the first named had addressed him, Mr. Stanley suddenly turned to Jacob and asked if he remembered him. No sooner had the boy's bright eyes lit on Mr. Stanley's face than a broad smile played over his stolid features and he stretched out his hand and said he perfectly remembered him ; and then commenced a conversation which was listened to with intense interest by all present, and which must have the effect of silencing for ever those persons, if any such remain, who affect disbelief in Mr. Stanley's story. Mr. Stanley began to question Jacob as to the last hours of the doctor, and upon the events which characterized the march of the Relief Expedition which Mr. Stanley sent to Dr. Livingstone after his return from Unyanyembe to Zanzibar.

Jacob said that the doctor expressed great joy when, after waiting so many weary months at Unyanyembe, he saw the caravan of freemen which he had been anxiously waiting for before the resumption of his exploration. After giving him a few days'. rest at Unyanyembe, Livingstone's party travelled southwest to Kasagera, Kigandu to Kesera, a district ruled by King Simba. While at this place the doctor had a relapse of his old enemy, chronic dysentery, which so weakened him as to compel him to take to riding a donkey. Mr. Stanley here said, when he heard this, "He ought to have returned then." But the doctor did not seem to think that this attack was very dangerous, and accordingly resumed his march in a south-westerly direction to Mpatwa, thence into the valley of Rungwa, where he found many boiling springs; then passed through Ufipa, and then Uremba, thence to Margunga. Mr. Stanley here asked Jacob Wainwright "which way the rivers ran?" Jacob said that they all ran to the right, which means to the west, into the Tanganyika. Along Moungo they reached a district called Kawendi, where a lion killed the only remaining donkey, the other having died in some of the oozy marshes of Uremba. Thenceforward Livingstone, continually growing weaker, was compelled to be carried in a hammock, but still urged on his way until he came to the headwaters which empty themselves into Lake Bangweolo.

Here, as he came to the lake, he made use of Mr. Stanley's boat, which he had carried with him a distance of 1,100 miles. He crossed over the Chambezi to the southern bank and attempted to push his way along the southern shore of Lake Bangu and towards the Fountains of Herodotus, reported to be at Katenga, where he thought he would be able to recruit his health, but perceiving himself to be growing weaker he determined to push back to Unyanyembe, towards home, and full of that intention he turned his face northward. But on arriving at a place called Kitumbo he seemed to have become suddenly conscious that his last hour had come, and he tried to settle there; but the chief would not permit him, and he accordingly proceeded further north towards Kibende. On his arrival at a small village in the district of Muilala he was placed in his tent; but thinking the sun was too hot for him, he ordered his men to build a hut for him to die in. His last entry in his diary was made on the 27th of April, 1873, thirteen months and thirteen days after Mr. Stanley had left him, wherein he describes how ill he feels and his inability to proceed further. After this entry Livingstone seems to have been too weak to have written more—seems to have resolutely prepared himself for death.

The boy Majwara, expressly commended to Livingstone, as a personal attendant whose fidelity would be undoubted, declares that, during the intervals of expressing his suffering by moans and sighs, prayers for his family were heard, and the word "home" was also frequently mentioned. Livingstone refused to have any other man come into the hut to him, but each morning they all came, according to custom, to greet him with the words " Yambo bana," or "Good morning, master," one after another.

The boy Majwara made some tea for him and offered him stimulants, which, however, seem to have had no effect on him. At midnight of the fourth day of his illness Livingstone passed away quietly to the land of spirits. In the morning the boy Majwara, hearing no sighs or groans, felt his master's face and found it cold. Then the solemn truth dawned upon his young mind that the " great master" was dead. The servants then seem to have held a consultation as to what should be done with the body. If they revealed the fact of the death to the natives it was feared that their superstition would cause them to prevent the servants from carrying their master away. So they kept it secret, and Farjalla, another of the men sent on by Mr. Stanley, proceeded to disembowel the body ; and, after leaving the village, hung the corpse in the sun to dry for five days, when they packed it in bark, and taking it with them proceeded on their long, long journey towards Unyanyembe. They did not arrive until the end of five months, many attempts to bar their passage having been made by the natives. Among the men whom Mr. Stanley sent to Livingstone, Jacob speaks in high terms of the good behaviour of the leaders Mabruki, Manwa Sera, Chowpereh and Susi. Livingstone was heard frequently to remark how very good his " boys" were. He praised them very highly, and was accustomed to promise them on the march that when he should return home he would reward

them well.   Jacob Wainwright was sent from Zanzibar to
England by order of the Missionary Society, of which he
was a pupil.   Among the things brought by Mr. Thomas
Livingstone, the eldest son, was the Winchester rifle
which Mr. Stanley presented to Dr. Livingstone.   Mr.
Livingstone means to keep it as a souvenir of his father.

The following is Majwara's Account of the Last Days of
Dr. Livingstone, by F. Holmwood, of H. B. M. Consulate,
Zanzibar; it was read at the last meeting of the Royal
Geographical Society in London, and is as follows:—

ZANZIBAR, March 12, 1874.

MY DEAR SIR BARTLE,—No doubt you will hear from
several interested in Dr. Livingstone; but, as I do not
feel sure that any one has thoroughly examined the men
who came down with his remains, I briefly summarize
what I have been able to glean from a careful cross-ex-
amination of Majwara, who was always at his side during
his last days, and Susi, as well as the Nassick boys, have
generally confirmed what he says.   I enclose a small
sketch map, merely giving my idea of the locality, and
have added a dotted line to show his route during this
last journey of his life.

The party sent by Stanley left Unyanyembe with the
doctor about the end of August, 1872, and marched
straight to the south of Lake Tanganyika, through Ufipa,
crossing the Rungwa River, where they met with natural
springs of boiling water, bubbling up high above the
ground.   On reaching the Chambezi, or Kambezi River,

they crossed it about a week's journey from Lake Bomba, also crossing a large feeder; but by Susi's advice Living-stone again turned northward, and recrossed the Kambezi, or Luapula, as he then called it, just before *it* entered the lake.

He could not, however, keep close to the north shore of Lake Bemba, owing to the numerous creeks and streams, which were hidden in forests of high grass and rushes. After making a détour, he again struck the lake at a vil-lage, where he got canoes across to an island in the centre, called Matipa.   Here the shores on either hand were not visible, and the doctor was put to great straits by the na-tives declining to let him use their canoes to cross to the opposite shore.   He therefore seized seven canoes by force, and when the natives made a show of resistance he fired his pistol over their heads, after which they ceased to obstruct him.   Crossing the lake diagonally, he arrived in a long valley, and, the rains having now set in fully, the caravan had to wade rather than walk, constantly crossing blind streams, and, in fact, owing to the high rushes and grass, hardly being able to distinguish at times the land, or rather what was generally dry land, from the lake.

Dr. Livingstone had been weak and ailing since leaving Unyanyembe, and when passing through the country of Ukabende, at the southwest of the lake, he told Majwara (the boy given him by Stanley, who is now in my ser-vice), that he felt unable to go on with his work, but should try and cross the hills to Katanga (Katanda?) and there rest, endeavouring to buy ivory, which, in all this country is very cheap (three yards of merikani buying a slave or a tusk), and returning to Ujiji through Manyema to recruit and reorganize.

But as he approached the northern part of Bisa (a very large country), arriving in the province of Ulala, he first had to take to riding a donkey, and then suffer himself to be carried on a kitanda (native bedstead), which at first went much against the grain. During this time he never allowed the boy Majwara to leave him, and he then told that faithful and honest fellow that he should never cross the high hills to Katanda. He called for Susi, and asked how far it was to the Luapula, and on his answering " three days," remarked " he should never see his river again."

On arriving at Ilala, the capital of the district, where Kitumbo the Sultan lived, the party were refused permission to stay, and they carried Livingstone three hours' march back towards Kibende. Here they erected for him a rude hut and fence, and he would not allow any to approach him for the remaining days of his life except Majwara and Susi, except that every morning they were all desired to come to the door and say " Good morning!"

During these few days he was in great pain, and could keep nothing, even for a moment, on his stomach. He lost his sight so far as hardly to be able to distinguish when a light was kindled, and gradually sank during the night of the 4th of May, 1873. Only Majwara was present when he died, and he is unable to say when he ceased

t.

h, in all this
ani buying a
gh Manyema

f Bisa (a very
Ulala, he first
ffer himself to
which at first
time he never
ad he then told
should never
ed for Susi, and
on his answer-
ver see his river

a district, where
refused permis-
one three hours'
y erected for him
allow any to ap-
life except Maj-
ing they were all
od morning!"
at pain, and could
his stomach. He
ble to distinguish
y sank during the
Majwara was pre-
say when he ceased

to breathe. Susi, hearing that he was dead, told Jacob Wainwright to make a note in the doctor's diary of the things found by him. Wainwright was not quite certain as to the day of the month, and as Susi told him the doctor had last written the day before, and he found this entry to be dated 27th April, he wrote 28th April; but, on comparing his own diary on arrival at Unyanyembe, he found it to be the 4th of May; and this is confirmed by Majwara, who says Livingstone was unable to write for the last four or five days of his life. I fancy the spot where Livingstone died is about 11.25 degrees south and 27 degrees east; but, of course, the whole of this is subject to correction, and, although I have spent many hours in finding it all out, the doctor's diary may show it to be very imperfect.

I fear you will find this a very unconnected narration; but my apology must be that the consul-general is not well, and the other assistant absent on duty, and there is much work for me to do. Mr. Arthur Laing has been intrusted with the charge of the remains and diaries, which latter he has been instructed to hand to Lord Derby.

Trusting that you are in the enjoyment of good health, and with great respect, believe me, dear Sir Bartle, your most obedient servant,

FREDERIC HOLMWOOD.

To the Right Hon. Sir BARTLE FRERE, K.C.B., G.C.S.I., &c., President of the Royal Geographical Society.

On the conclusion of the paper Sir Bartle Frere introduced to the meeting Mr. Laing, who brought the remains of Dr. Livingstone from Zanzibar.

A brief account may now be given of the two search expeditions sent in search of Livingstone, under the auspices of the Royal Geographical Society. In the beginning of 1872 this body issued an appeal to the public on behalf of an expedition intended to operate in earnest for the discovery and relief of the great traveller. The total amount at their disposal was very nearly £6,000 sterling, about £5,000 of which consisted of voluntary subscriptions. The society granted £500, and as over £500 remained of the £1,000 granted by Lord Clarendon, the late Foreign Secretary, this was also made over to the fund. The party was placed under the direction of Lieut. Dawson, Lieut. Henn, and Mr. Oswell Livingstone, the explorer's youngest son. Of course, at this time, the success of the *Herald* expedition was not yet known. As we have seen, however, Stanley and Livingstone, during the months of January and February, 1872, were journeying together between Ujiji and Unyanyembe. This first Relief party took its departure on the 7th of February, for Zanzibar. The officers in charge of the Expedition were Lieutenant Dawson, Lieutenant Henn, and Mr. Oswell Livingstone, the explorer's son. This enterprise came to nothing after spending over £2000 in stores. The Geographical Society determined to equip a second party under the command of Lieutenant Cameron, R. N., Lieutenant Murphy, R. A.; and Dr. Dillon, R. N. Sir Bartle Frere accompanied the expedition to Zanzibar, bound on a mission to the Sultan, and there they arrived early in February, 1873. In September they arrived at Unyanyembe where the sad intelligence of the death of Livingstone was related to them by his attendants; soon after the party arrived bearing the body.

There was one tragical event in connection with the expedition—the melancholy fate of Dr. Dillon. He was attacked by fever shortly after leaving Unyanyembe, and while under the influence of the delirium had committed suicide. The rest of the party arrived in safety at the coast in the spring of 1874.

The following account of the embarkation of the traveller's body was transmitted by telegram and published in the London papers :—

SUEZ, SUNDAY.

The body of Dr. Livingstone, arrived per *Malwa*, left this morning for England, *via* the Canal. Dr. Livingstone died on the 4th May, at Muilala, in the kingdom of Bisa, of dysentery, after five days' march through the marshy country. The body, which was escorted by Lieutenant Murphy to the coast, left Zanzibar on the 12th inst., in charge of Arthur Laing, who proceeds *via* Brindisi with his papers and effects. The body will go to Southampton, attended by Jacob, Dr. Livingstone's servant. The body was disemboweled and embalmed by a native, and was put on a bush to dry. Twelve days afterwards it was placed in two coffins.

The following is the copy of a telegram forwarded to the London office of *New York Herald* :—

"The *Malwa* arrived off Suez at eleven on Saturday night, having Mr. Arthur Laing and Jacob Wainwright aboard, with the body of Dr. Livingstone. He had been ill with chronic dysentery for several months past. Although well supplied with stores and medicines, he seems to have had a presentiment that the attack would prove fatal. He rode a donkey, but was subsequently carried, and thus arrived at Muilala beyond Lake Bemba, in the Bisa country, when he said, 'Build me a hut to die in.' The hut was built by his followers, who first made him a bed. He suffered greatly, groaning day and night. On the third day he said, 'I am very cold; put more grass over the hut.' His followers did not speak or go near him. Kitumbo, Chief of Bisa, sent flour and beans, and behaved well to the party. On the fourth day Livingstone became insensible, and died about midnight. Majwara, his servant, was present. His last entry in the diary was on April 27th. He spoke much and sadly of his home and family. When first seized he told his followers he intended to exchange everything for ivory, to give to them, and to push on to Ujiji and Zanzibar, and try to reach England. On the day of his death his followers consulted what to do. They determined to preserve the remains. They were afraid to inform the chief of Livingstone's death. The servants removed the body to another hut, around which they built a high fence, to insure privacy. They opened the body and removed the internals, which were placed in a tin box and buried inside the fence, under a large tree.   Jacob Wainwright cut an inscription on the tree as follows :—'Dr. Livingstone died on May 4th, 1873,' and superscribed the name of the head man, Susi.  The body was preserved in salt, and dried in the sun for twelve days.  Kitumbo was then informed of the death, and beat drums and fired as a token of respect, and allowed the followers to remove the body, which was placed in a coffin formed of bark, then journeyed to Unyanyembe about six months, sending an advance party with information, addressed to Livingstone's son, which met Cameron.  The latter sent back bales of cloth and powder.  The body arrived at Unyanyembe ten days after the advance party, and rested there a fortnight. Cameron, Murphy, and Dillon together there, latter very ill—blind, and mind affected, suicided at Kasagera, buried there.

"Here Livingstone's remains were put in another bark case, smaller, done up in a bale to deceive natives, who objected to the passage of the corpse, which was thus carried to Zanzibar, Livingstone's clothing, papers and instruments accompanying the body.  When ill Livingstone prayed much.  At Muilala he said, 'I am going home.' Chumah remains at Zanzibar.

"Mr. Webb, American consul at Zanzibar, is on his way home, and has letters handed to him by Murphy from Livingstone, for Stanley, which he will deliver personally only.

"Geographical news follows.  After Stanley's departure the doctor left Unyanyembe, rounded the south end of

Lake Tanganyika, and travelled south of Lake Bemba or
Bangweolo, crossed it south to north, then along east side,
returning north through Marungu to Muilala.   All papers
sealed  and addressed to Secretary of  State, are in charge
of Arthur Laing, a British merchant, from Zanzibar."

The *Malwa* arrived at Southamptom on the 16th of
April, and was immediately visited by the friends and
relatives of the departed traveller, the local authorities
and representatives of the press.  All the institutions of
Southampton took part in the procession which accompanied the hearse to the railway station.   On arriving in
London, the remains were taken in charge by a Committee
of the Geographical Society.   In order to be fully satisfied
with the identity of the remains, which had been preserved
in salt, an inspection took place at the Society's Committee
Rooms, when the disabled shoulder, badly united at the
fracture received from the lion on the eve of his marriage,
plainly proved the body to be that of the lamented Dr.
Livingstone.

The Dean of Westminster at once offered to give a
national recognition of Livingstone's labours in Africa, by
tendering to his family the honours of a public funeral in
the great Abbey.   The procession started from the rooms
of the Royal Geographical Society, on the morning of April
the 18th, 1874.  We extract from the London papers a
full and accurate account of the last closing scene when
all that was mortal of David Livingstone was laid in the
naveof England's mausoleum.

Yesterday  morning,  Dr. Livingstone  was  buried  in

Westminster Abbey amidst such testimonies of profound
respect and mournful veneration as have seldom been shown
for the fate of any one since the death of the lamented
Prince Consort. There was something touching in the fate
of poor Livingstone. His long absence—the loss of his wife
in the heart of the wilds of Africa—the rumours of his
death, which were only contradicted to be again revived,
the search of the gallant Stanley for him, which at length
set all anxiety and misgivings at rest, and then the last
news of all—the death of the great explorer. None believed in this, because none wished to do so, but kept on
hoping against hope, till the terrible calamity of the fate
which had overtaken the great man was found at last to
be but too true. The fate of Mungo Park, of Clapperton, of Lander, in no way excited any interest in their
discoveries, or more than a passing regret for their loss.
Africa was then an unknown land; and, to say the truth,
people cared as little about it as they knew. Lately it has
been opened up to us like a region of romance, by Baker,
Speke, Grant, and last, and greatest of all, the marvellous
man who was to rest in England's sanctuary of sanctuaries.
That the greatest of the great of this land lie beneath its
sandy soil we all know, but among the mighty dead whose
plain gravestones chequer its pavement, or whose monu-
ments adorn its walls, there are none more distinguished
for courage and moderation, for singleness of purpose and
the simplicity of his great philanthropy, than David Livingstone. How we have all followed him in his adventures from the time that the lion first seized him thirty

years ago and left such fractures in the bones of his arm
as led, even after the lapse of about a year after death, to
the instant identification of the body by the great surgeon
who attended him when last in England!   There seems
to be a sort of lurking suspicion among some that the body
after all may not be that of the famous geographer, and
this no doubt may be accounted for by the fact that so
many rumours have obtained credence as to his death.
But if there is anything that was incontestably proved it
is that the poor, emaciated remains which were yesterday
laid under the centre of the nave of our great Abbey, were
those of the most famous explorer of any time, ancient or
modern.   Not only has Sir William Fergusson identified
what he had done to the bones of the left arm, but with
the body the faithful servant, Jacob Wainwright, has
brought all the diaries, the instruments, the journals, and
even the poor clothes in which Livingstone breathed his
last.   If these are not proofs of identity, it would be hard
to say what is required.   They are but far too certain.

The Abbey had the usual quiet, solemn and stately aspect, that makes, as Coleridge says, a religion in stone.
The choir had a line of black cloth down it, which was
met by another from the door of the western cloisters,
where the body was to be received, and in the centre of
the nave was a black aperture, amid the black cloth, of
the shape of a coffin, and just rimmed round with a broad
band of white.   Without such a precaution one might
have inadvertently slipped into it in the early gloom of
the morning; but as the day wore on during service, the

sun came out in a flood of light, which, pouring through the
stained windows, tinted the columns and ancient monu-
ments with all the hues of the rainbow. The grave of
Livingstone is in the very centre of the west part of the
nave. The spot is in the central line, exactly half-way
between the western doors and the choir. On the north
side is the grave of the Countess of Clanricarde, and on
the other side that of Thomas Campion, a noted watch-
maker. Close by lie, Major Rennell, and Telford and
Stephenson, the engineers. Like all the graves in Westminster Abbey, it is not a deep one, for there are no vaults
under the Abbey, and the soil is so sandy that it is scarcely
safe to go far down. As it was, both sides of the grave
had to be shored to prevent the sand from slipping. These
supports, however, were hidden by black cloth, which
gave, as usual, a most forbidding aspect to the large aperture, and one of most unusual depth. The central position
of the grave made the whole ceremony far more conspicuous than was the case with the funerals of Lord Lytton
or Lord Macaulay. That of Dickens was absolutely private. Before the procession started from the house of the
Geographical Society in Saville Row, there was a funeral
service conducted by the Rev. H. W. Hamilton, Minister
of the Established Church of Scotland. The pall was
adorned with wreaths of flowers, one of them, composed of
white azaleas and delicate ferns, having been sent by Her
Majesty. The service consisted of the 39th Psalm, and
three other short passages from the Bible—Mark xiii. 33-
37, 1 Thessalonians, iv. 13-18, and Rev. vii. 9-17—followed

by an extempore prayer. The procession was then formed,
and passed slowly through the streets to the Abbey. It
was nearly twelve o'clock before those who were fortunate
to have tickets began to take their seats. Without a
single exception, all were more or less in mourning—that
is to say, some in deep mourning, others only in ordinary
black. The choir soon filled, and those beyond it made up
a throng in the nave and the aisles. But all was as silent
as the grave itself; not even the usual mild whisper of a
waiting congregation went round. Earlier than all came
a group of seven ladies, some very young, and all dressed
in the deepest mourning. They took their places in the
seats allotted to mourners in the southern side of the
choir, just in front of the two black velvet trestles on
which the coffin was to be placed. Each lady had with
her a large chaplet of myrtles and violets or camelias and
cypresses, which were ranged in front of them, and, in
spite of their beauty, were, with their associations, a mel-
ancholy-looking row. Towards twelve the Abbey began
to fill, and there was a faint though audible noise of the
crowd which was waiting without to watch the arrival of
what was most truly a melancholy procession. Soon after
twelve o'clock such of the public as had tickets were allowed into the building, and filled the aisles, while others
who were more privileged occupied the Sacrarium. By-
and-by all spaces were filled, and even in the clerestory
there were some lining the old monks' walk, and looking
down with a curious aspect from rather a dizzy height
on to the crowd below. At a quarter to one, the bells of

St. Margaret's began to toll. The bell of the Abbey, like
that of St. Paul's, never tolls but for Royalty. The coffin
was conveyed through Dean's Yard to the entrance of the
western cloisters. Thence past the time-worn fretwork of
carved mullions and pilasters, which were old and gray
when Africa was only a name, and America an unknown
sound. Through these cloisters it was reverently borne at
a very slow pace.*

The pall-bearers were Mr. Henry M. Stanley, who was
foremost on the right, the Rev. Horace Waller, Vicar of
Leytonstone, Dr. John Kirk, Mr. Edward Daniel Young,
who had been his companions on the Zambezi; W. C.
Oswell, Esq., Major-General Sir Thomas Steele, W. F.
Webb, Esq. (of Newstead Abbey), who had been his companions in South Central Africa, in the region of Lake
Ngami, and lastly Jacob Wainwright, the coloured boy
from Nassick School, who had been sent by Mr. Stanley
from Zanzibar, to form part of the escort of the great
explorer, on his last journey from Unyanyembe to Lake
Bangweolo.

Among the mourners, were Thomas Steele Livingstone,
William Oswell Livingstone, Agnes Livingstone, and Mary
Anna Livingstone, the dead traveller's children; Janet
and Anna Livingstone, his sisters; Mrs. Livingstone, widow of the Rev. Charles Livingstone; Rev. Robert Moffatt,
his father-in-law; Livingstone and Bruce Moffatt, young
relatives of the traveller; Sir W. Fergusson, Rev. H. W.
Hamilton, Dr. J. Loudon, Mr. James Hannan, the Duke of

---

* From the *Weekly Despatch.*

Sutherland, Right Hon. Sir Bartle Frere, K.C.B. (Pre
dent Royal Geographical Society), Sir H. C. Rawlin
K.C.B. (Vice-President Geographical Society), Mr. K
Murchison, General Rigby, Colonel J. A. Grant, C.B., I
J. Murray, Mr. J. Young, jun. (of Kelley), Vice-Admi
Baron de la Roncière le Noury (President French Geog
phical Society), Dr. Hooker (President Royal Societ
Mr. H. W. Bates (Assistant Secretary Royal Geographi
Society), Lord Houghton, the Provost of Hamilt
Mr. J. B. Braithwaite, Mr. C. R. Markham, Mr. R
Major (Secretaries Royal Geographical Society), Rev. I
Stuart, Mr. T. Nicholson, Mr. Ralston (friends of t
family), the Lord Provost of Edinburgh, Mr. Duns
M'Laren, M.P., Mr. James Cowan, M.P., Mr. Josiah Livin
stone, the Lord Provost of Glasgow, Dr. Watson (Pre
Faculty Phys. Glasgow), Baillie Walls (Chief Magistra
Glasgow), Baillie Bain, Mr. Edwin Jones (the Mayor
Southampton), Sir Frederick Perkins, Mr. A. Laing, I
Elliott (who brought the body from Southampton); I
George Sauer, Mr. Edmund Yates, and Mr. J. H. Ma
Gahan, Correspondents of the *New York Herald*; tl
Duke of Manchester, the Earl of Ducie, Lord Cottesh
Lord Kinnaird, the Bishops of Lincoln and Sierra Leon
the Lord Mayor and City Remembrancer and twenty ma
bers of the Corporation of London ; the Mayor of Nottin
ham, the Provost of Dumbarton, the Provost and Tov
Clerk of Ayr, Lady Frere, Lady Rawlinson, Lady Straq
ford, Hon. Mrs. Forester, Mrs. W. F. Webb, of Newstea
Abbey, Mrs. and Miss Goodlake, Sir Rutherford Alcock, S

Left column (edge cut off by the page margin and the dark band):

rere, K.C.B. (Pre
ir H. C. Rawlinso
Society), Mr. K.
A. Grant, C.B., M
lley), Vice-Admir
lent French Geog
nt Royal Society
Royal Geographic
vost of Hamilto
arkham, Mr. R. E
l Society), Rev. D
ton (friends of th
ourgh, Mr. Dunca
, Mr. Josiah Living
, Dr. Watson (Pre
ls (Chief Magistrate
ones (the Mayor o
s, Mr. A. Laing, Mr.
Southampton); Mr.
and Mr. J. H. Mac-
*York Herald;* the
ucie, Lord Cottesloe,
ln and Sierra Leone,
cer and twenty man-
he Mayor of Notting-
Provost and Town
linson, Lady Strang-
Webb, of Newstead
utherford Alcock, Sir

Right column (the text of this page; the first word or two of some lines is hidden by the dark band):

Fowell Buxton, Sir C. Nicholson, Sir C. Russell, M. P., W. Thompson, Sir Harry Verney, Major-General Sir Goldsmid, the Right Hon. Russell Gurney, M.P., the Hon. G. C. Brodrick, Hon. A. F. Kinnaird, Count Goaloff, Chevalier Cadorna (Italian Minister), Viscount Duprat Portuguese Consul-General), Mr. Moran (United States Chargé d'Affaires), Capt. Francis R. Webb and lady, from Zanzibar U. S. Consulate, Count Munster (the German Ambassador), General Scott, Admirals Codrington, Collin-n, Sir W. Hall, Sherard Osborn, and Ommanney; the Rev. Wm. Monk, who presented Dr. Livingstone in 1867 the Vice-Chancellor in the Cambridge Senate House; Colonel Ouseley, Professor Brock, and a deputation from the Anthropological Institute, and other deputations from the Royal Botanical Society of London, National Temper-ance League, Social Science Association, African Section of the Society of Arts, Reception Committee of Southamp-n, Church Missionary Society, London Missionary Society, British and Foreign Anti-Slavery, East African, and other societies.

Most notable among the throng, as they carry the coffin to the grave, are the African travellers who constitute such a natural guard of honour for this dead man. Foremost among them in right of gallant special service, and nearest to Livingstone's head, stands Stanley—sun-tanned new from Ashantee—whose famous march of relief gives America the full right to celebrate at this moment, as we know she is doing, simultaneously with England, the obsequies of the explorer. But for Stanley, Livingstone would have died long back, without aid or news from us; but near him are Grant, the discoverer, along with Speke, of the Nyanza; Young, who was with Livingstone in old days, and who sailed the Nyassa Lake and the Shire River in quest of him; Oswell, tanned and grizzled with hunting and exploring under an African sun; and beside them Rigby, and Moffat, and Webb, the godfather of the Lualaba, and the faithful friend who buried Mrs. Livingstone in the sad day of the separation of husband and wife; Colonel Shelley, of Lake Ngami, Waller, of the Zambesi; Galton, Reade—what a band of Africani! Such a gathering of sun-burnt visages and far-travelled men was never seen before; and, indeed, the list might be lengthened with the names of a hundred other famous travellers present, who listen with wistful looks round their great dead chieftain, while Tallis's hymn is being sung, after the lesson read by Canon Conway. It is a well-known hymn—one which sings of ultimate rest after wandering—the only real rest for all toils and travels. These are the words :—

> " O God of Bethel, by whose hand
>    Thy people still are fed,
> Who through this weary pilgrimage
>    Hast all our fathers led ;
>
> " Our vows, our prayers, we now present
>    Before Thy throne of grace ;
> God of our fathers ! be the God
>    Of each succeeding race.

JSTONE.

1 or news from us;
along with Speke,
Livingstone in old
ike and the Shire
and grizzled with
an sun ; and beside
he godfather of the
uried Mrs. Living-
on of husband and
ni , Waller, of the
d of Africani! Such
l far-travelled men
, the list might be
ndred other famous
wistful looks round
llis's hymn is being
n Conway. It is a
of ultimate rest after
ll toils and travels.

hand

lgrimage

ow present
ce ;
God

"Through each perplexing path of life
Our wandering footsteps guide ;
Give us each day our daily bread,
And every want provide.

"O spread thy covering wings around
Till all our wanderings cease,
And at our Father's loved abode
Our souls arrive in peace !"

After the conclusion of this hymn, in which the congregation joined with much effect, the coffin is borne down the choir into the centre of the nave, where towards its western end the grave has been prepared. Here also among the dead lying around are ancient, far-travelled worthies—companionable ashes for those which are now to be consigned to the same unbroken and majestic rest. Sir John Chardin lies nigh at hand, who saw Suleiman II. crowned Monarch of Persia, two hundred years gone by—a much-wandering Knight, "qui sibi nomen fecit eundo;" and Major James Rennell, who wrote on the geography of Herodotus and founded the African Society. The pall is withdrawn, and the polished oaken coffin is prepared for lowering into the dark cavity which opens so narrowly and so abruptly in the Abbey pavement, while the choir sing, "Man that is born of a woman" to Croft's setting, and then the tender strains of Purcell's, "Thou knowest Lord." This is the very last that will be seen of "this our dear brother," and now indeed strong men are fain to bend their heads, and sobs, not from women only, mingle with the alternate sighing and rejoicing of the solemn music.

The dizzy edges of the clerestory, eighty feet overhead, are crowded with people looking down from that perilous eminence upon the throng round the grave, and shadows are seen at many of the Abbey windows, of others peering through for a glimpse at the "last scene of all." As the precious burden descends the inscription on the plate may be seen—"David Livingstone, born at Blantyre, Lanarkshire, Scotland, 19th March, 1813, died at Ilala, Central Africa, 4th May, 1873." And then there falls the "dust to dust;" and, looking at the solemn dusky faces of the two Africans, Wainwright and little Kalulu, Mr. Stanley's boy, who are standing among the nearest, the mind reverts to that widely-different scene a year ago, when Livingstone, after much pain, which is not spared to the best and kindliest, gave up his gallant, loving, pious spirit to his Master and Maker, and when yonder negro lad read over him the very service which has now again been so grandly celebrated for him,

> "With pomp and rolling music, like a King."

The African—a simple-looking, quiet, honest lad—attracts many eyes as he stands by the grave; he knows alone of all present the aspect of that other burial spot, and to him more than all this one must be impressive. But he takes his wonder, like his duty, stolidly—his thoughts appear lost in his master's memory. Alas! that master did not dream in the supreme closing hour of loneliness and agony, that his body would find such honour and peaceful repose at home. Of that and of all other reward, however, he never thought while he wrought patiently and constantly, his appointed work for the sake of Africa—tramping, discovering, noting, hunting out the slave-hunters, and leaving himself and the results of his self-sacrifice to Heaven.   And Heaven, which has given him this sweet rest in English earth, will assuredly bring forth fruits of his labour—of that we may remain well convinced; meanwhile, the work of England for Africa must henceforward begin in earnest where Livingstone left it off.

The service draws to its end with the "Forasmuch" and the following prayers, read in a clear, sustained voice of the deepest solemnity and feeling by Dean Stanley; and then once more the organ speaks the unspeakable —as music only can—sounding forth, "I heard a voice from heaven." But the very finest musical passage of all comes last in the beautiful anthem of Handel, "His body rests in peace, but his name liveth evermore." Tenderly and meditatively the first sad dreamy sentence is set, as though it were utterly by some spirit of melody looking downward into the quiet, silent haven of the grave, where all the storms and toils of mortal life are over.  Radiantly and triumph- antly comes afterwards the jubilant antiphon, as though the same gentle spirit had conceived it, mindful of the sacred words, "Come ye blessed children of my Father, receive the kingdom prepared for you from the beginning of the world."  Last of all, there rains down upon the lid of Livingstone's coffin a bright and fragrant shower of wreaths and farewell-flowers from a hundred living hands;

21

and each of those present takes a long parting glance at the great traveller's resting-place, and at the oaken coffin buried in the spring blossoms, and palms, and garlands, wherein lies " as much as could die" of the good, great-hearted, loving, fearless, and faithful David Livingstone.

The following poems were intended as tributes to the memory of the deceased traveller.   The first by Lord Houghton (Monckton-Milnes) ; the second appears anonymously in *Chambers' Journal*.   We may remark that the name Ilala, also spelt Muilala is the name of the place at which Livingstone breathed his last :—

### ILALA—MAY, 1873 !

The swarthy followers stood aloof,
    Unled—unfathered ;
He lay beneath that grassy roof,
    Fresh-gathered.

He bade them, as they passed the hut,
    To give no warning
Of their still faithful presence but
    " Good Morning."

To him, may be, through broken sleep
    And pains abated,
These words were into senses deep
    Translated.

Dear dead salutes of wife and child,
    Old kirkyard greetings ;
Sunrises over hill-sides wild—
    Heart-beatings.

Welcoming sounds of fresh-blown seas,
   Of homeward travel,
Tangles of thought's last memories
     Unravel.

'Neath England's fretted roof of fame—
   With flowers adorning
An open grave—comes up the same
   "Good Morning."

Morning's o'er that weird continent
   Now slowly breaking—
Europe her sullen self-restraint
     Forsaking.

Mornings of sympathy and trust
   For such as bore
Their Master's spirit's sacred crust
   To England's shore.

HOUGHTON.

---

## LIVINGSTONE.

It is finished ! we shall gaze upon that dauntless form no more :
The dust that once was Livingstone alone shall reach our shore.
He has perished where no aid was—not a kindred spirit near ;
Not a word of friendly counsel to salute his dying ear !
Perished with his hopes unsated and his work still incomplete,
Afric's burning sun above him and her deserts 'neath his feet !
Who may say what tender longings filled his lonely heart at last ?
Thoughts of home and well-loved faces, visions of the sacred Past !
Yet we may not mourn the end that fitly closed so grand a life,
Nor begrudge him rest so welcome, wearied with a glorious strife.

He has fallen as falls the soldier, scorning to the last to yield ;
Sternly fighting, still unconquered, prone upon the battle-field.
Not for *him* the gradual failing that the feebler nature knows ;
Not for *him* the slow decadence whiah from meaner purpose flows ;
His to labour ever onward in Humanity's just cause ;
His to stride the lonely path where Duty led without a pause ;
His amid the forest-wilds to dare an ever-present death ;
For the welfare of his fellows to expend his latest breath,
Never in the blaze of battle was a truer hero seen,
'Mid the swoop of hostile squadrons—and the sabre's blinding sheen.
Such a life and such a death shall wreathe a glory round his name
That shall brighten unborn ages and illume the scroll of Fame.

# APPENDICES.

# APPENDIX I.



IN the time of Herodotus, and long … the general opinion was that Africa di… south as the equatorial line. There ex… …dition that Africa had been circum… …cians about six centuries before … … the southern promontory of Afr… …ed, it is difficult to conceive how … …sion could have prevailed … … … …nt. It is, therefore, most prob… … never succeeded; and, indeed, the circumstances … which it was prosecuted, according to th… … have come down to us, only add an addition… … improbability to th… story. Turning to … … we find, at the commencement of th… … that Europeans were only acquainted with that … the western coast of Africa which … from … of Gibraltar to Cape Nun — … … six hundred miles in length. The Portug… honour of extending th… … … …tline of the African continent. Th… … … this direction became truly a national … …eigns and princes of Portugal prosecuted their … singular enthusiasm. By the year 14… th…

# APPENDIX I.

## A BRIEF SKETCH OF DISCOVERY IN AFRICA.

IN the time of Herodotus, and long afterward, the general opinion was that Africa did not extend so far south as the equatorial line. There existed, however, a tradition that Africa had been circumnavigated by the Phœnicians about six centuries before the Christian era; but, if the southern promontory of Africa had really been reached, it is difficult to conceive how so erroneous an impression could have prevailed as to the extent of the continent. It is, therefore, most probable that such a voyage had never succeeded; and, indeed, the circumstances under which it was prosecuted, according to the accounts which have come down to us, only add an additional feature of improbability to the story. Turning to modern times, we find, at the commencement of the fifteenth century, that Europeans were only acquainted with that portion of the western coast of Africa which extends from the Straits of Gibraltar to Cape Nun,—a line of coast not exceeding six hundred miles in length. The Portuguese had the honour of extending this limited acquaintance with the outline of the African continent. Their zeal for discovery in this direction became truly a national passion, and the sovereigns and princes of Portugal prosecuted their object with singular enthusiasm. By the year 1471 the

Portuguese navigators had advanced 2½° south of the Line.
In 1484, Diego Cam reached 22° south latitude. The next
navigator, Bartholomew Diaz, was commanded to pursue
his course southward until he should reach the extremity
of Africa; and to him belongs the honour of discovering
the Cape of Good Hope, the name given to it at the time
by the King of Portugal, though Diaz had named it Cabo
Tormentoso (the Cape of Tempests). The Cape of Good
Hope was at first frequently called the Lion of the Sea,
and also the head of Africa. In 1497, Vasco de Gama set
forth with the intention of reaching India by sailing
round the Cape of Good Hope. After doubling the Cape,
he pursued his course along the eastern coast of Africa,
and then stretched across the ocean to India. The Portuguese had now ascertained the general outline of Africa
and the position of many of the principal rivers and head-
lands. With the exception of a portion of the coast from
the Straits of Bab el Mandeb to Mukdeesha, situated in
3° north latitude, the whole of the coast had been traced
by the Portuguese, and their zeal and enthusiasm, which
had at one period been treated with ridicule, were at
length triumphantly rewarded, about four years before
Columbus had achieved his great discovery, which, with
that of Vasco de Gama, amply repaid a century of speculative enterprise. This interesting combination of events
had a sensible effect upon the general mind of Europe.
The Portuguese soon formed settlements in Africa, and
began to acquire a knowledge of the interior of the coun-

try. They were followed by the French, and afterward by the English and the Dutch.

It is chiefly within the last fifty years that discoveries in the interior of Africa have been perseveringly and systematically prosecuted. In 1788, a society was established in London with the design of encouraging men of enterprise to explore the African continent. John Ledyard, an American, was the first person selected by the African Association for this task; and he set out in 1788 with the intention of traversing the widest part of the continent from east to west, in the supposed latitude of the river Niger. Unfortunately, he was seized at Cairo with a fever of which he died. He possessed few scientific acquirements; but his vigour and powers of endurance, mental and bodily—his indifference to pain, hardship, and fatigue, would have rendered him an admirable geographical pioneer. "I have known," he said, shortly before leaving England for the last time, "hunger and nakedness to the utmost extremity of human suffering: I have known what it is to have food given as charity to a madman, and have at times been obliged to shelter myself under the miseries of that character to avoid a heavier calamity. My distresses have been greater than I have ever owned, or ever will own, to any man. Such evils are terrible to bear, but they never yet had the power to turn me from my purpose." Such was the indomitable energy of this man, the first of a long list of victims in the cause of African discovery. Mr. Lucas, who was despatched by the Association to supply the place of Ledyard, was compelled to return home in consequence of several of the countries through which he would have to pass being engaged in hostilities. In 1790, Major Houghton, an officer who was acquainted with the customs of the Moors and Negroes, proceeded to Africa under the auspices of the Association, and had made considerable progress in the interior, when, after having been treacherously plundered and left in the desert, where he endured severe privations, he reached Jarra, and died there in September, 1791, it being strongly suspected that he was murdered. The next individual on whom the Association fixed was Mungo Park, who proceeded to the river Gambia in 1795, and thence set out into the interior. The great object accomplished during his journey was that of successfully exploring the banks of the Niger, which had previously been considered identical with the river Senegal. In 1804, Park set out upon his second journey, which was undertaken at the expense of the Government. The plan of former travellers had been to accompany the caravans from one part of the country to another; but in this expedition Park required a party of thirty-six Europeans, six of whom were to be seamen and the remainder soldiers, it being his intention, on reaching the Niger, to build two vessels, and to follow with his party the course of the river. If the Congo and the Niger were the same stream, as was then supposed, he anticipated little difficulty in his enterprise; but if, as was also maintained, the Niger terminated in swamps and morasses, many hardships and dangers were expected in their subsequent progress. Park

at length reached the Niger, accompanied only by seven
of his party, all of whom were in a state of great weakness from the effects of the climate. They built one vessel,
and, on the 17th November, 1805, were ready to embark
on the river, previous to which Park sent despatches to
England. His party was now reduced to five, his brother-
in-law having died a few days before. Park's spirit, however, remained undaunted. " Though all the Europeans
who are with me should die," said he, in his last letters
to England, " and though I myself were half dead, I would
still persevere ; and, if I could not succeed in the object
of my journey, I would at least die in the Niger." He em-
barked, therefore, with the intention of sailing down the
river to its mouth, wherever that might be ; but, after
passing Timbuctoo and some of other cities, he was killed
on the Niger, at a place called Boussa, a short distance below Yaouri. No part of his journal after he left Sansand-
ing has ever been recovered.

In 1797, the African Association had engaged Mr.
Hornemann, a German, who left Cairo in September, 1798,
with the intention of carrying into effect the objects of
the Association by proceeding as far southward and westward as he could get. In his last despatches he expressed
himself confident in being able to succeed in reaching a
greater distance into the interior than any other European
traveller ; but, after reaching Bornou, no certain intelligence was ever afterwards heard concerning him. Mr.
Hornemann learned many particulars which had not before been known in Europe respecting the countries to the

east of Timbuctoo.　Mr. Nicholls, who was next engaged, arrived in the Gulf of Benin in November, 1804, and died soon afterward of the fever of the country.　Another German, Bœntzen, was next sent to Africa.　He had bestowed extraordinary pains in making himself acquainted with the prevailing language and, throwing off his costume, proceeded in the character of a Mussulman, but unhappily was murdered by his guides on his way to Soudan.　The next traveller sent out by the Association was Burckhardt, a Swiss.　He spent several years in acquiring a knowledge of the language and customs of the people he intended to visit, and, like Bœntzen, assumed the characteristics of a Mussulman.　He died at Cairo in 1817, his travels having been chiefly confined to the Abyssinian countries.

In 1816, an expedition was sent out by the Government, under the command of Captain Tuckey, to the river Congo, under the idea, in which Park coincided, that it and the Niger were the same river.　Captain Tuckey ascended the Congo for about two hundred and eighty miles.　At the same time, Major Peddie, and, after his death, Captain Campbell, proceeded from the mouth of the river Senegal as far as Kakundy.　In 1817, Mr. Bowdich explored the countries adjoining Cape Coast Castle. In 1820, Mr. Jackson communicated an interesting account of the territories of Timbuctoo and Houssa, from details which he had collected from a Mussulman merchant.　In 1819 and in 1821, the expeditions of Messrs. Ritchie and Lyon, and of Major Laing, showed the strong and general interest on the subject of African geography. In 1822, the important expedition under Major Denham and Lieut. Clapperton set forth. After crossing the Desert, the travellers reached the great inland sea or lake called the Tchad, the coasts of which to the west and south were examined by Major Denham. This lake, from four hundred to six hundred feet above the level of the sea, is one of the most remarkable featur , in the physical geography of Africa. Lieut. Clapperton, in the mean time, proceeded through the kingdom of Bornou and the country of the Fellatahs to Sockatoo, situated on a stream supposed to run into the Niger. A great mass of information respecting the countries eastward of Timbuctoo was the result of the expedition. As to the course of the Niger, very little intelligence was obtained which could be depended upon: the natives stated that it flowed into the sea at Funda, though what place on the coast was meant still remained a conjecture. Soon after his return to England, Clapperton was sent out by the Government to conduct a new expedition, and was directed to proceed to the scene of his former adventures. Having reached the Niger at Boussa, where Park was killed, he passed through various countries, and reached Sockatoo, where he died ; and Lander, his friend and servant, commenced his return to England with Clapperton's journals and papers. Major Laing, meanwhile, had visited Timbuctoo, and transmitted home accounts of this famous city, where he spent some weeks ; but on his return he was murdered, and his papers have never been recovered. We have not space to allude to the many well-executed expeditions which have proceeded from Cape Town for the purpose of exploring South Africa, but have confined ourselves to those exertions which had for their object the elucidation of the question concerning the course and termination of the Niger, and were consequently directed to Central Africa.

The termination of the Niger had long been one of the most interesting problems in African geography, and we have now reached the period when, on this point, facts were substituted for conjecture and hypothesis. The river had first been seen by Park, near Sego, the capital of Bambarra. It was called by the natives the Joliba, or "Great Water;" and Park described it as "flowing slowly to the eastward." He followed the course of the river for about three hundred miles, and was told that a journey of ten days would bring him to its source. At Sockatoo, Lieut. Clapperton found that it was called the Quorra, by which name it is known in the most recent maps, it having received the name of the Niger in the first instance, from its supposed identity with the Nigir of the ancients. The want of information concerning the course and termination of this mysterious river, until determined by actually proceeding down its channel to the sea, was, as may be supposed, a fruitful source of speculation among geographers. By some it was supposed to flow into the Nile; others imagined that a great central lake received its waters. Major Rennell, an authority of great weight, came to the conclusion that, after passing Timbuctoo, the Niger flowed a thousand miles in an easterly direction,

ve proceeded
South Africa,.
ns which had
on concerning
d were conse-

en one of the
raphy, and we
is point, facts
pothesis. The
go, the capital
s the Joliba, or
flowing slowly
of the river for
at a journey of
At Sockatoo,
the Quorra, by
t maps, it hav-
e first instance,
of the ancients.
course and ter-
determined by
the sea, was, as
sculation among
to flow into the
ral lake received
of great weight,
Timbuctoo, the
asterly direction,

and terminated in a lake or swamp; others supported the opinion that its waters were lost in the arid sands of the Desert; while the Congo was said by many to be its outlet. Major Laing, by ascertaining the source of the Niger to be not more than sixteen hundred feet above the level of the sea, proved that it could not flow into the Nile; and Denham and Clapperton demonstrated that it did not, as had been supposed, discharge itself into the Lake of Bornou.

Richard and John Lander, in 1830, under the auspices of the British Government, solved the long-disputed problem of the course of the Niger by sailing down on its waters from Boussa to the ocean, where it was found to terminate in what was called the Nun, or First Brass River, from the negro town of Brass, situated on its banks.

An expedition under the auspices of the British Government, and headed by Dr. Henry Barth, attended by Dr. Overberg and Mr. James Richardson, was sent out in 1849 to prosecute discoveries in Northern Central Africa. Their travels and researches into the history and present state of the interior tribes were continued till 1855, and their results have recently been published by Dr. Barth. Dr. Overberg died in 1854, and was buried on the shores of Lake Tchad or Tsad. Mr. Richardson also fell a victim to the climate before the close of the expedition.

Dr. Barth visited the countries of Bornou, Kanem, Mandara, Bagirmi, and others previously explored by Denham and Clapperton, and carried his researches much farther, reaching the eighth degree of north latitude. His volumes contain much curious and minute information.

The following extract from the preface gives a summary of his travels.

"Extending over a tract of country of twenty-four degrees from north to south, and twenty degrees from east to west, in the broadest part of the continent of Africa, my travels necessarily comprise subjects of great interest and diversity.

"After having traversed vast deserts of the most barren soil, and scenes of the most frightful desolation, I met with fertile lands irrigated by large navigable rivers, and extensive central lakes, ornamented with the finest timber, and producing various species of grain, rice, sesamum, ground-nuts in unlimited abundance, the sugar-cane, &c., together with cotton and indigo, the most valuable commodities of trade. The whole of Central Africa, from Bagirmi to the East, as far as Timbuctu to the west (as will be seen in my narrative), abounds in these products. The natives of these regions not only weave their own cotton, but dye their home-made shirts with their own indigo. The river, the far-famed Niger, which gives access to these regions by means of its eastern branch, the Benuwe, which I discovered, affords an uninterrupted navigable sheet of water for more than six hundred miles into the very heart of the country. Its western branch is obstructed by rapids at the distance of about three hundred and fifty miles from the coast; but even at that point it is probably not impassable in the present state of navigation, while higher up, the river opens an immense high-road for nearly one thousand miles into the very heart of Western Africa, so rich in every kind of produce.

"The same diversity of soil and produce which the regions traversed by me exhibit, is also observed with respect to man. Starting from Tripoli in the North, we proceed from the settlements of the Arab and the Berber, the poor remnants of the vast empires of the middle ages, into a country dotted with splendid ruins from the period of the Roman dominion, throug.. the wild roving hordes of the Tawarek, to the Negro and the half-Negro tribes, and to the very border of the South African nations. In the regions of Central Africa there exists not one and the same stock, as in South Africa, but the greatest diversity of tribes, or rather nations prevails, with idioms entirely distinct."

The results of Dr. Livingstone's last voyages of exploration have greatly increased our knowledge of Southern and Central Africa, as will be readily seen by the readers of this volume, in which the condensation of these results has been given. Of course the chief objects which attract at first the attention of explorers are the broad geographical features of the country, the course of its rivers, the mountain ranges, and all matters which come more particularly under the head of physical geography. The mineral deposits, or the agricultural advantages of a country are, as a rule, discovered only after a more minute investigation of its natural conditions than it is possible for an explorer to make. The field of Africa has, how-

22

ever, been opened, and the recent discoveries in South
Africa of deposits of diamonds has attracted immigration
such as the modern world has seen attracted to California
and Australia by the discovery of gold deposits in these
two countries. As in both of these cases, the attraction
of a large population from the civilized portions of the
world has brought together specialists of various kinds,
and a wide spread and scientific examination of the territory has led to the discovery of various other sources of
wealth. In South Africa, near Cape Town, deposits of
gold, silver, copper, lead, and coal, the most important mineral deposit, since it affords the power absolutely necessary for our modern industry, have been found. Perhaps
the most startling of these instances of modern discoveries
is that of the diamond fields of South Africa. It is
impossible to accurately estimate the number of diamonds which have thus been thrown into the circulation of the world's wealth, but it is something enormous,
and hitherto in the modern world's history unprece-
dented.

When diamonds were first found here, the land was free
for any one to search over, but the news of their discovery led to the influx of such a large body of persons to
engage in this work, that, as in California and Australia,
the right of private property began soon to assert itself,
and claims began immediately to rise in value, until
a good one, thirty feet square, commands already
$15,000.

Already about Kopje is gathered a population of about forty thousand people. The New Rush is eight hundred yards wide, with eight parallel roads running through it, along which the dirt from the excavations below is carted away. At first there was no organization of the labour, and no arrangement by which the private interests of those engaged in it should be prevented from becoming detrimental to the public welfare. In consequence, the private excavations have been carried on so far, or in some cases, farther, than either safety or a fair prospect for profit dictated, and without any regard for preserving the roads. In many cases, also, these roadways were left so narrow that there was hardly room for two carts to pass, and now they are really dangerous, having become as they are, narrow causeways, seventy or eighty feet high, and being unstayed and supported by any but the most temporary appliances.

This place, New Rush, is the only one which is still considered as a profitable spot for diamond digging. Other places, as Hebron, Phiel, Klipdrift and Du Toit's Pan, have been chiefly exhausted, and diamond digging there requires too much patience to suit such an adventurous class as generally engage in speculative labour of this kind.

The gold fields are about three hundred miles from the banks of the Vaal, and the last town on the outskirts of civilization is Pretonia, about one hundred and fifty miles from Vaal. With the attention which has thus been

called to Africa, the next twenty years will most probably
lead to such explorations as will not only give us a complete knowledge of its physical features, but also lead to
an organized introduction of civilization into this country,
and an orderly development of its resources through the
appliances of modern industry.

# APPENDIX II.

## THE NEW ANGLO-AMERICAN EXPEDITION TO AFRICA.

### (From the London *Daily Telegraph*, July 4, 1874.)

WE are in a position this morning to announce that arrangements have been concluded between the proprietors of the *Daily Telegraph* and Mr. Bennett, proprietor of the *New York Herald*, under which an expedition will at once be despatched to Africa with the object of investigating and reporting upon the haunts of the slave traders; of pursuing to fulfilment the magnificent discoveries of the great explorer, Dr. Livingstone, and of completing, if possible, the remaining problems of Central African geography.   This expedition has been undertaken by, and will be under the sole command of, Mr. Henry M. Stanley, whose successful journey "in search of Livingstone," upon the suggestion and at the charge of the proprietor of the *New York Herald*, was the means of succouring the illustrious traveller, and secured to science the fruit of his researches, while it enabled our distinguished countryman to prosecute his latest investigations. Mr. Stanley will, in a short time, leave England fully equipped with boats, arms, stores, and all the provisions necessary for a thorough and protracted African expedition. Commissioned by the *Daily Telegraph* and *New York Herald* in concert, he will represent the two nations whose common interest in the regeneration of Africa was so well illustrated when the lost English explorer was rediscovered by the energetic American correspondent. In that memorable journey, Mr. Stanley displayed the best qualities of an African traveller; and with no inconsiderable resources at his disposal to reinforce his own complete acquaintance with the conditions of African travel, it may be hoped that very important results will accrue from this undertaking, to the advantage of science, humanity, and civilization.

We cannot, indeed, be mistaken in believing that the enterprise thus planned will be held by general opinion—not only here and in the United States, but throughout Europe—as one worthy to engage the efforts of modern journalism. The sphere of the press, as a minister to public interests and sentiments, is, of necessity, enlarging along with the widening range of those interests and sentiments, and while American liberality has well earned the right to share in reaping the fruits of Livingstone's work, the hunting-out of the African slave trade and the solution of the yet abiding mystery of the central portion of that continent are topics which obviously concern and attract every intelligent Englishman. To bring to light the wickedness of the traffic in human flesh is the best road towards its abolition; and we cherish the hope that this joint enterprise may furnish valuable information to the Legislature and to the British Government, whose credit is bound up with the final success of the movement set on foot by the treaty of Sir Bartle Frere. At present, as is only too well known, that treaty, concluded with the Sultan of Zanzibar, has not obtained the results expected. An infamous and lucrative traffic, but imperfectly revealed by the official communication recently communicated to Parliament, still thrives along the East African shores, and it will be part of the instructions of our joint commissioner to see with his own eyes, as far as possible, the methods, the haunts and the character of this nefarious trade, before advancing into the interior. This was assuredly one of the duties bequeathed to us by the noble-minded Livingstone. Everybody knows that the burning desire to rid Africa of that curse, the slave driver, lay even nearer to the great explorer's heart than his ambition to unlock her hidden secrets and to fill up the vast mysterious blank spaces of her map. For this he chiefly toiled—for this he sought to make his name weighty and his voice far heard—in order that, living or dying, it might be strong to urge England on to the completion of her historical duty. In the sermon which Dean Stanley delivered over the newly-closed grave of this great man, the subjoined words occurred:—"There arose in his noble breast as he wandered on among them, the passionate wish, ever mounting to a higher and yet higher pitch of burning indignation, and fierce determination to expose, and exposing to strike a fatal blow at that monster evil which by general testimony is the one prevailing cause of African misery and degradation—the European and Asiatic slave

trade. He grappled with it vigorously, and it recognized
in him its most formidable foe. In the struggle he perished,
too soon, alas! for him to know how nearly he had
succeeded—not, we trust, too soon for us to secure that
his success shall be accomplished, so that the work which
in its commencement and continued inspiration was the
brightest side of the name of Wilberforce shall, in its completion, shed the chief glory on the name of Livingstone."
It is one of the bequests, we say, of Livingstone to the
English speaking peoples that they should let the light in
upon this evil and extirpate it; and, therefore, one stead-
fast object recommended to Mr. Stanley—who, perhaps,
more than any other man, has the right to "administer
to Livingstone's testament"—will be to search out and
reveal what this slave traffic really is in its "dark places."

The second and scarcely less momentous bequest of the
illustrious dead is as certainly the completion of his geographical researches. This duty also stands intimately
connected with the future regeneration of Africa; indeed,
the two undertakings belong naturally to each other, for
when Africa shall once be delivered from the immemorial
terror of the slavers, then her uprise must depend upon
her natural resources and lines of internal communication.
Livingstone always saw and felt how intimately his mission of humanity and his scientific researches were linked
together; and the patient traveller who found rest at last
in Ilala worked for the future of Africa as directly as the
fearless pen which brought an English Plenipotentiary to
Zanzibar and the faithful hand which told us the truth

about slavery. In the course of his vast wanderings, Livingstone wrought also a stupendous work for science: but he felt it necessarily incomplete. The same eloquent discourse already quoted contains the following passage: —"The blank of unexplored regions which in every earlier map formed the heart of Africa is now disclosed to us, adorned with those magnificent forests, that chain of lakes, 'glittering'—to use the native expression—'like stars in the desert'; those falls, more splendid, we are told, even than Niagara, which no eye of civilized man had ever before beheld, where, above the far-resounding thunder of the cataract and the flying comets of snow-white foam, and the rising columns of ever ascending spray, and the bright rainbows arching over the clouds, the simple natives had for centuries seen the emblem—the glorious emblem—of everlasting Deity—the unchangeable seated enthroned above the changeable. And to Livingstone's untiring exertions, continued down to the very last efforts of exhausted nature, we owe the gradual limitation of the basin within which must at last be found those hidden fountains that have lured on traveller after traveller, and have hitherto baffled them all." Dean Stanley is quite right; the secret of the Nile—that is to say the key to the commercial road of Central Africa—has yet to be found. Burton and Speke, Grant and Baker, and even Livingstone himself have, with all their splendid discoveries, still left the ancient mystery unrevealed; it has ever more deeply receded as each of them approached it, the ultimate possibilities always becoming grander with each disappointment.   Thus it may yet prove that the far-off Lake Bangweolo, near whose shore the great explorer died, sends its waters to the wonderful Nile.   How that would enhance the pathos and the glory of his death, if it should turn out that Providence gave him his summons when his labour of love and duty were so much more thoroughly consummated than he knew!   He was wont to say in all his difficulties and doubts, " It will all come right at last."   In the belief that it will come right we are going to send the white man who was with him last, and whom he has blessed and called " as good as a son to me," upon the track of his failing footsteps to see if he can help Africa and geography, and finish Livingstone's task.

At this moment, in truth, the problem of Central African geography has become more fascinating, more absorbing, more important than ever before.   Livingstone has hunted this sphinx of science into a kind of corner, and six degrees of longitude westward of Lake Tanganyika now contain the solution upon which the future of Africa depends. Five magnificent lakes—the smallest of them, probably, as big as Michigan—and a long, superb, connecting lacustrine river, threading these lakes from the vast Usango plateau south of Tanganyika to the inland seas of Bangweolo, Moero, Kamolondo and the " Unknown Water"— have been made known to us by the same adventurous journey of rescue which prolonged the life of Livingstone· These glorious fresh-water seas, with the lordly river which strings them together, and with that other broad

stream which issues from Lake Lincoln and joins the
Lualaba—do they run northward to the Nyanzas and the
Nile, or westward to the Congo ?  Does Tanganyika find
some western outlet whereby to add her waves to them,
or are Tanganyika and Nyanza one ; or else by what
strange reason do her deep and mountain-shadowed waters
remain so sweet and fresh ?  These are not merely problems of the geographer's study—questions to while away
an evening of the Royal Geographical Society.  Upon the
right answer to them depends the proper road into the
heart of Africa—the destined direction of that commerce
which will some day rescue her and give her a place
among the civilized continents.  And when we add to
these primary inquiries the deeply interesting secondary
queries about the Katanga copper mines, those mysterious
" Four Fountains," and the underground habitations near
Moero, it will be seen at what an intensely interesting
stage of African discovery the expedition of the *New
York Herald* and of the *Daily Telegraph* sets forth.

It is true that the field of exploration is not quite at
this moment deserted.  In March, 1873, Lieutenant
Cameron was commissioned by Sir Bartle Frere, on behalf
of the Royal Geographical Society, to take supplies and
means to Livingstone, who was at that time, though none
knew it, near to die at Ilala.  Accompanied by Messrs.
Dillon and Murphy, this expedition started, but only to
encounter a run of ill luck and difficulties which brought
its resourses so low that at Unyanyembe it was already
nearly bankrupt.  To proceed at all Lieutenant Cameron

had to draw largely upon the Royal Geographical Society
and to buy his clothes at a ruinous price; and when, with
great courage and perseverance, he was at last going forward, the sad news came to him that the doctor was dead.
Of his two companions Dr. Dillon died overwrought by
suffering, and Mr. Murphy resigned and came back to
Zanzibar.   Cameron went forward to fetch the papers and
effects of Livingstone left at Ujiji, and reached that place
in February of the present year.   But he is, although not
aware of it, no longer now the emissary of the society.
That body had never expected to incur the heavy losses
of the upward march; and although its hesitation to
honour Lieutenant Cameron's drafts, felt and sustained at
first, was very properly surmounted in the end; still with
many other objects to follow, and the papers of Livingstone secured, it eventually resolved not to extend the
journey of Lieutenant Cameron or incur any further expense.   Letters to this effect have gone after him, which
reached Unyanyembe in June and Ujiji in July, so that
while we write the communication is perhaps being
delivered to this gallant officer which acquaints him with
the hard truth that he is no longer in the service of the
society.   He has faced a hundred obstacles with the
highest courage, and deserved, we cannot help thinking
a somewhat stouter support; and it will certainly be one
of the instructions of our commissioner, as it would
obviously accord with his own inclination, to be of use to
the brave young explorer if opportunity should offer.   As
to the chance of Cameron's solving the trans-Tanganyika

problem, it is, we fear, not strong.   He was to boat on the
lake for two months, and to make an excursion into Manyema, say down to May or June.   Then, if he waited at
Ujiji for letters, it would only be to receive that little
cheering one from Saville Row, practically recalling him,
while if he went forward without any news, his recourses
probably, would not carry him far unless he met with
much better fortune than in the first part of his trip.
Meantime, his friends at home have collected £600, which
will suffice to pay for his return journey from Lake Tanganyika to Zanzibar, and notice of this has been transmitted to the coast.   If he can, by any stroke of pluck or
luck, find the way northward to Gordon, he will have
solved one problem of African geography, and shown himself by a fresh proof, which was not needed, what all
know him to be—a brave man ; but it is extremely improbable that he has means for any such journey, and
much more likely that, not possessing them, and receiving
the letter of dismissal, he will have turned homeward by
next Christmas, so that our expedition may perhaps have
the pleasure of rendering service to him—possibly, indeed,
very timely service.

Meanwhile, the letters received from Cameron at Ujiji,
render the great problem of the Nile and the lakes more
fascinating than ever.   His observations show that Speke
was quite wrong in putting Tanganyika only 1,844 feet
above the sea level.   Livingstone was right; it is about
2,800 feet ; and, seeing that the same elevation, or nearly
so, is given for the Albert Nyanza—the difference between

Cameron's and Baker's estimate for the respective lakes is only twenty feet—the old possibility returns, that Tanganyika and Nyanza may, after all, be one. This was the report heard by Sir Samuel Baker, at Faloro, and telegraphed first to these columns; and if it were only true—if even the Lualaba and the southern lakes ran into the Nyanza—then Livingstone, after all, did find the real and ultimate fountains of the River of Egypt, and you may sail a boat, with certain portages, from Alexandria to the uplands of Usango, in the twelfth degree of latitude, south of the Equator. And this would mean that Africa, at the moment of her delivery from the slave hunters, had fair, and beautiful, and healthy highways, all ready and open to the north and to the east. If, on the contrary, the great inland seas and rivers of Manyema go westward to the Congo, it would still be deeply interesting and important to ascertain the fact. In every respect, for every reason, from every point of view, the sad continent seems to wait for the reading of this riddle. Then comes her long-deferred time of light and life! Sir Samuel Baker, delivering recently the Rede lecture at Cambridge, said: "She will awake when the first steam launch is seen upon the Albert Nyanza," and he added, that nowhere in the world does scenery exist more beautiful, or soil more fertile, or climate more healthy to the temperate and strong, than those vast and diversified highlands of Central Africa which inclose these glorious, sparkling seas of sweet water, and feed the mighty rivers whose course is so far winding that to this day no man has yet traversed them from mouth to fountain.

In full, and we hope, well-justified confidence, then, that our joint expedition will have the good wishes of all men, —we are about to send it forth. Africa is vast, doubtful and dangerous, and the best preparations cannot insure success, nor can the stoutest manhood command it. But whatever good equipment and sufficient resources can do worthily to continue Livingstone's work will not be wanting, and the commissioner employed will be a man who loves the great traveller's memory, who rejoices to follow in his footsteps, and who has displayed those personal qualities which can best overcome the hundred perils of an explorer. It was when Sir Roderick Murchison reluctantly announced, in 1871, that the Royal Geographical Society had no further intention of sending after Livingstone, that the *New York Herald* despatched Mr. Stanley, with the result of rescuing the good missionary, sustaining him in his last journey, and securing for his country, and for science, the rich fruits of his research. The society must not be blamed though another traveller is isolated, and an African exploration again suspended; its means are not inexhaustible, and it has done much and well for science. But then, the work of Livingstone, in its two aspects of humanity and discovery, is not a thing that must or can be dropped; and therefore, it is that, in this friendly alliance of resource and purpose, the proprietors of the two journals concerned have concluded their present arrangements.

**THE END.**

# EVERYBODY'S
# OWN PHYSICIAN;

### OR,

## HOW TO ACQUIRE AND PRESERVE HEALTH.

### ILLUSTRATED

### WITH ABOUT 250 FINELY EXECUTED WOOD-CUTS,

*Many of which are Engraved from Models in the Author's Private Cabinet, and correctly represent nearly all of the Organs of the Body, in Health and Disease.*

BY

## C. W. GLEASON, M.D.,

PROFESSOR OF THE INSTITUTES OF MEDICINE AND SURGERY, EDITOR OF THE PHYSIOLOGIST, AUTHOR OF THE LAWS OF LIFE, AND ART OF PRESERVING HEALTH, POPULAR LECTURES ON SANITARY SCIENCE, ETC., PHILADELPHIA.

### TORONTO:
### MACLEAR AND CO., PUBLISHERS.
### 1874.

*One large Octavo Volume, Price $3.*

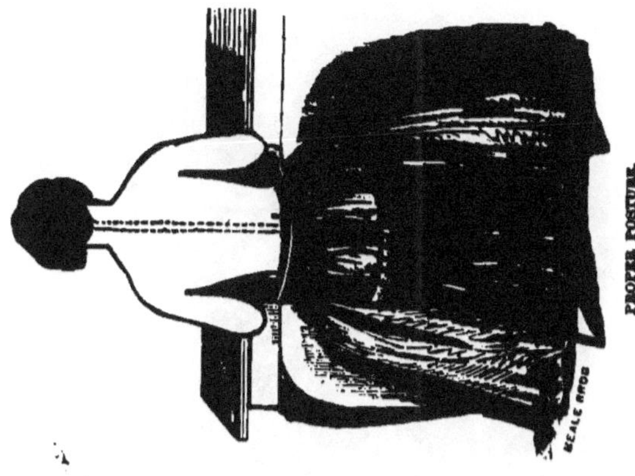

BEALE BROS
PROPER POSTURE.

IMPROPER POSTURE.

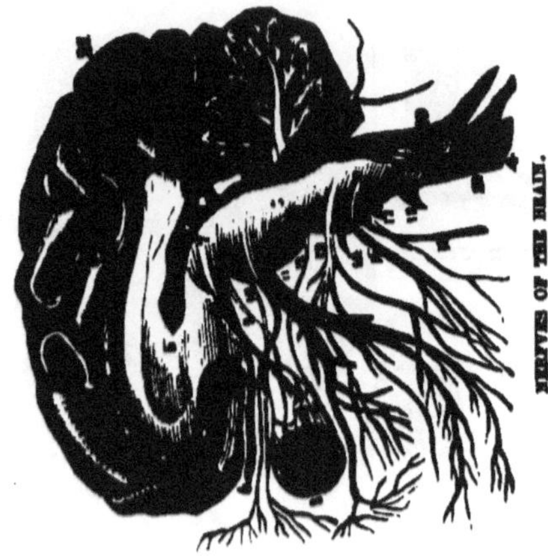
NERVES OF THE BRAIN.

DISEASES OF THE EYE.

RIGHT AND WRONG POSTURES.

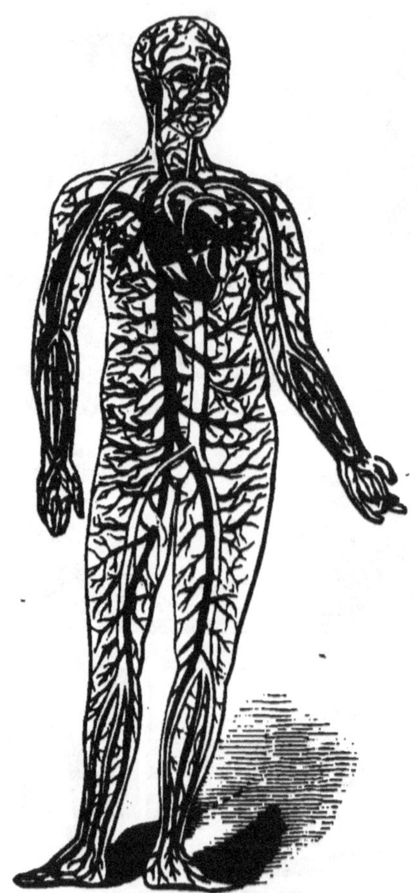

THE HEART, ARTERIES AND NERVES.

THE BRAIN AND NERVES.

DISEASES OF THE EAR.

THE

# PHYSICAL LIFE OF WOMAN:

Advice to the

## MAIDEN, WIFE, AND MOTHER.

—BY—

### GEO. H. NAPHEYS, A.M., M.D.

*Member of Philadelphia County Medical Society;
Corresponding Member of the Gynæcological Society of Boston;
Author of "Compendium of Modern Therapeutics," &c., &c.*

---

"Je veux qu'une femme ait des clartés de tout."
MOLIÈRE.

---

### PRICE $1.50.—POST FREE ON RECEIPT OF PRICE.

---

AGENTS WANTED EVERYWHERE FOR THIS AND OTHER BOOKS.

---

☞ Should these pages come into the hands of any one who may take no interest in
the books described, the Publishers will esteem it a favor to have them handed to some
one who may desire them.

---

TORONTO:
MACLEAR AND COMPANY.
1874.

# THE
# PHYSICAL LIFE OF WOMAN.

ADVICE TO THE

## MAIDEN, WIFE, AND MOTHER.

—BY—

### GEO. H. NAPHEYS, A.M., M.D.

*Member of Philadelphia County Medical Society ;*
*Corresponding Member of the Gynæcological Society of Boston,*
*Author of " Compendium of Modern Therapeutics," &c., &c.*

———

" Je veux qu'une femme ait des clartes de tout."
MOLIÈRE.

———


## *SYNOPSIS OF THE BOOK.*

It treats in detail the three peculiar phases of woman's life, viz., maidenhood, matrimony and maternity. Under the first head, the subject of puberty, its dangers and hygiene, and of love, are discussed from a medical stand-point. Valuable advice is given on the marriage of cousins, on the effects of marriage on woman and man, on "choosing a husband," on "the engagement," on the right time of the year to marry, on the wedding tour, and on many kindred topics. The physiology of the marriage relation is then considered. In the second part of the book, "the wife." It commences with some salutary hints on the "wedding night." Such inquiries of universal hygienic interest as, Shall husband and wife occupy the same room and bed ? What kind of bed is most healthful ? the dignity and propriety of the sexual instinct—its indulgence, restraint, and physiological laws, &c., are decorously but plainly treated. Well considered views are advanced in regard to over-production and the limitation of offspring. The author also gives much useful advice to sterile wives who desire to have children, and he answers the question, Can the sexes be produced at will? in the light of the most recent scientific research. Many pages are devoted to the discussion of inheritance, how to have beautiful children, twin-bearing, &c. The information in regard to the signs of pregnancy and the avoidance of its diseases and discomforts, the prevention of "mothers' marks" and of miscarriage, is of incalculable value to every woman. Minute, practical and careful directions are laid down as to the proper preparations for confinement, how to preserve the form after childbirth, etc. Under the head of "the mother" the rules for nursing, weaning and bringing up by hand, are copious, and would benefit every mother to know. The volume closes with a consideration of "The Perils of Maternity," and of the dangers and hygiene of "The change of life."

# TESTIMONIALS.

The following, among others, have been received indicating the scientific value and moral worth of this book :—

### SIR WM. STERLING MAXWELL,

*Recently elected Lord Rector of Edinburgh University,*

gave the usual address on being installed in that office. Among other things he referred to the medical education of women, and said he was in favour of teaching women everything that they desired to learn, and for opening to them the doors of the highest oral instruction as wide as the doors of book learning. So long, he said, as women would administer to their sick children and husbands, he must hear some argument more convincing than he had yet heard why they were to be debarred from learning the scientific grounds of the art of which they were so often the empirical practitioners or the docile and intelligent instruments.

---

### FROM PROFESSOR JOHN S. HART, LL.D.

STATE NORMAL SCHOOL, TRENTON, N.J.

GEO. H. NAPHEYS, M.D.,—

*Dear Sir :* I have read with attention the advance sheets of your book, "The Physical Life of Woman;" and take pleasure in saying that you have handled a most difficult and important subject with equal delicacy and ability.

Yours truly,

JOHN. S. HART.

## OPINION OF MARK HOPKINS, D.D., LL.D.,
*President of Williams College.*

"Your book is conscientiously written, and will be likely to do good."

---

### FROM THE N.Y. EVANGELIST, NOV. 18, 1869.

This is a plain and practical treatise prepared by a physician of skill and experience, in which he aims to furnish information to women, in their peculiar conditions and relations, married and single, so as to enable them to preserve their own health, and perform their duties to themselves and their children. The most delicate subjects are treated in language so chaste as not to offend any pure mind.

---

### EDITORIAL FROM PHILADELPHIA MEDICAL AND SURGI-
### CAL REPORTER.

It is a singular fact, that in this country most of the works on medical hygienic matters have been written by irregular practitioners in order to help on its legs some ism or pathy of their own. The public is really desirous of information about the great questions of life and health. It buys whatever is offered it, and cannot tell of course the tares from the wheat. In fact, as we have said, there has been very little wheat offered it. Scientific physicians do not seem to have taken the pains in this country, as in Germany, to spread sound medical information among the people.

We therefore welcome all the more warmly a work which, under any circumstances, would command our praise, advance sheets of which are now before us. The author is Dr. George H. Napheys, of this city. well known to all the readers of the "Reporter" as a constant contributor to its pages for a number of years, a close student of therapeutics, and a pleasing writer. The title of the book is "The Physical Life of Woman; advice to the Maiden, Wife, and Mother." It is a complete manual of information for women, in their peculiar conditions and relations, married and single.

The style is simple, agreeable, and eminently proper and delicate, conspicuously so when treating of such difficult topics to handle in a popular book, yet so necessary to be handled, as the marital relations of husband and wife, the consummation of marriage, etc.

We do not doubt that this work will find as large a sale both in and out of the profession in this country, as the works of Bockh and Klencke in Germany, and of Tilt and Chavasse in England.

### FROM REV. HORACE BUSHNELL, D.D.

HARTFORD, CONN., Sept., 1869.

GEO. H. NAPHEYS, M.D.,—

*Dear Sir:* I have read a large part of your book with interest. I shrink from expressing any estimate of it as respects its physiological merit, but it seems to be a book well studied, and it is written with much delicacy and a careful respect, at all points, to the great interests of morality. It will certainly be a great help to intelligence on the subject, and ought, therefore, to be correspondently useful.

Very respectfully yours,

HORACE BUSHNELL.

---

### FROM HARVEY L. BYRD, M.D.,

*Professor of Obstetrics in the Medical Department of Washington University of Baltimore, Maryland.*

BALTIMORE, Sept. 1869.

DR. GEO. H. NAPHEYS, Philadelphia,—

*Dear Sir :* I have examined with much pleasure and satisfaction your work on " The Physical Life of Woman," and do not hesitate to commend it most warmly to our countrywomen, for whose benefit it is intended. I congratulate you on the felicitous manner in which you have treated so difficult a subject, and would recommend it to the public as supplying a want that has long been felt in this country.

*Omne verum utile dictu,* and what can be more proper, or more useful, than that woman should be made acquainted with the great laws of her being, and the duties for which she was created?

Very respectfully, your obed't servant,

HARVEY L. BYRD.

---

### OPINION OF S. W. BUTLER, M.D.,

*Editor of the Philadelphia " Medical and Surgical Reporter."*

I have carefully examined " The Physical Life of Woman," and find it a work at once thoroughly representing modern science, and eminently adapted for family instruction. It is well suited to female readers, to whom it is especially addressed both in the matter it contains and in the delicacy with which points relating to their physiological life are mentioned.

S. W. BUTLER.

## EXTRACTS FROM LETTER RECEIVED FROM EDWARD M. SNOW, M.D., OF PROVIDENCE, RHODE ISLAND.

PROVIDENCE, Sept., 1869.

DR. NAPHEYS,—

*Dear Sir :* I have examined with much interest the advance sheets of your book, " The Physical Life of Woman ;" I am highly pleased with it. The advice given seems to me to be generally correct and judiciously expressed ; and in my opinion the wide circulation of the book would be a benefit to the community.

Truly yours,

EDWIN. M. SNOW.

---

## FROM REV. GEORGE ALEX. CROOKE, D.D., D.C.L.

PHILADELPHIA, Sept., 1869.

DR. GEO. H. NAPHEYS,—

*Dear Sir :* I have carefully read your work entitled " The Physical Life of Woman," and as the result, I must candidly say that I believe the information it contains is well calculated to lessen suffering and greatly benefit the human race. I know there are some falsely fastidious persons who would object to any work of the kind, but "to the pure all things are pure." You have done your part fearlessly and well, and in a popular manner, and I trust that your work may be productive of all the good you design by its publication.

Very faithfully,

GEO. ALEX. CROOKE.

---

## OPINION OF LLOYD P. SMITH.

*Librarian Philadelphia Library.*

LIBRARY CO. OF PHILADELPHIA, FIFTH ST. BEL. CHESNUT,

PHILADELPHIA, Sept., 1869.

It is an open question whether books *de secretis mulierum* should be written for the general public, but there is no doubt that when they are written, it should be done by the regular medical faculty and not by ignorant quacks. Dr. Napheys' "Physical Life of Woman" shows not only the scientific attainments of the author, but also a wide range of miscellaneous reading. The delicate subjects treated of are handled with a seriousness and earnestness becoming their importance, and the author's views are expressed in excellent English.

LLOYD P. SMITH.

## LETTER RECEIVED FROM REV. GEO. BRINGHURST,
*Rector of the P. E. Church of the Messiah, Philada.*

PHILADELPHIA, Sept., 1869.

DR. GEO H. NAPHEYS,—

*My Dear Sir :* I have perused with considerable care and pleasure the work on the " Physical Life of Woman," and feel no hesitation in pronouncing it admirably composed, honest, succinct, refined and worthy the companionship of every lady of this age. I hail its appearance with gratitude, and look upon it as a valuable contribution to those efforts which are making in various directions to elevate the tone of morals of the nineteenth century, and to enable mothers to discharge faithfully the duties they owe their children.

Sincerely yours,

GEORGE BRINGHURST.

---

## FROM THE MEDICAL RECORD, NEW YORK, JAN. 15, 1870.

Doctor Napheys, in his work on "The Physical Life of Woman," has acquitted himself with infinite credit. The subject, which for a work of its size takes a very wide range, is treated in choice, nay elegant language, and we have not noticed a single expression upon the most delicate matter, that could offend the most refined taste. There are, too, a great many interesting historical facts connected with the general topic, both in an ethical and physiological point of view, which show much discrimination in their production, and a good amount of sterling scholarship. To the medical reader there are many points in the book that are worthy of attention, prominent among which are remarks bearing upon the right of limitation of offspring. We sincerely hope that for the real benefit of women, it may meet with a hearty reception, and be productive of great good, in preventing many of these disorders now so rife in the community, which are solely the result of ignorance of the ordinary laws of female hygiene.

No one, however scrupulous, need fear to admit the work within the pale of his family circle, and place it with confidence, in the hands of his daughters.

---

## FROM THE NEW YORK MEDICAL GAZETTE,
JAN. 8, 1870.

Though professedly written for popular instruction, this book will not fail to instruct, as well the professional reader. We cordially recommend the perusal of Dr. Napheys' book to every woman seeking a fuller acquaintance with her physical organism.

## FROM H. N. EASTMAN, M.D.,

*Professor of Practical Medicine in Geneva Medical College.*

GENEVA, Sept., 1869.

GEO. H. NAPHEYS', M.D.,—

*Dear Sir :* I have just completed a careful reading of your advance sheets of "The Physical Life of Woman," and I unhesitatingly pronounce it an admirable work, and one especially needed at this time.

The book is written in a chaste, elevated, and vigorous style, is replete with instructions indispensable to the welfare and happiness of women, and should be placed in the hands of every mature maiden and matron in our land.

H. N. EASTMAN.

---

## FROM THE NASHVILLE JOURNAL OF MEDICINE AND SURGERY FOR NOVEMBER, 1869.

The outside of this book is more stylish and artistic than any the market has owed to the press this season. The type and paper of the inside are in keeping with the elegant exterior. The work contains much valuable matter, in a style peculiarly attractive. It is intended to treat woman as a rational being, to let her know much about herself as a woman, that from this knowledge she may prevent and therefore escape much of the suffering endured by her sex.

And who can do this but a physician? This may be regarded as the first attempt of the kind in this country.

---

## FROM THE CHICAGO MEDICAL EXAMINER OF NOVEMBER 19, 1869.

This work is written in a plain and pleasing style well calculated both to please and instruct. There is nothing of the *sensational* or imaginative character in it. On the contrary, its teachings are in strict accordance with scientific facts and good sense. Though designed specially for females, yet a careful perusal would be productive of much benefit to both sexes.

---

## FROM THE BOSTON MEDICAL AND SURGICAL JOURNAL, NOV. 25, 1869.

Most valuable for the perusal of mothers, and of those fathers who may be equal to the task of advising sons liable to commit matrimony. The style—of the text—is unexceptionable. Words are not wasted, and those used are to the point. The volume is not a mere *resume* of others' opinions ; but the author has made the topics of which he treats his own.

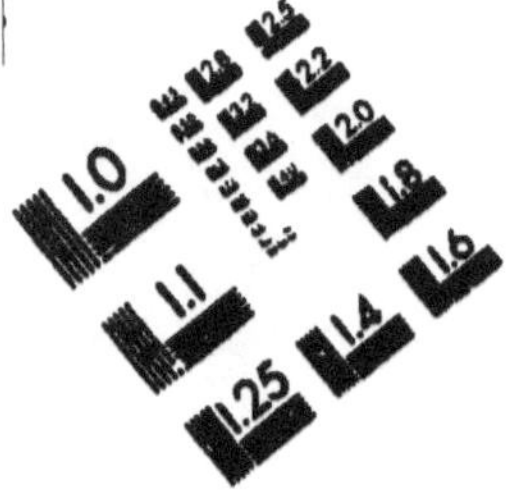

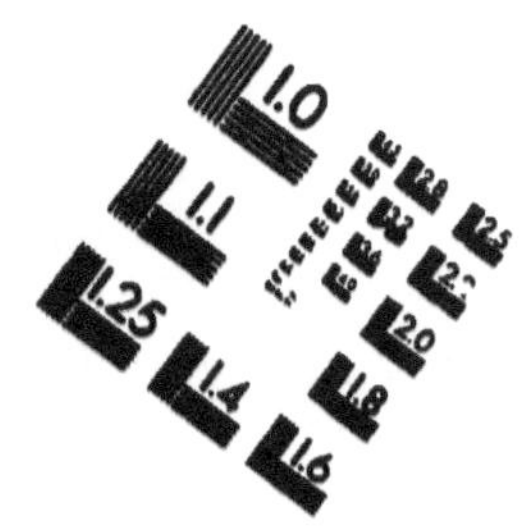

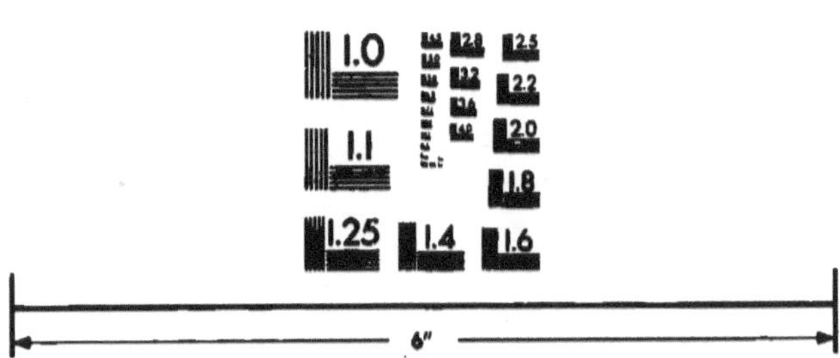

# IMAGE EVALUATION
# TEST TARGET (MT-3)

Photographic
Sciences
Corporation

23 WEST MAIN STREET
WEBSTER, N.Y. 14580
(716) 872-4503

## FROM THE NATIONAL BAPTIST, PHILADELPHIA,
### Dec. 30, 1869.

We join in the cordial welcome which this book has received. There is no other work which tells so well just what every woman,—and every considerate man also,—ought to know. Maternity is the one great function of woman, according to God's ordinance, and for this marvellous and holy mission, her physical, intellectual, and moral constitution has been designed. Dr. Napheys, in his wise "advice to maiden, wife, and mother," passes in review the cardinal facts respecting woman's physical life. The book is written in a very clear and simple style, so that no one can misunderstand it, while there is nothing to disturb or offend the most sensitive. A judicious mother would do her maturing daughters great service by first carefully reading this volume herself, and then have them read it under her guidance.

---

### OPINION OF MRS. R. B. GLEASON, M.D.

ELMIRA, N.Y., Sept. 1869.

The advanced sheets of "The Physical Life of Woman" have been read with much interest. In this book Dr. Napheys has well met a real need of the age. There are many things incident to woman's physical organization which she needs to know, and concerning which she still does not want to ask a physician, and may not have one at hand when she most desires the information. This book can be easily read and perfectly understood by those not familiar with medical terms. All matters of delicacy are treated with freedom, and still with a purity of thought and expression which is above criticism.

For many years we have been often asked for just such a book, and shall gladly commend it to the many wives and mothers who want for themselves and grown-up daughters such a book of helps and hints for home life.

MRS. R. B. GLEASON.

---

### OPINION OF DR. R. SHELTON MACKENZIE.

PHILADELPHIA, Oct., 1869.

Believing that such a work as Dr. Napheys' " Physical Life of Woman," giving a great deal of valuable information, explicitly and delicately, is likely to be of very essential importance to the fair sex, I cannot hesitate to express my favourable opinion of its object and execution.

## FROM THE METHODIST HOME JOURNAL,
### DEC. 4, 1869.

Hitherto, the subjects so honestly and so skillfully treated in this volume, have, to a very great extent, been ruled out of the realm of popular knowledge, and information of this class sought only in a clandestine manner. The people have suffered by deplorable ignorance on those topics, which should be as familiar to us as the alphabet. Dr. Napheys, by his scientific handling of the physiological points which relate to health, training, and development, has rendered a great service to the world. This, the press and public men have not been slow to acknowledge. This book has gained unquallified praise, and well deserves it.

## FROM THE INDEPENDENT, NEW YORK,
### NOV. 11, 1869.

It required a brave but sensitively pure man to provide for the want which existed for some reliable medical instructions upon points which every woman and every married man ought to know, and few do. Dr. Napheys we do not know personally. But his book is at once brave and pure. It is written in such a spirit that she who really desires to learn the truths of which she cannot with justice to herself or others be ignorant, may do so without being shocked; while he who hopes to stimulate a vicious imagination by its perusal will turn from its pages disappointed away.

## FROM THE PHILADELPHIA EVENING TELEGRAPH,
### OCT. 6, 1869.

This is a work by a physician of reputation on the hygiene of woman, designed for popular use, and introducing a variety of topics not generally discussed outside of regular scientific medical works. Dr. Napheys writes with dignity and earnestness, and there is not a chapter in his book that may not be read by persons of both sexes. Of course, such a work as this is intended for men and women of mature years, and it is not suitable to be left lying about for the gratification of ide curiosity. The author has been careful to write nothing that can possibly give offence, and he conveys much sound instruction that, if heeded by those to whom it is particularly addressed, will save much suffering.

## FROM THE PRESBYTERIAN OF PHILADELPHIA, DEC. 4, 1869.

A book which treats wisely and delicately of very important subjects, and subjects which ought to be treated by competent hands, instead of being left to quacks and the venders of nostrums. Dr. Napheys is evidently a conscientious and intelligent physician, and his counsels are such as may be put in the hands of all persons needing such counsels. We commend it, for its judicious exposition of the laws of nature.

## FROM REV. HENRY CLAY TRUMBULL,

*Secretary of New England Department of Missions of the American Sunday-school Union.*

HARTFORD, CT., Oct., 1869.

GEO. H. NAPHEYS, M.D.—

*My Dear Sir:* Understanding from my long acquaintance with you, your thoroughness of mental culture, your delicacy of sentiment, and your sound good sense, I was prepared to approve heartily the tone and style of your new work—"The Physical Life of Woman"—when its advance sheets were first placed in my hands.

A close examination of it convinces me that it is a book which can be read by every woman to her instruction and advantage. Its manner is unexceptionable. Its style is remarkably simple. Its substance evidences your professional knowledge and your extensive study. I believe it needs only to be brought to notice to commend itself widely. I think you have done an excellent work in its preparation.

Sincerely your friend,
H. CLAY TRUMBULL.

## FROM THE NEW YORK CHRISTIAN UNION, JAN. 8, 1870.

Society owes a debt of gratitude to this brave and scientific physician for the unexceptional way in which he has performed a work that has, up to the publication of this book, been a paramount need, not to be satisfied anywhere in the English language. If the volume contained only the chapter on the influence of the mother's mind upon her unborn child, we would recommend its purchase by every family in the land.

# THE TRANSMISSION OF LIFE.

### REV. CYRUS NUTT, D.D.,
*President of Indiana State University.*

I know of no work recently issued from the press, calculated to do so much good as "The Transmission of Life." It contains information of the utmost importance to the individual and the race, and should have a wide circulation.

---

### PROF. J. ORDRONAUX, LL.D., M.D.,
*Prof. of Physiology, Pathology, and Medical Jurisprudence, Columbian College, Washington, D. C.*

It was due to the cause of science, no less than morality, that some competent and honourable physician should reclaim this subject from the slough of pollution in which it has been dragged. Your work bears the impress of religious and scientific truth.

---

### PHILADELPHIA MEDICAL AND SURGICAL REPORTER.

This book is intended to meet a want which, during the last year, has been urgently expressed by several medical and literary journals in this country and England, namely, to place before the public, in popular yet irreproachable language, what information regarding the hygiene, nature, uses, and abuses of the procreative function in the male is necessary to protect the individual from the evil consequences of his own folly or ignorance. It will readily be conceived that to discuss such topics clearly, positively, and with benefit to the lay reader, requires no ordinary tact; and we must say that the author has succeeded beyond all our expectations. The work is characterised throughout by sound scientific views, and indicates extensive and careful reading.

---

### AMERICAN LITERARY GAZETTE.

PHILADELPHIA, March 15, 1871.

Those who are acquainted with the author's "Physical Life or Woman" will find this new book fully equal to that very popular and extraordinarily successful work, to which it may be said to form a sequel, being addressed to the other sex.

---

### NEW YORK INDEPENDENT.
*March 30, 1871.*

The book treats of an important and difficult subject with perfect delicacy of thougnt and expression, and its counsels are eminantly sound and judicious. It is, we believe, calculated to do great good.

### ANDREW D. WHITE, LL.D.,
*President of Cornell University.*

Your thoughtful and delicate presentation of the subject seems to me to merit great praise. That your discussion will do much good I firmly believe.

---

### REV. W. T. STOTT,
*Acting President of Franklin College, Indiana.*

I know no author who has succeeded so well in combining information with safe advice.

---

### PROF. JOHN S. HART, LL.D.,
*Trenton, N.J.*

I have been impressed with the care and discretion shown in the treatment of a very difficult subject.

---

### PROF. HARVEY L. BYRD, M.D.,
*Prof. of Obstetrics in the Medical Department of Washington University, Baltimore, Md.*

You have done your work well. I am one of those who believe the lay members of every intelligent community should be educated in a general knowledge of the laws of life. Hence I endorse your efforts in this direction.

---

### JOHN H. GRISCOM, M.D.,
*New York City.*

The numerous and important subjects have been nowhere, to my knowledge, as intelligently and effectively treated. The sanitary advice, so well inculcated, should be learned by every individual, especially by parents for the safety of their children.

### THE COLLEGE COURANT.

New Haven, Ct., April 8, 1871.

This work ought to be in every one's library, in every family throughout the country. No young man should be without a copy of it. *It has no equal.*

---

### THE CHRISTIAN SECRETARY.

Hartford, March 15, 1871.

Dr. Napheys has treated this delicate topic with excellent discretion, and his book comes highly recommended by some of the best and wisest men among us. Its perusal may save thousands of persons from untold evils.

### REV. HORACE BUSHNELL, D.D.,
*Hartford, Connecticut.*

"I see it to be a work immensely wanted, and think it will do much good. The subject, as related to family life, and the condition of posterity, is a really awful one, and ought to b just as much more awful to young men, as it more deeply concerns their welfare. Give it as g. eat a circulation as you can."

---

### REV. C. P. SHELDON, D.D.,
*President of the N. Y. Baptist Convention, Pastor of the Fifth Baptist Church, Troy, N. Y.*

"The subjects of which it treats are of great importance; and I am much pleased with the careful, candid, and able manner in which Dr. Napheys discusses them. The public need just such information, and in this work it is so imparted, that it cannot but be healthful and salutary. In moral and religious tone it is unexceptionable. I earnestly recommend its publication and circulation."

---

### PROF. NOAH PORTER, D.D.,
*Yale College.*

Dr. Geo. H. Napheys—

*Dear Sir :* I thank you for a copy of your work on "The Transmission of Life." There is in it much valuable information, carefully considered and industriously collected. The topics—of greatest delicacy—are treated with all possible refinement, while the much needed warnings concerning the offences against nature, which are practised in ignorance by many, and with shamelessness by others, are faithfully administered."

---

### DR. S. AUSTIN ALLIBONE,
*Author of " The Dictionary of Authors."*

"The subjects discussed are of great importance; the literary style is excellent—terse, vigorous, and perspicuous; the philanthropic zeal evinced is highly creditable to your heart; and the moral and religious spirit of the work is such as to give me a profound respect for the writer. The tendency of the book is good, and good only. It makes vice abhorrent and virtue cheaply purchased by all the wholesome restraints which it imposes."

### HON. T. W. BICKNELL,
*Vice-President Rhode Island Institute of Instruction.*

I have read "The Transmission of Life," by Dr. Napheys, and find the volume filled with truths which every man should know, understand, and daily practise. The author exhibits knowledge, wide reading, candour, and good sense. I can but wish for this work an immediate and wide circulation among the young men of our State, for by its teachings the causes of education, religion, and the purest morality will be advanced. A few friends who have read the book concur heartily with this opinion.

------

### THOS. W. PERRY, M.D.,
PROVIDENCE, R. I.

I have read with great pleasure "The Transmission of Life." The subjects are well arranged and handled with great delicacy and truthfulness. The book is worthy the perusal of all men, both professional and unprofessional.

------

### FROM THE PACIFIC CHURCHMAN.
SAN FRANCISCO, May, 18, 1871.

This is a book for honest, God-fearing men and women. Its subject is one of the most important and sacred in the world, and is treated with the highest scientific and professional ability; and, what is more important, is written from a Christian standpoint. It is one of the good signs of the times that such matters are written upon by honest, able hands, and the field not abandoned to quacks. Every young married couple should possess and read it.

------

### FROM THE CHRISTIAN ADVOCATE.
NASHVILLE, June 3, 1871.

The delicate and difficult subject is handled with great skill, prudence, and fidelity. The appalling prevalence of licentiousness in all its forms in our country shows that the question must no longer be allowed to rest. The reticence and fastidiousness which have characterised the pulpit, the press, the lecture-room, etc., must give way to earnest, well-directed efforts to stop the plague, which is sapping the foundations of society.

We call earnestly upon parents, pastors, and teachers to watch over the youth committed to their care with the utmost vigilance, so as to save them from the first transgression—and in order to this, you would do well to procure this volume and give it a serious and careful perusal.

### REV. HENRY A. NELSON, D.D.,
*Professor of Systematic and Pastoral Theology, Lane Seminary, Cincinnati, Ohio.*

" You have treated an important subject with great wisdom and fidelity. I could wish every young person to receive early the valuable—shall I not say necessary?—instruction which it contains."

———

### REV. ABNER JACKSON, D.D., LL.D.
*President of Trinity College.*

"I have found your volume both interesting and instructive. It contains a large amount of useful information and suggestion in regard to human welfare and duty. Matters of great delicacy, but of great importance in their bearings on health and happiness, are here treated of in a manner to instruct and guide, without shocking, or giving offence. The wide circulation of this work cannot fail to do good.

———

### REV. WM. A. STEARNS, D.D., LL.D.
*President of Amherst College.*

It is a difficult subject, which you have treated with propriety and success. The information which you give is of the greatest importance to the community, and especially to young men; and it is a thousand times better that they receive it from a work like yours, than be left to obtain it from sources of doubtful influence, or from bitter experience."

———

### REV. SAMSON TALBOT, D.D.,
*President of Denison University, Ohio.*

I have read carefully the advance sheets of "The Transmission of Life," and most heartily join in recommending its publication. The candour and learning of the author are very manifest; the information imparted is just that which the public most needs, and the moral tone of the work is altogether pure and elevating.

———

### REV. GEORGE W. SAMSON, D.D.,
*President of Columbian College.*

I have read "The Transmission of Life" with care, so has my son, who is a practising physician. I regard it as scholarly in its discussion, chaste in its expression, and unobjectionable in every respect. I cannot but commend this worthy effort in a field where faithful instruction is so much needed.

### REV. H. CLAY TRUMBULL,
*Missionary Secretary for New England of the American S.S. Union.*

"Your new work, on "The Transmission of Life," is one that every boy, and every man, every bachelor, parent, or teacher, should have and read and be grateful for. I have given sufficient study to the ways and needs of boys and young men, to appreciate perhaps more fully than most, the importance of your theme. I have been much instructed by your writings, and I desire others to be benefitted thereby."

———

### Rt. REV. THOMAS MARCH CLARK, D.D., LL.D,
*Protestant Episcopal Bishop of Rhode Island.*

"I do not hesitate to say that I regard it as a most timely and valuable treatise on an important and delicate subject. I do not see a line to which the most fastidious could object, and I believe that its general circulation among the young would avert a vast amount of misery and sin."

———

### BISHOP T. A MORRIS, D.D.,
*Methodist Episcopal Church.*

"The subject of this work is one of intense interest, and the manner of treating it is very proper. Both will command public attention and approval. May the book find a hearty welcome among all the wise and good."

———

### REV. LEONARD BACON, D.D.,
*New Haven, Connecticut.*

I think you have treated very judiciously a difficult subject. My belief that some such work may be useful is derived from the fact that the newspapers in all parts of the country overflow with advertisements addressed to the ignorance, the fears, and the guilt of transgressors. If your book can diminish the sale of the nostrums offered in those advertisements—still more, if it can put any on their guard against the vices which make such advertisements worth paying for, you will have done a good work."

———

### REV. J. AVERY SHEPHERD, D.D.,
*Head Master of St. Clement's Hall, Ellicott City, Md.*

The subjects treated of are not merely of great interest, hey are of *vital importance.* My decided impression is that this work *will do good.*

# THE
# GOD OF THIS WORLD;

## THE FOOTPRINTS OF SATAN:

### OR,

## THE DEVIL IN HISTORY.

*(The Counterpart of "God in History.")*

## BY REV. HOLLIS READ, A.M.,

*Late Missionary of the American Board to India; author of "God in History;" "The Palace of the Great King;" "Commerce and Christianity;" "The Coming Crisis of the World;" "India and its People;" etc.*

"Be sober, be vigilant, because your adversary the Devil, as a roaring lion walketh about seeking whom he may devour."—*1 Pet. v. 8.*
"An enemy hath done this."—*Mat. xiii. 28.*

## TORONTO:
## MACLEAR & CO., PUBLISHERS.

*One thick volume, crown octavo, Illustrated, price $2; post free on receipt of price.*

The Holy Inquisition.

Kicking the Bible out of the Public Schools.

# NARRATIVE

## OF

# MY CAPTIVITY

### AMONG THE

# SIOUX INDIANS.

BY

## FANNY KELLY.

WITH A BRIEF ACCOUNT OF GENERAL SULLY'S INDIAN EXPEDITION IN 1864,
BEARING UPON EVENTS OCCURRING IN MY CAPTIVITY.

TORONTO:
PUBLISHED BY MACLEAR & CO.,
1872.

# CERTIFICATE OF INDIAN CHIEFS.

Personally appeared before me, a Notary Public for the District of Columbia, Mrs. Fanny Kelly, who is at this time a citizen of the State of Kansas, and being duly sworn, deposes and says:

That in the year 1864, she started from Geneva, Allen County, Kansas, for the purpose of settling with her husband and family in Montana, and for this purpose she with her husband took all the goods and chattels they had, which are enumerated below, with amount and value.

She further says she is now a widow and has a family to support.

But she was for many months a prisoner, and taken captive by a band of the Sioux Indians, at the time at war with the white people, and with the United States, as follows:— On the 12th day of July, 1864, while on the usually travelled road across the plains, and west of Fort Laramie, she, with her husband and family, with several other persons, were attacked by these Indians, and five of the party were killed, while she was taken captive. That the Indians took or destroyed all they had. She was a captive for five months, suffered hardships and taunts, and was finally delivered to the military authorities of the United States in Dakota, at Fort Sully.

That the following is a statement of their goods and effects, including stock, as near as she can remember. The whole account was made out and placed, as she is informed, in the hands of Dr. Burleigh, late delegate from Dakota, but which she can not find at this time.   The amount and the leading items she knows to be as follows :

*        *        *        *        *        *

FANNY KELLY.

Subscribed and sworn to before me, this 24th day of February, A.D. 1870.

JAS. H. McKENNEY, Notary Public,<br>Washington County, D. C.

CITY OF WASHINGTON,<br>
  District of Columbia,<br>
    June 9th, 1870. }

We, the undersigned, chiefs and head men of the Dakota or Sioux Indians, do hereby acknowledge and certify to the facts set forth in the foregoing affidavit of Mrs. Fanny Kelly, as to her captivity and to the destruction of her property by members of our nation. We acknowledge the justness of her claim against us for the loss of her goods, and desire that the same may be paid her out of any moneys now due our nation, or that may become due us by annuity or by any appropriation made by Congress; and we would respectfully request that the amount as set forth in the foregoing bill be paid to Mrs. Fanny Kelly by the Department, out of any funds that may now or hereafter belong to us.

SPOTTED × TAIL,<br>Chief of Brule Sioux.<br>SWIFT × BEAR,<br>Chief of Brule Sioux.<br>FAST × BEAR,<br>Warrior, Brule Sioux.<br>YELLOW × HAIR,<br>Warrior, Brule Sioux.

ILLUSTRATIONS "FROM FANNY KELLY."

JUMPING BEAR PROMISING BY THE MOON, TO CARRY MY LETTER TO THE WHITE CHIEF AT FORT SULLY.

MY ARRIVAL AT FORT SULLY.

RED CLOUD, THE ORATOR SIOUX CHIEF.

A SCENE ON THE THIRD NIGHT AFTER MY CAPTURE.

ILLUSTRATIONS FROM "FANNY KELLY."

INDIAN FAMILY ON THE MOVE.

ILLUSTRATIONS FROM "FANNY KELLY."

ILLUSTRATIONS FROM "FANNY KELLY."